I0743891

SHADOWS & WOLVES

COMPLETE SHADOWLANDS SECTOR COLLECTION

MILA YOUNG

FORWARD

Shadows & Wolves is the complete collection of my Shadowlands Sector series, and I love writing in this world.

Wolves.

Fated mate.

Scorching hot scenes.

Danger.

I loved writing this series so much, and like all of my books, I always put my own spin on legends and myths.

Enjoy getting to know Meira and her three Alphas.

Love XOX

Mila

CONTENTS

SHADOWLANDS SECTOR

SHADOWLANDS SERIES

Three sexy Alphas' want to claim me, but will they be able to tame the monster inside me?

To survive, I had to pretend to be something I'm not—normal.

Only someone strong enough to fight the darkness inside me and savage enough to stay will be able to tame my beast.

The Ash pack Alphas claim I'm their fated mate and promise to help me, but these three ruthless wolf shifters are strong, powerful, and fiercely possessive.

Being submissive to them might be impossible, but I can't deny how their touch ignites a fire within me, how I burn to be with them in every way possible.

But will they still want me when they find out the truth of what I really am?

Shadowlands Sector is a three-book Wolf Shifter Sweet Omegaverse full of hot and gorgeous alpha males and a powerful woman who tames them all. Full of romance, non-stop action, and suspense, these diverse characters will tear at your heart and keep you reading until the very last page! Don't miss this chance to read the complete series today! Scroll up and grab your copy!

Shadows & Wolves is the complete collection of the Shadowlands Sector books.

SHADOWLANDS SECTOR

ONE

BOOK ONE

They claim I'm theirs to keep, but there's a monster inside me, one made of teeth and claws and terrifying need.

After my mother was brutally murdered, I fought to survive until I found refuge among the dangerous Ash Wolves. But that one move might be my biggest mistake of all. And I'm the queen of mistakes.

So I pretend to be something I'm not--normal.

I let them believe I'm broken, let them believe the lies. I let them believe anything they want... as long as it isn't the truth.

But I'm not normal. I'm anything but.

I need someone strong enough to fight the darkness inside me and savage enough to stay.

If I bond with the Ash pack, it might just save me but can I be submissive to them? All three men, ruthless wolf shifters, are strong, powerful and fiercely possessive. Yet, I can't deny that their touch ignites a fire within me that burns to be with them in every way possible.

They claim I'm their fated mate, that they can waken the wolf inside me, but will these wolves still help me when they find out the truth of what I really am?

CHAPTER 1

PROLOGUE

The creak of the door alerts me to someone entering my room. "Mama?" I roll over in bed expectedly.

But it's Jaine, our neighbor. She rushes to me with wild hazel eyes and messy blonde hair, still in her blue nightgown with patches. Her face is pale, her breaths shallow and raspy. I remember the blood and tears drenching her cheeks when she first came to our settlement after the Shadow Monsters killed her family. It still scares me to remember the fear on her face… and now, she has the same look as she hurries into my room.

The hairs on the back of my neck lift, and I draw my blanket to my chest, a whimper falling from my lips. "What's going on?"

"Meira, sweetie," she whispers, breathing heavily. She is a bit younger than Mama, but already looks out for me. "Death stalks the day. We must be swift and silent now." She chokes on her fast words as tears thread down her cheeks. There's a glint in Jaine's eyes, a window revealing a glimpse of her wolf lingering just below the surface. Her fear thickens the air in my room.

I shuffle to sit upright in bed, straightening my shoulders. "Where is Mama?" The morning light drenches my small room, and silhouettes darting past my windows outside. Their shadows are a frightening puppet show playing out across my drawn curtains.

They move fast.

There are too many of them. We're made up of a dozen females hiding in this settlement from the danger outside. The ten-foot metal fences lined with barbed wire have always kept them out.

"Jaine, what's going on?"

"The creatures are here." She glances over her shoulder to the ajar door. "You need to hide."

A chill fills my body. I hate the Shadow Monsters. I shiver, wrapping my arms around my pajama top and pants. We've been on the run from the creatures before, then Mama and I found this place. Our refuge. Or so I thought.

"I have to find Mama," I whisper.

But Jaine never answers me. She just snatches my arm and yanks me out of bed.

Pain flares through my limbs from the sickness I've suffered since birth. I wince as a pain, resembling claws, drags over my flesh. Mama insists it's related to my wolf side trying to come out. I'm already fourteen and still haven't experienced my first transformation. I shouldn't be alive as a result, but Mama says I'm her miracle girl. For years we've fled the wolves who will have killed me for what I am and we joined other random female settlements to keep me safe. Mama lies to the other women and says I'm only eleven and not at puberty yet so they won't want to kill me. I'm thin and look young for my age. Up to now, we've survived.

"Let's be swift and silent, Meira. Repeat those words in your mind."

My stomach hurts so bad. My gaze swings to the windows, at the commotion outside. Someone screams, and I cringe, grasping on to Jaine's arm. Why isn't Mama coming to get me? Where's everyone else?

This is a safe haven. This is our home.

But Mama was wrong. The Shadow Monsters broke in like they always do.

Jaine leans down, gripping my shoulders, and looks me in the eyes. "Repeat the words: swift and silent. Over and over."

Tears well in my eyes. One year of peace. That is all we've been granted, and now the demons are at our doorstep again.

Jaine takes my wrist, and we duck low as we hurry out of my bedroom and down the hall. She quietly opens the small cupboard door in the hallway where we keep brooms and winter boots. It's where Mama made me practice hiding until I could find it blindfolded. There's a lock on the inside of the door too.

"Swift and silent, baby girl, okay?" Jaine's voice is panicked and shaky.

I stumble into the hiding spot and spin to face her. My heart pounds in my ears. "I'm scared."

An explosive crash comes from somewhere in the background, rattling the whole house. Jaine shuts the door hastily, and darkness swallows me. With shaky fingers, I draw the metal lock into place and back away until my heels hit a bucket. Huddling down in the corner amid threadbare clothing, I hug my knees.

I rock back and forth, trying not to whimper too loudly.

Swift and silent.

We were meant to be safe here. Mama promised me.

A woman screams in the distance, and I shudder.

Thundering growls, smashing glass, and scrambling footfalls hit the floorboards. I inhale my cries and wrap myself around my bent knees.

Shadow Monsters are in the house.

I can't breathe… They'll rip me apart.

There's a scraping sound, like something is being dragged across the floor. Then it falls deadly silent.

All I hear are my breaths, the hammering of my heart.

Shadows pass over the wood slats just outside my door. With it comes a rancid meat smell. My stomach tightens so much, I think I'm going to vomit.

I flinch as another scream pierces the air, and I bite down hard on my bottom lip to stop myself from sobbing.

Someone slams into the wall just outside my hiding place. I shove backward, my spine pressing against the wall. Every inch of me is trembling ferociously, but I don't speak. Not a sound. Or they'll hear me.

A slurping sound mangled with screams fills my ears.

I want to yell, to run. My hands plaster to my ears and I tuck my chin into my chest, rocking back and forth.

Swift and silent.

Swift and silent.

Swift and silent.

Swift and silent.

I don't know how much time passes. Tears drench my cheeks. I can't stop trembling. I finally push forward and press my ear to the door. Sweat trickles down my back. My legs are cramping from sitting so long in one spot. *Mama, where are you?*

When I get too anxious to wait anymore, I unlatch the lock. The door creaks as I push it open. My heart stops.

I freeze on the spot.

Inhale.

Exhale.

Sitting here makes me an easy target. *Swift and silent.* So I force myself to look out.

The walls look like someone splashed red paint across them, but the sickening odor tells me it's blood.

Jaine lies on her back, her legs and arms twisted and broken. Her stomach lays splayed open. Shattered ribs poke up through the fabric of her pajamas. I'm going to be sick.

Terror bubbles on my throat.

"Don't be afraid of death," Mama would say. *"Our bodies are just vessels before we ascend to heaven. If you see someone dead, just look away and keep going."*

I whip my gaze away from Jaine and scramble out of the closet.

The silence is suffocating.

Moving fast through the old house barren of furnishings, I find no one around. I rush barefoot from one room to the next. Abandoned. *Mama, where are you?* Cold sweat sticks the fabric of my pajamas to my skin.

There are other homes in this homestead she may be hiding in, so I creep outside into the yard.

Rain falls as the bruised sky rumbles with thunder. A flash of lightning plunges across the heavens.

But I gasp at the sight before me.

Bodies lie everywhere, chaos all around me. Mothers. Children. Guards. A splitting ache tears through me. I should have tried to help rather than hide. I scan familiar faces, my stomach churning from the sickness, from seeing friends and neighbors torn apart and bleeding.

I hurry from one body to the next, searching for her face. Hope flickers inside me that she made it out alive. That she found a hiding space. I pivot around, and my gaze lands on a familiar face.

"Mama!" A cry bursts from my lips, and I rush forward, dropping to my knees by her side. Blood is pouring from the deep gash across her torn throat. I can't look at the injury, so I cup her face and place mine close to hers like she'd always do to me. Our noses touch; her skin is cool against mine. Tears fall and drip onto her cheeks. Dark brown hair spreads out around her head, her skin pale, tainted with blood. Everyone always says I'm beautiful like her with sharp cheekbones, small nose with a sprinkled with freckles, and a round face. But the only similarity I see right now are the light bronze eyes I look into.

"Mama," the word escapes my lips.

My insides shatter like glass.

"Mama! *Please*. Wake up." I hold her face, my arms trembling. "Please don't leave me." I won't survive on my own. I'm completely alone.

She never responds, and I just cry at her side. Mama is all I have left in the world. My breaths billow, and I hug myself. A cold wind cuts through my hair. The rain comes down heavily now, drenching me, but I don't move.

Mama will never drag me into her arms ever again or cover my face in kisses. She'll never wake me up with tickles. Or hold me tight at night when the storms come. I feel so lost. So angry. So scared. My breaths don't come easy as my heartbroken sobs float on the air.

Mama looks so peaceful lying down, her muscles relaxed as opposed to her always being tense when she was alive. My heart gives a painful throb when a gravelly snarl grows behind me.

I jerk my head up and twist around fast. Terror reverberates through my head.

A Shadow Monster stands at the corner of the house. Lanky and thin, his torn clothes hang loosely from his bony frame. He has no lips; they've been eaten away. Only teeth, broken and stained. That's all I see at first. Then the bulging eyes from the gaunt face. He is so skinny... starved.

I scramble backward up on my feet, panic kicking me in the gut.

He lurches forward, groaning.

Retreating, I want the world to open up and swallow me.

But the creature doesn't come to me. He falls to his knees in front of a dead woman and shoves his mouth into her torn stomach, eating. That slurpy sound makes me gag.

Bile hits the back of my throat. I recoil when someone brushes against my shoulder.

Spinning, I shriek to find another undead creature inches from me. Instinct kicks in, and I back away. Hair like straw dangles over her lifeless face. My heel hits something, and I fall. Hitting the ground, I shuffle backward, noting the fleshy, gory, torn-off leg I tripped over.

Fear pummels through me as my brain numbs. I can't do this. I can't.

The creature pounces.

I yell and flinch backward.

But it dives for the dead child beside me. My heart pounds in my throat.

The Shadow Monsters didn't see me. How? It's as though I'm invisible or something.

That's who I am. Invisible. I have to believe that or I won't move.

I scramble to my feet and find someone's disembodied finger stuck on my pajama pants with so much red gung.

Nausea pulses through me.

The undead's head snaps up in my direction, eyes falling to the stain. I shove the pants down my legs and toss them aside. I recoil as the creature eyes the pajamas crumpled on the ground.

Another creature who staggers on his feet bumps into me before pushing past me. A strangled cry escapes from my lips, and I slap a hand over my mouth to silence my sobs. I back away from the river of undead coming this way through the broken fence.

God, there are so many.

Shadow Monsters were once shifters just like me. Or maybe mere humans, or one of a number of other supernaturals in the world. Mama said the virus that destroyed our world didn't discriminate and took everyone it could, turning them into the undead.

Not one of the Shadow Monsters so much as looks my way, but they dart to the recently dead to feed. It's all they know.

My heart is beating too hard, too fast.

I don't know what's going on, but I have to get out of here before my strange luck runs out and they start noticing me. So I push past the horde of creatures.

Once clear, I run toward the main street, my feet now bare and bloody and in pain as I pound the worn path.

Jaine was right. *Swift and silent.*

CHAPTER 2

MEIRA

Five Years Later
When it rains, it pours.

I used to fucking hate that saying, loathed it with a passion. Mostly because I didn't understand how true it really was. How when life delivers one sucker punch, it quickly follows up with several more just to make sure you aren't getting up.

I'm not an optimist. I accept that. Living in a world ravaged by a virus broke my spirit when I lost everyone I've ever known… including Mama.

"Move," barks a muscular, white-haired Alpha as he snatches my arm, squeezing the hell out of it. He drags me down the middle of a small aircraft that reminds me of a steel coffin with wings.

The ropes binding my wrists at my back are too tight. The friction rubs against my skin and it stings. I want to say something, but I'm still tasting the blood in my mouth from his backhand at my last demand to release me. So I say nothing and stumble alongside him to keep up.

There are no seats in this small aircraft, just small, round windows and women sitting on the floor on either side of me. Eight women, not including me. They sit with their backs to the walls, their hands cuffed to a single chain linking them all and anchoring them in place.

They each stare at me with fear in their gazes. Their clothes are torn and filthy. Bruises and cuts litter their arms and legs… God, they are all

11

about my age, nineteen-twenty years old. Some are stunning, other ordinary, but they are all terrified.

Just like me, they were found in the woods at the wrong place, wrong time by the Ash Wolves. It's my fault for entering the Shadow-lands Sector… their territory. I should have known better, but starvation messes with your head. I've been living alone for the past five years, scavenging what I can, avoiding the monsters in the woods and wolf packs alike.

Female wolf shifters are commodities, and apparently, only good for two things.

Mating with the intent to breed.

Or trading, which eventually leads to point one.

And lucky me, I'm being traded to another wolf pack in the far west of Eastern Europe. Just delaying the horrible inevitable mating coming my way. I will fight to the end before I ever give in to any Alpha.

I grit my teeth, not caring whom they send me to. I'll escape and run. That's all I've known since the undead monsters stormed into my home and killed everyone I knew. My gut aches at the memory, and my wolf whimpers deep in my chest, but I drive the thoughts away. Not now. I refuse to drown in the grief I can't shake.

The white-haired shifter pivots me around, then shoves me away until I hit the wall.

"Sit!" he growls, darkness gathering under his ice-blue eyes. He's a wolf Alpha; I smell it on him like the electricity in the air after a storm. The scent of wolf lingers on him too, and my own beast responds, acknowledging him. But the rumble in my chest is a warning for him to stay away. His presence leaves a bad taste in my mouth.

I slide down to my knees and sit on my heels.

"Caspian, are we ready to go? Just brought in the last one from Mihai's delivery," the man who brought me into the plane suddenly calls out, his attention cutting to the open door leading to the cockpit.

"Mad, get your fucking ass in here."

I tuck these shifters' names into my mind for later because knowledge is everything in a world that has fallen apart. Information can be sold to the right buyer or to extract oneself out of a sticky situation.

Mad huffs and drags a hand down his rugged face. He's not an ugly man… quite the contrary. He looks to be in his mid- to late twenties with strong angular lines on his face and a square jawline, broad shoulders, and a body made of muscle. Except my skin crawls. There's an aura about him that doesn't sit right. Then again, most males I've encountered have a similar effect on me. They want one thing from me. While all I want is to drive my knee into their groins.

"Fuck, man," the other man in the cockpit snarls the words.

"I swear to hell, Caspian. We're already running late after Mihai insisted he got lost on the way here with the cargo. You better not fuck this up too." Mad's upper lip curls into a sneer as he marches forward and vanishes into the cockpit. From my angle, I watch him bend over to help the pilot, but I don't waste another second.

The fool has forgotten to link me up to the chain with the other women. A smug, satisfied smile spreads on my lips. Slowly, I lift myself to my feet, glancing the way we came, the main door still gaping open.

I glance over to the other women, their hands tied to a joint chain. I'll never release them without being caught first.

"Go," whispers the thin redhead next to me, her eyes flicking to the door and back at me.

An alarm screeches in my head that my chance to escape is narrowing the longer I wait.

My breath hitches, and I mouth, "*Sorry.*" I swirl around, my hands still tied behind me, and run as quietly as possible to the exit. Shivers ripple up my arms at the thought that I'll be caught.

I look behind me once more to find Mad still hasn't returned. Outside, the truck that drove us here is gone. I leap down onto the gravelly ground, my knees wobbling, but I manage to not fall over with my wrists restrained. Yay for me. Then I dart down the landing strip behind the aircraft. *Swift and silent.* I don't dare stop, and hope the pilot doesn't see me.

Running full tilt with my hands tied is harder than I expected, my shoulders swinging wildly back and forth in a see-saw manner.

Around me, pines stand tall and silent, the only witnesses to the direction I take. My pulse thumps in my ears. A quick look behind, and I'm far enough from the airplane to now slip into the dense woods and vanish from sight.

I don't know how long I've run, but I don't stop. The hill I'm scaling leaves my thighs burning. Ignoring the ache, I push forward.

The mistake is mine for going anywhere near a wolf pack in the first place. I've met enough females on my travels who have helped me out and told me whom to steer clear of.

Ash Wolves are at the top of this list in Romania. Their Alpha,

Dušan, is a controlling shifter who rules the biggest pack in the surrounding countries, and he gained that position for a reason. He takes what he wants without mercy.

Other smaller packs exist here and there in Transylvania, along with rogue wolves. Most small towns that once existed in the mountains have been overrun by the undead. Fewer safe zones exist now for free women.

I grew up terrified of these woods made of teeth and claws. Except now, it's my home. The Shadow Monsters leave me alone for a reason I don't understand, and I accept the universe's fate. Now, I just need to navigate around the wolves who also call this land home.

At the crest of the hill, I stop to catch my breath and stare out over the ocean of pines as far as the eye can see. Across the horizon, a small craft ascends. Mad and Caspian taking those women to their new home, stolen from freedom. Guilt flares that I couldn't do more for them. Except as I watch them fly away, I know I made the right decision. I made the only possible decision.

Dušan

"Well, only eight arrived on the transport," Ander Cain states through the comm unit, the flare of anger narrowing his eyes. His golden irises glint on the screen with frustration.

I'm seething, but I don't show it to the X-Clan Alpha of Andorra Sector. We are business partners, and it took me a goddamn long time to build this relationship, to gain his trust. Until I get to the bottom of this, I'll keep my cards close to my chest. I am the Alpha of Shadowlands Sector and I don't back down, but I also won't jump into a fight unprepared.

"Your Second is here to confirm," Ander continues before turning the screen on his end to face Mad.

My Second stares at me with a stoic expression and rattles off his explanation. "Meira wasn't part of the transport."

Anger flares over my chest, and I clench my fists by my side. He'd given me a list of all the female wolves we captured last week, all nine of them destined for the X-Clan Wolves.

"How is that possible?" I roar, then I school my reaction in front of Ander.

"You'll need to check with Mihai. He was the last one seen with the cargo before we took off," he retorts, and he's pissing me off, passing the blame off to someone else. My pulse rages through my veins to remind him of his place.

"I thought I charged *you* with that task, Stefan?" I rarely use his given name, but he's testing my patience. As my Second, I have to trust him, and he needs to be fucking on top of everything we do.

Mad explains he was busy with Caspian in the cockpit, which only has me grinding my jaw. I can almost see the cogs turning, which tells me he's hiding something. He speaks with confidence, smooth and believable. But today, something's off.

"I expected you to manage the shipment," I hissed. "Which clearly did not happen. Put Cain back on," I snap, sick of seeing his face.

Ander reappears on the screen. Running my hand through my short, dark hair, I have no choice but to return the cargo he sent me as payment for the girls. While the X-Clan pack have power, technology, and advanced medicine to trade, what they lack are Omegas. Their Alphas can only mate and impregnate Omegas. And that is one thing I have in my territory. Female wolves, with a good number of them being Omegas. Their scent gives them away. So our exchange benefits both our packs.

The X-Clan and Ash Wolves are both shifters, but genetically, we're different. The X-Clan are immune to the undead.

While Ash Wolves aren't immune and we need to find fated mates for our wolves to connect through marking and sex. But with all the shit going on and a growing pack to protect from the zombies trying to break into our home, I don't have time for that kind of involvement.

To maintain our relationship with Ander, I reluctantly say, "You can hold back one of my cargos while I locate our missing Omega." This isn't what I want.

Ander studies me cautiously. Thick, black hair sits cropped short to his ears without a strand out of place. I visited his compound for negotiations. They still live in penthouses in high security buildings, while we made our homes among old ruins and wilderness.

We are wolves, one with nature, and the wild is where we belong. I wouldn't exchange that for anything.

After more back and forth with Ander on how we'll do this, considering he's already sent the shipment—adding complications to the situation—Mad interrupts, stepping into view on the comm screen. "I have a suggestion."

"And that suggestion is?"

"Caspian and I will stay here as collateral while you find the girl. Once found, Cain can send his own pilot to retrieve her, and then we'll make our way back to you afterward."

I don't miss the tightness around Ander's eyes at Mad's offer. Such a suggestion would leave me uncomfortable too, considering Mad just invited himself to stay in the Andorra Sector. What doesn't sit well with me is Mad not consulting with me first. I won't forget this when he returns home, along with the chaos he just caused with the missing girl.

Ander drags a thumb over his bottom lip, the decision weighing heavily on him.

Having little choice, I lift my chin and answer, "I accept those terms, if you're agreeable."

"You have a week," Ander responds. "We'll renegotiate at that point should the girl not be in your custody by that time."

Squaring my shoulders, I grin because I have no plans on letting this go on any longer than it already has. "Oh, I'll catch her by then. I'll be in touch soon."

I end the communication with a click of a button on the small screen on my office desk.

"Fuck! I'm going to murder Stefan."

My Third, Lucien, an Alpha also, stands in the doorway like a sentinel. Legs spread, arms folded over his broad chest. His recently cut hair draws attention to the scar across his collarbone from when we fought an attacking pack on our territory a few years ago. I placed him in charge of my warriors to lead my battles. He swore his loyalty to me after I saved him from a horde of undead when he was ten, and ever since, he's been by my side. I trust him.

"Do you think Mihai lost a girl?" Lucien asks.

"I doubt it. He's completed dozens of cargo deliveries. So what was special about this one?" I want to believe he didn't have another agenda.

"What about Mad?"

I exhale a heavy breath. "Something's not right with this delivery. I can feel it." Mad's always pushing the boundaries… Being my stepbrother, he thinks he can, except whatever game he's playing at ends the moment he returns home.

Up on my feet, I move to stand by my window overlooking the grounds below.

We live in an ancient medieval fortress, the land barricaded with lofty stone walls to keep the zombies out and protect my pack. I glance out to the wooden shacks layering the land inside the castle walls. I welcome any wolf shifters in danger into my protection under one condition: They submit to me as their Alpha. In exchange, they gain food and shelter.

With that comes the need for resources. And this is why my partnership with Ander is crucial. He provides technology, vehicles, weapons, and much-needed medicine that we can't otherwise acquire. It's this trade that gives me the chance to protect those in my pack and gain an advantage over other warring packs wishing to claim my territory.

My stepfather was an Alpha, and he ruled with an iron fist. He gained followers through fear. But in the end, those men betrayed him.

Lifting my hand to my neck instinctively, my fingers run over the scar starting at my collarbone and going all the way up to the back of my ear. A little something from my stepfather when I was eight for disobeying his order. He slashed me with a serrated blade as punishment.

"This is why you'll never make Alpha. You had the chance to kill me and never took it."

I ball my hands into fists, then turn to my Third.

"Get a group of Alphas together to hunt down that Omega and fix this fucking mess."

CHAPTER 3

MEIRA

Three Days Later

My pulse races. Something is following me.

I twist around in the middle of the forest as a blur races amidst the dense woods toward me. Two legs, so definitely not an animal. A Shadow Monster? God, please don't let today be the day my good luck runs out.

I turn and run. The late-day sky cloaks the woods with an ominous gloom. I should have found a place to hide by now. Never stay out at night. All kinds of creatures slink out with the darkness.

My breaths are harsh and jagged.

A quick look over my shoulder shows a man is thundering toward me like a beast. Nostrils flaring, his mouth gaping, and those huge eyes are locking on me. A glint of wolf sparks in his gaze.

My stomach drops.

Shit, not again. Please not again. I've kept away from the packs, and I haven't seen any shifters for days since escaping from the plane. Where the fuck did this one come from?

He pounces, slamming into me. I tumble to the ground with a grunt while I convulse with terror.

Strong hands snatch one of my ankles to haul me backward. I jerk around and kick him in the face. Then I scramble away from under him and bolt, my feet pounding to the ground. Panic knots in my gut.

Sex is all he wants from me, and I shiver uncontrollably at the thought.

He throws himself on top of me, shoving me down. With a snarl, he rolls me over onto my back. The fuckhead clutches my throat and squeezes hard. Hot, rancid breath streams from his gaping mouth.

I punch his head over and over.

His lips curl upward, revealing razor-sharp canines, and he attacks. Teeth scrape and dig into the curve between my neck and shoulder. My flesh tears, the pain excruciating.

I scream and buck my body against him. He's so heavy and unmovable. Panic twists my mind.

Suddenly, he's ripped off me. I scramble to get up and reach the bite mark. It stings horribly, and I cup the wound to stop the bleeding that's worming through my fingers.

A cacophony of snarls and growls explodes in front of me. I recoil until I hit a tree. Fright paralyzes me as I clutch my wound.

Midnight-black fur is all I see from the wolf that rips into the other shifter. It's enormous, twice the size of a normal wolf, and in complete control of this battle. He leaps after the man, crashing down onto him and biting down onto his neck. The crunch of bone echoes, and I shudder.

Repulsed, I jump to my feet and charge out of there, the attacking man getting what he deserves.

A low rumble comes from behind me, and I spin around to find the black wolf trotting practically right on my heels. Trees crowd in around me, and I can't breathe. I'm suffocating with dread.

He growls at me, his nose creased, his fangs exposed. His fur bristles.

I cringe and almost die on the inside. I throw my hands out in front of me. "Please. I'm leaving your woods. Don't hurt me."

My heel catches on a tree root, and I'm falling. I scream as my heart slams to the back of my throat.

I hit the ground hard, and my hand instinctively seizes a thick branch near me. This isn't how I want to die. I hurl the stick at the wolf, who seems to be shimmering. His body convulses, fur shrinking, the long nose drawing into the body. Bones crack, the popping noise of skin splitting and knitting together. I've watched others transform, but I've never experienced it myself to know if it feels as painful as it looks.

Power pricks over my arms. The hairs on my neck shift.

It all happens in a heartbeat. Gone is the wolf, and in its place is a man standing over me completely naked. His icy blue eyes burn into me with the intensity of a raging storm.

My mind freezes over. I've avoided capture by wolves for the past few days by returning to the woods I'd been living in for years, so it's just my luck that I run into two wolves today. Fear twists my insides because I only barely escaped the others.

Shaggy, dark hair feathers around his chiseled face, cascading over his shoulders. He is huge, tall, and broad. Not that I expect anything else from an Alpha. His scent smothers my senses, and my wolf pushes and prods against my insides to get a closer smell.

He studies me, his attention falling to my mouth, then lower. My skin pricks with a shiver, my nipples pebbled in response.

His chest ripples with muscles. A faint sprinkle of hair covers his pecs and sweeps down his stomach into a tight V, all the way down. He's all there, out and proud. A black thatch of hair, a flaccid cock. Even soft, he is *huge*. Heat pulses through me, and my insides clench.

I shove to my feet, not wanting this wolf's groin in my face. No matter how much my body warms at the sight. No matter how much I feel the throb of arousal between my thighs. What I need is to get out of here because the way he stares at me tells me he wants to touch me, to impregnate me.

"Look at me," he demands in a deep, smooth voice as he reaches out toward me, his fingers brushing softly along my shoulder near the wound.

I flinch away and cry out with pain, even as goosebumps travel over my arm where he's just touched me. I've been running all my life for survival. Attention from an Alpha isn't what I want. Power flares from him in waves. It prickles over my skin and weakens my knees, as if my wolf senses his authority. She whimpers inside me with a desperation to obey him.

Total betrayal. My own wolf… She lingers inside me, responding to this Alpha, but still hasn't made a show of fangs or fur when I call her forward.

He sniffs the air, his brow pinching, before he glances over to the wolf he attacked to save me. Except wolves don't aid anyone without wanting something in return.

"He bit you to mark you into a forced mating," he states, as if it isn't obvious.

"You don't say? It clearly didn't work," I answer, still clutching my bleeding injury. "I don't need your help."

"What is your name, girl?" He steps closer, and my eyes don't know where they want to look. They move up and down his body of their own accord.

My mind is reeling, trying to come up with an excuse. Anything to get me out of his tangled chaos. But my heart is banging too hard, and I hitch my next breath all the way to my lungs.

"It's Meira, right?" He smirks, noticing my inability to even control my own body.

"I have no name," I say, cringing on the inside. *Oh, shit, shit, shit.* He's related to Mad and Mihai. The wolves who kidnapped me and shoved me onto the plane.

His laughter irks me… what irritates me worse is that I like the way he sounds, how he tilts his head upward to laugh at me. How I desperately need him to put on clothes so I can gain control of my gaze once again.

"Well, you've saved me, and I'm thankful. Have a nice day." I turn and quickly lunge into a run. Every male wolf craves the same thing. A female to mate, to keep prisoner, to impregnate. The thought alone infuriates me, and I pump my legs faster.

His hand snatches mine and he whips me back around. My feet stumble, and I jerk to face him, crashing right into his bare chest. So much flesh everywhere. He's burning up and so hot to the touch.

I shove my hands against him and reel back, then swing a fist at him.

He moves unimaginably fast and catches my balled hand in his, stopping it short from clipping his face.

He grabs me by the scruff of my neck and wrenches me closer. "You're not dealing with a Beta. Remember that, because next time, I won't take well to almost being punched in the face."

Only an Alpha would be so arrogant. "Let me go!" I shout at him. I get the impression he could easily pick me up and swing me over his shoulder. I'm not blind to the way he studies me, dragging his gaze up and down my body.

My fists clench, and I spit at him, managing to hit him square in the chest. He glares at me, and he grabs my arm and then hauls me with him as he pushes into a march. "You're going to get yourself in a lot of trouble."

I fight him, stumbling behind him. "I'm not yours to abduct and keep."

"Who said anything about me keeping you? I have an Alpha who might be very interested in you."

Edgy anger fills me. He's going to send me off again to god-knows-what-monster in another country. I strain against his iron grip, and though I know it's futile, I never stop fighting.

"This would go a lot easier if you learned obedience. It can be quite rewarding." He arches a thick eyebrow with amusement.

That time, it's me who bursts out laughing, all fake and for show. "Does that actually work on anyone?"

There's a pause as he cups the side of my face harshly, holding me in place.

He sniffs me, inhaling my scent. All wolves carry a distinctive smell that easily identifies them but also reveals their status.

"You smell like Omega," he declares with accusation, his nose scrunching as if I'm not worth his time.

I cringe and bite down on my cheek to stop from blurting out that I don't belong to his hierarchy. That I'm not the lowest rank in the pack, where everyone will feel like they can take advantage of me.

Alphas rule, one taking leadership and controlling a pack of other Alphas, Betas, and Omegas. The handful of Alphas in a pack usually don't stray from the top, and are ranked in order of his Second, Third, and so forth. Betas are the fighters, both male and female, the work dogs of packs. The Omegas, on the other hand, are the ones who have no power and do as they're told their whole lives. Majority of females are Omegas or Betas. It's why Mama and I always found settlements without men. She taught me to stay independent, to be in control of my own life.

"You will learn your place. Or I can personally show it to you."

"You're an Ash Wolf, aren't you? Of course you are." My voice is shaky, and I hate that my reaction is so obvious.

He cuts me a dangerous look, and all I can do is stare into those pale blue eyes, the darkness of his long lashes, at just how perfectly handsome this beautiful man is. He has a strong jaw, a perfect nose, and full lips that leave me frightened by the way he makes me feel. I hate that I think he's anything but a brutal barbarian.

"And if I am?" he asks casually.

"I've heard things about your Alpha, and I don't want to be

anywhere near that jerk." My temper flares at the thought that an Alpha like Dušan thinks he has a right to control everyone's life.

This man's gaze pierces into me, and I feel completely vulnerable under his scrutiny. "Really? What sort of things?" he probes, as if he's never heard the stories.

But I'll amuse him.

"That he's worse than the Shadow Monsters. That he kills all females after mating with them, terrified his child will eventually kill him to claim the position of Alpha. That he's ruthless."

"Those are severe rumors," he murmurs.

"Who said they were rumors?" I snap back at him.

His hand squeezes around my wrist, and I startle.

"So you've met the Alpha of Ash Wolves firsthand, then?" he asks.

"Well, no. Otherwise, I'd be dead. But I've spoken to enough people who tell a similar tale. Haven't you heard the saying, where there's smoke, there's fire?"

There he goes again, laughing, and I narrow my eyes at him.

I straighten my shoulders, trying another tactic since fists and screaming don't work. "*Please.* Can you find it in your heart to release me?"

"I suggest you come and find out the truth for yourself."

My stomach plunges to my feet, and the reality of him taking me to meet Dušan, Alpha of Ash Wolves, freezes my insides. The danger is real, my fate—sealed.

He hauls me deeper into the forest with long strides. My knees are shaking as I wrack my mind to find an escape.

"You're a monster," I snarl, digging my heels into the dirt as he drags me. "And when your Alpha kills me and I'm six feet under, I hope the guilt chews you up for eternity."

"That's a long time to feel remorseful. I'm sure I'll get over it quickly." He smirks my way, like my survival is a joke.

I look at him with a painful fury that he doesn't seem to notice. He just rushes me through the woods. Me, the victim. And him, the warrior dragging me to my death.

CHAPTER 4

ALPHA

*F*uck!

She's not what I expected. Gorgeous. Feisty. Tempting.

Her scent is like ambrosia, and it does something to me. Every inch of her calls to my wolf like no one has ever done before. My heartbeat races.

She's a wolf, yet the smell of humanity clings to her, along with something else. My nose pricks with the current of electricity beneath the smell, something almost sickly sweet. Every wolf carries a distinct scent that easily identifies their power, their status. We are born this way, nature dictating our future before our first breath into this world. But this girl… She doesn't carry the rippling power of an Alpha or Beta. Omega? Yes, but she smells differently.

She has no clue what she is either. I can see it in her lost, wild gaze. I feel it in her presence. Living day to day out in the woods. Like most of the female wolves we pick up, she's just trying to survive. On her own, she won't last out here. If the undead don't get her, the rogue wolves who lust over females to rut will sniff her down.

I'm doing her a favor by taking her. Though she doesn't think so, considering the way she fights me, digging her heels into the ground to slow us down. I'm seconds from tossing her over my shoulder and slapping that tight ass until she conforms.

The Omegas we catch become obedient almost immediately in the presence of an Alpha, their wolves taking control of them.

But not this hellcat. A growl rumbles in my chest, and I curl my fists.

There is something very different about this girl, and I intend to find out what.

Her obstinate behavior confirms she's grown up as a wildling in the woods and most likely hasn't been around too many males. I've searched the surrounding woods for the past couple of days and found no females. I only found her, once I extended the radius of my search. She has to be Meira. She fits the description perfectly, down to the beauty spot at the corner of her left eye.

"How far is your lair?" she asks sharply as she glances at the forest swaying in the breeze, the shadows dancing amid the trunks.

What is she searching for? The undead? Those bastards come out of nowhere. Where there's one, there are plenty. They travel like a swarm, so on the bright side, the numerous feet trampling the ground make them easily heard when they approach. My ears prick for any sounds in the distance… Nothing yet. The ones who survive the plague learn to assimilate and be quick on their feet.

Get bitten, and you become infected in a few hours. For that reason, we need to hurry. We have to get to my car down the hill before sunset. Otherwise, the other creatures that make the shadows their home will emerge. They don't make sounds; they attack without notice. Beasts who hunt only at night for fresh meat.

"If you'd stop fighting me," I point out, "we'd arrive sooner."

She watches my mouth as I speak but then tears her gaze away angrily. She's clutching her neck, blood trickling through her fingers, but it doesn't keep her from glaring at me with fury.

"I'm not afraid to remain in the woods," she says with venom in her voice. "Maybe we should spend the night in the forest?"

I shake my head. "Nobody wants to stay in the forest at night. I'm not buying whatever game you're playing."

I've only just met her and already, she infuriates me. She's just a tiny thing, five-foot-two or -three, compared to me at six-foot-two. A curvy body, her breasts high and round. Hair the color of the surrounding trees' bark flutters halfway down her back. Shorter strands hang loose around her beautiful face. My fingers tingle as I imagine twisting her locks around my hand and gripping them as I fuck her from behind.

Fuck! I don't need those thoughts in my mind, not while I'm naked. And walking around with a raging hard-on is not fucking comfortable.

"I thought you would have liked games," she teases, antagonizing me. "It's what you Alphas do, right? Chase down females to make them your possessions?" She pierces me with the most beautiful pale bronze eyes. I've never seen that eye color before, but it's so much more than just a shade. They're shaped to look permanently sad, like she's experienced too much sorrow in her life. When she doesn't snarl at me, she almost looks like she might start crying. Flawless skin with a sprinkling of freckles over her nose, and my gaze falls to the rosy full lips. Who is this girl?

The dripping blood from her neck catches my attention, the rivulets rolling down her shoulder and into the material of her tee. How long before she draws the undead to us with the scent?

I pause and pivot in front of her. She flinches back, clearly scared of me. I'll admit that her reaction both excites and upsets me. I'm a twisted bastard that way.

"What are you doing?" She looks at me with narrowing eyes, as if unsure whether she ought to trust me or not.

She wears a blue skirt that falls to her knees, the fabric torn from the fight, and a black tee two sizes too small for her, revealing a line of creamy silk stomach.

Like her clothes, her sneakers are stained with mud and long overdue for a wash. I reach down and grab the hem of her skirt where I spot a rip in the fabric.

"Hey!" She reaches down to push my hands away, but I tear the chunk of long material from the base of her skirt so fast, she doesn't see it coming. I shove her shoulder to turn her away from me before tearing the rest of it from all around. With a final jerk, I rip the strip free.

She stumbles on her feet, her eyes bulging out of their sockets. The earlier dress now sits above mid-thigh, revealing gorgeous, toned legs.

She snarls. "What the hell did you do that for?"

I seize her by the arm and haul her closer. "Keep quiet." Quickly, I wrap the torn material over the bite mark and under the opposite arm, twice over. She fights me, but I hold her roughly. I'm not playing.

I need this done fast, yet awareness of how close we are ripples over my skin. Her scent sinks through me, making it almost impossible to concentrate. A heady mix of pheromones flares within me in response to her. My cock throbs. A primal hunger pulses inside me to protect this female from all other males, to claim her. Take her.

No female has ever affected me this powerfully before. I grind my back teeth and I jerk her forward, a bit harder than I meant to.

"You have no right to—"

"I have every right," I growl and swing away, drawing her with me by the arm. "If it means it will save our lives and stop you from collapsing from blood loss, I will do what it takes." My pulse is out of control, and a possessiveness over her swallows me. What the hell is going on with me?

Her heartbeat accelerates. I can feel it beneath my fingers as I grip her wrist while she snarls at me, baring perfectly white teeth. No chipped or broken teeth. She will be a good exchange for the other pack.

Except adrenaline laces my blood, my wolf surging forward at the thought, demanding we claim her.

When our gazes clash, I get a glimpse of her vulnerability. And damn, it draws me in even further.

My wolf slinks through me, insisting she belongs to us and we need to mark her now. Except something feels off. She feels different. And I won't jump to conclusions about finding my fated mate that quickly.

I always thought I'd know when I sensed my mate... but this girl isn't what she seems, so how can I trust what I feel? It almost seems as if she's hiding behind an invisible veil.

Once we get back home, I'll work out what's going on.

Her cheeks blush each time she glances my way, her eyes dipping down my body. Her embarrassment at my nudity doesn't fade, and she keeps looking away. I don't understand her reaction. She's a wolf... after transformations, we are nude. Natural as breathing and yet her face is red. She has no control of her roaming eyes.

Once we eventually reach a valley with a small running river, I pause, holding her closer with one arm around her narrow waist despite her grumbles. No sign of rogue wolves or undead nearby. The woods surrounding us are silent. I sniff the air to confirm we are alone. I didn't realize how far I'd traveled to find this hellcat. A group of five of us went in opposite directions in the woods to track her.

"Drink and let's wash your wound. We have a fair distance to travel."

I expect her to argue, but instead, she crouches and cups her hands under the clear, running water and draws it to her mouth to drink.

Fresh water streams from her wet hands, falling back down to the surface of the river in large drops.

I do the same and fill my stomach.

She unravels the torn material I tied across her wound and pushes her long, umber brown hair over her shoulder. Then she cups more water and splashes it over the bite mark. It flows across her bare shoulder and soaks into her top. The fabric sticks to the perfect curves of her breasts.

My throat goes dry as I stare at the beads of water rippling over her collarbone and sliding beneath her top. A heavy desire closes in around me with the weight of a mountain.

The last streaks of sunlight glint against her raised face, and her bronze eyes seem to glow beneath the flare. Her gorgeous mouth parts as she exhales.

My groin clenches tight.

Such a beautiful creature. Whoever she is, I need to claim her.

I'm burning up to reach over and taste her, to mark her myself. The bite piercing her flesh bubbles with fresh blood. A fiery savagery rips through me at seeing the shifter's teeth blemishing her perfect skin. I crave to take her, to bury my face into her neck and taste her. To make her mine.

She runs her fingers over the injury and winces.

"How long have you been living in the woods alone?" I ask, trying to understand more about her, and also to distract myself from the effect she has on me.

She stiffens and doesn't look at me. "A few years."

"Alone? You've done well to survive this long." A few years? Fuck, that would drive anyone crazy.

She nods as she wraps the fabric back over her bite mark. I reach over and help her tie a knot to keep it in place. As a wolf, she should heal quickly.

"I have my ways," she says. I see the hunger behind her eyes, the wolf inside her wanting to make a connection. But something doesn't feel right.

The snap of twigs reaches me.

I freeze, my gaze shooting across the narrow river to where the sound comes from. A shadow flitters amid the trees. My lungs seize.

A figure lurches forward... an undead... A lanky man wearing no shirt, his decaying chest covered in open scratches. He moans loud enough to alert others nearby to join him.

"Fucking great." We'll be swarmed in no time.

Meira spins out of my grasp and runs back the way we came.

My pulse is on fire, and I throw myself after her. Seizing her arm, I drag her back into the woods fast. She fights me, as if facing an undead is a better option for her. I pray the blood in the water and near the bank distracts them enough that they won't follow us.

Fury churns in my gut.

"Let me go! They're after *you*."

I figure she's being her usual, complimentary self. "Where do you hide?" I demand.

But she says nothing, like suddenly the danger across the river isn't her problem. "If I shout right now, they'll be on us in no time." There's a challenge in her eyes, a threat. "Release me, and I'll tell you where you can go hide. Otherwise, you'll die tonight."

A sinister grin splits her mouth, and I have no doubt she means every word.

My wolf unleashes a low moan that bleeds up my throat.

I hear the splash of water, and my heart rages against my ribcage. A shudder rushes down my spine.

Squeezing her arm harder, I pull her close so we're face to face. "Listen. If I die in these woods, my entire pack will be scouring the woods to find you. Do you know what they do to Alpha killers?" I snarl.

She shrugs nonchalantly, and fuck, she is testing me. "They will hand you around to be taken by every single male." Of course I'm lying, but she doesn't know that. "Help me and I'll be sure you're taken care of."

She swallows loudly, the color draining from her cheeks. It takes her a while to think this through. "If the undead kill you, no one will think I'm to blame in any way."

I transfer my hand to her wrist and hold her. She thinks on her feet, and I like that about her.

The hatred she tosses at me makes me smirk. Then we're moving with haste through the woods.

She navigates the forest expertly, even with night closing in. She knows this location very well. We take a sharp left between two lofty pines into a denser part of the landscape. Pine needles litter the ground, and I note a small worn path. She's been living in this location for a while now.

We pause, and then she's reaching for a rope ladder dangling from an enormous tree. I glance up to find a platform overhead.

I didn't see *this* coming. She's built herself a treehouse to escape the dangers. Secretly, I'm in awe of her survival skills. How has she managed to go this long without an undead attack? She still had to hunt for food.

When the crunch of foliage comes from nearby, I grab the rope ladder and begin climbing. I glance up, only to see the perfect view of her ass in black underwear under her skirt. I shouldn't feel anything, but heat bursts through my veins until it feels like I'm on fire.

She scrambles up onto the platform, and I race up. I wouldn't be surprised if she cuts the cords and throws me down to the monsters.

CHAPTER 5

MEIRA

$\mathcal{N}$ight spreads her wings over the forest.

Usually, I sit up here, feeling safe in my wooden home, a simple box I made of thick branches I bound with rope to build walls and a roof. The branches are uneven, leaving gaps in the walls that blink at me with darkness. Just like me, it has imperfections. But I love it here.

I cut a glare across to the wolf shifter next to me, who's going to tear all this away from me.

He sits with his knees bent and arms draped over them, staring at nothing in particular. It must be killing him to have to hide up here with me instead of dragging me back to his pack to appear a hero to his Alpha.

"How have you survived alone so long?" he asks.

Shadows dance across his gorgeous face, and he doesn't even look at me, instead dropping his gaze to the wooden floor between his bent legs. I don't answer, except I remember Mama would always say: *Knowledge is power.* And this shifter has information that might help me understand the wolf packs so I can better avoid them.

"Life can be savage," he continues.

My response comes flying out. "You're an Alpha, working closely with the big wolf himself, so I doubt your life is that difficult." I regret the snarkiness in my voice immediately. I remind myself all of us who are left behind are still alive because we faced hell itself to not perish.

When he doesn't respond and guilt gnaws on my insides, I say, "Sorry, shouldn't have said that." We may be enemies, but in truth, are we any different? We're both making a life amid a horrendous virus that wiped out so much of the population. We're survivors, no matter who we are on the inside.

"This isn't where I wanted to end up," I admit. "But the endless strain of surviving forces you to make do."

"I haven't met many who are happy with their situation. But shit happens."

"Shit like kidnapping females and selling them to other packs like cattle?"

He turns toward me, and there's fire behind his eyes. I've touched a sore point. "No females are ever harmed. They're kept safe and looked after. That is part of our agreement."

"But we're still taken against our will, aren't we?"

"Aren't we all trapped by the undead? Forced to live in small settlements, make the best with what we have? So what's the difference?" His voice darkens, his words clipped.

"The difference is that we should get a choice if we go to the other pack or not. How do you sleep at night?"

He barks a loud laugh. "Count yourself lucky the Ash Wolves rule over Romania because things would be a shit show for everyone if we didn't. There are hardly any humans left in this territory after the virus, and the wolves moved in to dominate. But that shifter who attacked you earlier wouldn't care if you had food or shelter. He'd tie you to a tree and just rut you until you perished. Those are the kind of monsters that are out there. So, yes, I sleep soundly knowing I am making a difference." The depth and sincerity in his voice touches me more than I expect. It doesn't settle the fire in my chest about getting kidnapped and shipped off, but there's something almost beautiful about his passion to make a difference. My earlier hate for him eases a bit.

A sudden ache lashes across the middle of my stomach. It hits me with a sharpness pulsing through my limbs. The sickness has never left me after so many years. That feeling overwhelms me, and I hug myself, leaning forward as the wave rushes over me. It comes and goes, but as of late, I've noticed it hits me more frequently, as though it's building inside me. I'm scared it's my wolf wanting to come out, this damn beast who has tortured me my whole life.

"Are you hurt?" he asks.

I shake my head. "It's just hunger pains."

He reaches forward and grabs one of my green apples from the bowl I have in the corner. "Eat this."

I accept the offering and look over to him. Beneath the tough exterior, he does give a fuck about others. I bite into my apple, its sweetness coating my tongue and the juices dribbling from the corner of my mouth.

He stares at my lips, at the way I wipe away the mess. His lips part as he watches me. Is he going to lean in and kiss me?

The thoughts steal my breath, beads of sweat pooling between my breasts. My body has never reacted this way before, with such arousal and need all rolled up into a bubble ready to burst inside me. And just from a single thought.

But he never leans in closer or kisses me. He sits there, staring outside and biding his time.

By the time I finish eating, the ache settles, and I toss the apple core outside through the narrow doorway. A cool breeze curls inside the treehouse, and with it comes the shifter's woodsy, wolf scent. My heart skips a beat, blood rushing through my veins. What is wrong with me?

I rub my arms, noticing the goosebumps covering his skin.

I turn to the small bundle of clothes I've stolen during my searches from homesteads I've ransacked. I pull out an oversized black coat. It was made for a large man, and I've been using it as a blanket.

"Take this. It will warm you."

"I'm fine," he responds, staring straight ahead. "Cover yourself."

"I can see you're cold," I admit, hoping that if I show him care and compassion, he'll do the same with me if the time comes. He's opened up to me, so it's the least I can do. "You know, it's okay to accept help."

When he looks over at me, all I can focus on are his pale blue eyes, how much he reminds me of a wolf. This man screams *predator*, and he embraces what he is. Unlike me. I don't know what I'm supposed to be. I'm not a complete wolf since I still haven't had my first transformation, and I'll never be complete. I'm broken and unwanted because of what lives inside me from the lack of transforming.

"Will *you* accept help if I offer it?" he asks, his brow arching upward.

"Depends on what your offer is. Help is subjective and means different things to everyone. I love this home I built. It gives me the freedom to come and go, to not be controlled by anyone. So I don't need aid."

"But you're alone. We all need someone, no matter how strong we think we are."

"You know what happens when you get close to people? They end up dying, and it breaks you. So yeah, alone suits me perfectly fine." I drag the coat over my legs and up to my chin to keep the cold away.

"Better to have felt that pain. Then at least you knew love."

His harsh response sinks into me and resonates at my core. I had Mama, who adored me, but my father walked out on us when I was six after a huge argument with Mama. I remember the screams, the indents in our walls from his frustrated punches.

"I can't protect either of you!" he'd shout. *"Meira is weak because of me. She'll always be an outcast."*

Even after all these years, his words are a kick to the gut. My throat thickens at the memory that he was too weak, too weak to stay with us. He left because of me in the end. I bite down on my cheek until it hurts, just to stop the agony of the past.

We fall into another silence and I feel lost, unsure where I belong in this world. I know with certainty that being a slave isn't my destiny. I've been hiding for years behind the veneer of this forest, and it's exactly where I want to remain unnoticed. Here, I can do what I want and no one judges me.

My pulse races and now all I can think about is how I'll get away from this shifter. The moment I hear him sleeping, I'm out of here. Sure, it sucks that I will have to find a new forest to build my treehouse, but it'll be worth it to get away from the wolf pack. I don't need anyone.

"You should get some rest," he remarks. "We're leaving at first light."

Only I should get some sleep? So he has no plans of resting? He'll watch me. Gritting my teeth, I shuffle down and onto my side on the blanket I use for my bed. The small size of the treehouse doesn't permit me to sleep stretched out, so I curl in my legs and roll away from the shifter. I doubt he'll be able to stay up all night, so I'll bide my time.

He shuffles behind me, the wood groaning under his weight. Next thing I know, he's lying down behind me, laying with his chest against my back. Despite wearing no clothes, his skin is scorching hot against me, and the heat overwhelms me.

I stiffen, flexing my shoulders.

His hand loops around my waist as he drags me harshly against him.

I gasp and wriggle to escape, but he holds me in place. "You're not running from me," he growls in my ear.

My heart stutters.

"I can't sleep like this," I insist.

"Get used to it."

I freeze for a moment, then turn my head over my shoulder to see the smirk on his face. "What do you mean?"

"Come on now, little hellcat. You're not that naive. What do you think an Alpha will want to do with a gorgeous Omega like you?"

I grit my teeth and writhe against him. "I'm not a possession."

He laughs behind me. Asshole loves seeing me angry. Swinging a leg over me, he uncovers me in the process and pushes closer. His cock presses against my ass with only the thin fabric of my skirt and underwear between us.

I go to move, but he keeps me locked in place. A twitch pokes my ass cheeks, then another twitch, and it doesn't take long for his cock to become hard. And hell, he feels so large.

"You clearly have no control," I say.

"If you keep wriggling, you'll have a real problem on your hands."

His words have me stilling, and he just laughs at me.

"I hate you," I blurt out.

"Good. I wouldn't expect anything less. Now shut your eyes."

Drawing them shut, I know sleep won't come. Crap, why does he have to smell so divine? All I can think about is how good it could feel to have him against me, skin to skin. I imagine his cock sliding in between my legs, and a pulse throbs at my core.

His breath hitches behind me.

I freeze.

Oh fuck, he can smell my heat.

Alpha

Her sugary scent teases my senses and fills my nostrils. Her heat burns through me... little vixen wants me just as I want her. My balls are drawn up and feel heavy. I'm really not doing myself any favors here. She's promised to someone else. But she'll escape during the night if I fall asleep, and being a light sleeper, I'll feel her moving out from under me. So I hold her close.

She keeps wriggling that tight ass of hers, and the more she pushes me, the more I won't be able to control what I do next. All I can picture is me driving into her, filling her, making her scream. I've never felt so desperately fucking horny before. What I feel is that instantaneous lust, and my body is alive, ready to claim her. I do my best to hold on to my sanity. I glance down to where her coat and skirt has ridden up over her rear. The thin fabric of her black underwear follows the curve of her ass. My dick pulses at the thought of touching her everywhere.

My heart and I lie there with her in my arms, drowning in that sweet vanilla and clementine fragrance, mixed with her slick heat.

Holding her tight, my fingers graze the soft skin of her stomach, my cock pressing against her ass cheeks.

She suddenly shuffles to roll over, her ass rubbing over my dick, sending me ridiculously close to the edge of losing my mind. I hiss an inhale as she twists to face me.

"That's better," she grumbles as she curls her body to ensure no part of her touches my now painfully solid erection. She drags that coat over her and wraps herself up in it with just her head sticking out. Her mouth tugs into a grin with a look of satisfaction, like she's won. Hell, I haven't even started if that's the game she wants to play. But I won't let myself go there. Because if she begs me to take her, I won't stop until I have her beneath me and writhing.

Her breath sears across my bare chest, and she looks up at me with amusement. Her pale bronze eyes remind me of a sunset after a violent storm that shakes the earth. That's what meeting her feels like.

"Good night," I say, and with my hand still around her back, I wrench her toward me.

She gasps as her body slams up against mine, my dick nestled perfectly between us. With a grin curling my lips, I close my eyes.

I feel her hatred setting off sparks of awareness across my body.

"Why do you even care if I go back with you? You can tell your Alpha you didn't find me."

I crack open one eye to her glare, then another. "You want me to lie? I'm guessing you've never been in a pack environment before. You'll learn very soon."

"Heard enough to know the hierarchy." Those gorgeous eyes

narrow, and I know exactly why she's so angry. But in a pack, she'll be safer than out here. The X-Clan has agreed to care for all females I send them.

"No free animal enjoys capture," I explain. "But once they accept their new life, they realize the benefits."

She gives me a dubious look. "Really? You just referred to me as an animal needing to be broken in. Bet *you're* popular with the females." She huffs and flashes her vicious glare my way.

"Putting it crudely, some wild wolf shifters need breaking in for the benefit of the whole pack to work in harmony. Everyone knows their roles, and together, we are stronger." But she won't be my problem for long. Her new Alpha can have fun taming this one.

"You keep telling yourself that."

I grit my teeth. One more remark and she'll be lying over my lap and receiving my palm over that little ass. I tighten my grip around her. I came out here for one simple mission. Find the missing girl and return her.

She begins to fidget with the collar of the coat covering her, a nervous twitch, but soon after she settles down and closes her eyes.

Her heat continues to twist and curl through the air until I'm encased in it. I watch her face as her head rests on a folded hand. There is no denying her beauty—the dark hair spread out behind her, the perfect lines of her small cheekbones and nose, her full, luscious lips… the same lips that said everything she shouldn't have. Suddenly, her nostrils flare, as if sensing me looking at her.

I smile to myself.

Beneath the moon's hue, she looks intoxicating.

She is too perfect.

Too beautiful.

Way too distracting.

And not mine.

CHAPTER 6

MEIRA

$\mathcal{M}$y eyes flutter open, and I'm falling. Panic slams into my chest. I shudder, my arms jutting out to catch myself. Except my wrists are bound together with rope.

"Settle down," the Alpha growls in my ear, his arm looped around my waist as I realize I'm hanging over his shoulder while he climbs down from my treehouse.

He reaches the ground, and I slide down his body until my shoes touch soil. Our faces are so close, I can see the silvery flecks in his irises catching the sunlight. My heartbeat races in my chest.

I hate his quirk of a smile as my breasts drag down his chest. He may have the body of a god, all naked and insanely sexy, but I want nothing to do with him.

"Untie me," I hiss, jutting out my bound wrists to him. "I can't believe you tied me up while I slept."

In reply, he reaches over and grabs the rope dangling from my bonds, pulling me behind him. "Let's move."

"Are you fucking serious? A leash? I'm not a dog."

"You're my little wolf," he says with a small smile as he glances over his shoulder.

My feet stumble after him, and I'm seething on the inside. "Last night, I actually thought you might be an okay wolf. I even hated you

38

less. But now, I loathe you more than the Shadow Monsters roaming these woods."

He looks at me, his lips pinched. "That's a lot of hatred."

I tug against him, but he doesn't give an inch, hauling me into faster steps. Last night, I should have shoved him out of my treehouse.

"Just behave and this will be over in no time," he suggests, like he's doing me a favor.

Fuck him. I fight him the whole way, making him drag me and work for every inch.

We've been walking for hours, ducking low branches, trampling prickly shrubs, and stepping over dead logs. He brought with us several apples I've already eaten, and still my stomach still growls for food.

He even permitted me to relieve myself behind a tree. While he held the rope, of course. The shame. I will make him pay.

Coupled with that, how can we not have come across any undead yet? The sun sits directly above us when we finally step out of the thick woods.

He looks left and right down an old worn road, as if something is meant to be waiting for him. Overgrown grass and weeds press in at the edges, swaying in the breeze.

"Did they forget about you?" I say in a mocking tone. "So much for the pack who cares. Seems you're just another shifter who doesn't matter to the vile Alpha who's abandoned you out here. Is he really worth risking your life for?"

He stares at me, and those blue eyes flicker with the faintest smear of something dark. Something dangerous.

The threatening look leaves me trembling. This shifter carries power.

"Keep quiet and move fast. Or I'll carry you the whole way and you will not be conscious." The gravelly edge in his voice delivers his promise. He's worried about how vulnerable he is out here to the undead.

He swings left and tugs me behind him roughly.

I contemplate screaming and making a ruckus, but there are no guarantees the Shadow Monsters are even close enough to hear me. And I believe him when he says he will knock me out.

We walk onward, past lofty pines with the sun heavy on our backs. I suck in a harsh breath as a warm breeze swooshes through my hair. I swallow over my dried throat, and the muscles in my thighs ache from the steep downhill descent.

Twigs snap to my right, and I twist around to find a deer staring at us from the woods. The shifter guiding me doesn't even look at the animal, just sniffs the air.

"I may have no choice but to do as you say right now, but don't think that I am in any way obedient." I should have done more to let the Shadow Monsters take him yesterday. Slowed down. Fallen down. Something. But his words terrified me because the wolves would return. They'd catch my scent on him and never stop hunting me.

He looks over at me and considers my words. "If you follow my instructions, you will be safe. There's nothing for you to fear."

I want to laugh. I lift my bound wrists to prove my point. "And secondly, your Alpha is sending me to another pack, so don't lie to me."

"I can guarantee that you won't be harmed. I will never trade with brutes."

My heart pounds.

He talks as if he is someone who has influence over what happens to me once I reach the Ash Wolves pack. Except the stories I've heard of the Ash Wolves Alpha paints him as a barbarian. A different woman every night. He whips shifters who don't hunt for food. And any newborns in his pack are banished. Well, I struggle to believe that last rumor since that makes no sense to growing his pack. But the other stories sound real enough.

"Right, a lesser shifter can have such power over the Alpha of Ash Wolves." I tear my gaze from his.

But I feel him watching me from behind hooded eyes. "You need to know who I—" His words cut off, and I look around to see him staring down the road. A black vehicle is coming our way. The faint crunch of wheels on asphalt reaches me.

My stomach sinks right through me because now my capture feels real. With only this shifter, I feel I have the chance to escape, but once with the pack, I'll be watched. A shiver grips my spine.

The shifter draws me to the side of the road by an arm and holds me close.

"You don't have to do this," I say, my voice desperate. I'm about to be taken into the pack that rules this whole damn country. I won't be able to escape, and whatever freedom I thought I had will be a distant memory.

He waves at the approaching vehicle, ignoring me.

"Please! Set me free." I reach for his arm, touching him. "I don't want to be sold or be someone's slave. I'll die. Your Alpha doesn't even have to know you found me. I'll slip into the woods and you'll never see me again."

When he looks over at me, I search his eyes for sympathy…for anything to show me he isn't the monster I believe him to be.

"I can't do that, Meira." His words are sharp and clipped.

"I hate you."

The jerk just smiles as the black four-wheel drive vehicle grinds to a halt in front of us.

My legs wobble, and my mouth falls open to beg once more, but the driver pushes the car door open, stealing the words from my lips.

A man steps out of the car. Six-foot-three, slightly taller than the shifter next to me. His pale, steel-gray eyes scream wolf. He's broad-shouldered and rugged and smoldering. My heart is pounding wildly, my lungs gasping for air.

Despite his burly size, he stares at me with intense interest, like he knows something I don't. I'm surprised he's not burning hot in his long-sleeved, button-down shirt under this sun. Dark jeans hang low on his narrow hips, and he's wearing cowboy boots, which I find strange. He's got a head full of deep brown hair, a square jaw with strong lips, and a slight shadow covering his jawline, adding to the whole mountain man look. There is something extremely sexy about him, and mysterious… and that isn't what I ought to feel.

He stands tall and proud, his chin high, carrying himself with arrogance. Is he the Alpha of Ash Wolves?

Amid these two, I'm out of place, extremely short in my sneakers and completely breathless.

"Lucien, I was thinking you'd abandoned me," jokes my captor to the newcomer, and I suspect that little comment is a jab at my earlier remark.

I stare daggers at him.

Lucien does a double-tap of his fist to his chest before giving a slight bow of his head. "Dušan, I had no doubt you'd find your way back." He chuckles as if that's an inside joke between the two.

Wait!

What?

Did I hear right? My gaze flips between the two men and lands on Dušan.

The shifter whose arms I'd fallen asleep in. The man who had his erection poking my butt.

I can't breathe.

He was Dušan, the Alpha of Ash Wolves this whole time and he didn't tell me!

His expression is full of mirth, enjoying himself at seeing my shock.

Surprised? He may not say it, but I see it scribbled all over his face.

He let me say all that stuff about him, and he just listened to me. Heat crawls up my neck, but nothing compares to the anger burning in my chest.

Blinking at the men, I'm at a loss for words. I have no idea why my wolf seemed interested in this Alpha and wanted me to sidle up closer to him. She must have her wires crossed because this Alpha is everything I don't want in a partner. Arrogant. Dominant. Pushy.

I rip my stare from his and find Lucien's eyes piercing through me. His attention drags up and down my body, taking all of me in. A nervous excitement builds inside me, which is wrong. Nothing about either of these shifters should have my body responding to theirs, but it does. I overheat, and my nipples harden against the fabric of my top. Beneath their gazes, I feel exposed, as though I'm the one standing in front of them naked.

Lucien's gaze swings up to my eyes, and I can't look away from those hypnotic steel-colored orbs crowned by long dark lashes. "Is this her? Meira?"

"Yeah," Dušan responds, shooting me a satisfied look. "She's feisty, so watch the claws."

I sneer at him as he hands over the rope tied around my wrists to Lucien, then strides over to the rear of the vehicle.

Words graze my mind, but from utter shock, they refuse to come out. I'm stuck with two shifters who have my wolf rumbling for closeness, yet who are kidnapping me from my freedom.

"Put her in the back and let's get out of here," Dušan orders as he opens the rear door of the vehicle. He pulls out clothes, then steps into the blue jeans with frayed hems. As he tucks himself away, he lifts his gaze toward me and winks.

I'm fuming.

Lucien snatches my elbow and drags me to the back door of the vehicle before he opens it for me. "After you."

I lift my tied hands to climb in and push myself up, finding it harder to do with my wrists bound.

There's a shove at my back, and I fall forward onto the seat. I turn my head. "You're a real charmer, you know that?"

The door smacks shut just as Dušan closes the rear one.

"Assholes!" I yell as both men stand outside, whispering in private. I search the floor and back of the car for any weapons. Only clothes in the back. I shuffle across to the opposite door and tug at the handle. Locked. Of course it is.

The pair outside walk back to the car and jump into the front seats.

My stomach lurches as we take off down the road.

Dušan leans back and looks at me from the front. Blue eyes stare at me, burning like an inferno through me as he fixes his gaze on my face. "Get comfortable. It's a long drive."

I look away from him and stare out the window as we pass the forest. The place I once called home. Driving past it feels bittersweet. There is no way out of this for me.

CHAPTER 7

MEIRA

A shiver passes over me as we turn and drive up a long, narrow road. We've been going for hours up through the rocky hilltop of the Carpathian Mountains, and the closer we get to Dušan's pack, the more my stomach feels uneasy.

Outside, undead linger near and more stumble out of the woods. This is never a good sign, because it means they've sensed blood or they remember feeding in this location before. They remember areas.

We drive up to a pair of solid metal gates standing at least fifteen feet tall. A similar fence with barbed wire across the top stretches out on either side of the gate and around the whole settlement. The place looks ominous with a penitentiary vibe.

Gigantic pines lean low over our path, but the ones near the settlement have been chopped, with only stumps remaining. They've done everything possible to stop the undead and intruders from getting into their settlement.

I look ahead and spy an enormous medieval building beyond the fence and up on the hill. My mouth falls open with utter surprise.

"Your pack lives in a damn castle?" I gasp, staring at the steadfast stone walls, the pointy towers, the crenellations across the top. I've read about such places in books that Mama found for me when we'd ransack abandoned homes. But this is first time I've been near one.

"It's Râșnov Fortress," Dušan explains. "Knights built this place long ago to protect local villages against invasion from other countries. The Saxons later expanded the structure. And now, the Ash Wolves call this place home."

I nod, unable to stop staring up at the fortress that seems to take up most of the mountain. This whole time, I assumed the wolves lived in wooden shacks in the forest to keep safe from the Shadow Monsters in the most secure location. Not… in a *fortress*.

We come to a stop right near the gate. Movement from the right-hand side of the car draws my attention. Two of the Shadow Monsters are moving quickly toward us, mouths gaping open, eye sockets sunken, arms filthy and covered in dried blood and mud. One of them is half-rotten with a hole ripped out of his side, the bottom rib visible. I almost gag at the sight.

His head suddenly jerks sideways, then his body flops to the ground from the momentum. He lands in a ditch and doesn't move. Damaging the brain or decapitation are the best ways to kill them once and for all.

I glance up to the fence and spot a sniper with a rifle. The second monster goes down just as fast. It's easy when there are only a few…but facing several hundred at once is a different story.

I crossed a swarm once, caught off-guard as they poured out of the woods near a river I had been bathing in. They left me alone, but being invisible to them meant they shoved and pushed and stamped over me when I fell over. I don't even know how I survived, but that was the day I decided my shelter had to be in the trees.

A crow swoops down to the ground and hops over to the dead. It pokes at a wound on the man's side, then flutters off in an instant. Not even scavengers will eat the plagued.

The gates slide open and we are on the move again. I glance back as the doors shut quickly with a final sounding clink.

We drive along a curvy road that takes us farther up the mountain, and the more distance we cover, the more my chest clenches. Pine trees coat the hill in every direction, and amid them I notice wolves roaming about. Their heavy coats of black and gray are matted, and their lips curl dangerously over sharp teeth at our presence as we drive past.

At the top of the hill lies the fortress. An oversized drawbridge lowers in front of us and we drive inside before finally coming to a stop in a large cobblestone courtyard. Half a dozen other vehicles are parked here.

The two shifters climb out of the car swiftly. My stomach tightens as Lucien approaches and lets me out.

As I climb out, he takes my hand instead of the rope binding my wrists, then he moves with fast steps away from the vehicle. Gorgeous floral and fruit trees pepper the area, and they feel so out of place. Stone houses that resemble smaller versions of castles surround the court. We walk past them, and I note lanes darting between them to more buildings behind them. There are more and more people everywhere the farther we travel. Men only... My heart is pounding wildly. Where are the women and children?

All I want to do is cry.

Everything feels foreign. All I've known for so long has been the woods and small settlements here and there with only females. But this...this place is so immense, it intimidates me.

The other shifters glance my way, eyeing me head to toe. I bristle and shy away from them, only to bump into Lucien.

"We need to go fast." There's panic in his voice, which in turn has my pulse racing.

I take a deep breath, trying to control the tremors as I push back the fear coiling inside me.

Dušan strides ahead of us, all muscles and so tall—even the way he moves is attractive. All the shifters we pass tap their fists twice to their chests as they acknowledge their Alpha.

I try to remind myself of whom I'm dealing with now. Gone is my assumption that he's just a normal shifter. This is Dušan. The Alpha whom I've heard so many horrible rumors about. I haven't exactly seen that side of him yet, if I exclude the arrogance, dominance, and kidnapping. But as he looks back at me, I worry I might get to meet that monster very soon.

At the end of the yard stands a gigantic building comparable with a castle. It's made of sand colored stone and has three towers attached to it, with pointy roofs and numerous arched windows. A large balcony encircles the top third floor. Guards stand out the front as more male shifters are pouring out of their homes, many of them sniffing the air and staring at me with too much interest. The guards' expressions reminds me of the shifter in the woods who attacked me.

Panic chokes me as we quicken our stride.

The guards step aside, and Dušan pushes open the metal door so we can enter the castle. It's dimly lit inside, the walls stone and barren of any paintings or decorations. A grand staircase with black, curled railings sits ahead of us. There is an empty feeling about the place, and it's only when I look closely at the details that I see the claw marks on the stone walls and floor. The dent in the staircase banister. Three claw marks even streak the ceiling where a candle chandelier hangs.

Dušan pauses near the mahogany staircase and swings around to face us. Heat flares over me at the way his gaze slides over me, his stunning eyes blazing with fire. It seems he can't decide on what to do with me.

"What's going to happen now?" I ask.

He doesn't respond right away, and I see the wheels spinning behind those pale blue eyes. Does he remember how I offered him shelter from the undead, how he held me tight during the night? Just when I think he might ask me to join him, he walks away and tosses over his shoulder, "Take her to the others in the waiting room." He climbs the stairs two at a time. Heaviness sinks through me, dragging me lower and lower.

Bastard.

I open my mouth to say something, but Lucien is there, taking my elbow and leading me away.

"What's in the waiting room?" I ask.

"Just a place to relax and feel safe. You don't have to worry, Meira. No one will hurt you here."

I blink at this handsome man who walks me down a dimly lit cobblestone hallway. I don't even bother trying to remember the paths we take. How far will I get if I try to escape this castle with all the guards we pass? Muscular shifters dressed in all black watch our every move.

"That's not true, is it?" I answer. "It's where I'll wait until you fly me to the Alpha I'm being traded to."

He looks over to me but says nothing because I'm right. I sigh and tear my attention away from him. My insides are like tar, sticking to my ribs, and I just want to scream.

Lucien leads me to a door at the end of the hall, his steps heavy, matching his breaths.

The door creaks open and we're facing another guard, whose eyes meet mine. He's tanned with the sides of his head shaved. A healed scar runs across his nose and under an eye.

"The missing one?" He grunts.

Lucien nods. "First flight in the morning."

His words are like daggers, jamming into my back and twisting. I'm being sent away so quickly. I'm not ready to leave. I've lived in this country my whole life. I know these woods and the monsters in them.

Lucien turns to me and fiddles with the rope around my wrists. "Dušan has an agreement with every trading pack to ensure each female he sends is never harmed."

He draws the rope free from my wrists, but he captures my hands before I can pull away. He smiles at me, as if I ought to be grateful. But I am torn up. Scared. Angry. Confused.

"A captive is still a captive," I murmur.

He looks at me with an ache sliding over his face. Those steel-gray eyes seem to pierce right into my soul as his thumb brushes against the inside of my wrist. I swallow hard.

"If you get hurt, find a way to contact us," he points out. "We check in regularly with the packs and the women. Trust me on this."

Remaining under his gaze easily sways me out of my turbulent thoughts and leaves me at his mercy. The way his thumbs stroke my wrists ignites a heady feeling that overwhelms me along with his Alpha power.

My heart racing, I stare at him like there's more between us, but that's me skating on ice without knowing how thin it is. It's reckless and can only end badly for me. All male shifters want one thing—to claim a female and impregnate her. And I can't be that woman and bring a child into this horrible world. I shouldn't want to do anything with Dušan or Lucien.

His mouth parts to explain something, but I don't want to hear any excuse he has to give me. I'll be gone tomorrow and will never see him again. I draw my hands out of his and walk into the room, leaving him behind.

There is no reason for me to trust any of these Ash Wolves. Not now or ever.

At least half a dozen women I don't recognize lounge in the room, reading books or chatting. To my surprise they seem semi-happy with being here. Two sit by the fire talking, while a brunette sits alone near the window, staring out at the forest down below. All the couches are taken, and no one looks my way. Similar to the girls on the aircraft, these are a similar age to me, dressed in clean clothes with no rips or stains.

Fighting back a tear, I crouch in the far corner and rub at the soreness in my wrists from the ropes.

I don't know how much time passes when the brunette from the window stands to stretch her back and makes her way over to me.

"How are you doing?" She sits in front me, her legs crossed.

"I hate this place," I respond.

She half-laughs and nods. "I don't get how some of them can look so relaxed." She points her chin to the girls giggling on the couch. "I'm bouncing on my toes wanting to get moving already." She talks at a million miles a minute, her hands animated. She's wearing a yellow and white stripped dress with short sleeves. Not a single smudge of dirt.

"I'm Sam," she says, running a hand through her locks. She's beautiful with the longest lashes, and she's wearing a rosy lipstick. I've only ever seen Jaine wear lipstick. She let me try it on once, only it felt sticky on my lips.

"Meira," I admit, figuring there's no need to hide it any longer. It won't change my situation.

"You're doing well, Meira, to not be freaking out. Most women just brought in don't cope well at all and have a meltdown."

"Oh, I had my moment to freak out when Dušan caught me in the woods."

Her jaw drops open. "The Alpha himself? No way!" Her voice squeals with excitement. "What's he like? I've heard so many stories, all conflicting. A couple of the women have seen him and say he looks like a god. But he won't talk to anyone less than Alpha status."

I almost choke on my laughter. "He's more a prick, if you ask me." Just saying the words takes me back to us in my treehouse and his erection poking me in the ass. Yep, he's a prick, all right.

She looks almost offended by my words at first. "What's he like? Handsome?"

I blink at her. "You haven't seen him?"

She shakes her head. "Been three days since I was captured by a male Beta and brought here. All of us girls are going to a mating ceremony tonight to see if our soulmate is in the Ash Wolves' pack. If they're not, then we will be traded to another pack somewhere in Europe. Dušan has a few trade partnerships set up apparently."

I have no clue what the ceremony entails, but I get the gist enough to make sense of what will be going down. In truth, I hate the idea of the whole damn thing. "And you're okay with this ceremony thing?"

She nods enthusiastically. "I was in heat when I hid in the woods for the past two cycles and it caused me excruciating pain. My wolf is crying out for a mate and if I stay out there, a wild shifter will hunt me down and rut me until I die. So I'm excited to finally stop running and being scared. And I can't wait to see if my mate is in this pack." She reaches out and grabs my hand, her touch almost shaky from adrenaline. "I hear Dušan and even his Third, Lucien, might be attending. Both still have to find a mate." The glint of excitement gleams in her eyes.

I can't think of anything worse. But I don't hate the woman for her happiness, if that's what she wants. "Good luck with getting an Alpha."

Her face beams. "Are you not excited about tonight?"

I stare at the women around us. Most talking are just as excited as Sam. These females crave a mate. They want a shifter to join with and to have babies. I can't imagine living like this, to let someone else control me, to no longer feel free. Mama always said that until my wolf comes out, I ought to keep away from other wolves because they will kill me for being different. Which is why I fight for my freedom so much.

"You're being traded without a ceremony?" she asks.

Sighing, I say, "Yep. I'm being treated like an animal." Bitterness coats my words at remembering being caught in the woods and tossed into a truck. There, a male shifter interrogated me and made notes about me in his notebook. Then, I was hauled onto an aircraft. So while these girls get a ceremony, I got nothing like that.

"Oh, Meira." She lays a hand on my bent knee. "You're looking at this all wrong. You're gaining a life partner so you won't be alone anymore. Don't you want that?"

I shake my head, and her eyes widen at my response. "Really?" she asks.

"Don't you want more than just serving a man and having his children?" I try to keep the bitterness out of my words and not crush her dreams.

She blinks, staring at me with confusion. How nice it must be to live such an ignorant life. Maybe I'm the problem, fighting the primal call of my wolf, except I'm not like Sam or the other girls in the room. Things can never be that simple for me. What lies inside me isn't normal, but I push those thoughts away.

"Well, Meira," Sam says as she stands. "I'm sorry you get traded and don't get a chance to find your soulmate in this pack first. We wolves are all born to find our other half, not to be loners, so I will say a prayer to the moon that you will find your mate soon." With a short smile, she strolls across the room to join the others on the couch.

I lower my head and stare at the wooden floor, noting the scratch marks. Sam's words stay with me. Except I remind myself I'm not like her, and the only solution for me is to be on my own.

Time passes as I close my eyes and drift off into sleep. Now, it's night outside, and with it comes a lingering pain across my middle. It gets stronger, slicing deeper through me.

I push myself to my feet. Maybe walking will ease the ache. No one pays me any attention, but all I can think about is breathing slow and pushing past the pain. It always comes and goes. My sickness has never left me, even after all these nineteen years.

But the pain lashes over me as if someone whipped me. I cry out, clutching my stomach, and then fall to my knees.

Voices escalate around me. Someone is at my side, but I can't focus on anything. I hiss with the laceration tearing through me. It deepens, getting sharper, closing in around my stomach.

"Meira," Sam says, frantically waving at someone behind me.

I drop to the floor. Stars blink in my eyes, blurring my sight. My gut is on fire, feeling like someone is scooping out my insides. I hug myself, drawing my knees to my chest as I try to deal with the excruciating pain.

"I need help..." The words tear from my mouth as darkness feathers at the edges of my vision.

CHAPTER 8

DUŠAN

The Alpha in me demands I call Ander and confirm that I found his missing Omega. Except my wolf snarls with venom at the thought of not claiming her myself. That delicious mouth of hers says so many things she shouldn't—words that I've punished other wolves for. I ought to drag her aside and spank that tight little ass for her comments back in the woods.

That doesn't stop me from wanting to fuck her so hard the whole settlement hears her cry out in pleasure and knows she's been claimed. That she's mine. All those male shifters staring at her hungrily in the courtyard riled me up, and now I need to take care of that annoyance. She's an unmarked female, and her scent is ripe, calling males to her. Except for a true mating to happen, her wolf must accept the male.

I sigh and lean over the balcony outside my office, the wind still today, but I feel something brewing in the energy. Below, the evergreen pine forest stretches across the mountain. The old Râșnov city sits nearby, now abandoned and decayed. No one lives there aside from the occasional squatters. The streets are filled with undead, so humans left long ago.

Someone clears their throat, and I inhale Lucien's woodsy wolf scent as he joins me outside. "There's something different about her."

I know exactly whom he's talking about. I saw the look in his eyes when he first met Meira, the hitch of his breath, the acceleration of his heart. She's taken me like an unsuspecting storm, her scent refusing to leave me, her fiery attitude a challenge I want to accept.

I face my Third and school my thoughts on business. "Ander is expecting her delivery."

He bobs his head, but I don't miss the tightness around his eyes. "What if we hold on to her a while longer?" he suggests. "Discover what makes her different. I doubt Ander will appreciate us sending him faulty goods."

The wind drives his brown hair off his face, and he grips the railing alongside me.

"She's affected you that much?" I ask.

Steel-gray eyes raise to meet mine. "Not a fucking chance."

I almost believe him. Almost. He's always been able to convince others he's not impacted by the state of the world, as if he's immovable as a mountain, and that he just pushes on when life gets tough. But I know the man who stands before me. He's a friend who lost so fucking much that the only way to cope is to embrace denial. There's a reason he wears cowboy boots. They are the only thing he has left of his father, so he isn't as good at hiding his pain as he thinks.

"Mad and Caspian need to fucking return from the X-Clan." I growl. "I don't need a hothead like Mad ruining my trade agreements by doing something stupid." My shoulders stiffen. The only way I keep everyone in my pack safe is with this exchange. Delivering Meira fixes the problem. So why do doubts sweep through my mind about sending her to Ander?

My wolf snorts at my indecision. If he could laugh, he'd be howling. Wolves are meant to be mated. It's how we're built.

Wearing an irksome smirk, Lucien claps me on the back. "She's gotten to you too, I see."

"Fuck." I shake my head. "I don't need this." Pushing a hand through my hair, I stare out over the landscape. "There's something wrong with her. Her scent isn't right." And if I'd met my mate, I'd know. Which is why I think what I'm feeling is little more than lust.

"Part of me wonders if she isn't a cross between different wolf breeds," Lucien suggests.

I meet his stare, my gaze narrowing. "You think she's from an opposing pack?"

He shrugs. "You once told me to never dismiss any possibility."

Except she lived out in that treehouse. Well, at least, I thought she did. Doesn't mean she can't be aligned with another pack. There are many breeds of wolf shifters, many ready to kill and get their hands on my pack and territory. Kill me, and they have the right to fight for the spot of Alpha to my pack.

I grit my teeth and suck in a sharp breath, trying to control myself. She couldn't be a spy to let Alphas into the pack? But do I really know her?

Footsteps draw my attention behind me, ripping me from my thoughts.

Mihai is in the office, and I nod. Perfect. I'm about to find out exactly what happened with the delivery to X-Clan Wolves.

Lucien and I walk the length of the balcony and step inside to join Mihai.

Mihai double-taps his chest before bowing his head. He's a Beta and charged with managing my transportation and has been doing a damn good job for years. But Mad quickly blamed him for Meira missing from the delivery.

"Dušan," he says, as he waits for a command.

"Sit."

He does so across the desk from me. The rest of the room is empty. This isn't a place to lounge in—it's a place to get shit done. Lucien stands by the doorway to the balcony, his shadow stretching out over Mihai. He sits still, his back straight, never cowering.

"You've never let me down," I begin. "So, how did a girl go missing on the last delivery?"

He takes a deep breath, followed by a few moments of uncomfortable silence. Mihai's gaze slides from Lucien to me. "I delivered nine girls." He fiddles with something in his pocket and pulls out a folded-up piece of paper. Placing it in front of me, he unfolds it.

I read the list of girls, with the last one being Meira. Each has a tick on them, as per all other delivery slips. We've never had this problem before.

Looking up, I don't see a wolf who looks like he's hiding something. The telltale signs of lying aren't there; neither is he nervous sweating.

"So, you sure nine girls got on that aircraft?"

His eyes hold mine, never once looking away. "I supplied them to Mad at the plane like I always do, then I left. I didn't do a damn thing different."

Without Mad here, I can't corroborate either story. But I do have

Meira, who has no reason to lie about how she escaped. The only problem is getting her to open up.

"And Mad?" Lucien asks. "Anything different about his behavior?"

Mihai barks a laugh. "Mad was his usual prick self, telling me to fuck off because they were running late."

I blink at him, unaware of the flight being delayed. So, from what I gather, the girls arrived at the aircraft. Except somehow, Mad lost one between loading them up and taking off, since Meira was still in our woods and not two countries away. I don't need fuck-ups. I glance over to my video com and reach for it to call Mad.

"Excuse me." Jay, one of my close guards, abruptly sticks his head into my office. Panic crawls over his face. "I'm sorry for barging in, but we have an emergency."

"What is it?" I snarl.

"Something's wrong with the new female wolf. She was crying from pain and just passed out."

My heart clenches. Lucien steps closer, his breaths quickening.

"Bring her to my room," I order.

I stare at Lucien incredulously after our discussion that something is different about her. Mihai, still in his seat, furrows his brow in confusion.

"You can go," I tell him. "We'll discuss this later."

Meira

My eyes fly open, and my heart races. Sweat rolls down the sides of my face and neck, my whole body flaring with heat. I squint against the sunlight pouring into the room from the arched window. I don't know where I am at first. Slowly my surroundings come into view.

Stone walls remind me I'm in a castle with the Ash Wolves. A soft bed is beneath me as I lie on my side staring at a wardrobe made of dark timber, the corners carved ornately with wolves howling at the moon. There's a lush rug the color of fresh blood on the floor. I haven't seen anything so clean and new for a long time.

I smell him all over the bed. Dušan. His musky and wolf scent floods me, just as it did back in my treehouse. This is his room. The Alpha has placed me in his bed, which confuses me, considering he abruptly left me to be sent to the waiting room for shipping out.

"How are you feeling?" a deep voice asks from behind me.

I roll over to find Lucien sitting on the edge of the bed, looking at me with concern.

"You had us all scared when you passed out and wouldn't wake."

"My throat is dry," I croak, glancing around the room and finding a black leather lounge chair against the window.

Lucien reaches over to the bedside table next to him and picks up a glass of water.

I blink at him and shuffle to sit upright in bed. That familiar ache pulses through me. My sickness has come at me harder than before, the pain excruciating. What is going on with me? My stomach tightens because letting these wolves see me this sick will do me no favors. It will get me cast to the bottom of their pack hierarchy... too broken to be anything other than their slave.

He hands me the full glass. Our fingers brush, and a jolt of energy dances up my arm. It spreads through me and overwhelms me with a scorching heat. I lose my breath and swallow hard, trying to push past the sensation that draws me to this Alpha. Everything about him consumes me. Part of me wants to give in, to ask him to protect me. Another part hates those thoughts, but my body betrays me.

When I lift my gaze to him, I see his wolf stirring behind those stunning steel-gray eyes. The ones I want to fall into and get lost in.

I mentally shake myself, needing distance away from these Alphas.

"I'm feeling better," I lie as I drink down the icy water, chasing the heat that clings to me.

He looks at me as though he stares right into my soul. I hand back the empty glass and smile, fighting back the pain that leaves me groggy and exhausted. Normally, I'd stay in bed a few days to wait for the sickness to pass, but I've lost that luxury.

"Are you sick?" he asks, refusing to let go of the topic. Of course, he won't.

I shake my head. "Hadn't eaten for a while. I think it was just hunger pains."

He nods, but the way he studies me makes it clear he doesn't believe me. "We suspected that, so I gave you a small injection that should help."

My gaze instinctively goes to my arms and I look down at a small bandage on the inside of my elbow. I try not to overthink what he gave me, not wanting him to suspect me of panicking. But I have no clue how that will impact my illness.

With the small towel in his hand, he reaches over and moistens my brow. There's a tenderness in his strokes, in the way he looks at me.

Yet panic crawls up my spine.

"It's a bit hot in here," I say jokingly, but he isn't smiling.

I blink hard, and my thoughts seem to stutter.

"Don't worry. The injection was nothing more than vitamins to help boost your immune system."

Is that all it really was?

"And why am I in Dušan's bed?" The room has a warmth to it, a coziness, and it's been a long time since I felt this way. Sleeping on splintered logs can never replace the softness of a mattress.

"He insisted on it as soon as he heard you had passed out." Lucien is on his feet. "Let me get you some food."

When he turns to leave, I ask, "How long have I been sleeping for?"

"Two full days without waking."

I quickly steel myself and half-laugh, as I usually sleep for several days, which isn't normal by any standard. "I was clearly exhausted."

"Yeah, that must be it." He walks out and shuts the door, and the click of a lock resonates through the room.

Shit! I collapse back down in bed, my body throttling with pain. Curling in on myself, I bury my face in the pillow and want to cry.

Fear shakes me. This is why I avoided being caught for so long. The sickness makes me vulnerable, so how long before Dušan realizes this and works out that I've never shifted into my wolf? I've never been able to be whole. I'll be cast aside, and not even those starved males will want to touch me. I'll be locked up because someone like me shouldn't exist.

I draw the blanket to my chest and clasp my eyes shut, praying for the aches to leave. Then I'm finding a way out of here.

On the bright side, I didn't get shipped out to the other pack. Maybe that's a good omen. I ignore the mocking laughter in my head and cling on to the last threads of hope I have left.

Lucien

· · ·

The color of her bronze eyes reminds me of blazing fire. They stay with me, refusing to leave my mind. As does her heady scent, along with the smell of blood. I can't work it out, but she is definitely hiding something. Any other shifter and I'd have forced the answers out of them by now. But Meira does something to me. My beast calms in my chest, but she makes me anxious. Secrets get you killed in this world, so what secrets is the little wolf keeping?

I find myself standing outside the door to the bedroom she's in, like I don't have control of my own actions because my wolf insists I stay near. When she touched my hand, a buzz shot up my arm, slamming into me. She stole my breath away… My body went tight, and my wolf pressed forward as I curled my fists. An automatic reaction to protect her overwhelmed me.

Shock filled her eyes, and I burned to reach across the bed and take her into my arms. All I could think about was how beautiful she was, how I needed to taste her lips.

Fuck! My head is a heaping mess.

I still feel her presence. Now I understand Dušan's response to keep her safe in his bedroom, of all places. He feels what I do around Meira. Except, I've never heard of there being two or more soulmates for a wolf.

I push from her door and still feel the pull as I walk away. From deep inside, my wolf surges forward, aching for the shift.

Meira.

He calls to her, but I can't allow myself to want her. She'll be sent away, and if she doesn't, my Alpha gets first pick and first decision if he'll share.

As Third to the Alpha of Ash Wolves, I can't lose my head. Especially not when the Second is a fucking idiot. It frustrates me that Dušan keeps Mad in such a role, when this isn't the first time shit went south from his involvement. Just because he's his stepbrother doesn't mean he's deserving of the role.

Clenching my fists, I march outside and weave between the homes until I reach the edge of the fortress, ready to scream. Sucking in fresh air, I try to calm my racing pulse.

My head roars, while my heart yearns for Meira.

Great way to keep my head screwed on straight.

"Lucien," a male calls from behind me.

With a deep sigh, I turn to find Chase greeting me with a bow. He's a Beta who manages all festivities and pack runs. He's not a large shifter by any means, but his devotion to the pack is unchallenging.

"Everything ready for tonight?" I ask.

"Yes. I wanted to show you where we set up the circuit for the races. Make sure you approve."

The circuit is used for the younger wolves, the newly turned who aren't ready to run with the Alphas through the woods within the settlement.

He has a heart of gold, and even being in his late twenties, he lacks the confidence to make his own decisions. "You know what? I'll trust you."

He gazes at me with concern in his eyes.

I laugh and slap him on the shoulder. "You've done this how many times already?"

"At least a dozen," he says.

"Well, then under your guidance, this will be the greatest one yet."

He steadies himself and gives a nod. Then he's gone. I turn back to looking out to the Carpathian Mountains ahead of me.

Meira won't leave my thoughts. But I never expected any female to ever affect me in such a way. After losing my mate, Cataline, I shattered into hundreds of pieces and vowed to never find love again.

CHAPTER 9

DUSAN

I stare at my Fourth. "She may be an Omega, but there's more to her."

Bardhyl nods. "I've never heard of a wolf being sick like this before, except for Omegas who are in pain from their heat cycle. But not vomiting blood."

My body definitely responds around Meira's body, and my wolf insists we claim her. Her presence draws me with such compelling energy.

None of the other Omegas I've met have shown the symptoms Meira has during heat—bedridden and looking physically ill with pasty skin.

"Could she be carrying a virus? A precursor to becoming an undead?" I ask, my gut tightening at the thought that if she is, I'll have to get rid of her.

Bardhyl thinks about it for a second. He's from Denmark and looks every bit like his Viking ancestors… sandy blond hair worn loose over his shoulders. He's a warrior at heart and looks like one, towering over most. He's fierce and will never back away from a battle, which is one of the reasons he's on my team.

"Doubt it," he answers. "Otherwise, you'd show signs of being sick after the time you spent with her, and I've never seen an undead infection take this long to take over a new host."

"I guess," I say. We both stride along the outside of the fortress, my head trying to make sense of what we're dealing with. "I keep running every possible scenario through my head. Like she can't be a half-breed, or she'd be dead already at her age. So that can't be it."

The forest descends away from the fortress and goes all the way down to the metal fence, where there are more wolves running around in the woods.

"The blood sample Lucien took from Meira is still with our lab," he explains. "We're lacking all the technologies to do extensive testing, so it's just going to take a bit."

A black wolf darts through the woods inside the fence, followed by four others. As our pack grows, the space becomes limited for shifters needing freedom.

Bang. Bang.

I look over to the front gate, at the guards in the tower, taking out the approaching undead.

"There're more and more lately," Bardhyl says. "It's like something is calling them here."

I cut him a look, because I've had the same thought. For weeks now, the infected have appeared more frequently around our perimeter. "Can you look into that?"

He gives a quick nod, and his shoulders broaden. "I'm going down there," my Fourth says, then he lunges into a sprint down the hill—while I turn and march back into the fortress to pay Meira another visit.

Two nights. That's how long I've slept in the spare room, and each time I go into my bedroom, Meira is fast asleep, so what exactly is going on with that hellcat? I need to talk to her, so she better be awake.

There's no way I can send her to Ander in this state, so I've avoided calling him until I understand what I'm dealing with. Part of me wonders if I should swallow my pride and promise Ander a different female. He'll know no matter what… We send him a full spec sheet of every female we deliver.

I seethe at the idea of not keeping my word, since that doesn't make for a very trusting business relationship. We may be from different packs and wolf species, but at the core, we aren't too dissimilar. Which means my inability to deliver what I initially promised is a strike against our growing business partnership. I can't afford for the X-Clan Wolves to have any doubts about dealing with me. All the pack members under my care depend on me supplying medicine and technologies to better protect us and to hunt down food.

Morning sunlight pours through the arched window of the steadfast castle as I stride through its corridors, only the echo of my boots striking the cobblestone floor resonates through the fortress.

I push open my bedroom door and walk straight in out of pure habit, then halt, guilt punching me in the gut from just barging in here.

Meira is bowed over my trashcan, heaving into it.

I cross the room in three strides. "Meira, are you okay?"

She wipes the back of her mouth and straightens herself, meeting my gaze. Her eyes are watery, as if she's been crying.

Steeling her posture, she tries to smile, only I see the pain she's in. "I feel better now," she admits.

My chest tightens at seeing her in agony. I'll never forgive myself if she dies while under my care. I reach down and take her hand. It's clammy to the touch. "I know exactly what you need."

"Yeah, what's that?" she croaks, trying her best to act normal, but I can see right through her lie.

"You'll see." I take her with me, but not before I take a quick look into the trashcan and see blood.

Fuck! She's really sick… except, I don't understand *why*.

"Thank you," she says, distracting me from my thoughts. "Guess I'm just not used to living indoors."

Her excuse is almost laughable, but I let her have her moment. She doesn't have the strength to defend herself, and if I push, she'll grumble. So I say nothing and focus on her healing first.

She walks strong and tall, but her hair is damp and stuck to her head. This isn't the girl I found in the woods, but a shadow of her.

It isn't long before we reach the baths, located at the end of a hall on the ground floor. We step through an arched doorway and before us lies a large sunken bath large enough to fit ten shifters. Steam rises from its surface, and heat greets us as we walk inside. The water ripples from the regular filtering. Without the solar panels I traded with the X-Clan for energy—for things like keeping this bath constantly warm and clean—we'd still be living in the dark ages.

"Wow!" Meira's eyes grow in size as she pulls her hand free from mine and steps closer to the edge of the stone bath. At the back are the saunas and bathrooms, but right now, there's no one here but the two of us.

"A bath will help relax your anxiety," I suggest, hoping this will help her to start trusting me and eventually open up to me.

She looks over to me, her expression heartfelt, like she expected me to throw her into a dungeon. Even when she's sick and looks like death, there's an aching digging in my gut to claim her. Her presence alone drives me insane.

"You're going to watch me have a bath?" She arches a brow.

I laugh, because I'm not going anywhere. "The toilet and shower are in the back. I'll have a hot drink brought to you."

Meira nods and turns to the bath without a word. There's only one way in and out of the room, so she isn't escaping without going past me first.

I march out of the baths and head down the hall, finally tracking down a bulky guard.

"Send word to the kitchen to take a tray of peppermint tea and fresh bread slices to Meira in the baths. Also, speak to Alyna about finding a dress for her, and ensure no one enters the baths until I come out, understand?"

"Of course." He bows and marches down the corridor.

I walk in the opposite direction, taking long strides. I'm ready to find out everything I can about this shifter girl and what exactly her secret is.

By the time I return, Meira has her back to me, completely naked and stepping into the bath. My gaze slides over her shoulders, her tiny waist, and to a perfectly curved ass before she dips into the water all the way to her neck.

The image goes straight to my cock. I step forward. "Warm enough?" I ask, my throat suddenly thick.

She turns abruptly in the water toward me, her eyes wide. The shadowy outline of her body reveals itself below the surface in ripple effect as a gentle wave washes over her breasts.

She gasps. "Why are you in here?"

"It's a communal bath."

Her attention flips to the doorway and back, her arms lashing over her breasts. "So you're just going to stand there and watch me?"

"Would you prefer if I join you?"

"No!" Her response flies past her lips, and I laugh loudly at her nervousness. She doesn't realize how much that innocence affects me.

I stroll across the room, feeling her eyes on me. The restroom is a tiny room with two toilet cubicles, three showers, and a few sinks. I find her clothes piled on the floor, then I collect soap from the sink and a fresh towel from the rack. Back in the room, she's pressed into the corner of the bath, looking unsure of herself. I set the soap down in front of her as she looks up at me with those spectacular pale bronze eyes. She's searching for something in me, expecting something I don't understand.

"How are you feeling?" I ask.

"The water is soothing. I don't feel so sick anymore."

"Good," I murmur as I take a seat on a wooden bench alongside the bath and set a towel down beside me. Stretching my feet out, crossing them at the ankle, I recline and watch my hellcat. "You'd better get to washing or I'm climbing in there and washing you myself."

"You wouldn't dare," she hisses, her brows pulling together. Damn, she's sexy when she's angry.

I arch a brow and lean forward, my elbows resting against my thighs. "Is that a challenge?"

Her glare is like tossing daggers my way.

"Yeah, that's what I thought."

She clicks her tongue, and a mischievous expression slides over her face. Snatching the soap, she drags it under the water.

"So let's talk," I say. "What was going on? Are you injured, is that why you're sick?"

She shakes her head. "No, I'm not sick. I'm just having a hard time acclimatizing."

That's why she vomited blood? Right.

Someone clears their throat outside the bath, and I sniff the air. A timber-like smell… the guard. I jolt to my feet and find him waiting outside the entrance, carrying a tray filled with food and a midnight blue dress hanging off his arm. I reach over and rip off the store tag. We often do trips out to the old human cities to find clothing for our pack.

"Thank you," I say as I collect them from him.

"Will that be all?" There's a quirk at the corners of his lips. He's likely imagining that I want to be alone with Meira. Except my intentions are purely to find out information, even if my wolf insists something completely different is going on.

I nod. "Just keep watch so no one barges in."

"Of course."

With fast steps, I return to the bath, where Meira is starting to climb out. But the moment she sees me, she dips back in. Sneaky minx.

"These should help settle your stomach." I set the tray near the edge of the steaming bath.

I take a seat and place her dress on top of the towel. "So, you were telling me something about acclimatization making you sick?"

She glares at me and suddenly submerges herself under the water, then pushes back up. Her dark hair is slicked back, her face radiant and eyes full. Gone is the look of pained sickness from her expression. The woman in front of me is the one I caught in the woods.

Helping herself to the tea, she draws the cup into the middle of the bath with her, sipping away, her eyes never leaving me.

"Not sure what to tell you. Just had a bad couple of days. We all have them."

"Well, that's the thing, Meira." I study the way the corner of her eyes twitch with concern. "Wolves don't get sick," I say. "We're not built that way, and the only sickness to ever impact our kind has been the virus spread from a bite by an undead. But you..." I fold my arms over my chest. "*You* are sick with something else. How?"

She presses the cup to her lips and takes her time drinking it before returning the empty cup to the edge of the bath and moving to the shallower part of the pool. Her shoulders glide out of the water as she starts to lather herself with the soap.

"There's only one reason a wolf could be sick like this," I say.

Her gaze cuts over to me, fierceness flaring behind her eyes. "Don't know what to tell you. Maybe you're reading too much into it. Both my parents were wolves."

She pushes herself farther up to where the water cascades to her waist, exposing her breasts...the perfectly round and perky globes tipped with a deep cherry nipple.

My thoughts dissolve at the sight. Intoxicating. Fuckable. Dangerous.

She is perfection, and this beauty will haunt me for eternity. I never expected this from her. Those perfect full breasts are driving me wild.

I see right through what she's doing, but I can't stop my thoughts from falling prey. My wolf shoves forward, wanting to claim her. The spark in me flares awake, filling the emptiness I've lived with for so many years. I've bedded dozens of women, but none have touched me this way. None have roused my wolf to such a state of reckless lust.

Looking at her, I want it all. Every stroke, every taste, every desire. To be cock deep inside her, to make her cry out with pleasure, for her to be mine.

A growl flares from me as she lifts the soap and washes her arms and chest with a thick lather.

I can't look away. My cock punches against my pants, my breath hitches. I didn't expect her to be this conniving. She surprises me.

Her hands slide slowly and deliberately up and over her breasts. They jiggle with each movement, hypnotizing me. Her breasts bounce, the soft peaks hardening against their soapy coating.

Fuck me! She's teasing me, making a small moaning sound that goes straight to my dick. I can't breathe as a savage arousal rips through me.

"What were we talking about again?" she murmurs, like she's forgotten.

She's devious and manipulative. But has to be in order to survive in this world, and I'm enjoying her trying to distract me. My mind runs away with me as I picture myself pressing into her and filling her.

Her fingers dance under her breasts and over her narrow waist before dipping lower under the water. I ball my hands, digging blunt fingernails into my palms to stop from lunging forward and taking what I crave. Her eyes glint with mischief as she narrows them toward me. I try to stay still, to hold back, but it grows harder and harder.

"Wolf," I growl. "You're playing in dangerous waters."

She smirks and splashes me before dunking herself completely under the surface of the water.

A snarl abruptly escapes my lips.

I'm on my feet before I can stop myself, standing at the edge of the bath, drawn to her. Needing her.

She explodes back out of the water, shoving the water off her face, soapy bubbles running down her gorgeous body.

When she sees me so close, she blinks rapidly, forcing herself backward through the bath. Panic flares over her face, and my pulse is raging with the chase.

Darkness stretches over my mind.

Need drives into my gut. What spell has she put on me? She stares at me with fear... a fear that has my balls drawing up tighter, hurting like fuck for release.

My muscles tense, I watch her wade through the bath and hurry out.

Her gaze scans the bathroom, then she spots the towel on the bench, closer to her.

She turns toward it, and I drink in her scorching hot body. The small bounce in her breasts with each step, the tight stomach, the thatch of black hair between her legs.

Water drips down her body. I want her legs splayed open, to taste her, lick her, sink my teeth into her and take what's mine.

She moves quickly, but I'm faster, at her side in a second.

She gasps and backs away.

I press my hands to the stone wall at her back, caging her in. I inhale her slick desire, still unable to pin down her scent. But it doesn't matter to my wolf, who rumbles in my chest. I look down at her naked body, my cock straining against my pants. I groan beneath my breath at the way she stares at me, and holding myself back grows harder.

She's spectacular.

"You drive me insane with desire," I snarl. "My wolf pines for you, but there's so much more to you, isn't there?" I try to shake the fog out of my head, to think straight. "All I can think about is fucking you until you scream my name."

"Y-You w-want to mark me?" she whispers, her words shaky.

Meira

He steps back and turns away from me, leaving me breathless. His words and actions affect me more than I should let them. No man has ever spoken to me this way. Yet I don't back away, but instead, shiver with fear...with *need*. My wolf whimpers inside me, wanting to give Dušan everything we have. Except he's too close to the truth...

No wolf wants an impure shifter.

I will die before I give in to an Alpha or any male who wants me for nothing but slavery.

"Get dressed," he orders with his back to me.

My heart flutters with anxiety and my cheeks blush as I grab the blue dress on the bench and drag it down over my head. It cinches in around my waist and sits tightly over my chest. It has long, flowing sleeves and a skirt that dances around my knees.

"What do you want from me?" I growl. "I don't want to be here. Tell me how *you* would feel if you were ripped away from your life and forced to be a slave?"

He spins toward me fast, his eyes narrowing. "That's what you think this is? Being in a safe settlement is slavery? Then I've been a fool to think I was helping you."

My mouth drops open. "You plan to trade me to another pack, so how is that helping?"

His breaths deepen, but I won't back down to this Alpha. He lashes out and seizes my chin, forcing my head back. "You don't know what being a prisoner actually feels like. I grew up with a stepfather who was more terrifying than the undead outside. Who fucked every female in his pack and treated everyone around him like garbage. Who killed his own kind for not following his rules. What I offer is a longer life, whether in my pack or another pack that I know will treat females right." He swallows hard and releases me. A snarl tears from his mouth as he turns away from me abruptly.

I stumble backward, my heart shackled by his words.

"How long did you really think you'd last out there alone with the rogue wolves once they caught your scent?" he asks.

"I did well enough this long," I spit back.

"You want to know what I think?" He grabs my arm and drags me toward the doorway. "I think you're afraid to live in a pack. Afraid because you're a *half-breed*."

My heart starts beating, and I stumble alongside him, my words freezing up.

"That's why you're sick. Your human side is ill." He spins me around by the shoulders, drawing me against his chest. "You know what else your sickness tells me? You haven't had your first transformation yet, have you? Otherwise you would have shifted by now and healed from your wolf side."

I swallow painfully, looking up at him as my heart drops right through me that he's uncovered the truth. My father was human, and he met Mama when he saved her from a bear trap in the woods. He cared for her until she was conscious enough to transform and heal herself. Mama often told me it was the making of a romantic story… that was before he left us.

I lift my chin to Dušan, well aware that he doesn't know everything about me yet, but it's enough to set off alarm bells in my head. It tells me he's savvy enough to pay attention to everything I do. And that means I'm in trouble if I stay much longer in this settlement. What will he do when he discovers why the undead don't attack me? There is no way he can find out because I won't become anyone's lab experiment.

"What will you do to me?" I ask.

"That's up to you." He cocks his head to the side, staring at me sharply.

I blink at him, confused.

"You can stay as you are and keep getting sicker until you die. Or I can help you find a way to bring on your wolf with a forced mating." His gaze softens. He's looking at me as if he pities me.

Forced mating. The air rushes out of my lungs. After a male marks a female, she's forever under his command. Her wolf will obey him, and he owns her. Mama told me males can still mark a female with a bite that binds her to him even if they aren't fated mates. That's what lots of Alphas do, making a harem for themselves through a forced mating. So is that what Dušan wants? To keep me as his sex slave? I can't—I *won't*. I love my freedom too much to be owned by anyone. I stiffen. He will own me over my dead body.

"I'll be fine alone," I declare, as I lift my chin high, my mind stuttering and panic clutching at my chest. "My wolf will come out soon enough. I can feel her pushing, and I don't need your help."

"Half-breeds don't survive transformations on their own," he explains, his fury taming. "Maybe you need some time alone to think about your next steps. You don't have to be alone in this."

I'm lost, his words ripping over my mind. Fury punches me in the gut at his persistence, and my words come flying out. "There's a reason they don't survive. What lies inside half-breeds are monsters, not perfect wolves like you." It's what I've heard from shifters in other settlements.

He reaches for my hand. "That's not—"

"Don't," I cry out. "I don't need your sympathy or pity. I've lived with what I am for years."

The stone walls seem to close in around me. I can't settle down my nerves as I study his face. Shadows gather in his eyes and he doesn't say anything.

Because he knows what I say is the truth.

CHAPTER 10

MEIRA

I stumble into an empty room, the door shutting behind me with a clap, followed by the click of the lock.

"Fuck you, Dušan!" I yell as I spin around the empty room. Footfalls fade away outside.

"Sonofabitch!" I shout.

Four white walls, a small lamp, no window. My heart thumps wildly, and I'm drowning in so many emotions. Fear and unease uncoil within me.

He knows. He fucking knows I'm a half-breed. Half-wolf, half-human. When my kind don't transform once we hit puberty, like me, the animal inside of us changes and becomes a ruthless monster.

Old feelings flare through me, tearing at my heart. I've been happy hiding, letting everyone believe I was an Omega, a Beta, whatever they told themselves…anything but the truth.

I tremble, hating the pity Dušan gave me when he worked out what I was…I don't need anyone's sympathy, let alone this Alpha's.

My human father left us because I wasn't good enough.

Dušan now wants to force a mating onto me because I'm not enough as I am. The idea terrifies me. What if my wolf comes out? Will I die? Will she kill everyone around her? If by some miracle I survive, and then other shifters murder her, then I'm gone too.

It's why I've stayed so long in the woods, always alone.

No wolf will accept a half-breed as a true mate. I am nothing more than an outcast and weak.

I hate the world and loathe myself.

I feel desperate, more so than I have for a long time.

I don't want to feel used. It's hard enough living with what I am, let alone having others mistreat me for it.

Tears drench my cheeks. I don't remember starting to cry, but they fall like the broken shards of my life.

I squeeze my eyes shut, hugging myself tightly. In my mind, I see Mama in my vision from when I was younger and we had just moved into a new settlement, her face morphed into a furious frown. I had forgotten to shut the latch on the shed, and the chickens got out. They ran out of the settlement and into the woods that were crawling with undead.

I etch her face to the back of my eyelids. It has been so long since I had dreamed of her or seen her in my thoughts. Often, I lie in my tree-house for hours trying to picture her face, to remember on what side she parted her hair. But those little things fade with time.

My heart lurches like an undead. I miss her horribly. *She'd* know what I should do right now.

For so long, I have despised the world. But then what should I do? Cry myself into a puddle?

"Calm down," I scold myself. It's not as if I can control the way I was born, but what I can control is what I do with my life.

If I'm lucky, I'll be kicked out of this settlement, except I learned long ago that holding on to hope that things go my way is the quickest way to get myself killed.

I look up at the door and know exactly what I need to do.

To escape.

My sickness is tamed for now, so this is the time to move. Wiping my eyes, I stand tall, then blink at the lamp sitting in the corner, throwing light across the room.

I inspect the lamp up close before I snap off two of the metal brackets that cradle the lightbulb. They're hot to the touch, but I barely feel it when my whole body is flooded with adrenaline.

In front of the door, I lean over and jam the thin metal rods into the keyhole, twisting them left and right. Jaine taught me how to break locks, saying, *"This will save your life one day."*

A metal click sounds, and I smirk to myself as I push those two pins into my pocket then pull open the door. Quickly, I look outside. There's no one in sight.

I slip out and run along the corridor, remembering that I passed an arched passage to freedom this way. The walls are bare. Not a single painting, decoration, or rug adorns the place. The castle feels cold and nothing like a home.

A chill runs up my spine. I shoot a glance over my shoulder. No one follows, so I move faster.

Sunlight splashes the hallway ahead of me and my heart soars. I scramble up the stone steps two at a time, and swing right, following the light, bursting through the arched passage. I squint at first, adjusting to the brightness. I'm on an oversized balcony with a carved stone railing, at least three stories off the ground. Down below, the fortress grounds stretch out before me—the courtyard we walked through when I first arrived, the driveway and the metal gates. The metal fence encasing this territory shows just how enormous this settlement is.

Something creeps into my chest, a feeling I haven't felt since the last settlement I lived in with Mama. Where everything was safe and cozy. Until it wasn't.

But here, the settlement is enormous. How does Dušan control all these wolves? Where does he get the resources to feed and protect them? By the amount of homes below, there have to be close to two hundred wolves living here, maybe more. The sting in my heart pierces deeper for the simple reason that under any other circumstance, this could be a perfect home for me. Minus the small problem of me being a half-breed, putting me at the bottom of his wolf hierarchy and making me a monster in their eyes.

I need to get out of here. I swing around to find the balcony I'm standing on curls outward on either side of the castle.

Voices come from inside the building, and my heart pounds in my ears. I don't wait, running to the left, where the balcony vanishes out of sight.

Someone will see me!

Running, I breathe heavily as I push myself. Each time I pass a window, I duck to avoid being seen. I don't stop, hurrying on and praying I find some way down that doesn't involve going back indoors.

The castle is massive and I'm running out of breath by the time I reach the other end. I pause for a moment, sucking in breaths when I spot a set of metal steps a bit farther away. A desperate gasp escapes my lips.

"Someone's watching you," a male stranger hisses in my ear.

I jump in my skin from sheer fright. I jerk around, my arms raised to my chest. "Crap!"

"Boo!"

My whole body goes rigid at the shifter in front of me. Pale blond hair flutters over his strong, broad shoulders. He has pale skin, and his eyes are a vivid green, like he's one with the forest. The rest of him reminds of a Viking god. Built like a bear, he towers over me, dressed in jeans and a long-sleeved black tee. My knees weaken, and his presence alone leaves me utterly speechless. His closeness turns my reaction to a wash of heat.

I recoil, panic gripping me.

Seizing my arm, he hauls me toward him, my feet almost floating under me from his quickness. His eyes darken with the intensity of an Alpha, and the sensation of this power swarms me.

Face to face, his breath grazes over my brow, and my inhale hitches at his crisp wolf smell mixed with the fresh mountain air. My pounding heart leaves me breathless.

Clasping on to my bravery, I shove myself to my toes, lean closer, and kiss him right on the lips.

He flinches, not expecting that. I land a quick kick to his shin, and then rip out of his grip.

He grunts, but I'm already flying down the metal stairs, my hands sliding over the railing, my feet scrambling down so fast, I keep losing my footing.

"Get your ass back up here!" he orders.

My heart is racing. I hop down on the landing.

A heavy *thud* sounds behind me, the ground trembling.

I spin around, and he's right there, reaching out to grab me.

"Leave me alone!" I flick my arm up to block his, then pivot right out of his grasp.

He rushes up behind me, and large arms swoop around my middle, lifting me off the ground. Suddenly, my legs are flailing about midair as he has me tucked under his arm.

Irritation flushes my skin.

"Where are you running to?

My mind races. Maybe he doesn't realize who I am, so I can trick him into letting me go.

"Put me down. I'm on my way home and you startled me."

"What quadrant do you live in?" he growls, a hint of northern European accent coming through.

I sigh loud enough for effect. "Why are you grilling me? Isn't this place our sanctuary?"

He chuckles. "Why don't you come with me? I can help you out," he deadpans.

Setting me down on my feet, he drags his gaze from me to the path around the ground floor of the castle to where the houses are located. His expression is neutral, while my stomach is exploding with nervous butterflies.

I made a mistake—this gorgeous Viking definitely knows who I am. I see it in his eyes, in the slight tick in his jaw when he stares at me. He's about to take me back to Dušan.

"What's your name?" I demand to know, lifting my chin, all for bravado.

He spears a hand through his hair, narrowing his eyes at me, as though he sees right through to my thoughts. "I'm Bardhyl."

My gaze automatically swings to his powerful bicep, at the way the fabric pulls tautly over his strong chest at the slightest movement. My heart flutters at the sight.

I mentally shake my head—except my wolf is in my chest, pushing to get closer. Just what I need! She acts all coy and lusty while still living inside me, but what will she be like when she comes out?

The more I look at this shifter, the more I notice how handsome he is. My body screams out for him. My eyes do as well. So does my wolf. But he's just another minion to the Alpha.

I search the depth of his eyes for sympathy. When he pulls me by the hand toward the houses, I bite my cheek, reining in my anger.

"Where are you taking me?" I try to use my sweetest voice, hoping he'll find it in his heart to release me.

The smile he offers me melts me on the spot. His eyes seem to glint in the sunlight. With a strong nose and jawline, he is captivating. But he says nothing.

By the time we reach the courtyard with houses on either side of us, the sun is heavy on our backs. Around us, shifters are chatting, walking about, doing whatever it is they do. But panic is squeezing the hell out of my heart.

I trip over an uneven stone, and he catches my arm. "Please tell me where you're taking me. I want to return to my home. My parents will be looking for me."

He pauses before me, all strength and heat—dangerous. Arching a brow, he leans in close again, leaving me completely breathless. I shouldn't let his nearness get to me, but the image of him all over me is turning me on. "I adore the way you try to lie to me."

His grip doesn't let up, and suddenly we're flying across the cobblestones.

"Lie?" I huff, fighting to tear my hand from his iron grip. There's almost something intimate in the way he looks at me, as if he might sweep me up off my feet and carry me into the woods. I swallow, not completely averse to the idea…Wait! What am I thinking? Of course, I don't want that.

He turns and wrenches me across the open courtyard. I stumble behind him as we swing left between two homes, then turn left and then right, small stone houses all around us. Voices and cries of children come from inside the homes, as well as the succulent aromas of food cooking.

In seconds, he has my back pressed to the front door of a smaller home, his body trapping me. "I'm a fair man, and I owe you a kiss back." He smiles like a deviant before kissing me softly, teasing me.

I should push him back, or drive my knee into his groin. Instead, I'm losing myself to his affection, and he makes me forget all other thoughts.

My hands desperately clutch his tee, and I heave myself up on tippy-toes, taking his tongue in my mouth. Heavens, he feels incredible, tastes so delicious and masculine. My head screams this is wrong, to push this stranger away, but my wolf is pushing my body to taste him.

I groan against him as my whole body tenses. His lips drag over my cheek and to my neck just below my earlobe. His tongue flicks out against the tender flesh. I shiver beneath him. Dirty images fill my mind of what his mouth would feel like all over my body.

"I hate that I have to stop," he whispers.

The door behind me suddenly opens, and I'm falling backward into a dark room. I cry out, reaching for him, but I land on my ass as he stands in the doorway, grinning down at me. He grabs the door and shuts it, then he's gone.

"What the fuck?!"

It isn't long before the faint scent of floral perfume tickles my nose.

I freeze.

I'm not alone here.

CHAPTER 11

DUŠAN

Meira is a half-breed. *Fuck!* There's no way I can send her to Ander now, so trying to keep my word has been a damn waste of time. He won't accept her…not many will. She's a liability if her wolf does decide to come out. It will rip out of her body, killing her, but the beast that remains will be a savage brute that will kill everyone in sight.

This is why other packs kill half-breeds who haven't transformed once they hit puberty.

My wolf rumbles in my chest, shoving, pining for Meira. And I didn't want to see the truth smacking me in the face, didn't want to admit that fate had finally paid me a visit.

Her wolf has connected with mine. The precursor for mating for life. Now I feel the need in my bones, in the way my wolf hums in her presence, at how my body awakens at the mere thought of her. Back in the bathroom, I barely held it together to stop myself from claiming her. I'd hoped it was nothing more than lust because the growing desire inside me will soon make her insatiable to me. But she poses a grave danger to my pack. I'll have to make sure she is always with an Alpha when not closed off in her room.

I scrub a hand down my face. How is this going to work, anyway? An Alpha with a weak half-breed, who's a time-bomb waiting to go off?

I promised my pack safety. So why did the fates bring me together with Meira this way?

I pace up and down my office, fury burning through me.

"You will never amount to anything. No one will mate with you."

My Stepfather's words flare over my mind. With them comes rage, and I clench my fists. I promised myself I would make a difference to my pack, not become their burden like my stepfather did to his.

Memories roll right over me, giving me no chance to shove them aside.

"Don't," I yell, lunging at my stepfather who raises another hand to my mother. She's on the floor, bleeding and bruised, gasping for air. Her eyes turn to me as she mouths, 'run.'

The thought of her suffering excited him. I see it in his dark eyes. "I warned you."

I threw myself into my monster of a stepfather, a burly shifter, but still even my thin ten-year old body shoved him into a sideways stumble. Fury takes me, and I drive everything I have into him—punches, kicks, teeth. My fury simmers to a boiling point.

He shoves a hand behind me, snatches me by the scruff and hurls me across the room like I weigh nothing. I slam into the wall and slide down, my lungs gasping for air. I wipe away the useless tears...

"This is your fault," he growls, glaring at my mother. "You made him weak and useless."

His hand raises again, curled into a fist as he leans over my mother.

"Don't touch her," I scream, scrambling to my feet, but it's too late.

Everything is too late.

My world dies in that moment, ripped out from under me, and I know nothing will ever be the same.

The punches begin again and don't stop. The dull whacks soon turn to moist thuds.

The room tilts under me. My stomach lurches, and I run out of the room as I hurl out everything in my stomach.

Even today I feel the hollowness inside me, my muscles so tense they might snap. My throat thickens at the memory I've tried so hard to bury away. To push away the images of the blood seeping over the cobblestone floor. That isn't how I want to remember my mother, crumpled and bleeding on the floor. I want to remember her as the caring woman who loved me, who hid me, who protected me.

As broken as Meira is, as unpredictable as her wolf is, I can't push her away.

Whether she accepts it or not, she's in trouble, and I will help her.

I try to clear my head and make sense of what to do next. To push away the feeling of emptiness.

This is why I stepped up to the role of Alpha. Shifters now turn to me when they have a problem, when they need help.

A howl comes from somewhere in the woods outside. The wolf run is on tonight—at the full moon, when we are all at our wildest. When even my rules won't tame the wolves in my pack. This is a night of recklessness, of releasing and being one with our true nature.

And it's the perfect time to see how much her wolf controls her.

I can't stop seeing the blood in the trashcan from her sickness. So much of it, and any human with this illness wouldn't have many days left. I suspect her wolf side has kept her alive, but for how much longer?

Bardhyl appears at my office door, and I clear my throat, raising my head. "Everything went well?" I ask.

He nods. "You're right. The girl is feisty."

There's a fire in my Fourth's eyes when he speaks of Meira. She has this impact on those she encounters.

"Yeah. Try dragging her through the woods to our settlement like I did." I shake my head as he laughs. "Anyway, we now need a replacement for her to send to the X-Clan Alpha. Tomorrow at first light, take a small group of hunters out in the woods and find another girl." All the girls we had on hand either found their mate amid Ash Wolves, or went to another pack in Europe.

"Of course." He pauses for a moment, looking ready to ask me something.

"What is it?"

"What will you do with Meira?" Concern weaves through his words. His eyes hood as he breathes heavily.

"I'll find a way to save her. Otherwise, she can't stay here." Fear knots in my gut. I look down and stare at the comm video screen, knowing I have to contact Ander for an update, but I feel physically ill at the idea of parting from Meira. The world was meant to fall into place when I met my mate… Except it's just been a clusterfuck of a mess ever since I found her.

"You said she threw up a lot of blood, right?" Bardhyl asks. "That means the sicker she gets, the weaker she becomes. She'll be unable to stop the beast from finally breaking out."

Of course he's fucking right. "So we don't have much time. Tonight's the full moon. That's when I need to start."

Bardhyl nods. With a bow of his head, he leaves the office. He's a lot quieter tonight than usual, but I shake that off.

I'm left alone, and I can't stop thinking about Meira. How she affected me from the beginning, how there are so many things I want to do to her. My wolf demands I claim her before it's too late, but it's not that simple now. Panic fills me at the thought that I'll lose her before I get that chance, and that quickly turns to anger at her being a half-breed.

I've had my share of women. Enough of them that I don't remember how many. They eagerly take to my bed, and I fill them over and over. But I've never found the high I'm searching for, that feeling that ignites my fire and draws me to them, that awakens my wolf.

This hellcat is just that, and my whole body shudders in her presence. I can still smell her sugary scent from the baths, the slick that tightens my balls. I feel it in my veins, from the top of my head to my toes to the tip of my cock.

I know I'm not the only one whom Meira's allure has called to her side.

Meira

"Come close. Don't be afraid," a female's voice calls me from within the dark room.

I stiffen, blinking as my eyes adjust to the darkness. "Who are you?"

A flicker of candlelight erupts from the end of the room, revealing a woman in her mid-forties sitting in a rocking chair, her lap covered in blankets, her eyes shadowy and exhausted.

"I'm Kinley. Come join me." She nods to the wooden chair across from her. Nearby on the table is a collection of books, a pot of tea, and a single cup. She's been snoozing by the look of sleep still clinging to her eyes.

"I'm sorry," I say, retreating to the door. "I think there's been a mistake. I'll let you sleep." My hand reaches for the door handle to try to leave, but it's locked.

"Meira, this is no mistake."

I stand still and glance across the small living room. A curtain covers the windows, the fireplace is unlit, and this home has simple furnishings. The room smells stuffy.

"You live with death, girl," she murmurs. "You wish you were born differently. You believe that if you can just keep the wolf away, everything would be fine, don't you?"

"What do you know about it?" I whisper softly, almost unsure if I want to hear the answer.

She glances to the empty chair across from her, and I reluctantly cross the room, then take a seat.

"I know that if you keep ignoring the inevitable, it will be too late to save yourself."

Something tightens in my solar plexus, as she's way too close to the truth for comfort. My whole life, I've lived with the fear that my wolf hasn't shown, and that when it does, I'll lose all control. I accepted long ago that I am better off without her.

"It's worked this long," I answer.

"And what is your plan for the future? Keep running? A wolf won't stay at bay forever."

I study this woman with short sandy hair, wearing a white button-up shirt with frills around the collar. She's pretty and speaks with a kind voice, but frustration fills me with her vagueness.

"Kinley, I'm not sure what you want me to say or do. Or why I'm here in the first place. I don't even know you."

Her gray eyes glint in the candlelight. "My mother was a human, and she died when she gave birth to me. My father was killed and turned into an infected on my fifteenth birthday. My whole life has been survival, just like the lives of each one of the Ash Wolves outside. Just like you. And I'll be honest, Dušan asked me to talk to you."

Her admittance has a jagged edge to it, like she doesn't feel comfortable with it, either.

"Thank you for sharing."

"Go collect yourself a cup from the kitchen." She points her chin to the other side of the room. There's a plate with freshly baked flatbread and venison. "Bring that over too. You look starved."

Kinley speaks gently, and there's something almost comforting about her. She reminds me of my mother, and there's a warmth spreading over my chest. I'm on my feet and across the dark room, returning with the items in no time.

She pours me tea and the waft of citrus finds my nose. I collect one of the flatbreads, which is the size of my hand, and tear off pieces before popping them into my mouth. Hunger has me salivating, and I eat three in record time.

Kinley watches me as she sips her tea. "My neighbor makes them for me. She's ninety years old and still incredible in the kitchen."

Washing down the food with citrus tea, I set it back on the table. "Tell me about Dušan?"

"His stepfather was a ruthless leader, but after his death, Dušan took over and changed everything in his pack. *Everything*—including the pack rules and moving us all to this settlement, but especially when it comes to protecting females. He will kill anyone who harms a female." There's a knowingness in her expression, as if she's experienced that first hand.

"Why?"

"The old Alpha was violent, especially to his mate and children." She glances away for a moment, then clears her throat. I see the sorrow on her face. "But there's nowhere else I'd rather live now. Not after what happened to me." She lowers her hand and peels away the layers of blankets over her lap.

My gaze follows the movement, and underneath, she's wearing gray trousers. They sit loosely over thin legs. They're so bony, something tightens in my stomach.

I want to look away, but I can't. The top half of her body seems normal, but it looks like she's shriveled on the lower half.

"I'm paralyzed from the waist down," she says. "Happened when I was twenty years old and underwent my first transformation."

I blink at her words. "You survived?"

"Yes." Her eyes light up.

I'm completely stunned by her reveal.

"So even now, can you transform into your wolf?"

She smiles widely. "Of course. My legs will never work again in either form, but I'm alive."

My throat closes. I shift in my seat, unease curling over my spine. Just looking at her breaks my heart.

Is this my fate? I don't want to spend the rest of my life closed up in a house. I've always been on the run and lived in the wilderness. Being alone and unable to walk or run would kill me.

"I know what you're thinking," she murmurs. "But my transformation came when a rogue wolf attacked me. It was my fated mate's wolf energy, a wolf from the Shadowlands Sector, that saved me from dying when my beast broke out of me that day. The rogue wolf severed my nerves and put me here."

My hands shake by my side. "But I've heard of no half-breeds who've survived if they transform after puberty."

"I am living proof that it's possible, if you just believe."

My mouth dries as her words soothe my wolf, and for the first time in my life, I feel like maybe there is hope for me after all.

CHAPTER 12

MEIRA

"**P**lease don't lock me in there," I plead with Bardhyl, who shoves open the door to a seemingly random room in the castle. Once Kinley's mate returned home, Bardhyl collected me from her home and brought me back to the castle without so much as a word.

"Don't make me carry you inside. It's for your own safety."

There's an edge to his voice, which scares me. I step into the empty room. No furniture, just a lit fireplace.

He shuts the door and locks me in.

I dig my hand into my pocket and pull out the two metal rods from the last room, then make my way to the door. This palace has old locks which are ridiculously easy to pick. I wait a little while to ensure Bardhyl is gone.

I spent hours with Kinley, listening to her stories about living alone before her transformation. The similarities between our stories are uncanny. By the end, I decided I really liked her. But I also don't want to be closed up in a room and wait for Dušan to come and just mark me. I've met three Alphas who have connected with my wolf, and I want to understand that more.

Kinley suggested I spend more time getting to know my potential mates, as the transition will be easier. And tonight, I want to visit Lucien and talk to him to see if there's any way I can avoid a mating with Dušan. I hate him for kidnapping me, and I hate him more because of the way my wolf and body betray me around him. How they long for him. If I had my head on straight, I wouldn't dream about kissing him. It's best we stay apart. Lucien seems the most approachable of the Alphas I've met so far.

I jam the two metal rods into the keyhole and twist and fiddle with them until I hear the familiar clicking sound.

Quickly, I slip out of the room and speed down the corridor. The moon is full tonight. I can feel it on my skin, and the wolf inside me stirs more than usual.

A wolf bays in the distance.

Not stopping, I move in and out of hallways, up steps, and then repeat. It's only when I'm standing in a narrow arched door looking out into the woods behind the fortress that I quickly forget about Lucien. I've found a way out of the castle, and maybe while the night cloaks the ground, I can find a possible way through the surrounding fence.

I still haven't come to terms with the idea of an Alpha marking and owning me.

So I slip outside into the balmy night. Overhead, the enormous moon hangs low, illuminating the mountains in its silvery hue.

With quick steps, I head away from the main part of the fortress and rush into the forest inside the fence.

Twigs crunch, and I twist around to find no one there. I keep going as more and more growls and snapping of foliage move in closer. I pause and press my back to a tree, my heart galloping. Shadows dart around me. Maybe this is a mistake… I should come out first thing in the morning to find a way out.

A figure lingers near—out of sight, but whoever it is, they aren't leaving me.

I scan the trees behind me for escape.

There's no answer, but danger snaps in the dark across my skin. Still, I know the man is still there. I can now smell him, his scent…his desire. My boots scrape the soft forest floor as I step back once more. A howl cuts through the air in the distance. It's low and sorrowful, and the sound slices through me like a knife.

A desperate howl sounds…One call of a beast to another.

That's what is inside me—a beast that refuses to come out. I swallow the bitter tang of acid as a snap of a twig comes from somewhere to my right.

Shadows shift. I feel them more than see them, just like I feel every-thing around me now.

Like the moon…

The silver glow throbs in the air, sending shudders along my skin. My heart pounds in response, the tremors carving through my body.

Another sound cuts through the air, only this is somewhere behind me.

"They're coming for you."

I flinch at the words and jerk my gaze to the darkened thatch of trees. Dušan steps out of the shadows, striding with long, purposeful steps until he stands in the moonlight.

His soft blue eyes look almost silver in the night. I'm trapped in them, nailed to the spot as he steps closer. His long, dark hair dances in the air with the movement and my breath catches in my chest.

"I told you," I whisper, my voice hoarse. "I want nothing to do with any of this."

"And still, that won't stop them. Why did you leave your room?" He gravitates toward me in slow motion. My earlier fear fizzles in compar-ison to the delirious arousal burning through me for this Alpha.

That's how it is with us. Push. Pull. Gravitating one minute, and repelled in the next. Thoughts crowd my mind, panicked thoughts filled with the image of us.

"Other wolves, they'll keep coming and coming after you tonight. They won't know how not to. One way or another, your wolf has to come out. You have to be marked, Meira. For your own safety. Now that they have your scent."

"And your desire, right?" My response comes out as a whisper.

There's a twitch at the corner of his eye, a nerve flaring in response. He lowers his attention, taking in my body as I reach out and step backward.

"I'd be lying if I said I wasn't at least a little intrigued," he says.

Intrigued? A hard bark of laughter tears along my throat. "Nice choice of words. Only what's to say you aren't exactly like them?" I jerk my head toward the piercing call that dances on the wind.

My body thrums with power, like paws smacking the ground. Tonight, the wild wolves are set loose, just like Dušan said… and they're coming for me. Their hunger. Their need. Heat mingles with terror, and it's a dangerous cocktail.

"*I* don't know that you aren't." My voice trembles, needing and desperate. "I don't know that at all. I don't know you, don't know any of this."

Run. The need roars inside me. Take a chance on my own. I'm fast and lithe, able to scurry along the rocks and climb the mountain faster than someone like the bulky Alpha in front of me.

If I can escape the settlement tonight, I can find a crevice in the surrounding mountains and slip in. I'll wait until morning, wait until they finally give up the hunt...I can make my way back home.

Home.

The word resounds. Where is my home?

Dušan jerks his gaze to the right, his lips curling, a savage snarl spilling from his mouth. "Decide, Meira, and decide fast. They're coming."

Panic tears through me as a growl cuts through the trees. Dušan lifts his hands as long, black claws punch out from the tips. He turns his head and takes one look at me standing there petrified as another blur races toward us, cutting between the trees.

There's a moment that passes between us, one filled with desperation and duty before he rips his attention from mine and mutters, "Fuck."

He lunges away, lowering his head as he charges into the gloom of the forest. The heavy thump of his steps beats a panicked drum inside my head. Branches snap, mingling with a guttural roar.

A brutal thud comes moments later. Savage, primal growls fill the night. My stomach clenches with the sound as a howl comes tearing through the bushes in front of me.

I have no choice. I do the only thing I can—turn and run.

My throat tightens as a terrifying howl comes from the direction Dušan has disappeared. Is that him? The thunder in my head grows louder, crashing like a crescendo as images come to life. Dušan hurt, lying there bleeding and broken, all because he wants me for himself.

I shake my head as tears blur my view. I scan the tree line, finding a trail that carves a clear path to the part of the mountain within the metal walls. My knees tremble, locking as I stumble forward. I pray my legs will hold, and hurry, leaving the Alpha and the pack behind.

Guilt swallows me. I find myself slowing as I hit the bushes and turning back around. The unmerciful sounds are sickening. Fists and claws flay flesh until a piercing, shattering cry fills the night...and what follows is silence.

Empty silence.

Warmth slips down my cheeks as I look back to the trees. I'm on my own now, on my own with desperation and what little courage I have left.

Dušan's pale blue eyes haunt me as I stagger forward, my boots finding the worn path amongst the trees. A couple of other wolves come for me, swarming the forest all around me. Their male scent so pungent, it's like a rag down my throat. They smell so familiar.

I drive my boots against the ground and run as fast as I can. Nails pierce the flesh of my palm. Something emerges out of the infernal darkness.

"Where do you think you're going, female?"

The warning plunges like ice through my veins. His long, blond hair shines as he moves closer. I haven't seen him before, and I don't find him handsome in the slightest. I skid to a stop, my heart pounding so loud, I can barely think.

"Leave me alone," I warn, my voice cracking and trembling.

"I can't do that." He sucks in hard breaths and glides near, just like Dušan did.

But unlike the towering midnight-haired Alpha, this one keeps coming, lengthening his long strides. White fangs glow in the dark. "Now, I can tell you I'll be gentle." He jerks his attention toward the trees. "But the rest will be here before we know it…and I need to have my fill of you."

I shake my head as a tremor slices through me.

"God, I love the scent of your fear," the male growls, his voice savage and unkind. "Don't worry. You'll be wearing my mark before long."

He reaches up and grasps the front of his shirt. With one brutal yank, the fabric splits, tearing from his chest before he drops the ruined garment to the ground.

Muscles ripple in the night. All that power, all that lust. His dark eyes glitter like steel in the night. Panic floods me, clamping my insides tight.

"No," I whisper. "*Please*. No."

He's on me in an instant, lunging to close the distance in a panicked heartbeat. One hand goes around my arm, the other closes over my breast. He looks down at me. "I'll be gentle, *next time*, I promise."

Claws pierce the fabric of my dress. The sound of tearing cloth starts before a low and unmistakable warning growl comes from behind me. "Take your fucking hands off her."

I stiffen at the sound. Hope surges in my chest as a whimper slips from my lips. Dušan approaches, and the smell of blood and power washes over me. "I won't ask you again, Vin."

"She's not marked." The male turns to pierce me with his dangerous stare. "Not yet."

The sting from his claws cuts deeper, pressing in around my breasts. Is this what it means to be marked? Am I now this savage male's property? Terror drives in deep. "Please, no. Not you. Not like this."

Vin wrenches his gaze to mine as he curls his lips. "You don't want me, female?"

"No, she doesn't," Dušan answers for me. "Now remove your claws before I remove them for you…with your own fucking teeth."

There's a wince as fear drives to the surface of the wolf's eyes. Dušan smells savage, the thick, cloying metallic scent of blood hanging heavy in the air.

It isn't his blood.

Not his.

Relief courses through me as Vin unfurls his fingers and lowers his hand.

"Now let her go."

A low, pissed-off sound flies from the male's lips before he lets me go.

"Meira," Dušan murmurs.

A connection between us surges.

"Hurry," he whispers. "Run farther up the mountain inside the settlement, and I'll find you."

That bond between us throbs with life. Something crashes through the bushes behind us. I swallow hard, give a nod and step sideways, whipping my gaze from his in the last moment before I lash forward.

I race into the night, bounding over fallen logs and around thick, thorny brambles. Thorns snag on my dress, scratching deep. I push down the sting and keep on running, clambering blindly, pushing myself forward with the knowledge that the edge of the metal fence should be near.

The mountain towers above, a monolithic giant brooding and dangerous. I suck in sawing breaths and glance over my shoulder.

I can't hear them anymore. I can't feel Dušan.

My hands tremble as I climb farther, focusing on the motion of lifting my foot on the steep ground and pushing my body higher and higher, until I have to stop to catch my breath. I clutch a hold of the rock and lower my head to the surface.

Trees spread out like a blanket far below me. I'm high up...*really* high.

"Take your fucking hand off her." Dušan's words fill my head as I straighten and set my gaze to the task.

He hurt and maimed others for me.

All to save me.

Still, instinct leads the way. I move slower now, pulling myself up onto a small dirt ledge on the side of the mountain overlooking the fortress below. I just drop to my knees there, panting.

Silence finds me, clutching ahold of the edge. I barely hang on.

Down there. Down there, Dušan is battling one, two...ten of them to protect me.

I shudder. *"Hide. I'll find you."*

I hold on to those words, looking around. The soft glow of the full moon hugs the contours of the mountain. I can't climb anymore. I get to my feet and stagger backward from the edge, shoving my heels against the stone until my spine meets the coolness of the mountain.

Lightning flickers high up in the clouds, far off in the distance. Up here, the world spreads out before me, leaving only thoughts and memories behind. I drag my knees upward and pull them close.

Is Dušan still fighting? How many can he battle before one of them takes him down? I bite my lower lip as a shudder courses through my body. A snarl echoes through my mind, savage and unwelcome.

"No, stay away from me," I whisper, stilling the beast inside me that pushes forward.

Claws scrape under the skin of my knees before the tips push against my skin.

Fear bursts through me that my wolf will come now—tonight. *Here.*

I close my eyes as the faint echo of thunder rumbles through the sky, and that creature inside me reacts, lifting her head to inhale the faint scent of ozone.

I don't know how long I wait. Minutes feel like a lifetime as I watch the storm slowly creep closer, lightening the sky with neon flashes of white. As each second rolls it toward me, I feel that desperation inside.

I need to leave this place—leave Dušan—or by morning, there'll be no reason to leave. By morning, they'll have found me. Tears slip down my cheeks at the guilt I feel for sneaking out. I brush them away with the back of my hand and then shove against the ground.

"Don't tell me you're leaving already."

The low, guttural growl is punctured with slow heavy breaths. Dušan limps forward, coming out of the darkness like a god. Lightning cleaves through the sky behind him, and for a second, my heart pounds into the back of my throat.

He stumbles forward, holding his left arm against his body. He tries to hide the pain from me as he lifts his gaze, but wolves heal fast. A long scratch marks his cheek and his shirt is torn along the middle. One shoulder completely gone, torn by fangs and claws.

His boot scrapes as he stumbles forward, his ocean blue eyes searching my face before he slowly takes in all of me.

He saved me, protected me, and he could have died in the process.

"Why?" The word slips from my lips. "Why risk your life like that?"

"If I have to explain it, then I've done a pretty piss poor job of showing you before now."

My breath catches as he approaches me. Only this time, I'm not moving backward. This time, I'm not running.

"I don't want this." I shake my head. "I don't want any of this."

"And yet, that won't change a thing. You have a wolf inside you, Meira. One you can't cut out. One you can't deny forever. You're at the crossroads here. You can either die, or embrace what you are and learn that with the downsides, there are some pretty amazing positives."

"Yeah, like what?"

He reaches up, grasps the back of his shirt, and drags it over his head. Muscles cord, clenching tightly as he drops the ruined garment to the ground. "Faster healing abilities, for one thing." His arm doesn't droop as much anymore, and I catch him straightening. "And also smell," he continues. "For instance, I can smell the hares running frantically from the storm…can you?"

I draw in the air through my nose, letting the sweet scent carry me away. Panic tastes bitter under the sweetness. "Yes."

"Just like how I can smell your wolf. I can smell her hunger—her need. I can smell that she's ready to come through. That she *wants* to come through."

My pulse speeds up with his words. The thought of that—of being out of control—terrifies me. "I…"

"I can't fight them forever," he murmurs as he steps closer. "But I will for as long as I can, if that's what you want."

"Will it hurt?" I search for the truth. "I don't want to die."

"Not the way I want to do it." He lifts his hand. "And we don't have to…We don't have to have sex, if that's what you want."

"But you'll still mark me, won't you?"

Sadness flares for a second in his eyes. "Yes. My mark will show my claim. No other male will touch you. Not unless you want them to."

"Unless I want them to?"

"Don't worry." He swallows hard. "I won't force you into my bed, Meira."

My throat tightens. The thought of being in his bed fills me, just like the lightning floats in the sky over the valley. Do I want that? Do I want to belong to him that way?

My heart clenches tightly, answering for me. "What do I have to do?"

His eyes widen for a second before he steps near. I flinch as he lifts his hand. The movement is automatic. Still, that doesn't stop him from wincing. "Turn around and sit."

Turn around and sit? I don't know what I expected, but it wasn't that. "Can't you just bite my hand?"

A sad smile crests his lips. There's a slow shake of his head. "It doesn't work like that, unfortunately."

"Then how does it work?"

"Turn around, Meira. I promise, your wolf will lead the way."

I stare into his eyes, finding nothing but compassion and desire, and finally putting my trust in him, I turn around to give him my back. I sink to the ground, crossing my legs. I gasp as he moves. I become aware of him…intently aware of the close proximity of his body to mine. The way he towers over me and then drops to the ground.

I remember Kinley's story, how her mate helped her wolf cross. Maybe this is what I need. Help to release my wolf and no longer be an outcast.

"Hands on the ground in front," he orders.

My heart lunges. Still, I do as he instructs.

His fingers brush the hair from the back of my neck before he leans close. Warm lips meet my flesh. I close my eyes with the contact and try to remember to breathe.

Thunder growls overhead as he presses his chest against my back.

He pushes against me, making me lean forward until my hands take my weight. I rise up on my knees as he hunkers down above.

He is so gentle, so incredibly gentle and yet there is nothing soft about him. He's all power, all Alpha. The heat of his body melts into my spine, easing that constant ache in my body. His lips trail down, sliding over my shirt to press on my back.

"Mother have mercy," he growls, his voice husky.

My wolf moves closer. The sound of her soft, padding steps in my mind mingles with the heat of his body. A snarl slips from my lips, rumbling in the center of my chest before I realize it's there.

"That's it," he whispers. "Come to me."

I hunker down against the warmth of the stone. Heat radiates from within me, pooling between my thighs and spilling outward. Electricity dances across my breasts, making my nipples tighten as Dušan kisses the place beneath my ear.

"You ready, Meira?" he murmurs against my ear.

I don't register a word, don't realize a thing as he grinds his hips against the curve of my ass. Fangs graze that soft flesh behind my ear, unleashing a surge of arousal. I moan and drop my lower body to the ground.

Dušan follows me, bracing most of his body with his shoulders as he pins me down. There's a slow nip, playful and teasing. I curl my fingers as my wolf pushes closer. Raindrops smack the mountain with a hiss. The sky is alive, blazing neon white, and in the electric glow, my wolf lunges, driving herself higher.

With an unmerciful growl, Dušan bites down, sinking his fangs into the back of my neck. The orgasm comes out of nowhere, barreling on top of me as I grind my body against the stone. Pain slashes my palms, but the sting is gone in an instant as I feel my body shift.

Desire swallows the roar inside my head. Still, Dušan holds on, not letting me go. A shiver races along my arms until warmth moves in.

Dušan bites harder. There's no pain, no terror, just arousal, and as the neon glow of lightning dulls, he releases me...and pulls backward.

I lie there, his heavy breath on my neck, my wolf on the edge... so close.

"Something is wrong," he whispers into the moment that is perfect in every way. Except it isn't perfect, is it?

"She feels stuck," I say.

I feel his weight lift from my back. Strong hands clasp my waist and draw me to my knees. Arms wrap around my waist, his solid chest flush to my back.

Shadows move down below, flitting amid the trees.

His words are in my ear. "It's okay. It might take a bit more of a nudge."

I hear the smirk in his voice, and I know what he's implying. Heat surges through me at the thought of him taking me.

"Yes." I gasp the word.

His hold tightens in response, his breaths fast and shallow. "Not tonight. I won't rush this."

We stay like that for a long moment, and I melt against him. "You've marked me as yours, haven't you?"

He doesn't respond right away, instead sweeping the hair away from my neck. Warm lips find my ear. "Partially. Tomorrow, we will finish. But you are now mine. Everyone will know that now and leave you alone."

Mine. That is all I hear.

CHAPTER 13

MEIRA

"Are you ready?" Lucien asks from the doorway to Dušan's bedroom. Leaning a shoulder against the doorframe, his hands folded over his chest, he studies me with a strange expression. Hooded eyes, curved lips, and a mysterious glint in his stunning, gray irises. "It's a gorgeous morning, and Dušan asked me to take you to breakfast. He's got a few things to get done today."

For those few moments, I let myself drown in this perfect image of this specimen of a shifter. His biceps flex as he drops his arms by his side, then runs a hand through his short, brown hair. He is a wall of muscle. Captivating. Dangerous…because he puts dirty thoughts in my mind. My cheeks heat at the very possibility that somehow my wolf wants more than one man.

He's wearing dark jeans hanging low on his hips, a wrinkled blue t-shirt, and brown cowboy boots. Which intrigues me.

"What's with the boots?" I clear my throat and walk around the bed to collect the new lace-up sandals Dušan brought me last night. I'm wearing a sky-blue dress that falls to mid-thigh. The fabric is the softest material I've ever touched. He even arranged for black lace underwear and a bra. He then kept his word and let me sleep alone in his bed, which I appreciated.

"They're comfortable to wear," he answers, but I can tell he's lying.

I straighten and run my hands down the fabric. I can't get the

95

previous night out of my mind, and instinctively, I reach up to the back of my neck where he bit me. Where he left his mark. The skin is rough from his teeth marks, and just remembering the moment sends a shiver of excitement down my spine. I never expected the Alpha to be so gentle, to bring me to arousal with such tenderness. The night was a whirlwind of being swept into a perfect memory of fear and seduction.

Turning around, I find Lucien studying me, like he can read my thoughts. I try to swallow the lump in my throat, but it feels impossible. I'm torn between hating these shifters and desiring them. I loathe myself for it, but I can't seem to back away, either.

"Have you heard of the saying, '*wrong place, wrong time,*' gorgeous?" he asks.

"Yeah."

"I know you feel like a string of bad luck and bad decisions brought you to our doorstep, but do you ever think fate has a funny way of forcing things that are meant to be?"

"So you place your trust in fate?" I walk around the bed and note his gaze trailing down my body, all the way down to my gold sandals.

I know I shouldn't feel the things I do, but near Lucien, my breath catches in my throat and heat flares over my skin. He looks at me like he'll rip the dress off me and pin me to the wall as he fucks me. Fire curls up and over my neck at the image now smothering my thoughts.

"There are some things that are too strange, too powerful to be pure coincidences, don't you think?" he asks.

I lick my dry lips and nod as we both leave my bedroom and walk past the guard at my door. Maybe being so close to Lucien isn't such a great idea. Farther down the hall, we turn left toward a set of circular stairs heading upstairs. "Is that what you were brought up believing?" I reply. "My childhood was mostly about running and finding a new safe home. I didn't even know what fate was for the longest time."

He looks over at me with a soft look, brimming with sympathy.

"Don't do that," I say, my cheeks heating with shame. "I don't want your pity."

"That's not pity, Meira. It's understanding. We all have different stories, and I'm not saying one is better than the other. But some of us have had a shitty start in this infected world, even more so than others."

I open my mouth to speak, but I forget my words when we step out onto a small balcony jutting out from the base of the pointed tower roof. A gust of cool air hits me and swirls around me. My mouth drops open at the small table and chairs set up with plates of food, but my attention devours the sight from up here. I move toward the metal railing encircling the open area and stare out over the most spectacular view of the wild Carpathian Mountains surrounding us.

"Beautiful, isn't it?" Lucien stands behind me. I feel his presence so close to me. My skin ripples with goose bumps in anticipation—with the need to have him touch me and press himself against me. I shudder.

"It's spectacular." I glance down below to the woods just outside the metal walls of the settlement. Small movements down there catch my attention, and I squint for a better look since we're so high.

"Do you see that?" I point down.

Lucien steps beside me to look down, our arms grazing. His skin is fiery hot, and I resist the urge to lean in closer to him. He distracts me so easily.

You need to stop, I scold myself, knowing that I am in enough trouble after last night, and I need to rein in my desires.

The wind blows through my hair as we both stare into the woods, where half a dozen undead lurch closer to the fence. Two of them drop to their knees, hunched forward as if feeding. The others soon join them.

"Do you think it's a dead animal?" I ask, remembering that I saw undead emerging from the nearby woods when I first arrived. They've definitely fed here before, so they'll never leave if they keep finding food so close to the settlement.

Lucien doesn't respond for a moment but nods. "Yeah, maybe." There's a tightness in his voice.

I turn to face him, my back to the railing, and he straightens, standing so tall and so close to me that I can't think. My chest tightens at the dirty thoughts that play with my mind.

I dip my gaze to his full lips and my body trembles, then to the scar along his collarbone. This is a barbaric world when fighting is the only way to survive.

"Your heart is beating so fast. Are you afraid of me?" he murmurs.

"No, not afraid of you." I'm scared of the lack of control I have around him, at the arousal that leads me to draw my lower lip into my mouth.

The small growl that comes from him tells me I'm playing a dangerous game. He moves closer, and I don't draw away.

I lean forward with closed eyes until our lips press together. I can't think for those few seconds when the world seems to hold us prisoner in this perfect moment. In a moment where I'm kissing the shifter under Dušan's command, the Alpha who marked me as his last night.

He parts his mouth, and I do the same, our tongues mingling. Sparks flutter down my spine and fire melts between my thighs, coating my underwear in seconds. He isn't pulling back, and I'm not stopping. I don't want to end this, so I place my hands on his biceps as he wraps me in his arms. I press my breasts against his chest, my nipples rubbing over his muscular pecs.

I love the groaning sounds he makes.

Our breaths are racing, his kiss deep and dominating as he explores my mouth with his tongue—licking me, owning me.

He breaks away first, and I open my eyes to find doubt in his eyes. A chill settles in my bones.

"Even if I can't stop thinking of you, we shouldn't do this." The ache in his steel-gray eyes tightens my throat, and embarrassment crashes into me. It shouldn't, but an uncomfortable burning climbs over me.

"Why?" I ask.

"Because we'll both get hurt. I should never have kissed you." He looks away and turns abruptly toward the table. "We better eat before the wind carries away our meal."

I move toward the round table that's bolted to the stone ground, including the chairs. The metal is cold against the back of my legs when I sit down. The ache in my chest deepens, and I turn my attention to the food. There's a plate filled with cooked strips of meat, jam pastries, and even a round loaf of sliced bread with dripping butter.

"Lucien, we didn't do anything wrong." I surprise myself to find that I'm reaching out to him when I should be pushing these wolves away. My head hurts with confusion, with a need I can't comprehend.

"It doesn't matter," he says. "Eat up."

Did I hear him right? "Of course it matters."

He reaches over and fills his plate before eating.

"What do you mean?" I ask as he closes his eyes and makes a rumbling sound in his chest. When he looks at me again, there is sorrow in his eyes.

I don't know what to say. I'm getting myself in too deep, letting emotions carry me away. Lately, I've struggled to make sense of my body's reactions. My wolf may respond to these Alphas and yearn for them, but is she really that trustworthy? She's a beast inside me, refusing to emerge, and she could be the death of me.

Am I being foolish believing that what I'm feeling is anything but animalistic attraction?

We eat breakfast with small talk after that. He isn't opening up about why he pulled away, and maybe it's none of my business. Maybe he is doing me a favor. Because clearly I can't seem to control my instincts around the three Alphas I've met in this pack. I've kissed all three and my wolf insists she wants them all. Something must definitely be broken inside of me.

Once we finish, he walks me to Dušan's bedroom.

"Meira," he says from the doorway. "I think it's better this way." Then he closes the door and leaves. And I'm left utterly confused and hurt.

Dušan

Night drapes the heavens as I'm marching back to my bedroom after the longest day. Fire simmers in my veins. I finally got a hold of Mad, who insisted he and Caspian were simply being hospitable and planned to return soon. He gave me nothing and hid everything that was really going on. I can discern it in his eyes, in his voice. The idiot even tried to joke about Ander losing grip of his pack, all over an Omega he hadn't yet completely claimed.

What Ander does with his pack isn't our business, and Mad needs to check the mess in his own backyard before throwing stones.

When he returns, I'll make him tell me everything or he's out. Bardhyl is right. Unless Mad pulls his shit together, he needs to go. As my Second, I need someone whom I can trust, and right now, I suspect he's doing something really stupid that's going to come back on me.

My footsteps strike the stone, reverberating in the hall. Stopping in front of my bedroom door, I draw in a sharp inhale to calm down. I don't want to scare Meira. All day, she's been on my mind, her scent in my nostrils, her taste on my tongue. Tonight, I will bring out her wolf— our energies will merge. Knowing the danger she poses to herself and the pack means I need to do this tonight. Last night, her wolf was ready to come out, eager for escape. And I'm about to give it a big nudge.

I unlock the door with the key in my pocket and walk inside.

Meira turns toward me, surprise widening her eyes, her hand holding a ceramic jug on which the bottom has fallen out. The pale yellow nightgown she wears is drenched, the cloth sticking to her body, curving over her perky breasts, following the tightness of her stomach. I almost choke on my breath as I take all of her in.

I stare at the dark hair at the apex of her thighs, at the delicious circles of her areolas pressed to the wet material.

Fuck!

"I think the jug had a crack in it," she says with a crooked smile.

I kick the door shut behind me and lock it. My cock punches against my pants, balls tightening. At first, all I can do is just stare at the wet nightgown, at her gorgeous body.

Pulling myself back to attention, I hurry forward to where she stands barefoot amid shards of ceramic. "Don't move."

I kneel and pick up the large pieces first, then I meticulously find all the small ones. I try to ease back my own hunger and remember a question I have been meaning to ask her. "Meira, out of curiosity how did you escape from the aircraft?"

"Mad and Caspian were too busy arguing about being late so when I was dragged on, Mad forgot to tie me up, then as soon as he went to the cockpit, I ran."

"Appreciate your honesty." I dump the pieces of ceramic into the trashcan and mentally shake my head at Mad's carelessness. Though it does seem odd since he's usually so meticulous with details.

Meira starts to walk across the room.

"Didn't I just say not to move?"

She stiffens at my order. I march closer and sweep her into my arms and then carry her to the bed before laying her onto her back.

"Did you step on any broken pieces?" I ask, sitting on the end of the bed, where I lift her feet up onto my lap.

I dust her soles clear, including her toes, and she squirms, giggling.

"You're tickling me."

"Hold still." I run my fingers gently over her feet, to hear more of her beautiful laughter. I inspect the skin for any cuts. She has such small, adorable feet. Slowly I massage her feet and toes, and I feel her relaxing.

"I really appreciate your help, but I'm not hurt." She squirms from my tickly touch.

When I turn to face her, she's leaning back on bent elbows, the material of the nightgown pulled taught over her chest, its transparency hiding nothing.

Goddamn, she's fucking beautiful. Her tiny curvy body calls to me.

"So, what's the plan for tonight?" she asks. "Dinner, then a stroll through the woods?" That dirty smile gives me a painful hard-on.

"There's only one thing I plan to do with you tempting me like that." I stand up from the bed and start unbuttoning my shirt, never lifting my gaze from her widening eyes.

She quickly glances down to her nightgown, then hastily lashes her hands over breasts. "Crap! You distracted me when you came in."

She rolls away from me, but I snatch her ankles and drag her down the bed toward me where I stand. The skirt of her nightgown rides up her legs, and a flash of dark hair between her thighs appears. She gasps and quickly shoves the fabric down over herself, but my cock throbs so damn hard now. All I can picture is spreading those gorgeous thighs and burying myself inside her.

Our mating heat rises through me, lifting the hairs on my arms. My balls grow heavy with the promise of this hellcat. With the way she looks at me, she feels that connection, the arousal, the growing need.

A gasp escapes past those gorgeous rosy lips.

I pull open my black shirt, noting her dipping gaze. Her cheeks redden, and I can't hold back the smile as I unclip the buttons on my sleeves. I slip the shirt off and lay it across the couch behind me.

"Dušan, I d-don't know... No, I... Shit!" She stumbles over her words and it's adorable that she thinks anything she says will change what's coming her way.

"We're completing the mating tonight, Meira. We have to bring your wolf out. You know this."

She's shaking her head, but her body betrays her as she pushes the skin-tight fabric of her nightgown between her legs. Her hand slyly rubs her heat. Her slick scent fills the air, and I've barely touched her. The magnetism between our wolves from the marking has connected us, and now it's calling to her, to me. It's intoxicating, dragging me deeper and deeper.

She gasps, and my cock aches, digging against my pants.

"Take it off," I order. "Show me how you touch yourself."

"No!" She pulls back, while watching me like I'm the devil, but fighting against it will only bring her agonizing pain.

I reach out for her and snatch the thin fabric with two hands, tearing it in two with my bare hands. In one quick move, I rip it open all the way to her chest.

Those perfect breasts bounce, and I groan with unimaginable desire. She clenches her bent legs together, staring at me like a terrified deer.

"There are consequences if you don't obey, Meira. Now take it off."

"I... I shouldn't want you so badly, when all I want to do is shove you out that window."

A chuckle bursts past my throat, and it feels incredible to be laughing. "You can hate me, but tonight, we are bringing out your wolf. And you will beg for me."

"Never!" She spits the word at me, and I love her fierceness. It's exactly what I need by my side, someone who will hold her own, who will help lead my pack. She just needs to now grow physically strong.

I reach down and unbuckle my pants. "Take off the nightgown, Meira. I won't ask next time." I need her naked, need that luscious, curvy body to be all mine.

What we feel for each other is primal, our wolves seeking their partners, and the only way to help her heal is to remind her wolf I am the Alpha. The dominance with the energy tying us together will bring out her other half.

I unzip my pants, and my cock springs out. Her attention falls to my dick. There's hunger in her eyes as my scent twists with hers. She blinks, fear blooming in her irises, but she isn't pulling away anymore. I push my pants down my legs and step out of them before laying them alongside my shirt.

My hellcat looks at me, utterly lost.

"Now, show me, gorgeous. Show me how you touch yourself when you're alone and thinking of me. And don't fight me on this."

Her face pales, but her hand slips down her stomach and to the area between her legs. Then she pauses.

"No, no," I say. "That won't do. Open up."

"I know what you're doing. I will never submit to you!" She glares at me yet her body purrs for me.

"Then your wolf will never come out." I growl, needing her to stop fighting me.

She glares at me for the longest moment, and I don't back down.

Her muscles tense as she gradually pries her legs wide, her hand cupping her pussy. At first, she just lies there, battling her own arousal. Then her fingers work slowly, sliding along the folds. Her pussy glistens with arousal, so pink and wet.

"Good girl."

I grow harder and harder at watching, so close to coming all over the bed.

A moan slips from her lips as she works her fingers, her legs falling wider apart. I'm on the verge of fucking off my self-control and rutting her like a wild animal.

Her heady smell fogs my head, and I'm on the bed before I even decide to move. I'm on hands and knees, my head lowering between her thighs, and I take a deep inhale, letting every cell in my body recognize and imprint her onto me.

I drag my lips along an inner thigh, her whimpers driving me crazy. She draws her hand back, offering herself to me, needing this as much as I do. I push her thighs wider still. My tongue slides out, and I lick the length of her soft flesh. She quivers under my touch, clutching a pillow and pressing it to her face.

I kiss her softly, teasing, sucking on her clit. I hold open her little pussy lips and drag my tongue over them, devouring her. Her body shakes, her hips rocking. Clasping on to her thighs, I eat her out and plunge my tongue into her liquid heat. She smells incredible.

She is mine to claim, to take over and over.

The primal hunger from my wolf rises through me so powerfully, he leaves me shuddering.

With a roar, I pull back and lift myself to my knees, staring down at my mate. She's the most beautiful thing I've ever seen.

I reach over and rip the pillow off her face.

"I want you to look at me as I fuck you and make you scream."

She stares at me with such fearful eyes that doubt creeps over my mind. I'm not someone who backs down when what I need to do will help someone, even if they don't see it themselves. I charge ahead and get things done. But with my little hellcat, I smell her sickness, and I remember the blood in the trashcan. She needs this so badly, but I can't push her.

"No, you're not really ready," I announce. As much as my chest splinters and my rock-hard cock hurts like a bitch, I pull back. "We can try this another time." I draw her legs closed and sit on the edge of the bed, looking away.

I scrub a hand over my moist mouth and chin, still drowning in her arousal, but I don't want her remembering me this way.

"Dušan," she whispers, her hand tenderly settling on my shoulder. "I'm just…" She clears her throat and I turn to face her. She's completely naked and kneeling behind me. "It's my first time. And"—she lowers her gaze—"I'm scared it's going to hurt." The vulnerability in her voice affects every inch of my body, sending a fierce surge through me.

I cup the side of her face and she leans into my touch. Looking into those heartfelt eyes, her ache is mine. I understand fear all too well. "It will hurt a little bit, but it will then hurt in an incredible way, I promise."

"I want you. I want your help. I don't want to die from my wolf. Please." Her fingers press into my arm with desperation. She isn't accepting defeat, but facing the truth.

A deep ache in my chest rattles, and I'm impressed that she has finally come to accept her situation. That my intention isn't to just bed her, but to help her. I stare at the pleading in her eyes, at her messy dark hair, at her erratic breathing. I feel the energy between us in my bones.

"I will take care of you. You are mine now, Meira."

Her eyes never leave mine. She clings on to me as she closes in and kisses me. Soft lips graze my mouth. She shivers against me. Her tenderness squeezes my heart. I still have to learn of her past. We all have darkness in our past, and I want to discover hers. I want to show her she's no longer alone. I want her to feel safe.

"I need you, Dušan," she says against my mouth.

"And you have me." I kiss her back, one hand to the back of her head, the other on her arm. She tastes like the sweetest cherries. We kiss until she's breathless, until I'm so lost, I forget how to breathe.

I guide her back onto the bed and she shuffles up, grinding into the mattress. I press my weight between her thighs and run my tongue down her neck, across her collarbone, tasting her salty skin. I take her nipple into my mouth, gently gnawing on it.

She writhes beneath me, her hips rocking back and forth, my cock sliding against her slickness.

She is so perfect moaning beneath me. Her body responds to my every touch. I collect the other breast into my mouth, taking my time, needing her desire to build back up, for her to be drunk with need.

The room swims in our scents. Her fingers dig into my arms, her groans grow louder. I stare at her beauty, and she holds my gaze as I slip my hand down between our bodies and rub her engorged clit. It drives her insane as she slides underneath me. Her little pussy so wet. She's ready, so I press the tip of my dick to her entrance, feeling her soaking wetness. She gasps a bit, and the sound is an addiction.

"I promise to go slow at first," I say. "I will never hurt what's mine. Are you mine?" I ask, more to hear her say the words than anything. I already know it to be true.

She holds on to my arms, her wolf whining in her chest. She is so fucking arousing. When her lips finally part, a primal groan spills out. And I know she's ready.

She wrenches her head forward to meet me in a kiss, and I push gradually into her soft core.

"I'm yours," she cries out.

She is so tight, and the need to explode inside her thunders through me. My cock aches as I stretch her wider until my tip hits a soft barrier, and I know what that is. I am her first. I pull out and slide back in quicker this time, but not all the way. I need her close to coming, so she experiences less pain.

With her head tipping back, her throat is open and exposed to me. I watch her bouncing breasts, the tightness of her stiff nipples.

"Make it hurt more," she demands, spreading herself wider. "Please."

Goddamn, she is going to be the end of me. I lose all control around her. I am burning up, desperate to let myself sink in all the way.

"You smell so fucking beautiful."

She digs her nails into my arm, and with each moan she unleashes, I push myself, I go deeper. I fuck her faster now and thrust right past the soft barrier, sliding all the way into her.

Her screams fill the room, her back arching, her walls clenching around me. I'm losing myself to her, but I draw it partially out, leaving just my tip inside her, eager to fill her over and over.

"Are you hurt?" I ask.

Her eyes flash open, her breaths racing. I love how red her cheeks glow. "More. Don't you dare stop."

"Fuck, Meira." I plunge back into her on a hard thrust, slapping into her.

She cries out as I hammer into her, pushing her, taking her, owning her.

Her scent curls around me like a blanket smothering me. And my wolf is right there, his energy intertwining with hers, roaring in my chest. He senses what belongs to us.

Her body thrums as I lower my hand to her pussy, my thumb pressing to her clit, rubbing it in small circles, building her orgasm.

"Come for me, beautiful," I say.

She screams louder, and my cock twitches, the base swelling, knotting. At that same moment, Meira convulses and screams, and I explode with my own orgasm. I pulse into her, pumping rivers of seed, filling her up. The longer my knot remains in place and holds the seed inside her, the higher the chance she'll be impregnated.

Gods, she is stunning in that moment of pure bliss. Her inner walls clench around my cock, squeezing and milking me.

I hiss. Warmth floods my cock as her slick coats me.

I'm drowning in her arousal. Her head is back once again, and in a moment of pure desire, I bare my teeth and sink them into the side of her exposed neck, drawing blood and tasting her orgasm in the air. I pull back from her neck, the coppery tang on my tongue.

Energy flares over my arms. Time fades, and I don't know how long we are entwined together.

Except there's no wolf pushing for release, and I can't stop the disappointment from slipping over my thoughts.

Meira's sexy moans are endless. Her brow is a sheen of sweat, and I want to remain buried in her for eternity. But I'm missing something about her wolf, something that isn't clear.

"I'll never let you go," I declare, the knot easing, and slowly, I draw out of her. I sit back on my heels and admire her beautiful pussy, at the seed and her cum dripping out.

"Stay there. I'll get you cleaned." I climb to my feet, my legs shaky and my head dizzy from the intensity.

"Dušan," she says.

I glance back at her over my shoulder. "Yeah?"

"You better not let me go," she growls.

CHAPTER 14

DUŠAN

It has been three sex-induced glorious days since I first claimed Meira. Her heat is explosive, and she's on me the moment I join her in my room. But there's still no sign of the wolf emerging. It should have done so by now. She's in heat, her body preparing for motherhood… but I have no idea if she can even carry children with her sickness—with the wolf still inside her.

Her scent still teases my nostrils. Sweet honey and roses, with a hint of cinnamon, which is her wolf. I recognize her smell anywhere now as it's blended into my senses. So are the sounds she makes with her arousal, which sing in my thoughts.

She affects me so much that now her absence seeps through me, a constant calling to my wolf.

I've marked her as my own, claimed her temporarily. Until her wolf unleashes, our connection will never be fully merged.

Bardhyl joins me in my office and slumps into the seat across from my desk. A new scratch down his cheek blushes red. "Found a girl, just barely. Fucking rogue wolves are desperate out there for a female. I had to fight two to get this girl. She's twenty and is coming into her heat. So it's perfect."

"You did fantastically. We need her in a quick mating ceremony in front of Alphas to make sure none of them are her fated mate before we send her to the X-Clan."

Bardhyl dusts his hands for show. "Done. She's ready to go."

I nod my head. "I'm impressed. Okay, arrange delivery in two days' time. She'll need a wash, feeding, new clothes, and the lowdown on where she's going." I reach into my top drawer to collect my tablet.

"On it. You're calling Ander?"

"Going to do this now, then Mad and Caspian can get their asses back home."

Bardhyl's upper lip curls into a sneer at their names.

I speak before he does. "I know what you're going to say, but Mad was appointed by my stepfather before he passed."

"So? Fuck him and—"

"And what? Throw Mad out to the infected? You know I won't do that."

"Just so you know, if he does anything wrong on this trip to ruin our trading relationship, I'll put him in his place. I've had enough of his shit. You know before he left, the jerk changed all the locks on the sheds with a new password? It took us days to unlock them to reach our weapons."

I huff and shake my head. Mad is a prankster, but it doesn't make him malicious. He grew up with the my stepfather, his real father, given the same beatings. We had different birth mothers too, but they had no power over the previous Alpha of Ash Wolves. We all deal with the shit from our past differently.

I hit the call button on the video chat and sit back in my seat as Bardhyl leaves my office.

"Dušan." Ander greets me. His dark hair sits messily around his face. He's not wearing a shirt, and in the background is a kitchen. I must have caught him off guard.

"Ander," I answer, raking a hand through my hair. "I wanted to provide you with a brief update on the Omega. Is now a good time?" Tension flares across my shoulders that he won't accept a new girl over Meira.

A female's voice murmurs in the background of the video.

"No, stay," Ander insists, turning to look at someone at his side. "Please," he says softly.

The gentler side of Ander surprises me, as I've never seen him this way during any of our dealings. He's always in control, as any Alpha should be.

When he looks at me, I raise a brow out of pure understanding that only a female could soften an Alpha's heart. "Don't start," he mutters to me, then he refocuses on someone out of sight, stretching his arm out for them.

I can't help but grin at him, well aware that as much as Alphas try to hold these positions of power, we can all have our moments of weakness as well.

My gaze turns to a woman stepping into view. Her auburn hair, still wet, is draped over her shoulder. The dress she wears hangs loosely over her small frame. When she looks at me, all I see are blue piercing eyes. She's gorgeous.

"This is the Shadowlands' Sector Alpha," Ander says, drawing the woman into his lap. "Dušan, this is my Katriana."

It's good to see Ander has found his Omega. Seeing them together brings back memories of Meira and me last night. With it comes my rampant heart beating excitedly to visit her again, to take her to my bed every night until her wolf breaks free.

"Lovely to make your acquaintance, Katriana."

"You too," she replies, then she clears her throat. "Romania, right?"

"What used to be Romania, yes." I offer her a smile, and all I can picture is Meira, the urgency to go find her waiting in my room. "I'm sorry to interrupt you and your Alpha, but I promised him an update today."

"Indeed you did," Ander agrees, kissing Katriana's neck.

I avert my gaze as he finishes, letting my mind wander to the tenderness of Meira's skin under my lips. How I need to find a way to safely coax her wolf free so she can take her spot by my side. She is my mate, and now I need to help her. The longer her wolf remains at bay, the more worry churns in my gut. Survival for half-breeds is low... not impossible, but goddamn difficult. I drive those thoughts away, refusing to even entertain the possibility.

"What's the sensitivity level of our topic?" Ander asks, drawing my attention.

"Green." I understand right away he doesn't want his Omega to know all the details of our trade.

"Proceed," he murmurs, wrapping his arms around the Omega in his lap.

"We found your tenth promised wolf, but there's a complication. I need to switch out the product for a better fit." I study the Alpha for his reaction, not wanting this to ruin what we have set up.

He frowns. "What kind of complication?"

I stare at him for a long while, trying to work out the best way to explain without giving away too many details. Finally, I say, "A similar one to your current situation."

His eyebrows lift. "Oh." The way he intently looks at me, the corners of his eyes creasing, I can tell he understands. "Well, right then. A replacement is acceptable. How soon will you be transporting her?"

"Two days' time, unless you need her sooner?"

A quick shake of his head. "Two days is perfect. We have a social gathering planned that evening to introduce your wolves to my pack. Perhaps Mad and Caspian can stay for the festivities before returning to you?"

There is an eagerness in his voice, which tells me he's offering his hospitality as a confirmation he's content to keep trading more in the future. And this is exactly what I need. Maybe those two inviting themselves to stay with the X-Clan Wolves isn't completely a waste of time.

"They would be honored to stay," I say. "Thank you, Ander."

"You as well, Dušan."

"And nice to meet you, Katriana," I conclude in a softer tone before I hang up on the call.

Meira

I'm stir crazy closed up in Dušan's bedroom, and I miss him terribly. Despite it being days since I've seen Lucien, he's on my mind constantly as well. That kiss we experienced stays with me along with why he pulls away from me.

There's a guard at the door to stop me from sneaking out. Now I'm stuck in here with a desire that burns within me so wickedly, it never leaves me.

Dušan insists his bite mark and our sex makes me smell like a claimed female to other wolves for a few days only. Anticipation stretches inside me for his return.

Except worry is constantly coiling my chest. Why hasn't my wolf come out?

What if she never does? What if each time the sickness returns, it grows worse until it eventually kills me? I've never thrown up blood before. I know something is wrong—I feel it in my bones. So Dušan is right in trying to get my wolf out of me, to tame my human side that is carrying the sickness. Transformations heal any illnesses shifters may have contracted.

I turn and walk across the room before crawling onto the bed, feeling so many emotions inside from fear to anger to a desperation to have my Alpha near me. His markings have opened something up between us.

The pillows and bedsheets carry Dušan's masculine, woodsy scent filled with pheromones. The smell of his seed and my arousal lingers too. An instinct jolts awake within me, and my core clenches with need. I shut my eyes and curl in on myself, wanting to drown myself in his smell. Slick pools between my thighs at the need that sweeps through me for Dušan.

There is no doubt now that he is my fated mate. My body and wolf yearn for him, cry out for him. My breaths spasm in my lungs, and a burning heat sweeps over me. For so long, I tried to ignore what I was —an Omega, a shifter ravenous to find my mate, a half-breed in deeper trouble than I ever thought.

Dušan's scent sinks through me, and I feel like I'm going to burst with the ache curling in my gut. I push myself out of bed, needing fresh air, anything to calm myself.

A knock comes at my door before it swings open.

The hairs on my nape bristle and I stand there, half-expecting Dušan.

Except it's Lucien who enters. His nostrils flare with a deep, shaky inhale, and something glints over his eyes. He can smell my desire, my need, and his Alpha's as well.

"I had to see you," he says, his voice deep and gravelly, as though he's struggling with his emotions. "I tried to stay away," he admits, the corners of his mouth pulling tight.

I can't hold back the smile on my face at seeing him, at how much I missed him. "I need some fresh air," I plead as I step closer.

He nods and stretches his hand out for me. I accept, and the moment our hands touch, that jolt of desire sparks to life just as it had over breakfast a few days ago.

Our gazes clash. He feels it too, just as he sensed the attraction between us when we first met.

His fingers curl around mine, and he leads me out into the hall quickly. The guard standing there just watches me and doesn't say a word.

Next thing I know, Lucien and I are running down the hallway, my wolf fueled with adrenaline—with the need to hunt. Lucien glances back at me, that hunger lashing over his face. I've never felt like this before.

I should be scared and ashamed at wanting to be with Lucien as my body craves Dušan. I've become an Omega who mated with the Alpha of the Ash Wolves but who can't control her instincts or reactions.

Turn back! I yell in my head, but my wolf takes charge. The longing comes off in waves, and my scent of fear coupling with it. Still, we don't stop. Not when we break out of the fortress, not when we rush into the dense woods within the settlement, and not when Lucien's clothes rip off his body as his body transforms.

Crisp air splashes over my face. I suck in breaths, watching with awe. His body elongates, his bones crack, his skin pops. Deep brown hair explodes over his wolf form. On four legs, he runs alongside me. He's huge, easily reaching my waist, and utterly stunning.

Electricity races up my spine.

My bare feet hit the ground. I don't feel the pebbles or twigs I tread on. Only the exhilaration thrumming through me, the power driving me. Is this how it feels to take the form of a wolf?

I drown in the intoxication of my wolf—the primal instinct, the savagery, the familiarity. This is what I am meant to be. Free as a wolf, not hiding in trees and from my real form.

It hits me so hard…a feeling I've never experienced before.

When we finally reach the top of the hill where the metal fence blocks our path, we stop.

I gasp for air and collapse to my knees, half-laughing, half-trying to fill my lungs. "That's incredible. How could I have never felt this way before?"

Lucien in his wolf form curls around me, his gaze narrowing. I reach out gingerly and spear my fingers through his lush, thick coat. It's almost soft to the touch, and his skin is on fire.

He rubs himself across my back as he keeps circling me. My wolf surges in me. She's right there, whining for him, pressing against me for release. I sense her stronger now, like she's sliding right under my skin, desperate to tear out of me.

I breathe easy and open myself up as I did with Dušan last night. An ache comes with the concentration, and it burrows deep in my gut. I shut my eyes, squeezing them tightly. My heart hammers as sweat slides down my spine. Inside, I feel twisted and trapped.

A soft hand cups the side of my face, and I flutter my eyelashes open.

Lucien kneels in front of me naked, and all I can see is this big, powerful Alpha, a prime specimen that affects me. I drown in his woodsy, masculine scent. This beautiful man stares at me like he's inhaling me with his gaze.

"What's happening to me?" I swallow down a shaky breath.

"Your wolf is calling to mine… I can smell Dušan all over you, but I don't care. There's no jealousy, only the hunger to claim you as mine."

I blink at him. *His!*

I want to ask if he's toying with me, except I feel the sensation too. The intimate anticipation to reach over and kiss him just as I had wanted on our first kiss. My pulse races, because my body desires him while my brain tells me to push him away. To wipe that devious smirk off his face.

The inability to unleash my wolf plagues me—it scares me—but I don't know how I feel about being claimed by two Alphas. I'm struggling enough with Dušan's dominance and how my body melts around him—how my mind is not my own.

A cool breeze washes over us. My world spins as my heart beats quickly. I try to fight it and bite down on my lip to hold back.

"You can't fight it," Lucien says, his voice heavy and deep. He reaches out for me, his hand clutching my skirt.

I can't breathe from our proximity. I'm so nervous about what this means for us…for me… for my wolf.

Rising to his feet, he towers over me. "I will take you," he says.

My voice won't work, words won't come, because I don't trust myself to say anything but *yes*. But my body gives him the response he seeks. My chest thrusts out as if I no longer control my body, my nipples pebbled tight, pushing against the fabric of my button-up dress.

He reaches over and grabs hold of the material over my chest, then rips it apart. Buttons flinging wildly in every direction like hail.

I flinch at his aggression, while heat pours through me at his dominance.

I'm wearing no underwear, since the last pair was torn to shreds by Dušan, so I'm utterly naked underneath.

Lucien's gaze falls down my naked body, over my breasts, to my stomach, then to the apex between my thighs. He makes a guttural sound that adds fuel to my heat.

Our mouths clash, fire exploding between us, and I'm lost.

"Take me," I urge, seduction filling every inch of me. "Please."

His tongue licks over my lips, strong hands running down my back and to my ass cheeks, prying them apart. We kiss hungrily. I wrap my arms around his neck, pushing myself closer. Heat melts at my core, and I feel the slick sliding down my inner thighs.

His mouth is on my neck, a large palm on my breasts, squeezing until it hurts. I growl and bare my teeth at the deepening heat.

A hand slides down between us and covers my sex. I moan, desperate for him to be inside me, to feel that thick shaft thrust within me.

Fingers glide over my heat. His mouth is on mine, his tongue pushing between my teeth, and I take all of him. He pushes two fingers into me, and I scream from the sexual spell that has gripped me.

"Please, Lucien, fuck me." The intensity is unbearable, my skin burns, my stomach tightens.

He grasps the back of my thighs and lifts me off my feet. Our scents are so strong, so potent. I wrap my legs around his hips and fling my arms tightly around his neck as I cling to him. He walks us toward a sloping part of the hill before he lowers himself to his knees with incredible strength. He places me on the ground, and I lie back as he spreads my legs wider. His gaze falls to the slick.

"Fucking beautiful and all mine." He dips down and without ceremony, cups his mouth over my shuddering core.

I moan, my back arching as he licks the length of me over and over, then plunges his tongue into me. My scream comes again from the tension building and building within me. I grip handfuls of grass as I ride his face, my hips rocking back and forth. A growl rumbles from my throat and into the air. It coils around us, binding us.

My muscles flex with the tension clenching in my gut.

"Come for me," he insists. The moment his mouth clasps over my folds and tugs on them, I lose it.

A storm rages through me as the orgasm claims me.

Lucien forces my legs wider. A sharpness sinks into the inside of my thigh, the pain flaming over me, clashing with the climax. Yet somehow, the feelings work together into the perfect sensation that owns me, caresses me, heats me, fulfills me.

"Open your eyes," he orders, his dominance cutting right through me.

I do as he asks and lift my gaze to his. He's staring at me with such devotion, such protectiveness. His chin and lips glisten from my slick, and a drop of blood rolls out from the corner of his mouth.

The fear sinks in.

"You marked me?" He imprinted himself on my skin, took my blood. How can we be bound in such a small time? So fast? I want to pull away and hide, while my body begs me to stay where I am, to throw myself at him.

He pushes himself between my legs. "Of course. Could you not feel our wolves are fated mates? I tried to fight it, but it was killing me to stay away from you for so long."

Before I can even make sense of his words, he slips the tip of his cock into me. I tense, already sensing his size.

"Let me in."

Breathing deeply, I adjust my hips to better accommodate his girth as I lose myself in his steel-gray eyes. They call to me and I let myself fall as he slides into me, filling and stretching me. He leans forward, his hands pressing into the ground on either side of my shoulders. He's huge, and there is something exhilarating about having a man so big claim me.

Liquid heat seeps from my core, which helps him drive into me faster. I curl my toes as he thrusts all the way in. I can barely breathe, his shaft filling me completely.

My heart slams against my chest as he draws in and out of me, faster and faster, the friction igniting a blaze between us.

"I will take you again and again—until you can't walk straight, until you realize how much you mean to me. How much you are meant to be with both of us… until we help bring your wolf out of you."

His words barely register as my body thrums with pleasure. I moan with each thrust, but I am under no illusion that somehow I've gained myself two fated mates. I've heard of men having multiple women, but not the other way around.

Lucien fucks me, ramming into me. I wriggle under him as a shudder rips over me.

My sex quivers, every cell in my body pulsing. He leans lower and brushes a tongue over my hard nipple, flicking it. I cry out, desire pooling in my stomach.

Then I feel him growing inside me.

I freeze as he stops thrusting into me, but he remains over me, meeting my gaze.

"You're knotting, aren't you?"

Still, my need has me heaving to get closer to him, bucking against him. Fresh slick slides out each time he shifts.

His eyes roll back into his head, a snarl pouring from his lips. His mouth twists, his body shivering with the intensity of what's coming. A growl rips from his throat.

And my ache eases to have him so swollen in me, the keening sound smothering me, digging into my flesh.

"You're so tight."

My soft inner walls pulse against his knotted cock, squeezing him.

He roars, his chest puffing out, his skin shining with a sheen of sweat. I adore the way he looks as he floats in euphoria. His lips settle over my nipple, and he takes me into his mouth, sucking hard. That same pleasure and pain swallows me. My own climax surges forward once again, building, tightening. Then it crashes over me so fast, my vision blurs.

The orgasm rips through me. "Lucien!"

He breaks into a ravenous growl, his hips moving ever so slightly as he pulses inside me. I feel the warmth, the streams mingled with my own climax. I shudder beneath him as he keeps coming. That's the thing about Alphas—they produce an insane amount of seed, filling me completely.

I float down from my euphoria, and an ache strikes me in the chest. It has nothing to do with my sickness or wolf, but the reminder that the reasons Alphas knot and produce so much is for the higher probably of impregnating their mates.

I stay still, Lucien still inside me. He watches me the whole time, but his thoughts are still trapped in his own orgasm, I see it in his eyes. He stays inside me until his knot eases enough to safely pull out.

After a while, he comes out of me completely.

I collapse onto the grass, my body sore and my heart racing. Slick and seed slip out of me, and there's nothing I can do about it right now. When I look over at Lucien, I see so much more than an Alpha who needs to follow his instinct.

He collects me into his arm and holds me against his strong chest. I grasp on to him, inhaling his scent, listening to his heartbeat pounding inside his chest. I should be embarrassed by being out here naked and having just had sex in the wild. But in Lucien's arms, I feel safe and protected. My head is still spinning, trying to make sense of my emotions and thoughts.

I look up at the healed scar over his collarbone.

"How do you feel?" he asks as he brushes loose strands from my brow.

"Like I've been hit by a tornado." I smirk and half-laugh. "But I don't understand. If I have now been marked by two Alphas, why hasn't my wolf tried to come out yet?"

He kisses the top of my head. "You've got to remember, your body has been accustomed to her staying inside you. It's clinging on."

A shudder of dread pulls at my nerves. "And what if she never emerges? Then I stay as I am. I've lived this all my life, and I'm fine."

I'm barely thinking straight as my body still hums from our sex. But if she won't come out, then I can live with that. The question is… will the Alphas?

"How long have you been sick?" he asks with authority in his voice.

I look down, but he lifts my chin to look at him. "Meira, how long?"

"My whole life," I whisper, as if saying it softly will hide the truth. "My wolf has been holding back the sickness."

"And have you always vomited blood?" His gaze holds mine.

I blink at him, my voice vanishing. "I don't want to talk about this," I rasp out. I wriggle to get out from under his hold. Pushing myself to my feet, I collect my torn dress and slip my arms through the sleeves before pulling it tight around my chest since its missing all its buttons. Warm slick rolls down between my legs, and I need to wash.

"Meira." He grasps my arm and forces me to face him. "If you're getting sicker, what happens when your human side completely gives out?"

My gaze lowers to my bare feet, and my heart splinters. I lift my head and hold myself strong, putting on a brave face because I'm terrified of dying. "My mama always told me not to be afraid of death. That it comes for all of us." My face blanches at the memory of losing her, and that maybe I won't be far behind.

I swallow hard and turn away from him, but he catches my wrist and hauls me back to him. My hands jerk forward out of instinct and plaster against his solid chest.

His expression is furious, and his eyes look glazed over. "Do you know what happens when you die?" he barks, and I tremble in his grasp. "It's the people left behind like me who end up suffering, who pray for death every day. Fate can't fucking do that to me again."

Wait, what? *Again?*

CHAPTER 15

LUCIEN

"Whom did you lose?" Meira's tender words touch me more than she might ever imagine. Meira stands there, pulling her blue torn dress around her body and clutching the fabric at her chest.

She stares at me, waiting for my soppy story. We all have one in this godforsaken world. They call us survivors, but that's not what we are. We're the unlucky ones who get to see what it's like living in a rundown world that wants us dead.

"It's nothing. Don't worry about it. I shouldn't have said anything." I lick my lips and start picking up the loose buttons out of the greenery around us. I ripped her dress, so it's the least I can do.

"I lost my mother," she starts, her voice shaky. "I was fourteen when they attacked the settlement. I was the only one to survive, so I know how it feels to be left behind."

When I stand and turn to her, she's right next to me, her eyes heartfelt and glinting in the sunlight. "My mama was all I had left in the world," she says. "And I was forced to live alone in the woods, every day finding a way to survive."

My throat tightens and my mouth goes dry.

"How are you still so nice and put together after all of that?" I ask. "I still have nightmares of the things I've seen. I still try to tell myself that things might be back to normal one day. That's how I try to survive, by

119

lying to myself. Now you tell me that's not fucked up." I glance up to the sky, blinking hard. Cataline, my soulmate I'd lost to the infected, has stopped visiting my dreams, but the ache of being ripped in half has never left me. It reminds me that nothing is forever. That getting too close is a disaster waiting to happen. Maybe I was reckless and desperate, maybe too much time has passed to remember the ache I escaped so long ago.

I glance down at her hand on mine, at the thin healed scar from my inner wrist to my elbow.

She reaches out and her gentle finger finds my forearm. It comes with a surge of adrenaline, of pheromones, of the raw, primal instinct that drives shifters.

I have my suspicions that she has no clue how deeply imbedded a mating is. How her life will revolve around her mate's, and even being too far from them will be painful.

"You can talk to me," she murmurs.

I slide my hand into hers, our fingers intertwined, and draw her into a walk. "That goes both ways, my little wolf. Now, how about we go get you washed up and then eat, because I could eat a horse. Then we can talk late into the night. How does that sound?"

She tosses me a cute sneer, like she doesn't believe we're going to talk all night, but maybe this is my chance to be open with my past. To get her to talk more about her sickness, as I suspect that might have something to do with why her wolf remains stuck.

"Well, is that a *yes* to my offer?" I ask, ignoring the part in my head that's telling me I ought to speak to Dušan sooner rather than later.

But when Meira pauses to look at me while standing under a fern tree and the wind rips open her dress, revealing her delicious naked body, my heart hammers in my chest.

I quickly grasp the material and pull it back over her perfect curved body and she holds it in place with her small hands.

"What would happen if everyone in this pack found a way to become immune to the undead?"

Her question takes me off guard.

"Like, you know… imagine everyone living freely with no fear of the infected," she says.

My thoughts go straight to the X-Clan who are immune to the infected.

She continues, "I'm thinking how many more lives could be saved.

How going into the woods to hunt shouldn't be fraught with danger." She shrugs. "I don't know. I'm just thinking out loud. Stupid thoughts, really." I detect a hint of annoyance in her voice.

"You have a beautiful heart, Meira. And you want to know my honest thoughts?"

She nods eagerly, looking at me expectantly.

"If such an elixir existed, the battle over control of it would end in bloodshed."

She stiffens and her smile dissolves as she realizes how easily such power could lead wolves to war.

Shadows crowd under her eyes as she glances down and nods her head. "I'd like to think wolves are better than that, wouldn't you?"

The vicious fights I've seen between shifters for the single position of Alpha of a pack, the backstabbing in the hierarchy, the pain so many cause to get ahead is not indicative of a society who'd work in harmony. Under a strict rulership like Dušan's, it's possible, but it makes our fortress a target for every pack out there. We'd need a place that makes us untouchable.

"Maybe, and I really hope you're correct," I answer. "First, we need to find this cure, right? Let's head inside." We stroll through the woods within the settlement grounds, Meira staying especially quiet. I have so many things to ask her about her past, about things she likes, and we have time to get to know each other now.

Once indoors, we head downstairs and quickly reach the communal bathroom. Inside are two female Betas in the steaming water. They bow their heads at my arrival and continue chatting. I guide Meira to the showers at the back of the room and ensure that the room is empty first.

"I'll stay guard out here. There are fresh towels in there. I'll get someone to bring you some clothes too."

She steps toward me and has a look on her face like she's about to ask me something. I might be misreading the signals, but the words spill from my lips. "You want me to join you?"

A half-chuckle is her response as she strolls inside and vanishes into a shower cubicle.

I glance her way and scratch my head. Is that a yes?

Dušan

. . .

"**A**nder," I answer the call as I sit in my leather chair at my desk. The X-Clan Alpha doesn't greet me but just stares at me through video comm. He isn't alone as one of his own stands near. Something's wrong, and the tension in my stomach hardens.

"It's been brought to my attention that your Second and Caspian have taken twelve vials of my serum to create X-Clan Wolves," Ander finally says, surprisingly calm.

A chill shudders through me. "I'm going to fucking kill them!" I blurt out, regretting losing control so easily. I rein myself in and brace myself. Their actions punch me in my gut. I am going to murder Mad. I never should have trusted him. I should have demanded he return home the moment they made the delivery.

Thoughts rip over my mind about what Mad wants with the serum. Ander's team uses the serum to create X-Clan Wolves out of humans.

Shifting in my seat uncomfortably, I answer, "Ander, I know nothing about this, I swear on my life this was not coordinated under my leadership." A growl rumbles in my chest, my hands fisting at my side. "What Mad and Caspian have done has been of their own volition. I would never jeopardize our relationship this way."

His golden eyes pierce into me, and I square my shoulders.

"What benefit do I gain from stealing from you?" I point out as I realize that Mad must be searching for a way to make Ash Wolves immune to the infected since the X-Clan are unaffected. He must think the answer lays in this serum. We'd been talking about finding a remedy for years.

Sonofabitch! Why the fuck didn't he tell me first before pulling this stunt?

"I don't want to put a strain on our trading," Ander states. "And I do believe you weren't aware of their actions."

"I will personally deal with this issue quickly and return the serum to you. You have my word. I'm guessing the pair have already left your compound?"

My skin burns with fury.

He nods, and we continue talking about the severity of this situation and how to better secure our trading in the future. On the inside, I'm seething and ready to explode. Once I get a hold of those two, they will be lucky to breathe another day.

CHAPTER 16

BARDHYL

Sweat trickles down my back the moment I walk into the bathroom. Steam curls up from the surface of the bath and the first thing my gaze lands on are two young Beta women in a corner of the bath chatting. Many use the place for destressing. They're facing each other, the water to their necks, and only when they look my way do they bow their heads.

There's no connection for me to Beta females. They aren't compatible with Alphas...it all comes down to knotting. Their bodies don't release the pheromone to trigger our knotting and swelling. A while ago, Dušan told me of a barbaric story of a Beta Ash Wolf female raped by group of Alphas. They'd trapped the woman's daughter in the room to arouse the Omega inside of her to allow the men to knot. Thing is, Betas aren't built for the knot the way an Omega is.

The poor woman died, and the daughter, Daciana, was a shadow of herself afterward. Dušan had no choice but to send her to X-Clan, because there was no way she would accept living with Ash Wolves after that horrific ordeal. Dušan butchered the Alphas with his bare hands when he found out. I would have done the same, but I'd have taken my time so they would have felt every excruciating ache.

From what I've heard, Daciana is quite satisfied with her new arrangement in Ander's pack now.

Stalking past the bath, I meet Lucien's gaze from across the room.

He has his back pressed to the brick wall, but he straightens on my approach.

"You come to bathe with the women again?" he jokes and we hug with a clap to each other's backs.

"Maybe when the Omegas come to bathe, I'll return." I smirk and wink at him. Until Omegas find their mate, there's nothing stopping them from having a good time.

"So you tracked me down. Who's looking for me?" he asks.

"Hard not to track you down, bruh. I can smell her all over you and the entire pack is talking about you fucking Dušan's Omega up in the woods."

"Fuck!" He rubs a hand over his mouth. "So I'm guessing Dušan's asked for me, then?"

I nod. "But go see Mariana first. She has Meira's blood results you requested. Mad was in her lab room too, going over the results. When I questioned him, he told me to go fuck myself."

Lucien stiffens. "That prick is back?" Lucien spits. "Does Dušan know?"

"Fuck no. The sneaky rat came in without telling anyone. I only saw him since I went to check on Mariana after her mother passed."

"Hell, shit's gonna explode, and Dušan is gonna be fuming." Lucien's shaking his head, fury lashing his face. The cords in his neck twitch, as does the nerve on his temple.

"Okay, you stay here and take Meira to her room once she's finished in the shower."

"You go. I'll take it from here," I say.

He gives me a nod and marches out of the bathroom. In truth, Dušan called Lucien about a conversation he had with the Alpha of X-Clan. I doubt our Alpha has even been out of his office or spoken to anyone this morning to hear the rampant rumors. In truth, I'm not surprised since the small encounter I had with Meira left me completely mesmerized. And I've done everything in my power to resist going back to her… clearly, Lucien failed.

Back in Denmark, it's common for females to have more than one mate. The question is more if Dušan is open to it because it's not common here.

Movement from the shower room draws my attention to the door opening as Meira steps out in clean clothes and a purple dress hanging off her arm. Her wet hair is pushed off her face. Black leggings hug her gorgeous toned legs, and a wraparound blue top with a low V-neckline follows every curve of her sexy-as-hell tits.

I don't say anything, just waiting for her wandering gaze to meet mine.

"Hey, Angel Legs." My gaze drifts to the drop of water from her hair beading over her shoulders and rolling down the front of her cleavage.

The pulse in my neck jumps wildly, my groin aching.

"Last time I saw you, you pushed me into a house."

I raise a brow. "You fell inside after you kissed me."

The coloring in her cheeks reddens, and I enjoy watching her flush, wondering if she's that color when she's being fucked. The thought has my cock straining in my pants.

She lifts her chin high, her jawline tight. "Where's Lucien?"

"You're stuck with me, Cupcake. He had to go see Dušan."

Her eyes widen and she stiffens as her mouth parts, but the question never comes. I know exactly what she wants to ask, but her words never come.

"Come. I'll escort you to your bedroom."

She studies me, seeing right through me, then asks, "Maybe we can go sit outside for a bit? The inside feels stifling on such a nice day." I hear the fear in her voice.

"Of course," I say and take her purple dress, which I place in a corner basket for communal washing. Then, we stroll out of the bathroom and turn left down the hall. We walk past a couple, their whispers reaching us.

"She's with another man already?"

I shake my head at the gossip mill in this place.

"Dušan is very territorial, but he's also a generous Alpha," I say to Meira who doesn't seem to notice the couple we pass.

"Why are you saying that to me? Is there something you want to tell me?" She fiddles with the tips of her long, brown hair.

"Is there something *you* want to tell me?"

She half-laughs when she looks at me, then as we reach an arched alcove, she turns on me rapidly. "You know, don't you? About me with Dušan and Lucien. I can see it in the grin you're trying to hide. So tell me… Is Dušan going to hurt Lucien? God, you must know something. You need to tell me." Her voice climbs.

Her panic drives my pulse, but I hold my hands up in a playful surrender and offer her a small smile. "Well, I know once a wolf connects with another wolf, it's for life. And I also know that until you have your first transformation, neither Alpha can truly mark you as theirs even if you are fated mates, or stop others from trying to mark you as their rut partner."

The hum of adrenaline sounds in my head, along with my wolf pressing for release. He sees so much in Meira… I had hoped that my earlier feelings were just a physical attraction. Except I've never felt such intensity shuddering through me.

Her breaths hitch, and she feels it too. She backs away, her eyes widening with shock.

In haste, she rushes past me, careful not to touch me. I take her side when we reach the rear entry to the fortress that leads into the woods in the settlement.

Before we turn in that direction, an earth-shattering scream cuts through the air.

Meira flinches and bumps into me. I clasp a tight arm around her waist, holding her near.

Then an explosion of shouts and what sounds like a stampede swallows every sound. My heart slams to the back of my throat, and two Beta males dart past the arched entrance in fright.

My adrenaline rages and I turn to Meira. "Run upstairs to your bedroom. Lock yourself in and don't leave."

She's trembling. "What's going on?"

"I'm about to find out. Now go!" I turn her by the shoulders and push her to the steps. She grasps the metal railing and rushes up, glancing back at me with fear in her eyes.

"I'll come back for you. Go!" I bellow.

She turns and races upward while I lunge outside to find out what the fuck is going on.

Meira

*P*anic pummels through my chest. I know this drill. I've seen it too many times, and the fear I'm feeling isn't for my life. It's for this pack, for the Alphas I can't resist.

I abruptly stop halfway up the stairs and turn around to find no sign of Bardhyl. He's gone.

Terrifying screams erupt from outside, along with shouting and that skin-crawling groan that I know too well. The sounds of utter pandemonium shatter my world.

I'm clinging to the railing, my legs shaking. I feel the blood drain from my face because we are meant to be safe in this pack. The lofty metal walls, the powerful Alphas, the guards with guns. They promised fucking security!

This can't be happening again...please, not again.

I need to move, but for those few moments, I'm paralyzed to the spot as I remember losing my mama, the massacre in the settlement, and all those bodies.

My heart clenches with excruciating pain, my eyes welling with tears as every thread of grief I've been holding on to rips me apart.

All I can picture is Mama on the ground, blood pouring from the deep gash across her torn throat. My cheeks are soaking from hot tears, and I wipe them angrily away with my fingers.

Swift and silent.

But I won't hide.

I'm running back down the stairs before I can stop myself and dart outside. The woods within the settlement are right at the doorway.

Shifters are scrambling for their lives amid the trees, wolves in animal form, and the settlement fence on my left is smashed open, as if something has driven through it.

The undead pour into the settlement with such speed, it leaves me dizzy—nothing stops the infected. Torn clothes, broken skin, mortal wounds, missing body parts—nothing stops the infected.

Ice cuts through me, and I can barely draw a breath. My hands tremble as I clasp my stomach, fisting the fabric of my shirt, twisting it with pure terror.

A woman falls to her knees in front of me, a lanky undead lunging for her.

My heart stammers, and instinct kicks in. I rush forward and snatch a branch from the ground, then swing it wildly at the creature's face before it gets a chance to bite her.

The thing jerks backward, giving the woman time to scramble out of there. For good measure, I slam the stick into the creature's face over and over before I jam the pointy end into his face, piercing the eye and driving the wood into its brain. It makes a splattering sound as the

Shadow Monster silences and collapses. I stagger backward from the finally truly dead creature, swallowing past the boulder in my throat.

I sprint deeper into the forest, helping anyone I see in trouble the best way I can—with stones to smash in the undeads' heads, branches—anything to fight this battle.

An ear-splitting howl splinters the air, and I flinch around to find Bardhyl ripping his shirt off, his body already transforming into the biggest wolf I've ever seen. With a white pelt and black-tipped ears, he is stunning as he lifts his head and unleashes a howl.

A man with a gangrene arm and no lips charges up behind him, but Bardhyl snaps around in a heartbeat and swipes his massive paw at the monster, shredding its chest down to the bone. Another swipe, and his head is ripped right off. The headless creature crumbles and twitches, half its ribcage sticking out and broken.

Another Shadow Monster, with the contents of its stomach trailing behind him, lunges toward the Alpha. I'm going to be sick, but I still dart forward to intercept the attack, shoving my hands into the bony chest just as it reaches for Bardhyl. I knock it to the ground with my momentum and smash the rock in my hand into his head, over and over, blood and innards spilling free.

I scramble off it, feeling sick to my stomach from the sight, and suck in harsh breaths. Bardhyl brushes past me, his eyes narrowing and there is acceptance in his gaze, the need to attack our enemy. Then he lunges toward a horde of undead coming.

I don't waste a moment and rush toward the gap in the fence, needing to somehow stop more from coming in.

I shove past the undead and dart around the trees, past shifters fighting.

The twisted and warped fence is bent forward, clearly driven down by a vehicle.

Someone snatches my wrist and jerks me toward them aggressively, my heart blazing at the movement.

I grip the blood-stained rock over my head as I stumble to find my feet, then come face to face with the white-haired Alpha from the aircraft I'd escaped weeks before.

A gasp falls from my lips. "Mad!"

What's he doing here?

He whacks the back of my hand, and my stone flings out of my grasp. "So Dušan found you after all." He sniffs the air, then grins, sensing the Alphas' scents on me. "You haven't wasted your time, have you, bitch?"

I slam my fist into his chest, then slash my free hand at his face, nails scratching the side of his cheek, breaking skin.

Fury twists his expression into one of pure ugliness as his fist swings, then clips the side of my face.

My legs give out and I drop to the ground, my face an explosion of pain that ripples over my skull. Holding the injured side of my head, I cry from the agony.

He grabs my hair, then hauls me to my feet, and I tug back on my hair to stop the pain. Tears thread down my face. Fisting my hair, he tilts my head back violently, his face in mine. Ice-blue eyes slice right through me with venom.

"I know what's in your blood, why the infected don't touch you. Your blood tests show it all." He spits the words at me. "But I can't have you ruin my plans, Meira. I can't have you ruin them at all."

He seizes my jaw with his hand and squeezes. I whimper from the pain, from the fear of what this Alpha will do to me. The greedy look in his eyes is the reason I don't want anyone to find out the truth. Why I tell no one that I'm immune to the undead.

Someone slams into my back, and I'm shoved against Mad. In that sliver of a moment, his grip slips. I drive my hands into his chest and send him reeling backward.

Pivoting on my heels, I catapult myself into the river of undead at my back. Spinning back, Mad rises from the ground, his eyes spewing hatred, his hands fisted, but as the infected turn toward him, he retreats and runs.

The need to escape pounds in my head. I'll never be safe here, not with wolves like him, who see me as an opportunity once they uncover my secret.

Lucien's words spear over my thoughts. *If such an elixir existed, the battle to control it would end in bloodshed.* He was right. Wolves will kill to get to me...

I curse myself and whack a palm into the side of my head. *Stupid. Stupid. Stupid.*

Why did I let myself think this place might be different? Why did I get close to the Alphas?

My feet already recoil toward the broken fence behind me. My heart is shattering slowly.

These undead, the cause of the horrific state of the world, brush past me, unknowingly saving me.

I lift my gaze to the battle, only to find Dušan and Lucien staring right at me from the fortress doorway. They can see me swimming amidst the enemy without being attacked.

An army of undead swarms between us, more pouring into the settlement, shoving past me.

And the Alphas see it all now. They see me, my real secret. The one thing that promises to make me a lab experiment.

Adrenaline pumps through my veins, and a sick feeling dulls my thoughts.

I can't be here. I can't bring war to their home.

My heart splinters into a thousand pieces between escaping so their pack doesn't go to war and staying to help them save the settlement.

My throat thickens, already longing for the connection I have with the Alphas. I crave the intimacy. Adore that Dušan did his best to protect me. My head sways in two directions.

I shudder when I spy Mad from a balcony in the fortress watching me... he's a cancerous leech, and I know he will do everything to destroy me, even if it means eliminating the pack.

I straighten my spine and turn on my heels before running out of the settlement. This is what I should have done the moment I arrived here.

"Meira!" Dušan's voice fades behind me.

I can't stay here. I can't risk them losing everything. The Alphas are strong. They'll fight with claws and teeth.

The pain of leaving them behind squeezes my heart, but I don't stop running away. I never will.

Swift and silent.

Dušan

She's gone, and all I see before she goes is the fear in her eyes. The infected moved past her like she didn't exist. I lunge forward, but Lucien grabs my arm and stops me.

"Dušan, I have Meira's blood test results from when I arranged from the sample I took when she first arrived." Lucien chokes on his words.

"And?" I snap, unable to stop staring out into the woods. Except I need my head screwed on straight. "I have to fight for my wolves. This can wait." But I can't lose Meira. My breaths stumble inside me.

"Fuck, just listen to me for a second." He sucks in a deep breath. "Meira has leukemia. And it's spreading through her human form. Mariana says the sickness mingled with her wolf side is what makes her immune to the infected."

I shake my head, trying to hear his words as I turn to my Third. I smell her all over him, and I clench my fists. But I can't see clearly through my fury.

"So, what is it then? Her sick blood is immune to the undead? She's the cure everyone dreams about and can help all our pack? A solution that will bring war to our doorsteps when everyone finds out?"

"Yes. But there's a problem."

I swallow hard and growl. "What could possibly be worse?"

"The leukemia is spreading fast through her human side, and she doesn't have long before her body dies. Then her beast will rip out of her body." He stares at me, and we're both thinking the same thing before he mouths it. "There'll be nothing left of her."

My heart cleaves in half, and the world fades around me. Every emotion hits me at once—anger, frustration, fear, and heartache. They grip me, shredding my insides as everything Lucien said plays out in my head. The mess this will turn into, coupled with Mad's return and the coincidental breach of our fence, makes my blood boil.

"How long does she have?" I tighten my fists, my knuckles turning white.

"A week or two at most, Mariana thinks. I'm surprised she's survived this long." His words are strained.

Silence falls between us. All I can think about is the longing in my heart, the sharp ache that reminds me that she's meant to be one of us.

And she ran because she knew we found out her secret.

Sweet fuck, Meira. Why run? No secret could make us want you any less.

"Sonofabitch!" A howl tears from my throat. "Lucien, let's kill every motherfucking infected. Then, we're claiming our mate."

Lucien's eyes widen in surprise, then he nods. "We're in this together."

A terrifying scream rings in the air, and we both snap toward the sound. In front of us, the sheer number of undead is terrifying… I have never seen this many near our settlement. Wolves are running in every direction. Chaos strangles our home.

Shivers ripple up my spine, and I pray to the moon that we'll live to see another day. With one look at Lucien, we both lunge into battle.

SHADOWLANDS SECTOR

TWO

BOOK TWO

It's only a matter of time before I destroy them all...

A raging, bloodthirsty wolf isn't the only deadly thing inside me. So, I have to do what I've always done best. Run.

Leaving my alphas and the first taste of love I've ever known is the only answer now.

And even when Fate steps in and puts us all back together, including a sexy new alpha with troubles of his own, I can't stay. Even though it's killing me to go.

The pain of being away from them will literally kill me, but no matter what happens to me, I can't let them pay for my weakness.

I can't save myself, but I can save them. I can save them from seeing what I will become...

But my dominant alphas are better hunters than I am prey, and they're determined to keep me...whatever the cost.

CHAPTER 1

MEIRA

"Don't cry. Don't you dare cry!" I mutter under my breath, yet a sob sticks to my throat as my insides rip to shreds with heartbreak.

I'm running for my life through the forest, leaping over dead logs, ducking under low branches, never stopping. The sounds of screams and growls fill the woods behind me, and I can't stop shaking.

All I can think about are my Alphas. The two men I gave myself to, who protected me, who marked me. And now I'm fleeing from them. But I have no choice…because they know the truth.

I try to erase the images of the bloodshed between the Ash Wolves and Shadow Monsters, but they stain my mind. I remind myself I'm immune to the infected who plague this world, and remaining with the Ash Wolves will only bring war to their doorstep. Every wolf shifter will fight to claim a part of me for themselves, believing I can somehow make them resistant to the virus. I don't even know if that's true, but it won't stop the wolves from trying. Desperation drives everyone to madness.

I flashback to a memory of Lucien saying, *If such an elixir existed, it would end in bloodshed.* He's right… and I won't be responsible for starting a war amongst the wolves. It doesn't help that I'm a half-human, half-wolf and still haven't had my first fucking transformation into a wolf. Not even after two Alphas marked and mated with me.

That makes me a liability. If my wolf decides to show, it will rip out of me, killing me, and then it will slaughter everyone in sight. For those two reasons, I run to spare everyone the atrocities I'll bring to their home. Me escaping is offering them an opportunity to forget me, no matter how much fear closes my throat at the thought of never seeing my Alphas again.

My eyes water, and my insides shiver.

I'm doing the right thing.

I feel like shit on the inside for running, but I also know an opportunity to save lives when I see it. I don't belong in this pack. As much as my heart splinters in protest, I need to be clever and think about the consequences my actions will have. The knot in my chest tightens, and I swipe at the falling tears, my breaths turning to choked cries.

There's an ocean of undead pouring into Dušan's fortress. There's been a breach in the wall, and now the monsters infiltrate his compound. My gut clenches at the thought of innocents dying, but the Ash wolves are the toughest sons of bitches I've ever met. If anyone can survive such an onslaught, it's them.

Savage growls punch through the normally silent woods.

My chest feels ripped open and bleeds with agony for stealing away from them. A sudden flare of pain simmers through my body, deepening with each breath. Except I can't be sick again, not here and not now, so I fight past the screaming hurt.

I suck in each ragged breath and keep running, even though I feel like shattered glass.

Lanky, infected creatures bump into me in a frenzy to reach the wolf pack. I shoulder past them, shoving them aside, then I pick up a thick branch and cringe at the sting shooting up my side. But I don't waste the moment. I use it to take down a few creatures, slamming the weapon into their faces, sending them onto their backs. I thrust the branch into mushy, soft brains, the slushy sound sickening. I destroy half a dozen before the cluster heading to the pack fades behind me. I drop my branch covered in goo and blood, then dart away.

Screams and war cries bleed into the day, but I don't look back anymore. The Ash Wolves are my past, and I can only look forward. It's the only way I'll survive, even if my heart breaks. This isn't the time for emotions. I need to be strong and rational with every action I take.

My lungs ache and scream for oxygen when I reach the deep woods. I rest near an oversized oak tree, laying my hands on my knees and leaning over as I suck in deep pockets of air. My inhales wheeze, sweat coats me, and every muscle trembles. I squeeze my eyes shut tightly, the tears refusing to stay at bay, and I hug myself as I stumble into the tree at my back.

My time with the Alphas plays on my mind, and the memories just won't go away. I open my eyes to the trees and bushes surrounding me, the sounds of war replaced by utter silence and the occasional squawk of a bird. No scent of the wolves or infected. Still, the guilt of not helping them more sits on me like a mountain.

"Helping others is a weakness," one of the women I used to share a cave with once said. *"Danger comes, you run. Look after yourself because no one else will."*

I wrap my arms around my middle, remembering the enduring look in Lucien's eyes when he talked to me about his past, when he held me so close I couldn't breathe from desire. Dušan made me feel things no one else ever has, and he promised to keep me safe.

I had let myself believe them, but that was me fooling myself and them. Mama used to say promises are just disappointments waiting to happen.

I draw in deep breaths and stay there long enough to fill my lungs. I'm exhausted by these thoughts, and I can't keep dwelling on them, so I square my shoulders and make myself a promise to forget everything. Just as I have with everything else in my life.

Except my throat closes up and tears burn my eyes. I blink them away and stare at a rock face ahead of me, beaming under the glow of the sun. I see everything, every thin crack… every scurrying ant. I rub my arms, remembering how close I came to shifting… how I still feel my wolf stirring inside me. But getting her to make an appearance, even with the Alphas' help, just refuses to happen.

I don't need anyone. I keep repeating that in my mind like a mantra, hoping it will sink in. I push away from the tree and leap into a jog, putting more distance between me and them… *Swift and silent.*

The rest of the day, I keep moving, not knowing where I'll end up. But that doesn't matter, as long as it's as far from the wolves as possible. I've lived this long without them, and I'll continue to do so.

My heart gives a heavy thump at the thought.

By the time the sky darkens with the approaching night, I'm staggering, barely able to stay upright, and I stop near a river. I don't recognize the location or even how close I am to where I was living before.

That place I'd marked out, where I knew I'd be safe from rogue wolves. But out here, I'm an open target.

I drop to my knees in front of the river and splash my face, then take my fill.

A branch snaps on the opposite bank, and I jerk my head up, frozen in place. But it's only an infected staggering about. A young girl, maybe thirteen, wearing tattered clothes and only one shoe. Her braids are messy and stained with dark patches. Eyes void of life, she lingers on the spot as if trying to sense where to find her next meal. An animal, a human, a wolf shifter. It's all the same to her. But only the cry of a bird sounds in these woods.

She looks right through me like I am one of her kind, undetectable and non-existent. I climb to my feet and dust the dirt from the knees of my black leggings, while water stains splash my wrap-around blue top.

I scan the trees for the best sleeping location. Up there, I'm safe from rogue wolves and other creatures that come out at night to scour the woods. I have no weapons to defend myself, so I move quickly, having no time to waste. I scramble forward and use a tree's rough edges and lower branches to scale the trunk until I reach a natural platform made of three branches. At least twenty feet off the ground, I sit with my back to the trunk and fold my legs in front of me. Not the best spot, but it'll do. I survived for five years on my own, and I can do it again.

Deep breath, I remind myself and think back to the last time I scaled a tree for protection… It was the first time Dušan found me in the woods, when I should have run and never let him into my life. My bones seem to tremble at the memory of him close to me, his presence and scent swallowing me, claiming me before he ever marked me.

I reach up to the back of my neck where he bit me. The skin is smooth now, but the flesh feels sensitive under my fingertips.

After everything I've gone through—watching my mama be eaten by the infected, battling rogue wolves, and being captured—I was mistaken to think I might have found my fated mates.

Because there are no such things for me.

CHAPTER 2

DUŠAN

*Y*ou *fucking sonofabitch...* I unleash a growl, the sound thundering across the terrain, doing nothing to stop the onslaught of the infected. Dead, filthy things who are incapable of thinking but are always starved for flesh and blood race through the broken wall into my pack's yard.

I lunge at two of the bastards in my wolf form, my thoughts a mangled blur. On all fours, I charge headfirst and slam into one of their chests, tossing it aside, then snap around, teeth bared at the other culprit. I bite into his leg and tear it off, the slurping sounds nothing but a war song surrounding us.

Everyone will fight until we have slain every last fucking undead. Armed guards stand on the balcony of our fortress and take down one undead after another. *Bang. Bang. Bang.* They thin the herd as much as possible.

I leap from one creature to the next, taking down as many as I can, tearing the infected from wolves who have fallen. The screams are the worst, but Lucien has my back and we're fighting like a well-oiled machine. We've been at war against these monsters before, battling side by side since we were children.

The world is fucked. But we've adapted, become the killers we need to be. I feel nothing but hatred; everything else grows numb.

Bardhyl barrels into the fight, pelt white as snow charging in from the side of the house. He's a tank, taking down half a dozen creatures in one move. He's the most terrifying bastard I know. It's why I keep him close to my side.

Lucien releases a tremendous growl, and nothing will stop him once he's battling. Bodies scatter the ground around us, limbs twitching, eyes on decapitated heads blinking. But not much scares me anymore.

Wolves fight side by side, and I rip apart the creatures, leaving a pile in my wake. A scream rings through the air, and I swing my head in its direction to my right, my lips peeled back over fangs. Two infected have a female wolf pinned to the ground, biting into her body, ripping away flesh.

Fury slices me in half, and I'm flying toward them. I pounce on one and sink my teeth right into its back, ripping away flesh and bones. In my head, all I can picture is Meira being attacked. She's out there somewhere, and I need to get to her before it's too late.

Stupid woman… she never should have run.

She had so many secrets up her sleeve, didn't she?

One, she has leukemia, and her human body is dying. But I doubt she knows that.

Two, Meira is immune to the zombies because of the disease in her blood. I don't think her blood can be used as a cure, yet she runs because she thinks everyone will hunt her down for it.

Fuck! When I catch her, I'm spanking that tight ass so hard.

I throw myself at the second infected, my teeth latching around its neck, and I take its head right off with sheer rage.

I stare down at the female wolf I recognize as a new Beta who only recently found her mate. She's on the ground, gurgling blood while it pours out from the edges of her mouth. Her eyes peer into the sky, already turning glassy. There's nothing I can do for her. Once she dies, she'll reawaken as one of them. It's how the virus exists, how it expanded to infect the whole planet. Earth is nothing but a fraction of what it once was.

Nothing remains now. Only the virus-ridden creatures and survivors like us, trying to make a home amid the destruction.

When the Beta quiets down, I snap my jaw around her neck and rip her apart. I don't think about it. Just do what must be done. My brain sits barren for those few moments, choosing to ignore that these images will haunt my dreams for years to come.

But as the Alpha, I won't allow more of the creatures to be spawned. And sure as fuck not from wolves in my family pack.

Then I lunge into battle, forgetting every single fucking thing except destroying the enemy.

We fight.

Undead and wolves fall alike.

I don't pay attention as I plow through the dwindling masses.

I spin around on all fours, searching for my next victim, the heavy scent of blood blotting my senses.

All I find are wolves standing, injured and bloody, while the ground is littered with the undead.

I suck in jagged breaths, refusing to register to the small details. When I glance over to the broken wall and no more undead stagger inside, I tilt my head to the sky and call my wolf back with an ear-shattering howl that bleeds into the air. My flesh ripples as electricity pops over me like sparks. Black fur shrinks, bones crack, and I shudder with the transformation that rips through me in a split second. An explosion of pain swallows me, the agony excruciating, but I'm used to it now. Our changes are vicious.

Getting up to my feet, I stand in the form of a man wearing no clothes and stare out over the chaos. My third and fourth, Lucien and Bardhyl, take human form too, as do others. Bardhyl's white-blond hair flutters in the wind over his broad shoulders, and the way he studies the battlefield reminds me of the first time I encountered him up in Denmark, after he'd single-handedly slaughtered a small pack of Alphas. Lucien should have been my brother, as we are more similar than either of us would admit. He helps someone to their feet, then looks up to me. His steel-gray wolf eyes glint in the sun, and he runs a hand through his short, timber-colored hair.

Then the cries around us begin as wolves begin searching for their loved ones. My gut aches at the grieving sounds.

Lucien steps over a body to reach me. "Goddamn fucking infected." His expression twists with hatred as he takes in the massacre.

"We won. That's what counts," I say. "Arrange for all able wolves to take stock of how many we lost, and make sure they are really dead before families take them for burial. Take the rest of the infected down the mountain and as far from here as possible before their rotting bodies reek the air."

He nods, his attention sweeping over the fallen, his face splattered with blood.

"Bardhyl," I call out to the Viking wolf. "We need the wall mended immediately. See to it."

He taps his chest twice with his fist and turns abruptly to the wall. I have faith in my men to get things done. I swing to the dead, and Lucien and I start searching for wolves. They will be reunited with their families before receiving a proper farewell.

I spot a familiar face several feet away. It's a younger Alpha whose brain has been smashed in, meaning this brave soldier won't morph into a creature.

Bang.

The sound from behind me makes me flinch, and I lift my head, hating how fucking jumpy I feel. The guards are making sure all dead wolves stay that way.

We begin collecting the bodies and clearing out the mess. I don't keep track of how long we've been at this, but night starts to stain the sky and my muscles strain.

"We rest now." Lucien is behind me, his body covered in dirt and blood. Getting infected blood into our system doesn't turn us until we die. In truth, we're probably all infected already; many believe it spread through the air so long ago. And now it just lingers inside us until we perish and reawaken.

Around us, only the blood-soaked ground remains. The infected have been piled into trucks for disposing of tomorrow, and wolves are laid in the great hall for family ceremonies.

My head spins with so much to do, except this isn't even close to being over.

Meira comes to mind, and I look up to where the wall at the side of my yard lays smashed open. I keep picturing her running away, pushing past the infected, her gaze meeting mine with utter shock.

The look in her eyes screamed regret, guilt, and heartbreak—but still, she left. Except she never understood the pack rules of mating and marking. Now that she's been marked, she will feel the apprehension and a deep pain in her chest the farther she is from her mates. The problem is that because her wolf hasn't come out, hasn't accepted me or Lucien as her true Alphas, she's susceptible to other wolf attacks. Her slick heat will drive other Alphas to madness to claim her… and she's run out there alone.

"We need to find her." Lucien voices my thoughts. "The leukemia will claim her human body in a week or two."

A deep growl rumbles in my chest. I fucking hate this constant battle. If it isn't one thing, it's another. "We'll go after her tonight," I bark.

He doesn't protest because, like me, he feels the lacerating ache tightening around his chest from being away from his marked mate. I can barely acknowledge that he mated with my Omega, except it's not unheard of for females to pick more than one mate. But I shove those thoughts out of my head for now.

"Help Bardhyl and get ready. We leave in an hour and pray to the moon we're not too late."

"There's something you need to know," Lucien starts, but I shake my head, not ready to hear anything else right now. I'm tired of smelling like blood from the dead and need to get my head straight to work out how the fuck this happened before I take on any more shit.

Meira

A scream bleeds through the night, ripping me from my sleep. My breaths stutter in my lungs.

I rock sideways, my eyes flipping open, and my heart lurches to the back of my throat as I start falling out of the tree. Frantically, my gaze sweeps over the edge of the branch, and I lash out to snatch onto the limb overhead and steady myself. It takes a few moments for my heart to calm down and to make sense of where I am and why. Memories steamroll over me, crashing with incredible speed as I remember the insanity of what I've been through. But what I hate most of all is how easily my heart clenches at the thought of Dušan and Lucien. I'm not stupid—I know their marking me has done something to me, bound us somehow—but I don't understand the rules of how this works. Will the burrowing ache in my chest eventually fade, or will it drive me so mad I'll run back to them? So much for pretending I'll be fine alone. Even here they affect me.

Another scream rings out in the air, this time clearly coming from near the river. It's female, that much I can tell. I stiffen, a sliver of my survival instinct returning.

Is the girl facing a rogue Alpha or a small group of them? What if it's a trick by Mad to find me? Or is it a decoy sound Dušan is using to lure me out of my hiding spot? I can't stop thinking about the last words Mad said to me before I fled.

"I know what's in your blood, why the infected don't touch you."

His words stay with me. They cling to my mind like thorns, reminding me that to wolves, I'll always be one thing: a lab experiment.

All fantastic reasons for me not to move from my tree. This is how I survived so many years—by butting out of everyone's business. Maybe that makes me gutless, but I prefer to think it's smart.

Another scream, and this time, I chew on my lower lip, my mind starting to think things it shouldn't. Like contemplating ways to sneak down undetected to just see what's going on. But I wait a bit longer…

When the next ear-splitting scream comes, I start moving, climbing down the tree.

I remind myself helping a bit *will* reduce the guilt chewing on my insides at doing nothing.

I have no idea when I changed… the old me would never have done this.

My feet gently kiss the grassy ground, and when no one charges toward me, I slip forward and cut through the night. This better not be a mistake.

Pulling into a dark location under a massive pine, I stare out to the river, where shadows move about.

Someone's backing away, holding what looks like a sword. I squint. Nope, it's a branch.

I hold tight, sinking against the tree. My heart trips over itself, but I'm as silent as the night.

In a split second, the figure spins and runs in my direction, several others chasing right after her. I shudder, my brain firing off sparks and commands to run, but I don't dare move.

The girl darts past me, crying out, while three Shadow Monsters charge after her. Well, her first mistake was making a sound. It only attracts more of those things.

I breathe deeply and crouch, patting the ground. Finding a long branch, I snap it over my knee to create a sharpened point on one end. Then I lunge after the girl. The only reason I'm helping is because I feel shitty enough as it is, running from the pack, and everyone needs a helping hand sometimes.

Running after them, I come up on a shorter undead first and jab the pointy end of the branch into the back of its neck with ferocity. The sharpness cuts deep, breaking skin and sliding into him. Thing about the infected is, their bones and bodies are a lot softer than living creatures', so they're easier to penetrate.

It shrieks and falls over. Plucking the stick out with a gooey sound, I leap over him and run after the second one, shoving the weapon right into its back. A kick to the back of the knees, and the undead lurches forward, falling onto hands and knees. I shove my foot against its spine and grip the branch sticking out of its back. Then I drive down through its supple body and into the soft ground, pinning it in place. I have no idea if it will stay, but I swing and sprint after the girl's screams while stealing another branch off the ground. It's thinner than the last weapon, and the wood feels harder to the touch.

Trepidation crawls up my spine. This is madness on my part, running at night where other predators, including rogue wolves, lurk. But she's making enough noise to wake up the entire mountain.

So I scramble forward, where it's so dark I can barely make out my own hands. My foot catches on a root and suddenly I'm tripping forward, my pulse racing with fright.

I slam into someone, crashing into them hard.

Panic squeezes my lungs and a scream rises out of my throat.

But when the guttural growl of an infected spills into the night from the person beneath me, I quickly scramble back and plunge my weapon into the back of its head, where it's softest, over and over as the creature bucks and fights to get out from under me. But I don't pause, not even when something wet coats my hands.

When it quiets down, I finally stop and just sit there, straddling a dead infected, gasping for air.

I hate this day so much!

I don't know what took over me, as I've never reacted this way before—never acted so aggressively.

A sniffle comes from up ahead, and I lift my gaze to a dark bundle crouching near an oversized shrub.

"Are you okay?" I ask as I push myself to my feet and wipe my hands down my pants. "I'm not going to hurt you, I promise."

Slowly, I creep forward when a young girl steps out. She's maybe thirteen or fourteen years old… God, she's just a child. She only reaches my shoulders in height.

When foliage snaps behind me, I snatch her hand, drawing her to my side. "Shh. No words. Swift and silent, okay?"

She nods, and we both dart to the closest tree with low branches I can find. I swallow hard and help lift her, pushing her butt to climb up faster. I was her age when I lost my mama and had to survive alone in this world. With that thought, a terrible sorrow slivers over my heart at everything I've lost.

More than anything, I long for my Alphas right now, so agonizingly hard that I feel like my chest is cracking in half.

CHAPTER 3

LUCIEN

Dušan charges across the blood-stained field and vanishes in the fortress compound. Everything is fucked, and somehow amid all the chaos, Meira has run from us. I grit my teeth, and my wolf shoves against my insides at the thought that we're letting her get away. She's defenseless, sick, and so damn stubborn that it will get her killed if we don't find her in time. So we need to do everything here fast, because I need her in my arms again.

My stomach tightens each time I think of her against me, her hypnotic scent, the mark that binds us. But it means shit if she goes and gets herself killed. She only had to give us a chance to explain what's in her blood, but she ran. I want to kiss all that fear she carries out of her system.

Stupid woman has no idea how sick she really is or how close to the razor-sharp edge of death she walks.

As far as I'm concerned, we mend the wall and put the pack at ease, find that turd Mad, then go hunting for Meira. I growl, as the to-do list seems impossible.

And it's no coincidence Dušan's second-in-command appears just as everything falls into chaos. He visited the X-Clan pack across the other side of Europe, as Dušan has a trade agreement with them. But we were recently informed by their Alpha, Ander, that Mad stole serum from their compound.

The members of the X-Clan are a different breed of wolves compared to Ash Wolves, and something in their bodies allows them to be immune to infected blood. They have a serum that works only on their kind.

So that fuckhead Mad believed it was an immunity serum and that he could replicate it to use for himself. Except the serum is useless on Ash Wolves, and now his actions are jeopardizing our relationship with our strongest trader.

Dušan knows I want to rip Mad's head off, but he keeps protecting the bastard because Mad is his stepbrother. As far as I'm concerned, Mad deserves shit. They are related only by their parents mating after their were born. There is no biological link whatsoever.

Anyway, that doesn't mean Mad's not a dangerous fuck. He is responsible for the shit that went down today. I don't know how, but I'd stake my life on it. He's got shifty eyes. Bardhyl laughs at me when I say this, but you can tell a wolf's true intention by their eyes. They are the mirror into the soul, after all.

So how the fuck did Mad breach the wall to our compound? I don't know the answer, so I storm across the open grounds. Up ahead, the stone barricade lays tumbled inward as though something charged into it from outside. A large chunk remains intact, which should make putting it back together easier.

I push past the pack members collecting loose stones and rubble, and I step into the woods surrounding our home. Blood hangs ripe in the air from the battle, so picking up other scents here is close to impossible. But the tire tracks tearing up the terrain leading up to the wall are a dead giveaway. This is the only location with a clearing of woods, so it'd be easy to bring a vehicle up here and smash down the wall, then rapidly drive away before anyone really notices.

"Lucien," Bardhyl bellows. "Get your ass over here and give us a helping hand."

I turn to find him and half a dozen pack members standing in front of the fallen wall, most crouching low to start lifting it back into place.

"Of course."

My hands press to the stone barricade, and we push the goddamn slab upward.

I grunt and strain with the weight, but it doesn't take long for the wall to sit where it once was. Enormous gaps and cracks litter the broken wall, but it's nothing a lot of patching won't help.

Everyone's running around, cleaning up the mess, arranging for families to see to their deceased. Bardhyl turns to me, dust in his long, blond hair and across his brow. He stands slightly taller than me and could have easily stepped out of Viking times. This wolf is a warrior at heart and looks like one. He also has every available female chasing him in the pack... even taken women pay him too much attention. He fucking loves it, and who wouldn't? He's Dušan's fourth and my closest friend, next to Dušan.

I lift my chin for him to follow me out of earshot of others, and we move to the middle of the field where no one stands.

"Have you seen Mad anywhere?" Bardhyl's question comes in the form a growl as his gaze sweeps the yard around us.

I shake my head. "Dušan doesn't even know he's back yet. I didn't get a chance to tell him. But that dickhead won't be far, and he'll be lucky if I don't snap his neck when I catch him."

"I say we find him and chain him up before he gets a chance to do any more damage," Bardhyl growls, the muscled cords in his neck pulsing. His eyes sweep over to me. "Also, Dušan told me you and he are going to hunt down Meira. I want in. We capture Mad, then we head out. I know these woods inside out, and I have her scent. We split in three and cover more ground."

He's my equal, and I have no objection to more of us searching for Meira before it's too late, because it's killing me to know she's out there and we still haven't left our home. But I'm not sure Bardhyl is thinking this through. With Mad returned, someone needs to remain here to lead the pack.

"I know that look," he snaps at me. "Mad didn't fight alongside us, and that makes him the enemy in my eyes. We search for him now and start inside the fortress. We never should have trusted him."

"We didn't, but Dušan..." My words trail off because nothing is ever black and white. They are stepbrothers. Mad and Dušan are the only family each other has, even if not by blood, and those kinds of relationships are the most complicated. I breathe heavily, with dark thoughts sliding over my mind from when my first mate, Cataline, died... I still wake up in a sweat, swearing I can sense her near me. I vowed to never love again, but fate is unpredictable because she's made Meira my fated mate as well. And dealing with those emotions tears me up.

"If we do this, we move fast and grab that bastard," Bardhyl instructs, snapping me out of my thoughts.

I curl my hands into fists, and my heart surges into a race with the promise of a hunt. "Meira is running out of time, and we can deal with Dušan's wrath later if he doesn't like how we deal with Mad."

My friend nods, and we both lunge toward the fortress.

Dušan

We lost seven warriors during the battle, our home has been compromised, and the pack will go into a panic now. They don't feel safe, so it's my job to reassure them and ensure their fortress remains secure.

Though deep in my gut, worry clenches at me. Someone sabotaged us, and I'm going to rip their head off when I find them. Coupled with Meira running away, this whole catastrophe couldn't have come at a worse time.

I emerge from the shower and wipe down the water from my body with a towel, then I drag on my jeans and step into boots. I reach for a clean black tee and tug it over my head and down my body.

If I'm going to address my pack and help them calm down, I'm not doing it covered in blood. They need to know that despite today's tragedy, things will get easier. They have to. I need to believe this, because I can't charge into the woods after Meira if I'm worried about my pack's safety. The longer I take, the farther she'll travel, so I need to move fast.

I march out of my room and down the corridor. My plan had been to work with Meira and find a way to bring out her wolf before her time ran out. If she could just shift, her wolf would heal the blood disease that's ravaging her human side.

Well, that plan had failed miserably. Just thinking about it has me balling my hands into fists, my muscles throbbing with frustration.

Why run, little one?

From the corner of my eye, I notice a figure on the balcony as I pass the doorway. I turn to take a second look. Short cropped white hair. He's in all black, his hands gripping the railing as he stares out to the yard below, where everyone else is working tirelessly to bring back some semblance of normality.

My bristles rise, and my wolf shoves forward with aggression, growling in my chest. My blood boils as I charge toward him.

"You no longer pay your Alpha respect after a mission?" I roar.

Mad whips around to face me, his movement fast, but his smile slow.

My nostrils flare, and I march right up to him, face to face, and I'm breathing down on him. I'm trembling to rip him apart for defying me.

Hostility pours off him, fueling my anger, charging the air with electricity. His eyes narrow with a primal challenge. His mouth pulls into a sneer, accentuating the healed scar on his jawline.

"You stole from Ander." I spit the words in his face. "What the fuck were you thinking? Hand over the serum!" I roar. He's lucky I haven't ripped off his head yet.

My whole trade agreement depends on me returning the serum to the X-Clan. I don't plan to lose the ability to gain new technology and resources from Ander just so Mad can try to play god. This little shit has always looked out for himself. For so long, I justified his actions by telling myself he's younger than me, so he's still got a lot to learn. But this latest stunt might end my patience for him. I've had enough of saving his ass every time he does shit like this.

Mad doesn't move, instead looking me in the eyes, challenging me. "I did this for us," he snaps, like *I'm* the unruly one. "I saw an opportunity and I took it."

I grasp his neck, squeezing. "This isn't a fucking joke."

When I glare into his pale blue eyes, all I can see is my father. In my head, I hear him yelling at me, slapping me in the back of the head and telling me that I'm not good enough. That I'll never make a good Alpha because I'm too weak. Mad would crouch in the corner, whimpering while I got beaten, trying a few times to stop our father. But now he's changed, no longer the stepbrother I grew up with, but a wolf looking for his own path. And I wish him every fucking luck, but it's not going to happen under my roof.

He shoves a hand against my chest, and I release him as he stumbles to find his footing. His lower back presses into the metal railing, cracking a wry smile. "It wasn't like I could call you while in enemy territory and discuss stealing an antidote that could help all Ash Wolves."

That smirk and his words are like gas on my fury. "X-Clan is not the fucking enemy. If you're incapable of understanding a treaty, then I've wasted my time making you my second."

"Dušan," he growls. "That's not fair, man. I did this for us."

My heart slams in my chest, my adrenaline a ticking time bomb about to go off under my ribcage. "You did this for yourself. Otherwise, you would have told me. Instead, I heard it from Ander." A snarl spews past my lips, and he flinches at first, then straightens his shoulders, as if finding his bravery.

He's shaking his head.

I snatch his jaw and squeeze until he winces. "Listen very carefully so your brain understands: The serum from X-Clan does not work on Ash Wolves. It's made specifically for their wolves. It has no effect on us. If you'd asked me, I would have told you that before you went and almost ruined our relationship with Ander."

His eyes grow as wide as the moon at my revelation, and this is why I'm ready to tear off his head. I put him as my second for one simple reason: he's my stepbrother, and I believed he could step up and take the role seriously, keep the Ash Wolves leadership in the family. But that was a mistake, and I won't be making it again.

He yanks back from my grasp, bumping into the railing, a snarl peeling his lips back. "Fuck, fine, you can have them back. Get the hell out of my face."

I shake my head, my fingers curling with the urgency to beat sense into him, though I doubt it would make much difference. I see clearly now the mistake I made by giving my stepbrother this kind of power in the pack.

"Tell me what happened with the delivery of women to Ander. How did you lose one?" I stand tall, my voice rising and patience thinning.

He shrugs. "No idea, but I'd say it's fate considering that little bitch has blood that could be our cure." He leans closer. "Think of the possibilities, brother. I'll take one for the team and fuck her to claim that Omega's cunt, and we use her blood for the cure to help all Ash Wolves."

I'm fuming and throw my fist into his face without hesitation. I clip him in the head, and he lurches backward from the strike, clutching the side of his face. His wolf awakens behind his gaze.

That's what I want… for him to attack. I'll destroy him.

He pulls from my reach, his lips a thin line as he spews hatred at me.

"You want her for yourself? So why didn't you claim her? She smells of heat, her slick so sweet on the air."

He's antagonizing me. I see it in the way his mouth quirks, but I won't fall for it this time. He's manipulative, and everything he does comes with motivation. There is no way Meira just happened to escape from the plane by accident. We have protocols that have never been broken before.

"You know what I think? You made it easy for Meira to run away when you weren't looking so you had a reason to stay with the X-Clan, knowing I'd scramble to find a replacement female for Ander. You counted on me doing anything to save our trade agreement. All the while, you set up your little plan to steal the serum. This wasn't an opportunity you stumbled on, was it?"

There is no other way to explain how Meira never made it to Ander. I've been wracking my brain over this, as our plans are straightforward… females get on the plane and are tied to a chain, end of story. Mihai confirmed he delivered nine women to the aircraft, which can only mean Mad didn't do the one step he was meant to on purpose.

A stoic expression slips over his face, the one he uses when he's lying. Behind him, down in the yard, pack members work tirelessly to bring order back to a chaotic day.

"You've become paranoid, brother," he grumbles, his shoulders bunching up like he's about to transform.

"Were you responsible for the breach in the wall too?" I bellow, anger burrowing into my bones.

He scrunches his nose and scoffs at me like I'm making this up. "You want to blame me for the spread of the virus across the planet, too?"

I'm on him in seconds, my hand on his neck again, and I push him into a backbend over the railing. "There are no such things as coincidences when it comes to you, Stefan. And I can't ignore that we have our first breach on the day you secretly sneak back home."

"Don't fucking call me that!" he snaps, baring his teeth. He loathes that name, as it was my asshole father who gave it to him.

Straining against me, his hands grip my arm for support to avoid tumbling over the balcony. "There was no sneaking inside," he mutters. "What the fuck is wrong with you?"

I can barely control myself as he lies over and over.

"Come on, Dušan. This isn't you. Growing up, we had a goal, remember? Find a way to end the curse. I tried and failed with X-Clan.

Shoot me for wanting the best for Ash Wolves. But that bitch, Meira is out there, so let's go hunt her down." There's a glint in his eyes... My stepbrother is a master of deceit. I see this clearly now.

The more he talks about Meira, the more I think about gnashing out his tongue. I don't want her name in his mouth. All I hear are his threats against my fated mate, and that's not going to work.

I wrench him up from his backbend over the railing, and I feel the trembling anger in his body, his wolf growling for release. To my surprise, Mad strains to hold back, the lines on his brow giving him away. His gaze spears over my shoulder. Footsteps close in behind me and I sniff the air, inhaling the earth and wolf scents of my third and fourth.

Lucien and Bardhyl have joined us. Perfect.

Grabbing Mad by the shirt, I swing him around and glance over to the two pack members I trust with my life. I kick Mad's legs out from under him so he drops to his knees before us.

"You're stripped of your fucking title as second to Alpha," I roar. "Your position is at the bottom of the hierarchy in the Ash Pack. Even Betas carry rank over you."

"Fuck you, Dušan. You can't do this! This was my father's pack too. I belong at the top." He starts to get up, but I drive another fist to his face to keep him down, an ache from the strike reverberating up my arm. He groans and stares at me, unflinching.

"About damn time," Lucien growls.

I look up at him. "Lucien, you are now my second-in-command, and Bardhyl, my third. Take care of this turd. I want him chained up in the dungeons."

Bardhyl smirks as he reaches down and grabs Mad by the arm, yanking him to his feet. When Mad swings a punch, Bardhyl laughs and snatches his fist, then twists it behind Mad's back. Mad cries out with pain, and Lucien takes the chance to land a fist into his gut.

I turn away, frustrated to high hell. I just want Mad out of my fucking face. Taking a deep breath, I ground myself and get ready to speak to the pack and put them at ease.

I hate that I'm fuming on the inside at having to imprison my stepbrother when we should have been one team. For once, I want something to go in my favor.

My thoughts swing to Meira and time ticking away. She's fucking gone! Fury coats my mind. Knots tighten in my gut. She's been gone for

me. Overgrown shrubs smother the land with evergreen vines crawling up the pine trunks. But there's no sign of a body or remains, so I trace my way toward the river. I need a wash, and that's likely where the girl has returned to.

Once there, I kneel and splash the crisp water onto my face, then scrub the back of my neck as well. I take my fill just as a twig snaps from across the river.

I snap my head up and spy a small deer with white spots dotting its back. I'm mesmerized, as it's been so long since I've seen a deer. The little thing has survived this long, and I hope she manages to continue doing so for a long time. When I climb to my feet, she flinches and bursts back into the woods.

I'm up on my feet and turn away from the river. The deer might have been lucky until now, but all our luck runs out eventually. This isn't a world with butterflies and unicorns, but zombies and sex-starved wolves. I hastily rush up the bank and dart into the woods and out of sight so I'm not easily spotted.

But the girl lingers on my mind. Where has she gotten to? As selfish as it sounds, I'd enjoy her company. It sounds strange to think that when I've lived in the woods by myself for years, but if I'm honest with myself, being with the pack was a nice reprieve, even if it was short. Knowing I wasn't alone and that we all worked toward survival in a protected area started growing on me. I sigh at what a hypocrite I am.

My emotions straddle the fence now, when once I couldn't even fathom the idea of joining a pack. It's ridiculous to even have such thoughts, considering how things ended with the Ash Wolves.

I march quickly over the dried foliage and shrubs, my hands swinging by my side as I sweep the woodland for any sign of the young girl. With each inhale I take, I search for distinctive wolf smells and the putrid stench of the Shadow Monsters. My trick to survival has been living next to the undead creatures, as they tend to keep to small herds in the same location. Their presence makes it more likely rogue wolves won't be around to hurt me. It's a simple trick, but it's kept me alive this long.

I keep the river to my right and head straight hoping I'm heading in the right direction to where I used to live in the treehouse. I'll collect what few belongings I have and find a new home where no one will be able to track me.

Step after step, I keep going, needing to forget the Alphas who've affected me in ways that surprise me. It's my fault for letting myself believe I could even have a normal life. The truth stings worse today because I miss them, and I hate myself for having such emotions. I curl my hands into fists against the ache rising through my chest. It's the same sensation as last night… a longing that threatens to rip me apart. With it comes a desperate sensation of leaving behind what belongs to me, but I don't stop walking. I keep pushing, one foot in front of the other.

It's the stupid markings Dušan and Lucien gave me. I sense the prickling over my skin where they bit me, and an unmerciful energy floods me, reminding me constantly I am theirs.

I jerk my focus to the woods, but my head lifts with darker thoughts.

My throat thickens as fear collects into a ball. I could die at any moment if my wolf comes out. But then again, I'm surviving the apocalypse, and death is coming for everyone sooner rather than later. I try to ignore the worry simmering in my mind that I'll be caught. I wrap my arms around my waist, surveying the land with every few steps I take.

Having walked most of the day, the sun is now descending, and with it comes an icy cold. I focus my energy on moving faster through the quiet woods. My weary muscles strain, and I keep going until dusk settles around me. The loose stones on the slanted earth slide under my feet, and I slip, my stomach lurching. I snatch onto a nearby branch and catch myself. Quickly, I hurry down the hill into an open valley where the river roars and foams around the boulders it crashes into.

I kneel at the edge of the water to fill my stomach when I glance over to my side and find the dried-up carcass of a deer, its skin peeled away and rib bones clean of flesh. It looks as though someone tried to find a meal out of the remains.

Near my foot something white glints, and I reach over to the bone that must have once belonged in the animal's leg. It's been snapped in half, but the shattered end sticks out sharply. I tighten my fingers around the bone that fits nicely in my grip.

Sticking it into the waistband of my black leggings, the pointy bit upward to avoid poking a hole through the fabric, I'm up on my feet and heading off quickly again. A small field of wild grass and shrubs surrounds me, the river at my back. I trudge toward the broad oak trees that populate this part of the woods, standing shoulder to shoulder, thick with heavy branches covered in lush green leaves. These lofty guardians will be my home for the night.

Under the protective shadows of the woods, I search for the perfect tree to scale and settle into, preferably one that has multiple branches crossing. But my attention snags on a rose-red fruit hanging from a tree several feet away.

My mouth salivates instantly as I rush to the plum tree, branches heavily ladened with bright red globes. A cry of joy falls from my mouth, and I jump up and snatch a fruit from the branch. The skin is smooth under my fingers, and I take a big bite, the crisp skin breaking between my teeth with a satisfying snap. Sugary-sweet juices burst in my mouth and drip down my chin. I moan with contentment and finish the fruit in three more bites before I grab two more.

Tossing the seeds to the ground, I help myself to more, unsure how many I've eaten when I finally stop. Juice runs down my fingers, and I wipe them down my pants before collecting half a dozen more to take up into a tree with me.

Mama and I would go fruit picking all the time. She'd stand watch for Shadow Monsters while I scaled trees and threw the fruit down. If we'd known then that I was immune to the undead, it might have made more sense for me to keep guard, especially after Mama had a few close calls.

I miss her terribly, miss hearing her voice, miss her mixed fruit pies. Cradling my plums, I resume my search for the best tree to settle in when a sudden excruciating sharpness digs into my whole body. I shudder, the fruit tumbling out of my grasp and plonking to the ground as my knees buckle.

The ache pulses, and I hold myself tight, riding the pain that shudders through me like broken glass. My lungs tighten and I'm coughing, spitting blood onto the ground. Just as I did back at the Ash Wolves fortress. Something's really wrong with me. These attacks are coming more frequently, and I don't feel like myself.

I stare at the blood splattered on the dried leaves. This is a recent thing—spewing up blood. I wipe my mouth, my hand shaking as fear slides into my thoughts.

My wolf refuses to come out. I'm broken. But as much as I run away from the safety of the pack and know that wolf could rip out of me at any time, which will kill me if my Alphas aren't near, I don't want to die.

I live at the end of the world and tell myself every day that death could come any moment now, but when I face it head on, feeling it clawing inside me, my bravery fades.

Tears blur my vision and I hiccup a strangled cry, the throb curling around my heart. All I can think about are my Alphas and how crawling into their arms would ease the ache. My emotions don't even make sense, yet I sit in the middle of a darkening forest on my own and wonder if I've made the right decision.

I cry in my hands because I didn't run away for me. I did it to protect them from me. No matter what I tell myself, that's the fucking truth. I am a danger to them, but on the inside, I'm dying to be with my wolves.

My chin trembles as tears slide down my cheeks.

I'm tired of the constant fear and stress, wishing I could have been born a normal Omega. I remember the female wolf I met on my first day in the Ash Wolves compound, and her words about mates stick to my mind.

"You're gaining a life partner so you won't be alone anymore. Don't you want that?"

I arrogantly said *no*, that I wanted freedom instead. But now that I can't have Dušan or Lucien, my chest cracks with heartache.

The woods are all I've ever known, yet I've let myself experience something I can never have. And going back is impossible. I abandoned them during the attack because it was my only chance to put distance between us, to keep them safe.

The wind shrills around me as I quietly cry. The mistake is mine... I never should have let myself fall for the wolves, because now I don't know how to get them out of my heart and soul.

CHAPTER 5

MEIRA

A chill hums in the air tonight, pressing in around me, the leaves rustling wildly. I tip my chin up as I get to my feet and wipe my eyes. Mama would always say, *"Fate will happen whether you fight against it or not."*

If my wolf plans to burst out of me tomorrow and kill me, then it will happen regardless, and I can't live worrying. So I exhale, letting out the stress and energy bubbling in me, and collect my plums off the ground. With them in hand, I hurry through the forest. The light is fading fast, and I scan every tree I pass for a possible place to sleep.

Pain shoots through my gut and my back seizes, hitting me so fast, I stumble on my feet. Everything freaking aches, but I always feel better after sleep. I reach a great oak with dozens of thick branches spiking outward, two of them crossing over near the trunk. It's perfect. The only thing that would make it better is if I had a blanket, but I've slept in worse conditions.

But when a shattering scream cuts through the silence, I flinch and drop a plum from my grip. My heart starts pounding as I turn and scan the forest. When the sound returns, I can tell it's definitely female and is coming from deeper in the woods behind me. My thoughts fling to the young girl from last night, and bile rises to my throat.

Is it her?

A third shriek comes, and I drop all my fruit to the ground before seizing the sharpened bone in my waistband.

"Hell," I murmur under my breath, because despite what I did for the girl last night, I'm not a hero. I hide and survive. That's what I've done all my life.

I've run away. I've stayed away, but I can't do that any longer. Something in me has changed, and I'm already running through the woods in the direction of the screams. Fading streams of light guide my path. I cut around trees and leap over shrubs, unsure what to expect, but there's only one way to find out.

Another cry echoes around me, louder this time, so I'm getting closer. Trees crowd around me, and my only saving grace is the rustling leaves, covering my thumping footsteps on dried foliage.

I'm running, but the screams don't come again, and a shiver zips up my spine at the thought that I'm too late. That I should have run faster, or maybe I've gone in the wrong direction. I sniff the air, but all I inhale are the smells of timber and soil. My senses have never been as strong as the wolves'.

I want to call out to her, but that's just foolish.

In an instant, someone slams into my back with such speed, and I'm tossed off my feet.

It's me who screams this time, out of pure shock. Sharp rocks scrape my hands and knees, then I collapse flat on my face into the dirt. I push myself up, gritting soil between my teeth and spitting it out.

A dark shadow looms over me, the sudden movement smothering my earlier bravery. I scramble to get up, but I only get as far as to my knees before the wolf prowls closer, moving silently and with deadly intent.

Pale eyes lock on me, wisps of hot breath curling up from lips peeled back over razor-sharp teeth.

Black as the night, this wolf is enormous, fur shaggy and knotted. Half his ear was torn off long ago and has healed to sit upright, not flat against his head like the other. The Carpathian Mountains fall under Dušan's jurisdiction, and for any other wolves to move in, they'd need to challenge him first. So this can only be a rogue shifter.

"Get the fuck away from me," I snarl with a powerful voice. Facing a wolf with fear only gets you killed faster. But what I really need is a distraction, because monsters like him don't walk away from a free meal or a female to rut just because of a strong demeanor. My fingers remain tight around the weapon I grip by my side, a shiver trailing up my legs.

A whimper comes from farther to my right.

The beast turns his head in that direction for a split second. That's all I need… a sliver of time.

I scramble to my feet, energy bleeding through me, and I lunge at the creature.

I slam into his side just as he snaps his head around, and I plunge my sharpened blade into his back, tearing flesh, blood bubbling. Quickly, I wrench it out to strike again, adrenaline propelling me to keep going. To fight and never give up.

But it all happens too fast. His thundering snarls fill the night as he swings around before I can stab him again. Huge jaws snap at my side. I flinch out of the way, then throw myself over his body and into a forward roll before leaping to my feet and running.

I'm trembling, running on adrenaline and terror, the bone slick with blood in my hand. I turn my head quickly to look back. The wolf chases after me, his eyes narrowing with hatred.

I don't stop sprinting. My skin crawls, and I've never moved so fast.

His paws hit the earth, and he growls at my back. This time, I scream. Stuffing the weapon into the back of my pants, I frantically leap up into the closest tree, my hands grasping the lowest branch. I swing my legs up as the air swooshes under me with the ferocity of the beast's attack, but he misses.

I scramble up like a mad squirrel, my hands scraping raw against the bark, branches cutting into my knees, but I can't stop or I'll die.

Suddenly, flesh and fabric tear across the back of one calf. I bellow and lose my grip on the tree, arms and legs whipping about as my heart lunges to the back of my throat. All I can picture is the wolf destroying me the moment I land, and I'm shuddering all the way down to my bones.

Thump.

I strike the ground hard, my back taking the brunt of the pain, and my cries fill my ears.

A shadow hovers over me, the threatening growl stealing all sounds. Fury ripples off him in waves. But I'm on the move, rolling away and scrambling on hands and knees.

Teeth latch around my leg, slicing into my flesh further.

I yell, my back arching, and I shove myself onto my hip, kicking him in the face with my other foot. My hand grabs for my weapon, and I raise it high then drive the sharp end of the bone into his face, right into an eye. The weapon sinks in with a sloshing sound. I shove it all the way in, trying to hit his fucking brain.

He jerks backward, releasing me, and convulses as he shakes his head madly, blood pouring out. The sounds he makes are horrible.

I push myself away and grab onto the tree, dragging myself to my feet.

The wolf is shifting, and in moments, he's turned into a massive man, crumbled off his feet.

Short, black hair sits messily around his square face. He has thick thighs and too much hair across his body. He's yelling with agony as he tugs at the weapon. But I can't bear to look and instead dart to where the girl's cries came from.

I stumble upon her several trees away, and it's the same young girl from last night. My heart bleeds to see the gash across her neck, her lip busted, and her top ripped down her front, revealing her tiny chest. Her hands are tied by a rope around the tree at her back. Her head is down, and she's crying hysterically.

She flinches as I lunge toward her.

"It's only me."

Tears drench her cheeks, and I rush to untie her, constantly looking up in case that bastard comes charging back. My fingers shake as I tug at the knots. I get them loose in seconds, then I rush to the girl who is sitting down and pull her to her feet. "We need to run. Remember what I said last night, swift and silent. Keep repeating that as we get out of here. Stay with me, and please don't run away this time."

She doesn't say a word, just hugs herself with an arm and nods.

I hold her wrist, and we're on the move through the woods, me limping from my calf. It will heal soon enough. My ears prick for any sounds, my eyes sweeping left and right. I spot the rogue wolf in the distance, lying on his side in human form, his body twisted, his mouth parted. The bone still sticks out of his eye. I guess I struck his brain after all. Fucking asshole... He deserved that, and not a sliver of guilt fills me. He isn't my first kill, and if I intend to survive, he won't be my last.

By the time we stop to rest, I have no idea how far we've gone. We're heaving for breath, and that's when I see she has blood over her chin and chest from her busted lip. And my hands are red from the attack. I feel it rolling down the side of my face too, and I hastily wipe it away with my shoulder.

A river gurgles nearby, so I take her hand. "He's not going to hurt us anymore. But we need to clean off the blood before the infected track the smells to us. Okay?"

She remains glued to my side this time and nods, so I guide her out of the woods, where the last streaks of daylight cling to the world.

Scanning the small open area with the river, I find there's no one else around. So we rush over and crouch near its bank, then begin washing ourselves. The rushing sound of the river floods my ears, the water icy against my skin. It's a deeper, greener color in the darkening light. I stare at my reflection, at the wildness of my dark hair and how much longer it hangs than I remember. It easily reaches down past my chest now. Dirt mars my cheeks and brow, but I'm caught in how pale my bronze eyes have become. Thick lashes crown them, and when I look into them, all I see is my wolf peering out at me. *Why won't you come out?*

I glance over to the young girl as she washes herself. "I'm Meira. What's your name?" I ask as I scrub the blood off my hands. Then I sit on my ass and check the damage on my bitten leg. I hiss as I peel back the torn fabric that sticks with blood, hating how close I got to that dickhead killing me.

"Here, let me do that," the girl offers. "I'm Jae," she answers while she pushes the fabric of my leggings to my knee and starts washing my wound with fresh water. It stings, and I bite down on my lip to bear the ache.

"It doesn't look too bad. Think you'll live." She grins at me, and already I like her. Anyone who makes a joke after almost being rutted by a freaking wild man is my type of friend.

I reach down and rip a strip of material from my pants. It's a bit of a strain, as my arms are trembling with exhaustion, but I need to stop the bleeding. I use the fabric to tie up the fang marks that sit around my calf muscle, wrapping it tightly. "So, Jae, how have you survived this long on your own?"

"I'm not alone," she answers quickly, her voice light and almost chipmunk-like. It's a strange comparison, but it's the first thing that comes to mind. Maybe it's her cute, round cheeks and tiny nose. She has a heavy smattering of freckles over her nose and cheeks, and her dark bronze hair has been cut super short. She looks adorable.

"Is your family around?" I ask.

"My sisters are looking for me. We've heard about a place up in northern Romania where there are no undead."

"But there'll be rogue wolves like that asshole back in the woods."

"I know. I just got separated from my sisters, and they have my knife. But we have a place to meet again we agreed on if we ever get lost, and I'm not too far. Thank you for helping me."

"Want me to take you there?" My mind is buzzing with a possible chance to encounter others like me. Omega or Beta, I can't tell what Jae is, but the idea of being in my own small group of females is exciting. No Alpha bullshit to deal with.

"No, it's okay," she responds in a clipped tone, turning back to the river to wash her hands.

I don't push the topic. I understand that in this world, the easiest way to survive is to not trust anyone. And as much as my throat tightens at the rejection, I swing my gaze to the woods behind us and turn my thoughts to the both of us getting up in a tree before nightfall. I'm no fool and suspect she won't be there when I wake up in the morning, but I accept that. In her shoes, I'd do the same.

She's on her feet, and I then remind myself it's best she doesn't want me to help her further. I'm a danger to anyone I'm near, and the last thing she and her sisters need is a ticking time bomb.

CHAPTER 6

DUŠAN

The crisp scent of the wood fills my senses. Everything from the pines to the soil and even the decomposing dead rabbit somewhere to my right.

I sniff the air, searching for the sweet, slick scent of my mate.

But I pick up on not a damn thing, and the sinking sensation falls deeper through me.

I turn and head right because I've been tracking a dead trail for the past few hours. We left our compound just as night settled over the land, splitting up and running in three different directions. We're in human form, but we still have the advantage of our wolves' sharp senses, so we use our noses to try to catch Meira's scent in the dark woods.

I'm hoping the new direction I'm going in brings me across a path Meira has traveled.

Time passes too fucking slow, searching and not finding a single clue. Back in the fortress, Mad is locked up, and my chief of the guards has stepped up and will work on implementing routine as soon as possible. Order helps people get back into their lives and deal with disaster.

I announced to my pack they are now safe, and I will be implementing further security measures to ensure a breach never happens again. And that comes in the form of deciding what I'll do with my stepbrother. I can't trust him any longer. That was my mistake before, and he may deny being responsible for letting in the undead, but everything points to him. And to be on the safe side, I locked up Mihai and Cassian, who both had dealings with Mad during the transport of the women to the X-Clan. Right now, I don't have the luxury of time to interrogate them for the truth, so that will have to wait until I return. I can't take any risks while I'm away from the pack.

Finding Meira comes first, and everything else must be placed on hold until I find her. I can't lose her. A piercing fear pinches in my chest that I am too late. That I waited too long before I began the search.

A growl thunders in my chest out of pure frustration. My boots slap the ground with each step I take.

It isn't long before I pick up the decrepit stench of the undead, the smell choking me. I gag, but I swing toward the scent and not away. Meira isn't foolish, and she knows among the undead she is safer from other wolves. It would be my strategy as well.

My ears prick up at everything because I'm alone, and being cornered by those things would be my undoing. But for Meira, I'll risk it all.

The air grows thicker with their decay, and I slow my pace now, making no sound.

I reach to my belt and draw a blade, my fingers curling tightly around the hilt.

There's movement ahead… I count four shadows stumbling through the woods. Bile rushes up my throat, and I hold still. There are no other noises from around me, so is it just them?

A ferocious snarl cuts through the night, deep and guttural, full of menace and warning. I lift my chin and sniff the air, and the familiar musky, wet dog scent that belongs to Lucien hits me. *Fuck, yeah!*

I'm moving before I even make the decision to, darting around trees, keeping my eyes on the undead. Listening… listening… listening.

Footsteps from my right. I pivot and lunge in that direction, rushing past the filthy undead. Where there are a few, more linger. These things tend to move in herds most of the time.

My heart races as I sprint through the dark, slivers of moonlight lighting the way. I grip the knife in my hand tighter.

Another growl shatters the silence. I hurry, my wolf shoving against my insides, demanding release to tear these fuckers apart. To cover distance quicker. Except I need to know what I'm dealing with first.

A figure slams into a tree only a few feet from me.

I freeze and don't make a sound.

Moans come from the creature slumped to the ground, but already it starts pushing back to its feet.

With my heart beating, I lunge in its direction, my knife raised, and I plunge the blade right into an eye, driving it into the brain. Quickest way to eliminate these things.

It drops back down, and I wrench my weapon free, the action making a squelching noise. I wipe the blood on the torn fabric that hangs off its shoulder as I scan the woods up ahead.

Four undead approach Lucien in a semi-circle, and there are more in the woods on their way here. I tense up. All it will take is one mistake, one slip, and they'll be on him. Then more and more will come until it'll be too late to escape.

I whistle low and sharp to catch Lucien's attention. Moonlight glints off the two blades he grips.

He barks out a laugh. "Took you long enough to get here," he teases. "You're getting slow." But I hear the shakiness in his voice. Being out here alone is never a good idea.

"Four more coming this way," I say. "You take the two on your right. I'll take these two."

He gives one nod. "A small group is just to my right. They'll be here soon enough. We need to get the fuck out of here."

Then we charge into battle. It's what we've always known, and this is no different than the hundreds of times before. Except his mention of even more of the undead nearby worries me. They'll come toward the sounds—they'll *rush* toward us.

I kick the back of the legs of one creature. It falls, and I hurl myself onto the second one, locking an arm around its neck as I stab him in the eye. Pulling the weapon out, I turn and jump at the one on its knees, shoving my blade into the back of its neck in an upward motion.

Someone slams into my back. I'm tossed forward, my pulse spiking.

"Ggffff."

The sound is in my ear, frozen hands yanking at my head.

Panic smothers me. I swing back an elbow and buck at the same time. The weight rolls off, and I scramble up, but another crashes into me, and I'm stumbling about as if I'm drunk, trying to twist around.

The deep moan is right in my ear, fingers digging into my flesh.

My wolf flushes against my chest, but I hold him back. To change now would make me an easy target, as I'd be defenseless during the transformation. I kick my leg back, heel connecting with brittle bone as I hear the clear snap.

I shove the undead off me and whip around to see Lucien leaping at one of his undead, stabbing it over and over in the face with fury.

Two more of them come at me.

I dart around a tree and grab a handful of one of the undead's hair, except it comes free in my hand with some of the skin.

Disgusting creatures.

As it turns toward me, eyes sunken, skin pulled taut over its cheekbones, I slam its decayed head into the tree trunk. Three times for good measure.

It makes gurgling sounds before it drops to its knees, then I spin around and lash out with my knife. The blade cuts through the throat of the last monster. But not all the way.

"You fucking piece of shit." I kick it in the gut and it falls, and I'm there to finish the job in seconds.

I roar and straighten myself to find Lucien wiping his weapons on the grass. "I bloody hate these things," he snarls as he tucks his knives back into the sheaths on his belt. Bodies litter the woodlands around us.

Unintelligible voices come from the woods on the other side of Lucien, and my stomach drops. The small group Lucien mentioned is on the move.

Hastily, I wipe my blade clean and tuck it away.

He slides in alongside me, and we run in the opposite direction.

No words at first, not until we get far enough to not be heard.

We sprint through the woods, but the sounds coming up behind us seem to grow louder.

I look over my shoulder as a swarm of undead rises behind us where we've left the bodies. There have to be at least a hundred of the bastards.

"Hell! Lucien, you said a *small* group."

He snorts a nervous laugh. "Didn't want to scare you."

I cut him a glare but then smirk, because he's always played down any danger. That's how he deals with shit. Tells himself and others it's not so bad, then he doesn't panic when he faces a wall of damn undead.

I'm the opposite and need everything laid out before me.

He draws in a shaky breath as he looks behind us.

We don't stop, knowing that if we get far enough, they won't be able to trace our smell to follow.

I swallow thickly, praying they don't track us.

Meira

$\mathcal{A}$s expected, Jae isn't with me in the tree when I wake up in the morning. I'm not surprised she took off, but I really hope she's smart and makes it back to her sisters. Unease settles in my gut. I'm worried that she's walking into more danger, but I can't spend all my time searching for her when I have to get away myself.

I rub the cold out of my arms and glance down below to the quiet forest. My stomach rumbles, and all I can think about are those sweet plums.

I scramble down the tree and return to the fruit, where I gorge until I sate the hunger pains.

The day is new and bright, so the plan is to make as much headway through the Carpathian Mountains as I can. First, I make a quick stop to wash by the river, then relieve myself. But the whole time, my longing for the Alphas burns through me like a storm.

This feeling for them can't last forever, right? If I put enough distance between me and them, maybe the bond between us will fade.

I remain within the woods and avoid the open land by the river, but I follow its path. I don't remember how long I've walked, but all the plums I carried with me are now eaten, and the sun sits brightly overhead. My fingers are as sticky as honey, so I slide out of the woods and rush to the water for a quick wash.

Something in the knee-length grass catches my attention from farther ahead. It's lying down, unmoving.

My legs stop working, and I don't breathe for a few moments as I squint for a better look.

A wolf? Except that's not how these fiends hunt. They have too much ego and testosterone to ever crouch and hide. They charge like a fucking bull and take what they want.

Long grasses sway in the breeze. The water gurgles and branches behind me rustle in the breeze. But everything else is dead silent.

Might be a killed animal. But when my thoughts fly to Jae, I lunge forward.

I stare down at the figure. She's twisted, lying on her back. My gaze focuses only on her face, because staring at the shredded body, the bones picked clean, repulses me.

Frantically, I search the features, my heart pounding so hard. Dead eyes stare up into the sky.

This isn't Jae.

It's not her.

A sob chokes past my throat because for a moment, I thought I'd stumbled upon her remains. Whoever this is has been dead for a couple of days, judging by the stench and foam slipping out from the corners of her mouth.

I retreat, but the gagging reflex kicks in strong, and I hurl my breakfast. No matter how many deaths I've seen, I can never get used to it, and the sorrow for whoever that was crashes into me like powerful waves.

With fast steps, I leave that place and return to the safety of the shadowy woodland. I bolt and don't stop until my chest aches from exhaustion. Then I press my back to a tree to catch my breath and can't think of anything else but that poor girl. What if she had been one of Jae's sisters?

I know in my heart there's nothing I can do about it. Still, the grief sits heavily over my chest.

When something sounds in the distance, I tilt my head up.

Thump.

My heart thuds inside my ribcage. There's no sign of the river, and I don't know which way I've been running. Where am I?

I'm in the woods, I tell myself, *so there are lots of noises.* Except these are woods of claws and teeth, and anything out of the ordinary is a potential danger.

A muffled scream comes.

It's clear that someone is in trouble. My thoughts strangle on Jae, on the dead body I found, on remembering how I survived this long on my own in the forest.

By keeping to myself and minding my own business.

I draw in a breath of frigid air, and a tingling buzzes at the base of my spine. And that's when I head toward the distress call to investigate.

Maybe I no longer want to be that person, the one who turns away when others need help.

The forest here is denser, and the land is populated with more birch trees than pines. The scent of the forest isn't strong, but it's also closer to where I live…. well, at least in the right direction. Though while there's that benefit, it comes with the knowledge that rogue wolves chose this terrain. I never understood why and figured it had something to do with the low branches, making it an easy getaway should they be chased by the undead.

My body rattles the more ground I cover, convinced this is where the sounds came from. Somewhere in this vicinity… Taking short, sharp breaths, I slow down and dart from one tree to the next.

Cautious, I slowly make progress, but when I find nothing out of the ordinary, I start to backtrack.

A groaning sound comes from just ahead. I slide in behind a tree and peer out from behind it, studying the evergreens and shrubs. That's when one patch of land catches my attention farther away. It's flatter, darker than the rest.

I know right away what it is… a trap that rogue wolves use to capture animals or females. That's how those fuckheads capture women to rut.

And that knowledge alone raises the hairs on my nape. They're around here, but something—or someone—got caught in the trap.

I move quickly before I can think about it too much. From the edge of the deep hole in the ground, I can see that someone down is there, but the shadows make it too hard to see much else. It's definitely not an animal.

"Jae?" The word slips past my lips, and I curse myself for not thinking before speaking out aloud.

"Meira!" a male voice responds.

I freeze and stare intently into the hole as Bardhyl, of all people, steps out of the shadows.

"What the hell are you doing here?" I blurt out. This is horribly bad. If a rogue wolf comes along now, he'll kill this Alpha.

"What do you think, angel legs?" he answers with that Norse accent, and all I see are those deep green eyes staring up at me. There are gashes in the side of the hole where the earth came away from when he tried to climb out.

"I don't need you to come after me, you know. Are Dušan and Lucien nearby too?"

"Never mind that. Be a good girl and get me out!" I hear the panic in his voice. He knows as well as I do that he's in a shitty situation.

I nod. "Be back in a sec." I turn and scan the area for something long and sturdy. I find a fallen log. It's not too broad, but it's freaking long. And he needs something sturdy to climb up.

I run over to the log and snatch the end closest to the hole. Hands wrapped around the rough trunk, I tug, but it barely budges.

Shit, shit, shit.

I can't believe Bardhyl is even here… How did he track me so accurately? Did Dušan send him after me while he stayed with the pack? Well, if I intend to keep that distance from the pack, then this is my chance to just hightail it out of here.

That thought alone sends a twinge of despair through me.

Fuck. My own body betrays me. Okay, fine. I'll get him out, then I'll bolt out of here.

Sucking in a deep breath, I pick up the trunk and heave it once again. It shifts and I shuffle backward, dragging it with me.

If I break my back carting this log, Bardhyl owes me everything.

My heart flutters each time I keep thinking back to his green eyes and that white-blond hair draping over his rounded shoulders.

I hate to admit it, but seeing him has awakened something inside me. Butterflies, mainly. The pesky things flutter frantically in my stomach.

Pulling the log, I jerk it over the ground a bit at a time until I reach the hole, then I dump it down and breathe heavily. Sweat drips down my spine, and I glance down at Bardhyl.

"How are you doing there, baby cheeks?" he asks.

"I don't even know why I'm helping you since the last time I saw you, you manhandled me. Then you shoved me into someone's house."

He chuckles at me, and as much as he infuriates me, gods have mercy, that is the most delicious sound I've ever heard.

"I can indulge you all you want when I get out. Now stop wasting time."

I huff and turn back to the log that has my muscles trembling. I move to the other end of the dead log, which is close to twenty feet long, and try to work out how to do this.

Bending over, I lift the end up and push it onward. Slowly, the timber shifts over the edge of the hole. I push it, straining in the process, and sluggishly lift my end higher so the base goes into the hole at a descent. It slides forward, and suddenly the base slams into the inside wall and sits there, jammed.

"Crap!" I run toward Bardhyl, gasping for air. "Can you jump up to grab it?"

He arches a brow as if I've asked him to jump to the moon. "Did you get the longest log in the forest?"

"Excuse me? I'm trying," I huff and turn back around. I loop an arm around the log about halfway and heave it backward a bit, then use every inch of strength to lift my end higher.

Sweat rolls down the side of my face, and exhaustion coils right in my chest. I don't know how much longer I can do this before I pass out.

A sudden blur comes from my left.

It slams into me, wiping me clear off my feet, the log falling from my grip.

I scream. My back hits the ground so hard, all the air from my lungs escapes.

Panic strangles my chest, and adrenaline kicks in as a burly form straddles me.

A meaty hand strikes me on the cheek. Stars dance behind my eyelids as pain shoots across my face, and my screams never cease.

I throw punches and thrust against the rogue wolf shifter, who's ripping at my clothes.

He growls, and an overpowering stink of wolf and earth collides into me. I frantically swing my fists into him, never stopping. But it seems to make no difference to this rock of a man.

He's not massive, but he's so fucking strong, it terrifies me.

"Woman," he snarls in my face, like somehow he's forgotten how to speak because he's become the animal he is known for.

Boldly, I rake my fingernails across his face, breaking skin and making him bleed. He hits me in the face again, but I won't stop. I won't ever go down like this.

I pat the ground around me.

My hand latches onto a branch. I snatch it and drive it into his face, hitting him square in the eyes.

The asshole squeals like a banshee and jerks back, clasping his face. I shove against his chest and use that exact moment to slip out from under him.

Scrambling around, I push myself up from my hands and knees.

A strong hand seizes my ankle and yanks me backward. A foot pushes down on my ass, flattening me onto my stomach.

I yell and writhe to escape.

He's tugging on my pants to drag them down my ass.

My terrified screams strangle me. I snatch the first rock I find nearby, then I twist just as his weight vanishes off me.

In a rush, I roll over onto my back, shuffling backward, my hand clutching tightly around the rock. I'm shaking hard, my heart a machine gun shooting off rounds.

Before me stands Bardhyl, as tall and broad as a bear. He towers over the rogue wolf and shoves his fist into the man's face over and over, blood splashing from the deathly hits.

My hero's face twists into fury as he snatches the man's neck, fingers digging into his throat.

The rogue wolf's eyes bug out with terror.

Bardhyl rips his throat out, holding the thing in his grasp.

There's blood and sinew everywhere.

My stomach twists in on itself.

The man drops to the ground, gurgling, bleeding to death, and his end comes swiftly.

Bardhyl tosses the throat aside and spits before wiping his mouth with the sleeve of his coat. More dots splash over his cheeks, and when he looks at me, the hardness in his expression eases.

"Are you hurt?" He leans over and takes my arm, pulling me to my feet, and my hands instinctively reach up against the hard muscles of his chest. He studies me from head to toe, checking for wounds, I guess.

"What you just did was…" I swallow hard.

"That fuck deserved a million times worse for touching you."

"It was incredible." I shouldn't find something so disturbing exhilarating. But this Viking wolf saved me, and watching him destroy the freak made my heart sprint. He did that for *me*. I ought to hate myself for enjoying such a show, but I don't. My body buzzes when I stare at him, and there's exhilaration from the knowledge that a powerful man is protecting me.

I glance over to the hole, where the log sticks out.

Bardhyl's arm slides across my back, and he draws me close to him. "We need to go now, because more are coming."

Hastily, we leave behind the chaos, and only as the adrenaline starts to fade from my body do I feel the aches and the fear as I realize with stunning clarity that I was almost raped. I push the thought far away because I can't permit those emotions in. I got away, and that's what matters.

When I look over to Bardhyl, my heart pleads with me to return with him back to the Ash Wolves.

Except in my mind, I know the truth that if I join him, I'll bring them death. Returning is not an option.

CHAPTER 7

ARDHYL

My wolf has always felt a connection with Meira, beginning with our very first meeting back at the pack home. I caught her trying to escape, resisting me from the onset. Hell, that drew me to her instantly. She's a survivor and has been one all of her life, which means she's a little spitfire and doesn't back down. That's how someone exists in this world on their own.

I grew up fighting to see another day, so I can relate to her. My pack up in Denmark was slaughtered by a neighboring pack. I only survived because I'd been out hunting that morning. When I found the destruction, I lost myself.

I run a hand through my hair, my fingers brushing over the scar on my ear from the battle that came afterward.

Revenge turns the most controlled warrior into a Berserker. For weeks, months, I hunted down the Alphas responsible, not caring for my own life. I saw red, burned up with fury, until I caught them.

I heave a loud exhale at the memory. Only Dušan knows the truth of what happened, of the massacre in my wake. He's witnessed the real monster that lives inside me. He had arrived to talk to those Alphas after they betrayed him, and they turned on him.

Yeah, I like to think my interference saved him, but in truth, I lost control and butchered all the Alphas in that pack. Dušan saved me before I could do something worse that I'd never come back from.

My stomach clenches because, after all this time, I like to think that person isn't me anymore.

Shit, I hate remembering those times. I loathe myself for what I was back then.

Meira presses up against me, distracting me. This small Omega has stirred up so much dust in her wake since arriving at our compound.

The majority of the Omegas I've met are passive, and right now Meira is behaving more like other Omegas than she usually does. A typical Omega accepts her role to mate with an Alpha and be his. The union brings enormous pleasure to both but also alleviates the growing aches an Omega goes through if she doesn't get her fill of an Alpha. Quite literally.

But this little fire starter has me all wound up tight and making me feel so much more than I have with any Omega before. I've crossed paths with many, fucked them, but meeting that perfect one hasn't been my fate.

Now, when I look down at Meira holding on to my arm, a monstrous protective nature crashes into me. I'd fight through hell and back to keep her safe.

Except she's taken… Well, spoken for by my True Alpha, Dušan, as well as Lucien. Though this little woman is a complicated mystery because she still hasn't transformed into her wolf. That means the union with her mates isn't complete. That makes her body still release a pheromone that draws males to claim her, to take their chance that they might be her mate.

From what I feel deep in my chest, I worry that my heart is expecting something that won't happen.

I'm not her mate. I can't be, and what I feel is purely a result of her out-of-control pheromones.

"You sure you are all right?" I ask, as she hasn't insulted me in a short while.

She nods and quickly wipes at her eyes.

"I won't let you out of my sight again," I say. "I promise to keep you safe, but you will do as I tell you and not run off, understand?"

"Do you know where the river is?" She ignores me and looks up at me with huge bronze eyes that remind me of a russet sunset. Her features are delicate, and yet there is always fire behind her gaze. Even now, it burns brightly.

"It's not far. I'll take you there. It's on the way back home."

I feel her stiffen beside me, but I say nothing more of it. She is magnificent in every way. She's not mine, no matter how much my craving intensifies for her. But despite having two Alphas who've already marked her, she is ready to run again. I see it in her downward gaze, feel it in her escalating pulse.

She's wild and has no idea what being an Omega means.

"You were never taught the roles of wolves in packs?" I ask, gaining myself a glare.

"I know plenty enough," she remarks. "Alphas are at the top of the food chain and Omegas are meant to be subservient to them. Is that about right?"

I snort a laugh at her feistiness. "Once an Alpha meets his Omega fated mate, he would do anything for her, fight an army, bring her the rarest berries from the deadliest area if she asked. Don't you see? Omegas are the ones who control the Alphas."

She doesn't respond, but the surprise in her eyes says everything. I hope this helps her start to understand how crucial her partnering in a pack is.

We travel without talking, my attention and senses on the forest surrounding us. Danger is everywhere, and I need to get her out of here.

She finally breaks the silence. "Did they send you alone to find me?"

"Dušan and Lucien are also searching for you. I picked up your scent a little way back and was tracking you until I stepped into that damn trap." I should have seen it coming, but I was on the run from a group of undead and wasn't paying attention.

"I can't return with you," she explains casually, like I have no say in the matter.

She makes me want to laugh at how adorable she is to think she stands any chance of getting away from me now that I've found her.

"And I won't stop hunting you down."

She cuts me a threatening glare. Boldly, she peels away from me. We move quietly through the dense forest, over shrubs and under branches. Occasionally, I glance over to Meira, who seems miles away with her thoughts.

"Why did you run?" I ask. There's so much more I want to tell her, but I won't discuss her sickness while we're rushing through the woods.

"I'm sure you're aware of why or you wouldn't be out here. Dušan would have told you everything."

"Running away isn't the answer."

"It is to me. And you've wasted your time. I appreciate you helping me. I owe you everything for that, but I won't go back."

I don't push the topic, as I suspect she will change her mind once she's in Dušan's and Lucien's company. After an Alpha marks an Omega, the connection between them is unbreakable. Even if she hasn't closed the connection yet, the allure of their initial mating has fused their fates together.

The gurgling river comes into view beyond the treeline, and seeing it brings me warmth. If we follow this, it will bring us directly to the Ash Wolves compound.

What I wouldn't give to be back home and have a hearty meal then a sweet minx in my bed. I look over to Meira, who marches alongside me. She's small but has all the curves a man could want. This woman is goddamn beautiful, and the idea of her locked in my room with me sends a twitch through my cock. The more I look at her, the more I can't stop my mind from wandering where it shouldn't. To hear her screams when I bring her to orgasm, to feel her body jerk and shake beneath me.

Shit, those thoughts aren't going to help me keep my distance. I've done well enough on my own this far, and I don't need the complication of an Omega responsibility. Plus, she's already taken.

We carry on to the river in silence. Once there, I scan the area for the undead and wolves, then lift my nose and sniff the air. We're alone. The sun is at noon, so that means we need warmth and food because we won't reach the pack compound tonight.

I toe off my boots as I pull off my shirt, stained with dirt and blood. When I tug at my belt, Meira clears her throat.

"What are you doing?" she grills me while arching a brow.

I cut her a glance, my grin beaming at the thought of making her squirm. "We're both going to wash ourselves and our clothes. We need to clean the scent of blood from our flesh. Then we'll sit in the sun to dry off a bit."

"Just leave your clothes on then," she retorts, gripping her hips. I adore her aggressiveness. It calls to my wolf, who wants to break her, to dominate her.

"And where would the fun be in that?" I say.

The hitch in her breath makes me smile as I tug down my pants and step out of them. I'm naked. Meira's cheeks are blushing, and despite her stiffness, her eyes dip to my cock. It's half-erect, and judging by her gaping mouth, she's impressed.

I laugh at her inability to hold back. "Your turn, cupcake."

She scoffs and rolls her eyes at me, backing away. "In your dreams."

Giving in doesn't work with me, so I close the distance between us, invading her personal space. She frowns and tries to retreat, but I grab her arm before she takes off.

"We can do this one of two ways. You strip, or I strip you."

"Get off me. I'm going to wash with my clothes on."

"That's not an option. You won't wash properly, and drying will take longer." I reach for her top, but she slaps my hand away.

Fire flares in my chest, and I snatch her jaw, forcing her to face me. I'm not used to Omegas fighting back, but this wolf pushes and pushes me.

"Have you made a decision?" I say through my gritted teeth, leaning down closer to her.

"I'll do it myself," she hisses back at me.

I release her. "Good."

She huffs, and I watch the fury cross her face, but she doesn't say anything else. Instead, she starts undressing.

I look up ahead to give her some privacy, but she remains in my peripheral vision. Next thing I know, she strolls right past me, bare as a baby, and my attention falls to her perfect ass, moving with each step in a way that hardens my cock.

She steps into the water and looks back at me over her shoulder, her delicious, pouty lips parting with a smirk. "Are you happy now?"

My lips split into a tight smile. "I can think of a few things that would make me happier."

Meira sucks in a deep breath and jerks back into the water. My eyes latch onto her tiny waist and the curve of her ass, and all I can think about is how much I want those toned legs wrapped around me. The water moves gently, lapping against her hips, and she keeps going deeper.

I join her, the water fucking freezing when I step into it. *Goddammit.*

She turns to me as she dips into the water that now reaches her neck, and the pale bronze orbs of her eyes study all of me. So I march forward, despite feeling like I'm about to pass out from hypothermia. My balls are going to shrivel up to peanuts.

"Are you struggling?" she mocks, the challenge clear on her face.

Accepted.

I dive straight in, not giving a shit that it feels like I've crashed into a tub of ice. I glide underneath the surface, the water murky, but I spot her legs up ahead. I burst out of the water inches in front of her.

She's moving backward, splashing like a drowning fish, and loses her footing.

I can't stop laughing, and when she pops back up, she's furious, but all I can focus on are those pretty little tits tipped with deep red cherries, pointy and hard. Blood dives south, and I start to think that maybe this wasn't such a good idea after all.

Quickly, she covers herself with her hands. "Maybe you should focus on cleaning yourself," she instructs. "And maybe make yourself useful and go collect our clothes to scrub clean."

Oh, she is good at testing my patience. Even so, all I can think about is burying my face between her thighs. So I turn and wash my body and face clean of blood and as much of my scent as possible. Then I collect our clothes. She snatches hers out of my hand, and I shake my head because Dušan and Lucien will have their hands full with this Omega.

Now, I just need to keep my hands off her before I make a terrible mistake.

Meira

*B*ardhyl is crazy dominating, just like Dušan and Lucien, which is why we're both naked in the cold river. I see my mistake now... I never should have saved him from that pit. Now he always has one eye on me, and escaping is going to be damn hard. But I'm not blind to the way he studies my body, how his large cock grows harder. Seriously, these three wolves are packed with enough ammunition to impregnate every female in this country. But I can't ignore the desire he rouses within me.

I splash my face, running my fingers through my wet hair. Bardhyl doesn't move far enough from me to help calm my sprinting pulse. I swallow hard, my throat feeling suddenly dry in his company.

A twig snaps behind me. Adrenaline kicks in, and I flinch forward, stupidly pressing myself against him. His cock nestles against my lower stomach, and now I'm blushing ridiculously.

His large hand wraps around my back, drawing me even closer to him as he laughs. "It's just a rabbit, little bird."

I twist my head back around as the brown furball bounces into the woods.

Bardhyl slides a finger under my chin to look at him, while his hand sits splayed against my lower back, holding me in place against him. His thumb tenderly caresses my back, sending excited shivers up my spine. I feel his erection twitch between us.

"You don't need to be scared."

I stare up into those deep green irises. I may still be shaken, but I'm furious at myself for being so jumpy. It's Bardhyl distracting me that makes me feel so off-kilter. I've survived this long by noticing every-thing around me. But then again, I never had a delicious man who has me fluttering with heat each time he looks at me. I have to pull myself together, not think about what it would be like to kiss him, or climb him, or…

Maybe it's normal to feel this attracted to these Alphas since my wolf won't come out to play, which in turn has my hormones going haywire. Though what I have noticed is that since finding Bardhyl and being in his company, I haven't felt the agonizing ache for the other Alphas, or even my own sickness.

Inhaling, I wriggle myself out of his grasp and splash away, even though my body trembles with a need to just give in to the desire pumping through my veins.

But I won't let myself fall prey again. I already suffer from missing the other two Alphas, so what am I thinking? Adding a third one to the mix? *Great idea, Meira.* Why not make myself a harem, while I'm at it?

"Meira," he says, flashing me a sexy grin.

"Yeah?" I wait for him to speak, clueless as to what he's going to say, but I can only imagine it will be something to embarrass me.

"If you're curious, you can touch—"

"Are you kidding me?" I snap back.

"Don't be shy, sweet lips. Many women who meet me want to, and seeing as we are both naked, I give you permission."

My mouth hangs open at his arrogance and directness. I've never had anyone talk to me the way these Alphas do—mostly because I never grew up with Alphas. They're full of smugness and are always propositioning me. And my body betrays me, of course, lighting up in a fiery blaze on the inside at the smallest of touches.

I raise a brow, hardening my expression. "I'm sure you're well versed in touching your own cock."

He bursts out laughing like he's the king of mirth, grasping a hand over his stomach while he enjoys himself.

What the hell is wrong with him?

"I knew you couldn't stop thinking about my cock. And I was talking about you touching my guns." He smiles deviously as he flexes his biceps.

"Sure you were." I splash him with water, drenching his face and chest, but he keeps laughing at his own stupid joke. Seriously, I should have known he was the joker of the Alphas. When he keeps chuckling, I change the topic.

"Are there Vikings in your bloodline?" I ask, staring at this mountain of a man scrubbing his face. The water reaches his waist, his biceps flexing with huge muscles. His chest is easily twice the width of mine, with light hair across powerful pecs. His stomach ripples with more muscles. With his sandy blond hair draping over his shoulders and strong angular cheekbones, he *screams* Viking.

"My ancestors are said to have been Vikings, yes." He lowers his head to look my way, waiting for my reason for asking.

"I'm curious about your wolf," I begin. "There are stories about Berserkers, fierce warriors known for going into a battle in blind rage, howling like wild animals, biting their weapons."

"And you think I lose control when I take my wolf form?"

I shrug. "Do you ever feel that call from the past? Mama once told me the wolf that forms inside us is a creation of our bloodline."

"She was a smart woman, and correct. If my pa still lived, he'd tell you that Berserkers live fiercely in our bloodline." He snorts a laugh, as if he's remembered something about his father.

I can't stop thinking about him calling my mama smart. From what I've seen, most males see women as property, things to be claimed. So for him to say this leaves me curious to understand more about who he really is.

"My pa trusted only those in his pack, which was why he kept a small tribe. But sometimes trust isn't enough to save you from death when the enemy is bigger than you. It's one of the reasons I joined Dušan. He believes in building a large community of wolves to make us all stronger." He smiles at me as though even the sorrowful talk about his father can't bring him down.

"I'm sorry about you losing your father."

He shrugs. "Shit happens when you live in a broken world."

"If there's one thing all the survivors in this world have in common, it's that we've all witnessed the deaths of our loved ones. And that stays with you."

He turns from me abruptly and walks out of the river. "Time to get out," he orders, clearly not liking the direction of our conversation. "Before you turn into a prune."

After he wrings his clothes of water, he kneels on the wild grasses near several large boulders, where he proceeds to place his clothes to dry in the sun.

Still clutching onto my clothes, I climb out, holding them against me as a shield, feeling insecure about walking naked in front of this hunky wolf.

All wolves insist that being naked is normal, but it sure as hell isn't for me. I'm the woman who's never transformed, so nakedness doesn't come so naturally to me.

Bardhyl's eyes are on me. Always on me. I shuffle forward and hastily lay my clothes out to dry on the warm rock, then sit down quicker than I have my entire life. My heart is pounding loudly, and so much of it has to do with how attracted I find myself to this wolf.

He's flexing his muscles again.

I can't help but laugh at him. "Do women really ask if they can touch your muscles?"

"Why does that surprise you?"

"It's not something I would ever do."

"Yeah, but you aren't exactly the typical wolf shifter, either, my cupcake. You grew up living alone out here."

I eye him carefully. "Not sure if that's meant to be a compliment or insult."

"Neither," he confesses, his voice hard. "It's a fact."

I hug my knees tighter to my chest as the long grass sways around us. The sun is warm on my shoulders while I hold his gaze.

He clears his throat. "On a scale of one to ten, how bad would it be if I—"

"Fifty," I respond, smirking at him because the moment he mentions something being bad, it would be horrendously bad, I suspect.

He arches a brow. "I didn't finish."

"Didn't have to. I got the gist to know it involved doing something I wouldn't agree with."

My stomach flutters at the wicked thoughts that play on my mind. Despite myself, I want to know exactly what he was going to propose.

He studies me intently, the corners of his mouth curling upward mischievously. Yep, whatever it was he had in mind, it was dirty. "Do you ever stop being so serious and just enjoy someone's company?"

His question catches me off guard, as it never occurred to me until now that I came across that prickly. But when he looks at me with a raised brow, I can't help myself and say, "And do you never cease joking?"

His expression hardens. "Sweet cheeks, you may not love me if you see who I truly am."

CHAPTER 8

MEIRA

ove! Did Bardhyl just say that four-letter word?

Of course it's a figure of speech and he doesn't mean actual love, but the word sticks with me. Maybe because the only person to ever say it to me was Mama. I've never had anyone to whom I've felt close enough to even joke about it.

Bardhyl makes me want to sit around and talk to him for hours, even if he annoys the hell out of me.

He's lying on the grass now, his eyes closed, enjoying the sun for the short period of time as our clothes dry.

I'm staring out toward the river, my back to the warm rock.

Running away now would be stupid, so I'll bide my time and wait until this big guy next to me is really asleep. Then I'll escape.

I am so tired of always looking over my shoulder. Exhausted of feeling like a rabbit on the run in a world filled with wolves. What I need is to find the biggest colony of Shadow Monsters and move in near them. Sure, they aren't the prettiest sight, and their constant gurgling, moaning sounds are annoying, and they stink, but beggars can't be choosers, right?

And I refuse to give in to my emotions, reminding myself that getting away is for the safety of the Alphas. They'll eventually get over me. They have to… I have to believe that so I know it's possible to do the same.

"It's time we get a move on," Bardhyl orders. "We find shelter for the night, and tomorrow we should reach home." His shadow falls over me as he grabs his clothes from the rock next to me.

I reach up with one hand while still covering my chest with the other and take mine, then hastily drag the top over my head, threading my hands through still-damp sleeves. I could have done without wearing moist clothes.

"You're not my favorite person right now," I say to him as I wiggle my feet into the pants and drag them up my legs before getting up to quickly cover myself.

"Then I'm doing my job right. I'm not trying to make you like me," he grumbles.

I turn to face him as he buttons up his jeans and partially tucks his shirt in, his head low, blond hair cascading forward. All I can see are strong, powerful arms and muscles. This bulking man towers over me easily, and he'll use force to keep me by his side. For that, I hate him. But my body responds to him in beautiful ways, and a thread of arousal rises inside me, licking over my skin, hinting at a desire for more.

His offhanded commands irk me, though. "I don't expect you to like me, but I'd hope you'd have some compassion. I'm broken, Bardhyl. A danger to the pack. Can't you see that's why I can't return with you?"

I shift to walk away when he reaches over and grabs my jaw, not hard enough to hurt, but enough to keep me locked in his hold. His thumb caresses my cheek, and he gazes at me with such passion, I can't bear to work out where things stand between us. I don't want to know, in truth, because I'm already grieving over leaving two Alphas. So please, universe, don't throw another into the mix. I sense my body responding to Bardhyl in ways it has with Dušan and Lucien. Heat burns between my thighs. The wolf inside me may not have come out yet, but she isn't shy about letting me know which men she craves.

"What do you think is going to happen when you don't return to your Alphas?" he asks.

"What are you talking about?"

All I can focus on is where he touches me and that while I'm under his gaze, somehow I'm the most important person in his world.

Bardhyl reminds me of the other two, and rather than letting myself trip over myself for this wolf, I have to remain strong. Summoning my strength, I tear free from his grasp.

"They will get over me and find someone else. All the females in your pack would love to mate with them." Even as the words leave my mouth, an ache spears over my chest. I've heard of wolves living happily without a mate. Unmatched Omegas make perfect companions to Alphas without that deep-felt connection. It's possible.

Bardhyl shots me a puzzled look, like I've lost my mind. "I think you and I need to have a long conversation about the birds and the wolves."

I laugh. "It's called the birds and the *bees.*"

"Not where I come from, and clearly you know very little about your own kind. Or that if you don't return to your Alphas, the ache you feel from your distance will grow so intense that you'll wish you were dead."

No, distance will break our bond. It has to.

With frustration, my response rips out of me. "Scaring me won't make me change my mind. You can twist words into any form you want, but they don't mean something different."

"I never took you for being philosophical. You're the kiss-and-run kind of girl to me."

"Ha. Goes to show how little you know of me." I turn away from him, my insides blazing with anger that he sees me as someone so fickle. I flip him the finger. "Don't mistake my admiration of your naked body earlier for something it's not. I hate you. No matter how big your dick is."

His footfalls fall in behind me, and he's chuckling to himself. I'm cringing on the inside for blurting out the last part. I wanted to insult him, but instead I complimented him. What is wrong with me?

Oh, I know. The vulnerable, sexually deprived side of me has me saying ridiculous things.

"If you want, cherry lips, I can show you later how much bigger it can get if you think *this* is big."

I refuse to give in to him and don't respond. Out here, I carry the upper hand by being immune to the Shadow Monsters, and that is my strength. Now, if we could just run into some undead, all would be dandy again.

Everyone has their own path in life, and mine is to be alone in the woods. I'm not afraid of the dark or the virus. What scares me the most is other people.

Getting too close.

Then losing them.

That heartbreak is worse than death.

After losing everything once, I vowed to never go to war with my heart again.

The far-off memory of my mama faded, and I let it dance away. Now, I keep walking and wait for the right moment to make my own move.

"You smell different," he says out of the blue, and when I glance his way, his eyes focus on me.

"Every wolf has a unique scent," I correct him.

"But yours is more than a wolf smell, Meira."

I pause and raise my chin to him. Something in the pit of my stomach hardens. "What are you saying?"

"That when I inhale the air around you, my wolf goes crazy to claim you, but he also whimpers at the sickness you carry."

My cheeks burn. "I already know. It's my wolf who refuses to come out. But thanks for reminding me how obviously different I am."

"That's not what I'm saying."

He falls behind as I march ahead. But then he's suddenly at my side and snatches my wrist.

"Have you never wondered why you're feeling sick and throwing up blood? Dušan told me how sick you were back at our compound. But no shifter has that kind of illness, even when a wolf hasn't shown itself yet."

"Yeah, so? What do you want me to say? I don't know why I'm fucked up."

"Oh, baby girl." He clasps the sides of my face, but I've had enough of everything, and I shove my hands against his chest.

"Just stop."

"No. I won't until you properly understand."

"What the heck are you talking about?" I'm yelling now, my body trembling. "Don't talk in circles. Tell me what you know."

His expression grows stoic. "Dušan ordered tests of your blood while you were at the compound, and we think we know why you're sick and why the undead don't touch you. It may also be why your wolf won't come out."

My stomach drops right through me. "What did the test show?" My voice comes out lighter than intended, and I hate that there's fear behind my words.

Except a chorus of moans rising from up ahead of us distracts me.

I jerk my attention to a gang of at least twenty Shadow Monsters rushing toward us. We're out in the open, talking too loudly, drawing their attention.

Bardhyl draws me by the hand in the opposite direction, but my mind screams at me to pull away from him and run toward the undead. This is my chance to get rid of this Alpha. To be on my own and hightail it out of the Shadowlands once and for all.

But I can't get his words out of my head. He knows what's wrong with me. Since losing Mama, I've wanted to understand why I'm different. What if Dušan's discovery can provide me with a cure to my wolf being stuck inside me?

I choke on the hope curling in my chest.

"For fuck's sake, Meira, move your ass!"

The undead come fast, and panic twists Bardhyl's expression, heavy with the dilemma of if he should leave me behind and save himself.

But if we split up now, I'll never know the truth of what is wrong with me.

Goddamn Shadow Monsters. Of all times to attack, they come now?

I spin away from them, and then we run.

Bardhyl holds on to me tightly, as if to keep me safe, but *he* is the real one in danger here. If I want to hear about the blood test, I need to make sure he survives. Funny how irony can be a pain in my freaking ass.

Bardhyl

My breaths come hard. I shove my feet to the ground, covering the ground fast, hauling Meira alongside me.

For those few seconds, I swore she'd take off and use the undead as a mask, but me telling her about her blood test couldn't have come at a better time. I'll use that to keep her by my side for as long as possible and ensure I get her back to the pack.

I dare a glance behind me. Those fucking assholes aren't giving up, though we've put a fair distance between us through the dense woods. They won't stop until they lose sight of us.

"What did the test show?" she asks between gasping breaths. "Tell me."

"Later," I retort.

"No, now. It's the perfect time," she huffs beside me. "What if you die and I never find out?"

She infuriates me. I have a mind to toss her over my lap and make that pretty little ass of hers pink.

I cut her a harsh look, seeing right through her plan. "Then you better make sure I don't die."

She narrows her gaze, and I know that if we weren't running at full tilt, she would have punched me. I might have enjoyed it, too.

I leap over a dead log right after her and swerve to follow the downward slope of the land.

When she twists her head toward me, the smile on her face is cunning and not something I expect. But she doesn't faze me. If she wants to play this game, she won't know what hit her. I can push her buttons if that's how she wants to do this.

The foliage-covered ground rushes out from under my feet, and I crash onto my ass, a grunt rolling over my lips. I scramble back up just as Meira tumbles over the steep descent. I lash out and snatch the back of her top, seizing her against me rather than letting her fall.

She's breathing heavily, and I stare behind us to where a scattering of the undead track after us. The herd has definitely thinned, but even with my blade, I couldn't risk a fight here. Too many followed. What we need is a means to hide and conceal ourselves until they disappear.

"There!" Meira yells out, pointing to something slightly to our right, but all I see are trees.

In moments, we burst out of the woods to a small clearing at the edge of a cliff, spearing outward on either side of us.

My eyes lock on a dilapidated bridge made of ropes and wooden planks that looks like it might crumble if I step foot on it. It spans about a hundred feet over a gorge, to a side that seems free of the undead. But it looks so high, I'm not sure how safe the bridge is.

Meira goes first to cross this rickety thing, which is brave of her.

I smirk to myself, but that moment of cheer evaporates when a guttural moan comes from behind me.

Quickly, we rush onto the bridge, the wood groaning under my weight, and the whole thing starts swinging from side to side with our fast steps.

I make the mistake of looking down to the snake-like river down below, and my head spins from the distance. I clutch onto the rope, my legs locking in place as I picture myself falling over and plummeting to my death.

I fucking love my life, and I fight tooth and nail every day to survive. But now, I can't get the image of me falling through this broken bridge and dying out of my head.

My heartbeat pounds in my ears.

"Bardhyl, what are you doing? Move your legs," Meira berates me, her voice irritated.

But my eyes are set on the river so far below.

Soft hands touch mine as I hold on to the rope with a death grip.

"Listen to me." She yanks me by the hand. "Look at me. You need to move, and now, or *I* will be the one to push you over the edge."

When I meet her gaze, I believe she means every damn word. "Is that how you help someone off a ledge?"

"Well, it got you moving, didn't it?"

Only then do I realize I've taken steps forward.

"Don't look down. Seriously," she says. "Just focus on my voice and travel fast. They're right behind us."

I don't look back. I do exactly as she says. I shake all over, one hand holding on to Meira's and the other on the rope. Step after step, we're closing the distance.

With a sudden sway, the whole bridge shifts beneath us. I latch on to the rope harder and look back to find three undead stumbling onto the damn thing. There are half a dozen more on their heels. Will the bridge even take all our weight?

"Hurry up," Meira ushers me. "Let's go. You can do this, Bardhyl."

Focusing on her voice, I do just that. Quickly, I step after her, the bridge swinging, my stomach lurching with each movement. With only a third of the distance left, we start rushing.

My heart slams ferociously in my chest.

Don't look. Don't look the hell down.

Meira pushes ahead of me and is waving me to hurry, and in seconds, I'm alongside her on the other side. I could kiss the damn soil beneath my feet.

I seize the blade from my belt and turn around as the creatures stumble wildly toward us. I lunge to the edges of the rope and in one swipe, I cut the top rope on one side, then I crouch down and draw my blade through the cord tying the bridge to the timber pole near me.

The bridge suddenly collapses on its side, sending the undead hurtling down to their final deaths in the valley. They fall like blobs, smacking into the river and the overgrown banks.

One of the suckers is hanging on to the bridge, while others are still climbing on.

I cut the ropes attached to the stakes on the other side, and the whole thing collapses away, taking with it the last undead.

There's another bridge closer to the pack fortress. Getting home is going to take longer than I want, which fucking sucks.

"Okay, we need to go." I'm on my feet and spin around as I catch Meira going in the opposite direction.

I snatch her wrist and haul her toward me. She spins in my direction, her hands slapping against my chest as we collide. All I see are those eyes, those bronze irises, and I don't know what comes over me, but I'm leaning down and kissing her before I can find my senses.

She freezes at first, taken aback by my kiss. Fuck, I am too, and I start to pull away just as she kisses me back, parting that delicious mouth. Her small hands curl around the back of my neck, pulling me closer, pressing her gorgeous breasts against my chest.

Fuck me!

I shouldn't be doing this. But my cock twitches and I hold her tightly, against my better judgement. It's she who finally pulls away. When I let her go, I'm short of breath, and my head fogs with what I've just done.

"We leave now!" I grab her hand and start marching. My heart hammers in my chest and my dick presses against my jeans. What the fuck is wrong with me? I freak out about dying on the bridge, so my response is to kiss her?

The woods grow denser as we follow the line of the gorge while I try to get my head straight. To remind myself whom Meira belongs to. And it sure as fuck isn't me. No matter how much I want to rip off her clothes and claim her right now, to make her scream my name.

Hell. Those images in my head of me taking her aren't helping. Just need to clear my mind, that's all.

"I'm surprised the big bad and powerful Bardhyl is afraid of heights. I thought you were indestructible," she jokes and half-laughs, but I hear the strain behind her voice. She kissed me back, so I'm not alone in this sudden awkwardness. But if the only way to deal with our mistake is to pretend it didn't happen, then I'll play along.

"Baby cheeks, everyone in this world is flawed, and I never said I was perfect." Case in point, right now I want to swing her in my arms and kiss her, no matter the cost.

I am completely flawed.

CHAPTER 9

DUŠAN

I fucking hate the woods. I never thought I'd admit that, considering I live in the Shadowlands forest, but *fuck!*

"Where the hell can Meira be?" I bark, frustrated to hell.

Meira is nowhere. I've only found these damn undead and a rogue we ran into. Kicked his ass and kept going. With our heightened sense of smell, we ought to have picked up on her scent by now. But that tells me we're going completely the wrong way, even after changing directions several times.

"I bet Bardhyl found her," Lucien murmurs. "He's the luckiest of us. He always wins on card night."

I cut him a glare, but hell, his reasoning might be more accurate than us wandering aimlessly through the woods. If Bardhyl tracks her first, he'll keep her safe and protect her with his life. But not knowing if that's the case is driving me insane.

A bird chirps somewhere around us, followed by another. There are no other animals. "We follow the river. She would have made stops to drink and wash, so we'll pick up her scent." My initial thought was that she'd gone to high ground, as there are pockets of caves up there, offering protection. Except I'd been mistaken.

"Agreed." Lucien nods and we cover the ground quickly, sticking to the riverbank.

Aside from a few animal prints, the pebbled shore shows no marks.

We've walked for a long while when Lucien asks, "What are we going to do with Mad?"

Just thinking about my stepbrother raises the hairs on the back of my neck. I never should have appointed him so highly in my pack or ever trusted him with delivering Omegas to our trade partners.

"He'll have three options. He submits and will be under constant guard, he leaves, or he pisses me off so much I'll kill him." The words taste sour in my mouth, but he's fucked up before and I always give him another chance. The fault is mine for treating him differently than my pack because he's family. But my pack is family too, and I've had enough.

"About time," Lucien snarls. He and Bardhyl have warned me about Mad for years, and I chose not to listen. Well, that shit changes now.

We push on, the surrounding trees swaying in the breeze. It feels like we've walked for hours when Lucien pauses and stares down at the bank. The ground is all torn up, footprints going in and out of the water. I crouch down and trace my finger along the edge of a bare footprint that's too small to be male. The steps are perfectly aligned, no stumbling, meaning this hasn't been made by the undead.

I take a deep inhale of the mud, the freshwater, the sweet grass, and beneath it all is another scent. It's faint, but it carries a wolf signature and that sickly blood smell. It's gone in seconds, but that's all I need.

"She was here." I shoot to my feet, scanning the area for a clue, something.

"Someone was with her," Lucien states, pointing his chin at larger footprints. No shoes, either. "Told ya. Bardhyl got to her."

Thank fuck, if that's the case.

"These barefoot markings have them going into the river on purpose. To wash off blood, perhaps, and stop the undead tracking them. Or they had wolves on their heels and needed to hide their scent."

"The tracks had to be made today. They're still fresh," I say. "We're close." Hope that we might finally find Meira spears through my chest.

We exchange quick glances and head down the river, toward the direction of our pack. It's where Bardhyl would have taken her.

Together we pick up our pace. Lucien and I have been inseparable since we were kids. After losing his mate, he was withdrawn when it came to finding another partner. It didn't stop him from seeking out Omegas to fuck—he never had a lack of females eager to fill his bed—but it's never been anything more than one night.

Until now, with Meira. I should be furious that he touched what belongs to me, but fated mates don't work that way, do they now? Wolves will choose each other irrespective of what the heart wants. Yeah, it fucking burns to picture him taking her.

What choice do I have if the wolves have picked their mates? I can't lose Meira or my closest friend, so I swallow my damn pride. We'll find a way to make this work.

"Who made the first move, you or Meira?" I can't help myself and want to know.

He doesn't meet my gaze when he responds, knowing too well what I'm asking. "Do you have an issue with us?"

I've always thought one day I'd find my fated mate and it would be just the two of us. But it's rare for my dreams to become reality, as the universe likes to fuck with me.

"Fate has a wicked sense of humor and kicks you in the teeth when you least expect it," I respond.

He throws me a stare from hooded eyes and huffs. "I knew you'd bring this up. I don't need your jealousy crap. I just…" He glances up at the sky. "I don't fucking know. It's just that when I'm with her, the heaviness I've been carrying around with me lifts." He shrugs. "I haven't felt this for a very long time, Dušan. I would never step on your toes, you know that. You're like my brother."

When he meets my gaze again, there's a hardness behind his eyes, like he doesn't know what to make of his feelings. Of how Meira swept into his life and knocked him off his feet without warning. How both our wolves connect with her…

Everything about her should send off alarm bells, but instead I want to take her, strip her down, and claim her over and over. To mark her so many times that her wolf has no choice but to goddamn show itself already.

"What if we lose her to the disease?" Lucien murmurs, as if reading my mind.

"It won't happen." My spine stiffens. "I'll tear the fucking world apart before I lose my fated mate."

Bardhyl

snap of lightning spears over the darkening sky, quickly followed by a thunderous growl. The earth trembles in response, and the first drops of rain hit my face.

Meira is running alongside me while I scan the area for shelter. Hiding in a tree isn't going to cut it, not with the storm rolling in. When I look across my shoulder to Meira, her gaze is sharp, taking in our surroundings.

Farther to our right, the mountain climbs harshly, a rockface appearing behind the trees. My hand slips into Meira's, and I guide her in that direction. Maybe we'll be lucky and find shelter.

We swerve through the thicket of the woods when the land suddenly ascends severely, rising and rising into the cliffs overhead.

The rain comes down in fat drops, soaking us. My skin pricks with cold, and I draw Meira to my side.

"There," she calls out, dragging me to her left. I spot the darkened hollow in the side of the mountain. Four other caves lay waiting for us, and I'll take any at this moment. I release her hand and hastily pick up small branches and twigs near the trees not yet wet. Wet timber is a bitch to make fire from, so I rush with haste, grabbing an armful. Meira does the same, collecting larger branches covered in leaves. We're soon rushing into the nearest cave with our bundles.

I exhale as cold water drips down my back from my hair. I move in deeper and dump the wood on the ground, then sniff the air for any indication of an animal or the undead being in here. It's pitch black, but all I smell is the stale cave.

I take out the lighter from my pocket. I'm not a caveman; I came prepared. A quick flick and the cave illuminates, revealing a long, narrow area that offers us the chance to be farther from the entrance of the cave.

I get to work and build a small fire in the middle of the cave, giving us plenty of space to sleep behind it.

By the time I finish and kneel in front of the flames, bathing in the heat, Meira has made a makeshift bed of large palm-like leaves layered on the floor.

Outside, the rain pummels the land, coming down in sheets.

"That storm came out of nowhere." Meira joins me by the fire, warming her hands. The orange glow beams over her beautiful face.

And this is exactly where I want to be… enjoying the rays of her smile when she glances at me with a question on her pouty lips.

"Food would be amazing right now," she says, and I think she's batting her eyes at me. Does she think that's going to work? I'm not going out there in this weather to search for an impossible meal.

"It would be," I respond. "When you come back with something for us, I'll have a small spit over the fire."

She glowers at me, and I chuckle at how predictable she is sometimes, though I've been with her long enough to know she doesn't typically flirt to get things she wants. Is this a sign that she's growing comfortable in my presence?

"You're not exactly being a gentleman," she answers while sitting down in front of the fire, crossing her legs.

"Never claimed to be one, or a hero, or anything else. I am what you see in front of you. An Alpha following orders and keeping you in check."

She tilts her head in my direction. "Then why did you kiss me?"

"To show you that you're wrong."

She stiffens and folds her arms over her chest. "Excuse me?"

"You think you have everything sorted out and that running away will solve your shit. But nothing in life goes as we expect it, now does it?"

She narrows her eyes, that cute little nose wrinkling.

I push loose strands of hair out of my face. "You never expected me to kiss you, and now you can't get me out of your mind. I know you can't. It's written all over your face." And it's constantly on my mind, the sweet cherry taste of her lips, her racing breaths, and how she clutched on to me, desperate for more.

"No, it's not. Don't kid yourself," she barks in response.

I laugh, and already I smell her desire on the air, the faint slick, delicious scent that stirs my wolf. It calls to him, and here she tells me she's not thinking about me. Right.

I shift toward her, and she responds by scrambling to her feet, backing away.

"Are you afraid that you'll lose control, and when you start, you won't be able to stop?"

"Remember, *you* kissed *me*." She tightens her arms under her chest, pushing up her perky breasts, the dampness of the fabric gluing itself to the curve of those perfect tits. I can't help myself. My cock springs up and twitches in my pants.

I get to my feet. A few quick steps, and I close the distance between us. A warning bellows in my head to back away. That I'll be the one who won't be able to stop.

Except when she looks at me like a mouse trapped by a lion, the excitement in my veins propels me forward. It has been too long since any woman has made me feel this alive, this addicted, this fucking captivated.

I reach out and snatch the back of her neck, wrenching her toward me. She gasps, that little sound driving me crazy with need. Goddamn, where did this hellcat come from?

I take in her slick smell again, and fuck, she's going to be my undoing. I should have known the first time we met that I would never walk away from this Omega.

And now that I have her in my grasp, I don't know how to pull away.

The unbearable ache in my chest demands we take her as ours. This is the right time, the perfect moment for us.

She looks me in the eyes, challenges me with her stare, having no clue about her place in the wolf world. Maybe that's what attracts me to her so much.

There's so much difference between us that it's refreshing to have an Omega who fights me, who doesn't just do as I order. Most Omegas have lost their fire, accepting their fates. And as such, most just search for an Alpha, desperate to find their matches and fall into their routines. That isn't what I want…

"Are you going to tell me about my blood test results?" she demands.

Lightning steals the shadows around us, the rain drenching the woods outside.

"Here's the thing. I'll make you a deal," I begin, not releasing her from my hold. She shoves her fists into my arm, but I'm not letting her go just yet. "You and I will kiss, and then you will beg me to touch you, to finger that tight little pussy. When we get to that stage, you tell me to stop, and I won't touch you for the rest of the night."

"Are you fucking insane? I'm not agreeing to that." She shoves her hands against my chest, and I release her. She stumbles, her cute breasts bouncing and drawing my attention.

"If you don't tell me to stop, I win. Then you are mine for the night. How does that sound?"

She stiffens, blinking at me blankly. Oh, she's good. "Is that your standard pickup line?"

I look her up and down. "I've never had a woman reject me, if that's what you're implying."

"And if I don't agree to this ludicrous idea?"

"Do you have another suggestion to keep us entertained all night?"

She tilts her head back, her chin high. "Um, sleep."

There's no way I can sleep when all I can think about is our earlier kiss, and I dip my attention to her parted lips. I should back away, but I've let myself go this far, and pulling back is as easy as getting starved wolves to back away from an escaping deer. In other words, it's impossible. Hell, I don't fucking want to pull away from Meira. She's affected me so much, and maybe I just need to get her out of my system.

She makes a humming sound. "So, when I win, you will tell me immediately what my blood tests said, right?"

I lean forward and whisper in her ear. "Sure. But cupcake, you won't be able to resist. I promise you that. You'll be screaming my name well into the night."

CHAPTER 10

MEIRA

I must be insane to even contemplate this. Bardhyl is a freaking horny wolf who sees this as an opportune time. Why can't I get the memory of our kiss out of my head? How I desperately clung to him, needing so much more of him, how I sensed the ache easing while in his arms, just as I did with the other two Alphas.

I sidestep to get away from him, to catch my breath because I'm drowning in my own arousal. When I look at him, a fogginess clouds my judgment. Even now, his smell is all over me—the musky wolf, the freshness of rain on his skin, even the mud on his shoes.

There's no denying it. I've thought of kissing him since our first encounter at the pack fortress. Then again, I felt that way about Dušan and Lucien. And, well, look where that got me. Now I'm stuck in a cave during a storm with a Viking hunk, and instead of flat-out driving him away, I'm contemplating some crazy game where he turns me on and I have to tell him to stop. Who does that?

"Meira," he calls to me, but I keep my back to him, needing to find some sense of rationality about this situation and for my cheeks to cease burning.

"I don't think this is…" I start, but then he steps close in behind me. The heat of his body pours over me, and I seem to have lost my ability to think.

"What's that, cupcake?"

Inhaling deeply, I reach inside and track down a sliver of common sense, then manage to say, "I vote for sitting by the fire and trying to sleep. Your idea is crazy. We're not doing it."

An ache sits heavily in my lower stomach, just like it did before Lucien and Dušan took me, and now it stirs again. It's my wolf, rising to the occasion.

Maybe for my wolf, I should give this a go. If Bardhyl's presence awakens her, I'll regret never attempting to bring her out. I want to laugh out loud at my ridiculous reasoning. As much as part of that is true, I can't get the image of his nakedness by the river out of my head. His large cock, his large hands, his promise of what he'll do to me. His presence alone squeezes my libido.

Maybe some women can push away such a man, and I always thought I'd be the same. Apparently, I'm wrong. I'm just a wolf in heat. My resistance is a thin façade with cracks threading through the surface.

I turn to face him, my chin high, wearing my bravery, which is a terrible mistake. That earlier resistance has crumbled around me.

The moment I lay eyes on him and discover he's just in his jeans, the top button open, I forget my argument. When did he take his shirt off? "That's very presumptuous of you." I eye his Adonis-like chest that leaves me weak. "I haven't agreed to your crazy idea."

"Let me tell you what you're thinking." He reaches over and slides a strand of hair that was caught in my lashes behind an ear, but I bat his hand away. "In your mind, you will slip away from me and never see me again. Yet the idea of finding out the truth about what's in your blood is tempting, isn't it? Should you play my game and gain some information, or forget it because you've lived this long without knowing? What difference would it make, right?"

I narrow my gaze at him.

"You know I'm right."

"And if you are, then you're an asshole for using a piece of important information to get into my pants."

He *tsks* at me. "I said you would be mine for the night. Who said anything about sex?" He smirks evilly. "When I win, you will give me a full body massage all night long."

I roll my eyes hard at him. "You love playing games, don't you? I can see the way your eyes twinkle as you twist everything around your words. But I can tell you now that when we kiss, you will be shocked at how quickly you will lose."

"So that's a *yes* then?" He sticks out his hand to make this official, and I accept because he may be right about my intentions, but I will burn in hell before I let him know he's right. He always brings out the competitive side of me, I've noticed.

He suddenly backs away and stands by the fire just in his jeans. Even his boots and socks are off. My toes wriggle around in my wet shoes. I follow suit and toe them off before returning to the heat.

"So," I say amid the strange awkwardness, "are we doing this?"

"Whenever you're ready. I always let the woman make the first move so it's clear they want this and I'm not forcing them to do anything against their will."

He stares into the fire as he talks, his hands stretched out, and I'm trying to decipher the expression on his face. He gives nothing away.

"Did you learn that from Dušan?" I ask, remembering my first time with the Alpha and how he pulled away when I hesitated after he went down on me. It had nothing to do with pleasure, because I still shiver at the memory of his tongue on my pussy. It was the fear of what my wolf would do.

But a simple kiss with Bardhyl I can do with my eyes closed. I move toward him, and he doesn't even look my way. He stands so tall and muscular, his nose slightly crooked, which only adds to his attractiveness. Spectacular green eyes that I want to dive into, and long, blond hair tumbling over his shoulders and falling to his chest. But my gaze lingers on his bicep for a bit too long and then shifts over to the tightness of his abs, the way the firelight dances over his perfect body... all sharp angles and cuts. He has to be a Viking god, because how else can one person be so perfect?

But if anyone is not going to be able to say *no*, it will be him. I press closer to him, nudging my breasts against his side on purpose. He swings an arm around me while pivoting his whole body to face me.

Danger and arousal swirl behind his gaze. I push myself against him once more, my hands planted on his hardened pecs that twitch beneath my touch, which he does for show.

"Bardhyl." I breathe his name on a moan. "You are not doing a good job of winning me over."

"Oh, have we started?" He mocks me, and I'm fuming, angry words rolling over my throat, but he turns on me so fast, I lose my voice.

Strong hands grasp my hips and lift me in a heartbeat, just enough to place my feet on his. He smiles wildly as he walks me backward until I hit the wall, and I'm pinned in place by his huge frame. I shouldn't enjoy this, but I love his aggressiveness.

With each inhale, I smell his muskiness, and my body trembles before he even kisses me.

He plants one hand on the wall above my shoulder, and the other strokes my jawline. His eyes devour me, and beneath his stare, I start to feel absolutely tiny in comparison.

"I've been trying to figure you out," he says, his voice dark and raspy.

"Yeah, how so?"

"To understand what would make a woman like you happy."

I lift my chin higher. "That's easy. Freedom."

He nods. "I got that part, but I mean sexually. The feistiest of people love to be dominated when it comes to being fucked."

"We can't sleep together. That was part of the rules you made up." I smile cheekily.

"There were no rules about talking about it." He leans in closer, his cheek brushing against mine, his breath heavy on my ear. He doesn't touch me anywhere else, and already a hot flush flares over me.

"I'm going to mark you as mine, and when I wake you up in the morning, it will be with my tongue."

I half-huff and half-gasp, making a strange strangled sound as my knees weaken beneath me. He presses his body against mine, the thickness of his cock rock-hard against my stomach. My insides are melting, and I know this shifter will go to any length to win. But that is never going to happen.

Even if my body is begging me to kiss him first and then beg him to strip me with his mouth.

"A shame you won't win," I state.

"No?" His response taunts me.

The heat from his body is like an inferno, and his heavy breaths on my neck have me squeezing my thighs together. This man is a warrior, ripped and made for war, so I can only imagine how incredible it would be to have sex with him.

His fingers trail down my arms, and goosebumps rise over my skin.

"Are you all right?" he whispers, while his thumb scrapes innocently over my stiff nipples.

It takes my breath away, and a shudder of pleasure drives straight to the apex between my thighs. Gods, I'm so wet. "You're not playing fair."

"This is how I kiss, cupcake." He leans his brow against mine. "I need to make sure you want this just as much as I do."

"Well, that's where you're mistaken. I feel nothing."

He throws his head back and roars with laughter. "Little woman, I can smell sweet slick filling the air. If I slid my hand to your tight pussy now, I would bring you to orgasm in seconds."

Swallowing hard, I try to hold myself together and not give in to him. "You make me so angry and horny at the same time, but that doesn't mean I can't resist."

"You want my touch, don't you? Clenching your thighs won't give you the release you crave."

His words send a shiver of excitement over me, and I want to wriggle so much and unleash the building pressure.

"You're struggling already," he tells me.

"Will you just kiss me and get this over with?" All I can think about is feeling him up against me. I'm high on the fumes of my own desire right now, and this Viking promises me things I desperately need. A rush of heat pours out of me.

His mouth clashes with mine suddenly. He kisses me harshly, violently, beautifully. His hands aren't on me, just his lips.

They kiss me with an unbearable passion, sucking on my lips, biting into the flesh, and there's something exhilarating to be with a man with such wildness.

I want to be lost to him, to have him carry me into this intoxication he promises.

When his tongue sweeps into my mouth, he explores me, and hell, his tongue is so long. I shake as he expertly draws mine into his mouth and sucks on it in a way that makes me think how glorious he will be going down on me. He seems like a biter, and shit, but I want his mark all over me.

With a grunt, he breaks away.

My lips feel swollen and sore in the most incredible way.

"Have you decided?" He growls, his eyes wild with lust.

I'm still battling the inferno of desire swallowing me while the ache between my thighs pulses. I'm so horny, I don't think I can stand it, and all he's done is kiss me.

"Maybe you need a bit more convincing," he says, his hand reaching for my pants, his fingers curling in over the band around my waist and pulling at it. "A bit of finger fucking?"

When I try to speak, my voice comes out all breathy, and I hate that all I can think about is needing release. The ache burrowing through is my wolf responding, calling to Bardhyl, needing him.

My pussy clenches at the thought of Bardhyl taking me.

"You lost for words, cherry pie?"

He pulls on my leggings, leaning in for another kiss. I hungrily cup his face and kiss him back this time. I can't even think straight, because the way he kisses is like being shot into the sky and floating on clouds. Like nothing can touch me. Like I am all he cares about. And I crave that feeling again and again.

His hand slides down the front of my pants until he finds the heat between my legs, the slick wetness that coats me.

My nipples tighten as he rolls a finger over my clit.

I kiss him harder, my world spinning with intensity. My hips rock back and forth as I clutch on to his shoulders. "Goddamn, Bardhyl," I murmur.

"What is it? You like the way my touch feels over your creamy pussy?"

"Stop talking, fuck!" I push down on his shoulders, needing him where I am about to explode.

But he fights me and looks me in the eyes. "Just so we're clear here, I've won, right?"

I pause for a second, my heart speeding, my desire crashing into me too fast. I can't even speak properly.

"N-No!" I shove against him, panting softly. But I'm fooling myself.

I've never seen a man stare at me like Bardhyl is now, promising me raw, primal sex. And shit, how the hell am I meant to come back down from this? "You play dirty."

His hand slips under my top, his palm so huge, I shiver with anticipation. "You're mine tonight, and you know it." He tugs on my top and rips it up and over my head, then tosses it somewhere behind him.

"You have perfect tits." His hands are on them, and I'm moaning, adoring the way he pinches my nipples to the point of pain, but I need more. "Say it," he says.

"What are you talking about?"

He pulls back his hands, and my skin quivers with the cold.

"That I won and you are mine for the night."

He grabs the top of my pants and yanks them down my legs, leaving me naked. I gasp as he glances up from where he crouches in front of me.

"You haven't told me to stop yet."

But when his hand trails up my thigh and clasps my pussy, a whimper escapes my lips.

"That's what I thought."

Bardhyl

Her pussy is soaking wet, her slick driving me wild. She steps out of her pants, and I clasp on to her hips. Then I turn her away from me. She looks at me over her shoulder, her bronze eyes questioning me.

"Are you ready to say it?" I remind her, but when she doesn't respond, I run a hand up her back and force her to bend forward for me. She is spectacular, so stunning, and I now understand why Dušan and Lucien couldn't hold back.

"Place your hands on the wall."

She obliges, and I nudge open her legs with my foot, then I drop to my knees.

"Good girl. Now let me hear the words."

I take in all of her, her lips pink and swollen. Slick glistens on the inside of her thighs with her need.

Leaning forward, I take her scent inside me, my wolf shoving forward, well aware of what he needs to claim. I smell it too, a lot more than before… and I realize now that I have been wrong to think I had any resistance when it came to Meira.

My wolf snarls, bringing with it a sensation that rolls over my chest.

She's mine. She's my fucking mate, whether I wanted that or not. Our wolves are fated to be together.

Holy fuck! That complicates things, doesn't it?

"No more teasing," she moans. "You won. Are you happy? Now please, Bardhyl, fuck me."

I smile and love hearing her say those words. "Not quite yet, sweet cheeks."

"What more do you want? I'm giving you what you want. You can choke me, slap me, tug on my hair—anything."

Her eagerness sends pulses of arousal through me, and my cock punches hard to full erection. It hurts so much, and I'm dying to sink into her. But first I need to taste her. Grasping her ass, I pry apart her cheeks, seeing all of her. Then I press my mouth to her pussy, my face buried against her heat. She's like candy, sweet and musky and everything I could want

She moans instantly. I devour her, tugging on her folds, loving the sounds she makes, how she grinds herself against my face. My cock hardens, and I'm dying to fuck her. I eat her out savagely, her addictive screams turning me on even more.

I lick her from her little pussy all the way to her ass, taking all of her.

She trembles under me, and I feel she's close, but I'm not ready to have her go there. Not yet. So I pull away.

She groans in protest.

"Told you, gorgeous, that we do this my way." Up on my feet, I lift her with me, her back against my chest. My mouth is on her shoulder, licking her, taking mock bites. She has me wound us so tight that I'm barely holding on.

I carry her across the cave to the nest of leaves she built for us.

I twist her around in my arms and lay her down on her back. She stares up at me, her cheeks flush, and I see the hunger in her eyes. But there's something else. Her Omega side is controlling her.

Her breaths come heavy, and she clutches the ache in her stomach.

"Your body is craving an Alpha, and I'm going to be that for you, little Omega. It might even help your wolf."

"It won't make a difference. There's something wrong with me. This was a mistake." She moves away from me.

I lash out and take her arm, forcing her to face me. "Hey, enough. You're everything to me."

She scoffs. "Why? I told you before, I'm broken, and you shouldn't want me. I'm an idiot for letting myself get this far and believe that..." Her words trail off.

"Meira, I don't give a shit if you're from hell and sporting horns. I will dive into the darkness for you and with you."

She blinks at me, uncertainty flashing over her expression.

"Spread wide for me. I will show you."

I see the struggle behind her eyes where she wants to fight me, but she's way past the point of coming back. She's riled up, her wolf on the edge, and the pain she's feeling will worsen if she does nothing about her arousal. She obeys and her knees fall open. Light from the fire dances over her naked body. She's so beautiful.

Things are different now.

I should have sensed this before, but I refused to.

I'm not saying I have the answers, or even that I'm ready for dealing with a fated mate or Dušan's reaction.

But the answer stares me in the face. It curls around my heart like barbed wire.

Regardless of what tomorrow will bring, right now, it's all about Meira.

I get to my knees between her widening legs and lean forward as she watches me, worshipping my goddess. I take her heat into my mouth once again as she writhes, moaning louder, her hips rocking back and forth.

She tastes of euphoria, and I let myself fall.

I've been with enough women to know when someone special lands in my lap, and every lick, every inhale, every touch I make strengthens the bond between us. Energy lifts the hairs on my arms as it slides through my veins.

Her excitement escalates fast now, and I push a finger into her. She gasps, her chest arching, and fuck, I love the way her body reacts to me.

"You taste so damn good." I growl and kiss the inside of her thighs as I finger her faster. She's so juicy, and I add a second finger, squeezing it in there.

"Oh, Bardhyl." Her legs widen, and she shifts to fit me.

Meira's a delicious morsel, and I finger her quicker now, driving into her as she thrusts her pelvis with each push. Her cries grow louder, more intense. Fuck, she's gorgeous.

"God, you are so tight. When I stick my cock into you…"

She screams with her orgasm, and I bare my teeth then bite just above her small mound so she will always see my mark.

I taste her slick and blood, taking her into me, bonding us.

Her body convulses, her beautiful cries a song to my ears.

Before she finally quiets down, I pull my sticky fingers out and kneel in front of her. I wipe my mouth with the back of my hand, taking in her soaking cunt, the line of blood rolling from my bite, and this gorgeous naked woman spread out for me.

She draws in her lower lip between her teeth, grinning at me so sexily. Gods, she wants this so badly.

I slide my hands under her ass and prop her up slightly for an easy angle to take her.

"You smell and taste so fucking incredible, cupcake. And I'm going to fuck that pretty, tight pussy," I rumble as I palm my cock and run the tip over her fire.

"I want you," she admits. "Please don't make me wait."

My heart hammers in my chest at her words, and I inch into her, slowly at first, until I get the right fit. Her walls squeeze around my dick, and I growl with desperation to drive into her.

She watches me, her hands clutching the blanket of leaves around her, her eyes dilated. She's as sexy as fuck. And she needs this.

I push into her all the way and fall forward, my hands on either side of her shoulders. She cries out, her body arching. Slowly at first, I draw out of her and go back in, then I pick up my pace to match her quickening moans. Her hands curl around my arms, holding on to me.

I fuck her harder, slamming into her. A blaze surges through me, and I roar as the intensity swallows me. She's so small, but she takes all of me, and her sweet groans wrap around me like a warm blanket.

She moans, curling her legs around my hips, while my gaze fixes on her bouncing breasts. Waves of bliss crash into me, sending shivers of power across my skin. My wolf shoves forward, calling to hers, craving her.

It doesn't take long for her to shudder, her head tilting back with the orgasm tearing through her. Just watching her, feeling her constrict me is the most magnificent feeling. And that's when I know I've come too far to back the hell away from her.

The tip of my cock swells inside her. I sense it pushing deeper and locking in place, knotting. Then it hits me, the climax racing through me like steaming water, my seed gushing out, ribbons of it filling Meira. I hiss, my body humming with ecstasy. It's how it works with Alphas and Omegas, how we ensure each fuck is a success to breed.

A howl bursts past my lips, my body shivering uncontrollably. White lights spark behind my eyes and I fill my little wolf.

When I finally float back down, I'm hunched over her, buried deep. It's where we'll stay until my swelling eases.

It takes us both a few minutes to ground ourselves back to reality and readjust to our surroundings.

We're breathing fast, and her smile matches mine. I rub her nose with mine like Eskimos as I hold myself on all fours over the top of her, and she laughs. The sound is delicate and comes from in her gut.

"Fair to guess you don't have plans to fall asleep after this?" Her words are raspy, and her walls every so often clench around my cock, sending me into a frenzy of hisses as I lose the small amount of restraint I hold on to.

"You keep teasing me like that, squeezing me, and I'll keep you here for a week with me."

Her eyes widen. "I suspect Dušan wouldn't take too well to that."

I shrug. "He has to find us first." I'm talking out of my ass, but my head is still floating on the arousal, with lots of my blood filling my cock right now.

Meira clings to my arms, making no effort to pull back. Our faces are inches apart, her breasts squished to my chest.

"This is your fault, you know? Your stupid idea didn't go so well."

"From where I'm standing, it worked perfectly."

She sticks her tongue out at me, but her eyes are still glazed over from her orgasms. "Will you tell me about my blood test?" She whispers the question as though she's afraid I won't tell her.

"In the morning, I will. Not now." There is no way I can dump such news on her while I'm buried all the way inside her and we're locked together for a little while. I want her to focus on the joy she experienced, not what tomorrow will bring.

Waves of energy surge through my veins, the essence of my Alpha feeding her Omega the strength to eliminate the aches in her body. We're made for one another; it's as simple as that. No matter how pissed Dušan or Lucien may be, I can't change the nature of wolves and that we are fated mates as well.

After a long pause, she says, "You marked me, didn't you?"

"Of course. You're my fated mate, Meira. Have you not sensed this?"

Her grip tightens. "While we were having sex, I felt the connection like with Dušan and Lucien. But how can I have three mates?"

"It's common practice in Denmark. Women often take several husbands, and in some cases, men might take several females. But it all comes down to the selection of our wolves, and whom we were fated to mate with from our birth."

"That's pretty deep, to think our lives have been predestined for us."

I kiss her nose. "To me, it feels natural. We were meant to be together from the moment we took our first breaths. The hard part is finding each other."

She chews on her lower lip, a habit I notice of hers when she's worried about something, then she squeezes my cock as she shifts.

"Fuck, babe." I growl. "You keep doing that and I am never going to pull out."

"Oops." She smiles too beautifully to get mad at her.

I scoop an arm under her back and in one swift move, I roll onto my back, taking her with me, her legs still straddling me.

Now she's lying on top of me, me still embedded inside her gorgeous pussy.

She places her cheek to my chest, and I wrap her in my arms. I feel her thumping heart, hear the softness of her breaths. There's nowhere else I want to be. While we're locked together, she softens, and I like this side of her as well. We can't fight all the time.

"Tell me a story," she says.

I hold her tight and begin. "There was once a wolf, but she was so much more than she ever thought, for you see, she was half-beast, half-human."

She cranes her head up. "Is this a story about me?"

I hold back the laughter. "You'll find out if you keep quiet and listen."

She sticks her tongue out and squeezes her sweet pussy to prove her point. I hiss a breath, and if she keeps this up, I'm spanking her ass raw.

CHAPTER 11

LUCIEN

The woods around me bleed with shadows. Dušan trots alongside me, both of us in wolf form and carrying our clothes in our mouths. My jaw tightens, as I've been carrying my boots as well. They once belonged to my father, and there is no way I am leaving them behind. He had this obsession with the cowboy boots that he found on the side of the road. He took them, and they strangely fit perfectly. I lost him so long ago, and the boots are all I have left of him.

Morning brings blessed heat. The storms stopped just before dawn, but it was a wicked night of heavy rains pissing down and cracking thunder. Dušan and I had sheltered in an old abandoned shack, and in our wolf forms, we chased away the cold.

The rain washed away most scents, but when we discovered the fallen bridge, we knew we were definitely on the right path. There's a smaller rope bridge farther along the canyon's ridge that I discovered on my last visit to this area of the woods, which Bardhyl most likely wouldn't know about. That means they're still on the other side of the gorge. We move fast and cross over the narrow bridge made of rope and old wood panels.

Bardhyl would have shit his pants crossing this. Dušan takes rapid steps ahead of me, making the whole damn bridge wobble and shake.

Then we're running along the gorge, well aware Bardhyl would be headed in the direction of our home. My heart beats faster at the thought of seeing Meira again. I intend to keep her by my side every minute of the day until she accepts what she means to us and that being apart isn't going to work. She belongs to us and we to her. She just doesn't seem to realize that yet.

A twig snaps, and we freeze. I lift my nose and sniff the air, Dušan doing the same. Fresh rain. Muddy soil. And wolf. A she-wolf, more specifically, carrying a heavy air of slick. Meira. My heart gallops at the thought of finding her.

The cold wind blows directly in our faces, so she's ahead.

One look at Dušan, then we're off. We each spear outward to cover more ground.

The air thickens with her scent when I spot her racing alone through the woods at least fifteen feet away. My muscles ease at having found her, the tension rolling off me. Thank fuck! All I want now is to snatch her and kiss her until she sees sense.

She glances over her shoulder then keeps going. Has she ditched Bardhyl so easily? He's getting sloppy—or is something else chasing her? I wait a moment, studying the forest behind her, listening, but nothing comes.

She's running away. That's what she's good at, what she's always known, and it breaks me to see her doing it again after we offered her everything.

Fear strangles people, I get it, but she's our fated mate, and for that I will fight to the ends of the Earth to make her believe we won't let her walk away from us.

Not again.

Never again.

A growl rumbles through my chest as I watch her running. On the other side of her, Dušan moves in her direction. That's my cue, and I dart toward our girl.

We travel like the wind.

Minimum sound.

Hunting what is ours. What belongs to us.

Dušan reaches her first, and she startles, a cry falling from her lips at seeing his wolf form. She backs away, hitting a tree, but she slips past it only to arrive face-to-face with me. I drop my clothes in front of me and call back my wolf.

"No!" she mutters as she looks over to Dušan standing before her as a man, naked.

"You are not supposed to be here," she continues, her voice quavering. Defeat finds her—it's written all over her face. And my heart aches to see her disappointment that we've found her. That's not the homecoming you want from your fated mate.

My body shakes, bones stretch, skin splits, and I bear the excruciating pain because it's gone as fast as it starts. Pain comes hand-in-hand with being a wolf, and I learned a long time ago that being afraid of it makes it worse. Now I embrace it. The more the change aches, the stronger it'll make me.

I rise to my feet in human form as Meira swings her attention my way, the tears in her eyes breaking me.

"This wasn't meant to happen," she murmurs. "Why can't you all see? I'm nothing."

With three long strides, Dušan reaches her, taking her arm. But she pushes him away.

I drag on my jeans, then pull on my long-sleeved tee and shrug into a jacket as I step into my boots. I stroll over as I straighten my shirt and jacket, my gaze again scanning the area for any sign of Bardhyl. Nothing. He's not around.

When Meira looks my way again, our gazes clash as mixed emotions crawl over her face. She's so scared that it's driving her decisions.

"You don't need to be afraid," I say as I stretch out an arm to her, but she just shakes her head.

"Don't. It drives me crazy standing here and not touching you. It wasn't this bad before." Her chin trembles as reality crashes into her thoughts. "If we just keep apart, our bond will break. It has to."

Her legs tremble, and Dušan scoops her up before she falls. He's still naked, which intensifies his connection with Meira, aiding her in healing quicker. The energy from my Alpha and me are overwhelming. Omegas *crave* Alphas. They need them for survival, and she's been away from us so long.

The ache she's experiencing is like someone has lit a match in her chest, causing the fire to spread wildly, burning her from the inside out. It comes from spending too much time away from the ones you're bound to. This is why we can't have her run away again, why she needs to fathom the danger.

"You're going to be all right now," Dušan coos, and she cradles against his chest. She looks so innocent and small. The opposite of her usual self.

I follow my Alpha out of the woods, grabbing his clothes off the ground in the process, and head into an area of land where the sun beams brightly. He drops to his knees and holds her against him. I kneel in front of him and reach over, pushing hair out of her face. Her scent hits me, heavy because she's so close. Sweet candy, just as I remember from when I went down on her, but there's something else. A masculine smell on her too. Bardhyl's.

He's claimed her. Fire slams into my chest to think he's laid with Meira. I've known him for years, know he wouldn't force himself on her… He wouldn't dare. What the fuck went down?

I meet Dušan's gaze, his eyes reflecting back my sentiment.

Bardhyl's smell is strong and reminds me of snow and dirt. Every wolf carries a unique signature, so there's no mistaking it was he who was with Meira.

Meira twists her head and looks at me, and I forget everything else. The primal instinct living inside me awakens, the savagery, the familiarity of what we have together. She feels it too, our connection like taffy pulled to the point of tearing.

"We missed you," I say, but she winces and pulls away, curling in on herself in Dušan's arms.

"Give her time," he says.

I dump Dušan's clothes near him and get to my feet as I stare into the surroundings, looking for any movements that would indicate undead are near. Time is what she needs for the pain of our reunion to settle down, for her to come to the realization that what we have is real and isn't going anywhere. I won't deny, though, that it stings like a bitch to have her pull away.

My thoughts slip back to my first fated mate, Cataline, taken by the undead. When she died, it felt like someone had scooped my heart right out of my chest while I watched. I never want to experience that again, yet here I am, connected to Meira, that same feeling crawling through me again.

"Go find him," Dušan orders, and I know exactly whom he's talking about.

I nod once and march back in the direction from which Meira came. I don't for a minute believe Bardhyl forced himself on Meira, but rather they had a similar connection as I have with her. Our wolves drew us together like magnets, the call impossible to resist.

We're animals programmed to breed. That's the core of what it comes down to. And sometimes, that connection is split. Bardhyl told me of women taking several men as mates in Denmark. Admittedly, it pains me to share Meira with two men, because I'm a greedy bastard—it makes me want to steal her away from everyone. Having her other mates being my best friends does ease the ache, though. I wouldn't accept them if they were strangers, or worse yet, someone I disliked. But I won't walk away if she takes Bardhyl into our relationship. I just need to make sure that is what happened between them.

I've been walking for over fifteen minutes, and my gut instinct tells me to return to Dušan. He's alone with Meira, and out here, we're the vulnerable ones.

A few more steps forward and a wall of stone peers back at me in the distance.

Caves.

I speed up and dart into the first one. It's empty, as are the next two, but in the fourth one, I hit the jackpot. The waft of a fire lingers in the air, as does the musky scent of sex. Twigs and a pair of boots litter the ground, and there are burned-out remnants of a small fire.

The sunlight behind me illuminates a figure rolling over onto his back, groaning like a bear.

Bardhyl squints in my direction. "Lucien?"

"Who'd you expect, Santa?" I tease, stepping deeper into the cave. He once told me he used to believe in the jolly bearded man, even when he was twelve.

Now that I'm closer, I can see his wrists and ankles are bound by vines. I chuckle while he growls at the realization that Meira attempted to tie him up. He rips the vines with sheer strength and his bare hands, then drags himself off the ground. He's naked, and his long blond hair resembles a bird's nest.

"Where is she?" he snarls, his shoulders squaring, his chest pumping rapidly with breath. His expression morphs into one of dread.

"Dušan has her. Get dressed, man. We need to go," I order.

His wide brow furrows, watching me. "She ran, then? Of course she did. That little minx is a fucking handful." He bends over and collects his jeans before climbing into them, followed by his shirt and boots.

"What the fuck happened in here last night?" I need to hear the truth from him.

He lifts his chin toward me. "Fuck, Lucien, she crawls under your skin. And being alone with her, it was impossible to resist the allure."

He steps closer, rubbing his fingers through his hair. "It wasn't my intention to touch her. Her wolf called to mine like never before." He gives me a lopsided grin that makes him look stupid, but I know exactly what he's saying.

"You marked her?" My voice rises with a hint of jealousy.

"Yes," he admits immediately. Bardhyl has always been a straight shooter. Says it as it is. "As soon as I sensed she was my fated mate, I left my mark, hoping it would bring out her wolf. No fucking luck there."

"Shit. I've never faced someone with her condition before. What if her wolf is throwing off signals to all Alphas, and we're getting mixed signals too?"

Bardhyl snorts a laugh and claps me on the shoulder. "Have faith in the wolves, my friend. She may not be completely put together yet, but our wolves are smarter than you think. The mating game needs both sides to feel the eternal calling."

I shake him off and we march outside into the sunlight. I missed Meira like crazy, and now jealousy burns through me, but this is my darkness to deal with. If Meira's wolf selected Bardhyl as well as Dušan and me, then we're all in this together.

I shove him in the arm. "Fair warning. Dušan might be pissed. Your scent is all over her."

Bardhyl licks his dry lips and rolls his shoulders. "Won't be the first time he and I have clashed."

CHAPTER 12

MEIRA

I've never felt this level of intensity, and pain, and longing all at once. My body shudders, and the only relief comes from pressing as close as possible to Dušan. I can't even begin to make sense of how my wolf side works, but it's clear that I have zero control.

"You'll be okay," he reassures me as I loop my arms around his neck.

I breathe in his scent, and with each inhale, the aches dissolve. His presence is like oxygen to me. I take everything I need and he gives it to me, knowing exactly what will help.

Lifting my head, I stare into the bluest of eyes, brighter than the sky above us. His pitch-black hair flutters over his shoulders, and now I remember why I fell so easily for this Alpha. He's captivating and makes me forget that I am broken beyond repair. I mated with three Alphas who are my fated mates, who make me cry with desperation to be with them, and yet I've still failed them.

"You shouldn't have bothered," I whisper, my throat tightening.

"I had no choice, Meira. I need you like the air I breathe, and I would have gone insane if I never found you again. You know what I'm talking about, so how can you say that?"

A pulse dances in my neck, and I hate that my eyes prick. One moment, I finally escaped from Bardhyl. Next moment, I'm in Dušan's arms and drowning under his attention.

"I'm not enough for you, Dušan. Can't you see? Three Alphas

marked me, but I'm still not good enough. It still wasn't enough for my wolf to come out." My voice trembles at how I don't feel complete. This is why it's easier to live alone. No one judges me, or reminds me of everything I'm not. "I want so much to hear you tell me you need me, that our life will be perfect, but I can't even promise you I'll be here tomorrow."

"Hush, don't say that shit," he coos. "Everything is fixable."

"You're not listening." I push my hands against his chest and wriggle out of his grasp. My feet are unstable at first, but I manage to stand on my own. "It kills me to leave you. My wolf is a stubborn bitch. She won't come out, yet she makes me suffer, longing for you, insisting I need to be with you. But then what?"

He reaches an arm out to me as he stands, looming over me. But I push his hand away.

"How's it going to work, Dušan?" I grip my hips. "We pretend all is good, then one night when we all sleep happily my wolf decides to tear out of me, killing me, and then slaughtering my Alphas? And if not that, wolves will start a war when they find out I'm immune to the undead and see me as some kind of cure." I wipe away the tears leaking out of the corner of my eyes. "Why do you want to live with a ticking time bomb?"

He snatches my arm and forces me against him. I stumble forward, our bodies colliding. "If I'm going to die, I couldn't think of a better way than at your wolf's teeth."

I frown at him. "Don't mock me."

His hand around my back strengthens. "I mean every word, Meira. But that's not going to happen. We need to keep trying to help you. Now that we know why you're sick, it might be the key to unlocking this situation with your wolf."

Bardhyl's words about the blood test come to mind. "What did my bloodwork show?"

But instead of responding, he twists his head to look over his shoulder as Lucien and Bardhyl stroll toward us. I push myself out of Dušan's arms, torn in too many directions, my emotions a tangled mess.

Stay.

Buy myself time.

Escape from these three is impossible. So that option is gone.

What I need is to understand what Dušan discovered in my blood.

Maybe there is a chance to make this work and heal me by some miracle.

The air suddenly grows thick as Dušan turns to Bardhyl with a sense of hostility I don't expect.

"With me!" Dušan barks at Bardhyl, who glances my way and winks before walking off with his Alpha.

"What's going on?" I mutter toward Lucien, who doesn't pay them attention but only has eyes for me.

"Are you hurt?" he asks.

I shake my head. "Tell me what's going on with them." I don't mean to snap, but I don't want Bardhyl hurt because of what we did last night. What happened was mutual on both sides. And if he's one of my fated mates, then Dušan and Lucien need to accept that.

"Dušan is Bardhyl's True Alpha, and that means answering to him."

I jerk my head up. "Answering to him about being with me last night?"

He nods. "About marking what's his."

Fire fuels my words. "From what I understand, you three are mine as much as I am yours, so we should have a say in this together."

Lucien smirks. "You've been listening to Bardhyl too much. What the Denmark pack does and what Ash Wolves do are not always aligned. But they will sort it out, even if it comes down to a fight."

I stiffen. "What the hell? Did you fight Dušan too? That's barbaric!"

As though he can't stand it a second longer, he reaches over and takes my arms, drawing me against him. "We are barbarians, my little bird, and our Alpha Dušan has the right to accept or reject another man for his fated mate."

"But it's my wolf who picks!"

"And Dušan gets the final say, even if it breaks your heart and Bardhyl's. What Dušan says is law. You will have Dušan and me, so your Omega wolf won't suffer."

I hate the sound of this. Fury churns in my chest because what I felt with Bardhyl is animalistic and wild and… well… I don't know what to make of my feelings, but I should get to make that choice, not Dušan.

I spin on my heels and march in the direction of the woods where Dušan and Bardhyl vanished when strong arms clasp around my waist and whip me up off my feet.

"I can't let you do that," Lucien whispers.

"Why the hell not?"

"Trust me. Men just need to get shit off their chests sometimes, and both Alphas have dark pasts they may not be ready to share with you."

That statement leaves me stunned, and suddenly I feel like I don't know any of these men.

I shove myself out of Lucien's grasp. How in the world can I be so needy for their attention, have their presence physically eliminate the pain their absence caused, and yet have them seem like strangers on another level?

"What's *your* dark secret then?" I blurt out, eyeing him up and down. "Is it related to your cowboy boots?"

His face loses some of its color at my question, and it's clear I've taken him off guard. He never blinks his steel-gray eyes, while the breeze ruffles his short, brown hair. He's six-foot-three, rugged and smoldering, everything about him screaming *wolf*. My attraction to him started the second we met by the side of the road when he picked up Dušan and me. Even now, standing before him, all I can think about is going to him, tasting his lips, remembering how he claimed me. But I stand my ground, wanting answers. Lucien is everything I've ever desired in a man, and he looks at me with hunger.

But he doesn't make a move, either.

"The boots are all I have left of my father," he finally answers. "And if you need to know the truth, I lost my first fated mate not that long ago to the undead. So yeah, we all have dark shit in our past, Meira. And we deal with it the only way we know how. It's why you run, isn't it? It's all you've ever known."

I can't move or even find my voice, as what he's said weighs heavily on my mind. There are so many questions I contemplate asking, yet only one pushes forward. "Y-You already found your fated mate?"

He runs a hand through his hair and glances to his feet momentarily before meeting my gaze. "Until I met you, I still dreamt of her. They say a true fated mate is for life, but that isn't the case. Look at us. We all come from twisted pasts, and we are bound to you." He stands tall, and his stormy irises lock on to mine, making it clear he wholeheartedly believes every word he says. But part of me worries that maybe I can't live up to his initial mate. He loved her first, and she will always be with him. What if I'm not good enough?

I want to apologize for my earlier anger at him, to draw him in my arms, because I struggled severely from being away from the Alphas over a few days, and it would have been a lot worse without Bardhyl next to me. I can't even imagine how losing her felt. But the thought of losing one's mate brings back the heartache from when my mama died. It was so long ago, yet it feels like it happened yesterday, and that familiar sharpness in my chest rises again.

Striding closer to him, I slide my hands in his, our fingers interlacing, and I just hold him, because no words can ease the grief.

Three Alphas, each so similar but so different.

Dušan is the one in charge, dominating and never letting his guard down.

Lucien brings patience and understanding to our group, but there's a fire in his eyes that makes him unpredictable.

Bardhyl's the joker, but he's using that to hide the real him. It's so obvious.

And me... I complete the circle of misfits by being shattered and lost.

Maybe I'm where I should be, among these three. After all, we're all trying to find out where we belong in this world, right?

An ear-piercing howl slices through the silence, and I flinch, my head jerking in the direction of the woods Dušan and Bardhyl disappeared in.

Dread flares over me, and I jump into a run toward them.

"Meira," Lucien yells, his footfalls hitting the ground right behind me. He snatches my arm and swings me back around, but my fury lashes out.

I slam my palms against his chest and catch him off guard, judging by his widening eyes, but he doesn't let go of me. My breaths are coming out as pants, and all I can think is that Dušan is beating up Bardhyl, deciding *for* me who I can or can't be with. Pent-up tension has me thrashing to free myself.

"Let go! He's going to hurt Bardhyl."

Lucien breaks out into a laugh at my expense.

"Meira, it'd take an army to physically hurt Bardhyl. That's the first thing you need to know about your Viking warrior. Now come here." He wrangles me roughly and spins me around so his chest is flush against my back, his arms clasped around the front of my shoulders, keeping me in place.

"Then why can't I go—"

Two wolves burst out from the woods with such ferociousness, I flinch against Lucien, losing my words. One as black as night, Dušan, the other with the whitest fur and black-tipped ears. Bardhyl. Together, they're a jumbled ball of teeth and growls, the battle savage.

My heart hammers and I go rigid, but I'm not backing away. Lucien's lips are on my ear. "The thing about Ash Wolves is that most things between Alphas are resolved through battle."

I shudder and clench my teeth. "Why the hell isn't Dušan accepting Bardhyl? It's my call!" Writhing against Lucien does nothing to free myself.

"Quite the opposite," he murmurs, his chin resting on my shoulder. "Watch them fight. It's all mock. There's no blood. This is a fight of power and aggression and reconfirming hierarchy. Bardhyl took something that belonged to the Alpha, and now Dušan must reestablish his position before he accepts the Viking being with you. Bardhyl has to kneel."

The more I watch, the more I start to notice he's right. The pair roll on the ground in a tangle, biting at each other's necks and sides and hides, ripping fur but not drawing blood.

Looking at it through different lenses now, there's an aggressive beauty about the fight.

I don't understand most of these pack rules or the power struggle, but I'm slowly learning new things every day. Things I missed out on while growing up mostly with other females and then on my own.

Dušan latches on to the back of Bardhyl's neck and tosses him across the ground with ridiculous strength. Bardhyl slides into a tree and stays down as his Alpha trots over to him and sniffs him.

"See here," Lucien says. "He'd normally unleash a howl of victory, but that's not going to work in our favor out here."

I swallow hard as Bardhyl climbs up, head low, and darts past his Alpha to vanish into the shadowy woods. Moments later, Dušan comes toward us. His body shakes as he pulls himself up into a human, transforming so fast that by the third step, he's completely taken human form. Fur has vanished, his face morphed back to his gorgeous self.

Bite marks and bruises mar his body, but it doesn't distract from how powerful and utterly naked he is. My gaze falls to the thatch of dark hair above his cock, flaccid but still big... and of course, I lack any ability to act discreetly.

He catches me staring, and my cheeks flush with fire.

I shift to move out of Lucien's arms, but he holds me still as Dušan approaches. Strong and powerful, he stops inches from me and grabs my chin, forcing me to face him. A fresh scratch under his eye blushes red. He only has eyes for me.

I'm pinned between these two Alphas, and I need to ask what the resolution was with Bardhyl and if he's coming back, but instead I'm lost under Dušan's wild, hypnotic stare. My body hums with energy, their energy blending in with mine.

"You've selected three of us as your mates, and I accept that. But no more, understand?" he growls.

"It's not like I consciously wanted three," I respond, my muscles tensing. I don't know if it is or isn't, but my wolf seems to be in heat around these three Alphas.

"Maybe not, but I won't tolerate another."

Bardhyl returns toward us, already dressed. His head is low, and I find it fascinating how loyal and dedicated wolves are to their Alpha.

Dušan lets out a deep, throaty growl, filled with dominance, sexual desire, and a reminder of all of our positions in his pack. I feel the vibrations of his power like never before, and my breath catches in my throat.

He nods to Lucien, who releases me, and it's Dušan who takes hold of me now, by my neck, and draws me to him. Our lips clash with a savage hunger. And just like he put Bardhyl back in his place, I know exactly what's coming my way.

His canine nicks my lip, and he licks my blood, the pinch stinging. His hands tighten on my hips. I can barely breathe from the heat he pours over me.

"You are mine." He snarls in my mouth and pulls back, his eyes taking wolf form.

Instinct has me wanting to kiss him back harder, but I stand my place in front of him. My wolf picked him and the others, so that means finding a way to make this work.

"We should leave," Lucien says, interrupting the buildup. The way Dušan's hand has grabbed at my top, it's like he might rip it off me here and now.

"Time isn't on our side with her sickness," Lucien continues.

Sickness? My blood runs cold. I turn around, surrounded by my three shifters, and look at each of them. "What did my blood test show?" I ask, meeting each of their stares.

"She doesn't know yet?" Dušan asks Bardhyl.

"Nope," Bardhyl answers, his voice hard.

"Is this the place to do it?" Lucien questions.

"Hell yes," I say, butting in. "I'm not moving from this spot until you tell me."

Maybe I'm a comedian, because all three of them laugh at me, but I don't appreciate being mocked for standing up for myself to three powerful men.

I dig my heels in. "I'm not kidding around," I snap. "Someone tell me what the fuck is going on with me."

They exchange looks, and it's Dušan who cups my face and leans in. "Meira," he starts off tenderly, and already I can tell he's going to say something bad.

"Just say it. Don't sugarcoat it, please." My stomach coils in on itself. The longer they take to tell me, the worse the scenarios my mind comes up with are.

He kisses me on the mouth, then pulls back with a look of regret washing over his face. "Meira, baby girl, you have leukemia."

CHAPTER 13

MEIRA

"Oh, Meira," Dušan murmurs, his hands sliding over my shoulders. His attempt to smile comes out crooked and holds a sense of guilt, as if the news was somehow his fault. "This is why we had to find you so quickly. The disease is slowly working through your human body, and your wolf is the only way you'll survive."

I read about human illnesses when I once broke into an old library for shelter. The building had been ransacked, but some books still remained. From what I recall, it's a blood disorder, a cancer of blood cells. It stops the body from fighting bacteria and viruses, and… I know there was other stuff in the book, but I can't remember the rest.

"Meira," Dušan says softly.

But as the information sinks through me, the tears fall. I must have done something awful in my previous life to have so much bad luck in this one.

I sob into my hands, and Dušan gathers me into his arms, his chin over my head, his hand rubbing my back. Here he is, still naked like it's natural, and I'm falling apart. Everything feels surreal. He kisses my brow and my fingers. But all I can think about is if my wolf had just come out, it'd have solved everything.

"Leukemia is what's been making you immune to the undead, and your wolf side has kept you alive this far."

I raise my chin and lower my hands while he wipes my tears with his thumbs.

"Your results showed that your human body is starting to break down and…" He licks his lips, seeming to struggle to find his words.

"What is it?" I ask, needing to know exactly what's going on with me.

Lucien and Bardhyl approach us, one standing on each side of me.

Dušan says in a whisper, "It's progressing quickly. Within maybe a week or two, it will spread to your organs. It's why you've been vomiting blood, why we need to find a way to bring out your wolf."

Dread throbs under my skin. It's one thing to hear I have a disease that might be stopping my wolf from coming out, but now I'm being told I only have two weeks left to live at most. I can't fathom the news. Here I worried that staying with the Alphas put them in harm's way, while a bigger danger lurked over me.

I can't breathe. My knees weaken, threatening to collapse.

As if my illness wants to remind me this is shit is real, a tremendous ache spreads through my whole body, ripping at me as if someone has whipped me.

My legs give out and I cry, hugging my middle. I wrench over, and the pain spews out past my throat, coating the grass with blood. I feel better getting it out of my system, but it doesn't remove the reality of my shitty situation.

Lucien is at my side, pulling my hair over my shoulders.

Everything is too unbearable now. Numbness crawls through my limbs, and I look from one Alpha to another, each offering me hope. But I sense their fear, too, that it may be too late. How could things have gotten so bad?

I've been different my whole life, and I never let it stop me.

When I look up and wipe my mouth with my sleeve, I blink at my three men.

Powerful Alphas here to help me.

They owe me nothing, but they don't turn away. The burning in my chest lingers, but it's less painful now.

Every second ticks away in my mind.

Bardhyl offers me a reassuring smile, and Lucien takes off his jacket and hands it to me to wear while Dušan dresses himself. Then he stretches out a hand to me.

"Let's go home."

I doubt anything will be the same again. How can it be? I tried to go back to the way things were, believing I was doing the right thing. But I was wrong.

So now, I'll take these wolves' guidance and try it their way. I slide my arms into Lucien's black leather jacket. It floods me with warmth, his wolf scent like a reassuring blanket cocooning me. It falls to my thighs and keeps the cold at bay. Then I place my hand in Dušan's.

"I'm ready," I admit. Ready to survive. After all, there are two options in front of me, right? The one where I continue following Mama's instructions to keep running, to not trust anyone, to use what I have to continue living. Then there is the one where I place my trust in these stubborn, dominating Alphas who won't give up on me. Who promise me a new world.

Me.

Meira.

The lonely girl who lived on the fringe of the world.

Who's now desperate to find a way to survive in Shadowlands while everything else tries to kill me at every turn.

I squeeze Dušan's hand so he knows I'm set on following him. This is my last chance, so I take it.

He offers me a smile that warms my heart and sinks down into my soul.

"First thing I'm doing is eating half a goddamn boar," Lucien states.

Bardhyl chuckles. "Only half? You've grown soft."

There's comfort in their banter, like somehow I belong here, though at the back of my mind, I have mixed emotions. I barely know these Alphas, even after everything we've been through. This is new, and giving in has never been something I do.

But going with them... It doesn't feel like *giving in* right now. It feels like hope.

Dušan

F*uck.*

The word just keeps sliding over my thoughts. It never occurred to me once that Meira might gain yet another fated mate. I'd seen no signs of it back at the compound.

Fated mates are for life.

This bond is not just between Meira and me, but with Lucien and Bardhyl as well.

I don't cross swords, and I'm sure they don't, either, but that's not even what bothers me. It's not having Meira all to myself all the time that I need her.

What the hell am I meant to do? These men are my closest friends, and I won't lose them or have Meira hate me for denying her the ability to be with them.

Yeah, the situation is bullshit, and fuck yeah, I'm jealous. But like most things in my life that don't go to plan, which is a fucking lot, I improvise.

We've been walking for a few hours now, and I can't stop staring at Meira, even if I try. She's constantly on my mind. And it bothers me a hell of a lot that I don't know how we're going to work out our situation. Allocated visits? Fuck that. The decision will come to me once we get home, so I shove those thoughts aside for now.

Priority is getting home in one piece and finding a way to save her. And until then, I sure as fuck don't want her thinking I'm an asshole. I swallow my jealousy and distract myself by surveying the woods we pass through, listening to sounds, anything that will give us an edge to get the hell out of here fast.

I crave her, and the savage urge to drag her into my arms and claim her right now up against a tree grows by the second. The urge to strip her and fuck her so she remembers her Alpha grows through me.

Timing sucks.

Location sucks.

Fuck, I just need a damn break, a minute for things to stop sucking.

Lucien walks ahead of us, Bardhyl at our backs, and we travel silently.

Her eyes flicker in my direction, then look away quickly when I catch her staring. What is she thinking? That I'm a monster?

We live in a world full of dark creatures, and in order to survive, you must become one. She'll either accept that or she'll struggle to find happiness.

For fuck's sake. I have to get my head straight and stop whining.

We're downwind, and the next rush of air brings with it a new smell... wet dog fur, muskiness, perspiration.

Wolves.

My hands fist into balls, and fury rises along with my wolf within me. The presence of any uninvited wolves on our land is a hostile sign and a declaration of war against us.

We all cease our marching in unison. Lucien's head lifts as he takes a deep breath. "At least five or six of them. A small pack."

I clasp Meira's hand and draw her to me.

"Rogue wolves?" she murmurs.

"Those bastards rarely work together, and if they do, never in these numbers." I glance over my shoulder to Bardhyl. "Scout out the pack," I order.

He lifts his chin, his jawline clenching. "Think it's in any way related to Mad?"

"Doubt it, but I won't discount anything right now. They wouldn't have picked up our scent yet, so we have the element of surprise on our side."

One nod and he sidesteps past us, then darts into the woods without a sound.

Dread lifts the hairs on my nape. Not for me, but for Meira. We don't have time for this shit, and I don't want her harmed.

"Anywhere we go, they'll track her scent down," Lucien says.

"Then we fight and rip their fucking heads off." I suck in rapid breaths, and my wolf bristles at the mention of a battle. "And one eye on Meira at all times."

"If we could track down some undead, maybe I could hide among them if we tie them up?" she suggests.

"Love the idea, but we haven't encountered any. We stay low until Bardhyl returns."

Lucien charges ahead of us, searching for a safe spot. We know the drill, have done this too many times when we hunted for Omegas. We've been ambushed before by rogue wolves, but we've never had a pack on our land.

My muscles knot up, and a pang of fury has me riled up.

"I need a weapon," Meira states. I draw a blade from the back of my belt and hand it to her, hilt first.

"Don't hesitate to use it. Don't give the enemy a chance. You see an opportunity, strike." I push a hand through her hair and draw her closer to me. "Nothing will happen to you, I give you my word."

"Does she have a name?" she asks, lifting my blade.

I want to laugh at her cuteness. "No, but I've always seen it as a male over a female."

She studies the leather hilt, running her thumb over it. "Feels feminine to me."

I eye her, not sure if she's insulting me or the army knife that is thick and razored on one end, but I let it go. "You can call it what you want, babe, as long as you use it when needed."

Taking her elbow, I guide her to a shadowy part of the woods, where dampness fills the air and will mask our scent easier.

Lucien returns to us in moments, wild-eyed and nodding. "There's an old rundown farmer's cottage down the hill close to the water. But we'd be spotted going down there, so it's not an option for now."

"Then we stay low and wait," I say.

Meira tucks my knife into her boot, and we sink down to our knees near several oversized shrubs. They'll conceal us in case someone moves fast past the area. The problem is more to do with the smell my little Omega emits, calling to others like a dinner bell.

First, work out what the hell we're dealing with, then we finish this. We're too far from our compound, but I have two of my strongest warriors with me. I could do with a good fight right now.

Meira bites down on her lower lip, staring out into the woods around us. "If we can bypass them, maybe that's for the best," she suggests.

Except that's not the world I live in. Running away isn't an option. Intruders are in my backyard, and no one else will drive them away before they cause damage. My pulse is thumping, my heart pounding with adrenaline at what's coming our way, and I can't fucking wait.

"We never run from the enemy," Lucien whispers to Meira. "We always fight."

"When we go back, I want someone to teach me how to fight properly and use weapons," she says, and hell, I might just love her for that.

I lean over and kiss her cheek, then sweep over to her lips. "You got it."

A leaf crunching draws my attention behind me, and I jerk my head up, my hands fisted, ready to lunge, Lucien doing the same.

Bardhyl bursts out of the shadows, and I stand to meet him as he speaks. "Seven males. Two are Alphas, others are Betas. And they're coming this way."

"Good. We spread out and wait, then we jump. Go for the Alphas first." I flick my hands at my men to show them the best spots to wait before we attack.

The wind direction is in our favor, and I want this over with fast.

I crouch back down next to Meira. "Stay here. I'll be close. Anyone comes near you, you scream."

She nods quickly and her cheeks pale. I don't blame her for being afraid. I'm so damn tired of these complications preventing us from getting home.

I kiss her on the brow and jolt to my feet, ready, leaving her kneeled down.

It's barely a split second that passes when a guttural growl erupts from behind me.

Blood drains from my face, and I whip around to find a huge timber wolf shifter standing over my startled Meira, his teeth bare as a growl rolls through his chest, ears pressed flat to his head. Sonofabitch... He has every intention of taking Meira.

CHAPTER 14

MEIRA

I dig my fingers into the soft soil as my heart hits the back of my throat. Coldness sweeps through me, bringing with it the reality of how much shit I'm in.

I flinch and look over my shoulder as a gray wolf stands inches behind me. Hot breath washes over my back, his growl reverberating so loudly, it seeps into me. I can't stop shaking. My gaze swings back to Dušan, who stands six feet away, blood draining from his face. Bardhyl is close by, and Lucien is nowhere in sight.

Dušan straightens, his shoulders broad, his demeanor transforming into a powerful Alpha before my eyes. Anger now lashes his features, his upper lip twisted.

"Why are you on my land?" Dušan barks loudly, nostrils flaring, voice flooded with menace. Shadows gather under his eyes, and there's no way in hell I want to ever cross him when he looks this furious. But right now I welcome it, want him to tear apart the creature looming over me.

"You get one chance," Dušan warns. The air thickens with the scent of his wolf and the energy of an oncoming transformation. His eyes have already morphed into his wolf's.

My skin is littered with goosebumps from the war I'm in the middle of.

Fear swells inside my mind, slipping into my veins, except I'm not alone anymore. I have three Alphas who will fight for me... *with* me.

I feel the weight of the knife in my boot, but I don't reach for it, not yet. I stay kneeling on the ground, waiting for the right moment. I have no damn idea when that is, though.

No one dares move an inch.

Shadows slink around the woods surrounding us, circling us, cornering us. More wolves.

I want to warn my men, but I am under no illusion my Alphas aren't already aware of the additional intruders.

My heart speeds.

Then in a crazy moment of silence, everything changes.

Thundering steps strike the earth at my right. I turn just as Lucien, still in his human form, lunges at the wolf behind me.

Lucien slams into him, dragging him away, but not before the enemy bites into my shoulder.

Sharp pain slices into my flesh, and my screams bleed into the air as I'm dragged down from the momentum.

I'm drowning in agony while commotion explodes around me. I hit the ground with a loud smack, and I swear I'm going to scream from the exhaustion of constantly getting hurt and being in danger.

For those few seconds, I feel nothing but the racing adrenaline taking me over.

I rush to my feet, my hand going to my boot. Knife in hand, I stagger backward, shudders tearing through me.

Lucien strangles the wolf with his bare hands as the creature jerks to his feet, and I can't breathe from the terror colliding into me.

Sounds of battle burst from my other side. I whip around as Dušan battles two wolves. Bardhyl, in his white wolf form, roars with fury as another two wolves collide with him.

I should go help, but I can't even stand upright steadily.

When a shadow emerges from my right, I turn in its direction. A brown wolf with white-tipped ears and dark eyes prowls toward me. I lift my weapon because I'm not fast enough to outrun him.

I know better than to run, anyway. It would only further spark the wolf's desire to show his dominance over me. Doesn't stop my legs from shaking.

"Don't come any closer," I threaten, my fingers tightening around the knife's hilt until my knuckles turn white.

This is my fight as much as the Alphas'. I edge past a pine tree, my eyes never leaving the enemy.

Head low, he slinks closer, a deep, guttural sound rolling from his chest. I twist away, the air rushing out of me as an overbearing fear squeezes my chest.

Then he charges.

An involuntary scream spills past my throat as I swipe my blade, the sharp edge catching the animal on the side of his nose.

He growls and bowls into me, knocking me over. In seconds, Lucien wrenches the wolf off me just as fast.

I scramble backward on my ass over the forest floor, gasping for air.

Lucien lifts the wolf and tosses him away from me. How the hell does he have such strength?

He's at my side, blood smeared across the cuts on his neck and arm. He smiles like somehow everything will be all right. In that very moment, a burning ache from the bite on my shoulder sinks through me, like someone has poured boiling water over my skin. I wince at the blood staining my top.

"Stay close to me." Lucien heaves each breath. He grabs me, his fingers tightening on my wrist as he hauls me alongside him.

Dušan howls victoriously with two wolves slain at his feet, then leaps to Bardhyl's aid, as the white wolf has four attackers surrounding him. Lucien doesn't go to his aid but holds me close while my head whirls with fear that we'll be captured.

That's when a shrill whistle pierces through the woods.

We freeze, listening for more sounds.

A figure strolls out of the shadows, a shifter in human form, dressed in jeans and a gray hoodie. The stranger is tall and may not be as broad as my men, but there is an energy around him. More wolves in animal form join him. The shuffling sound behind me draws my attention to the small pack pulling away from Bardhyl and Dušan to join their Alpha.

Only when this stranger fully emerges from the darkness do I see him clearly. He's not old—maybe in his early thirties—brown hair parted on the side messily and hanging over one eye. His chin is wonky, like it's healed from a bad accident. And he looks familiar... like we've encountered each other before. I wrack my mind, but I've crossed paths with so many people, most for short periods of time. They flash in my thoughts, except most memories I pushed away long ago. Most fall into one of two categories. Those who've hurt me, or those who died and left me messed up. Which means whoever this guy is, well… he's got to be an asshole.

"Meira," he says, sending my stomach plunging to my feet because he remembers my name when I can't recall his face. "I've been searching for you. Heard from a little girl who spoke of a Meira in these woods, so we came to investigate."

"You better not have hurt her," I snap, my weapon raising. I'll gut the weasel if he did something to Jae.

"You actually care? Since when?"

At hearing the slight lisp he has, I start to remember. Not long after Mama died, I met him during one of my stays in a town in northern Transylvania, where small fractions of packs appear all the time. It's a wild area where fights for small pockets of land just outside Dušan's territory occur daily. I met this man in a small community area. I was younger, lost in the world, and I trusted him when he offered me shelter and food.

But in exchange, he wanted what I wouldn't give. That night he called me his Omega and tried to rape me, so I kicked him in the balls. The bastard beat me up until my eyes were so swollen, I couldn't see a thing. All those memories, the ugliness of the world, my fear, blended into a mess I tucked in the farthest recesses of my mind. I had intended to forget them… and I sure as hell don't want to bring those memories back now.

That's the reason I ended up living alone, why I made a treehouse, why I never helped anyone else. It's been so long, but now seeing him again, I'm trembling.

"You owe me," he snarls. "And I'm here to collect."

"What the hell is he talking about?" Lucien snaps, holding me closer to him. Dušan in human form, Bardhyl as his wolf, join us, confronting the intruders. Four of us against maybe fifteen of them. Are there more wolves out there, watching us from the shadows? How long have they been tracking us if Bardhyl only spotted a handful earlier?

I spit on the dirt and offer him a sneer. It's more than Evan deserves. "You're a bastard. You beat me up and tied me to a fucking tree, then left me for days."

Dušan stiffens beside me and steps forward. "She owes you nothing. But you are trespassing on my land. I'm the Alpha of Shadowlands Sector, and you will pay with blood."

Evan scoffs as if the threat means nothing to him. "I protected her from the men who planned to steal and rape her between them. And she screamed bloody murder when I touched her. Frigid bitch." He looks over to me, flicking his head in an attempt to shift the lock of hair out of his eyes, but it never moves. "I tied you up as a lesson. But you escaped, didn't you? You know how much I had to pay those men in resources to leave you alone, to not go after you? You should be thanking me." He sets a splayed hand to his chest like somehow his words are heartfelt. "Now, I come for my payment, which I'll take in the form of rutting you over and over."

Bardhyl unleashes a snarl that comes so sudden and loud, it makes me jump in my skin.

"I don't have fucking time for this bullshit," Dušan growls. "Leave, or you end up like them." He points his chin to the dead wolves at my left. "That's my only peace offering."

No one responds, and Evan rolls his eyes, slouching on one leg, eyeing his large group and then the four of us. Yeah, that part worries me too. But I'll die before I let this asshole claim me. Looks like I'm fighting.

Lucien's hand is on my waist, and he has me glued to his side. He looks down at me for a smidgen, whispering while Evan talks shit to my Alphas. "In a second, all hell will break loose. Get up a tree as fast as you can. It'll be easier for you to defend yourself, as you can fight them back with a branch to keep them from climbing after you. Understand? I'll try to stay near."

Before I can even respond, energy collides into me from my Alphas transforming. The air ripples with their musky, powdery scents.

"Your time's up," Dušan declares. He shifts into his wolf form and jumps into attack, Bardhyl and Lucien on his heels.

I dart backward. Running, I scan for the best tree and spot one with lower branches and thicker clusters of leaves for concealment.

But before I can reach my haven, someone slams into my back, throwing me forward onto my face.

My cries are muffled by the mouthful of dirt I just ate. I whip around the moment weight lifts off my back and swing my blade, catching the unsuspecting bearded man across the gut. It's not deep, but it's enough to draw blood and distract him.

I kick him hard in the shin, and as he bowls over, I run to get out of there. Choosing a different tree to simply escape this asshole, I skid around the battle and finally climb up a perfect one with enormous high branches and lots of foliage.

My hands grasp the lower branch as my legs quickly swing up and around, when a sudden sharpness bites into my ankle and tugs down on me. But I hold on desperately and kick wildly. I look down to the gray wolf latched on to my leg, and another coming closer. I kick him aggressively in the nose, and with a whimper, he releases me.

Hastily, I scamper up the tree, shoving past the prickly branches ladened heavily with round, deep green leaves. The bark on this trunk scratches the hell out of my skin.

From up here, I scan the area.

The wolves battle. Teeth and fur and growls.

The aggressive sounds they emit leave my skin crawling. I don't know if I can ever fight that way.

A growl sounds below me. I look down, and the damn bearded man is back, his eyes as gray as his stormy skin, his upper lip sitting at an odd angle from an old injury. I shake with anger.

I tuck my knife into my boot and reach up to grab a thinner branch with spiky offshoots. With both hands, I yank down on it, the wood cracking and snapping free. Lurching backward from the motion, I fling out a hand and snatch the trunk to steady myself.

"No use hiding, bitch," he snarls.

I sidestep to stand on a branch directly above him. He's not so skilled at getting up here, luckily. So I haul the branch, shoving a shoulder against the tree for balance. My feet spread over a platform of crisscrossing branches, and I spear my weapon downward.

It jams right into his head and scrapes down the side of his face. He cries out from the shock, his hands cartwheeling as he falls and hits the ground hard. His face is bloody, and *ouch*, I did a lot more damage than I thought. Fuck, yeah.

Lucien was onto something in telling me to hide up here.

The torturous sounds from the battle have me twisting around toward other wolves who are rushing my way. I clutch onto my branch, my insides wound so tightly, I might be sick.

They snarl at the base of the tree while the bearded man gets up. I shove the weapon at him, but the dick grabs it and wrenches it away with unimaginable strength, taking me with it as I lose my footing.

My death flashes before my eyes as the ground flies up toward me. A shrub breaks my fall, poking and stabbing me. I groan, as every inch of me feels like it's on fire. I keep expecting teeth to tear into me and rip me apart.

Strong hands grab my ankles, and I'm wrenched across the ground. I cry out and reach for anything to use as a weapon. Fistfuls of dried leaves aren't going to help me.

I spin on my side, thrashing against the bearded asshole who's smirking at me with blood-stained teeth from where I'd hurt him. He deserves a hundred times worse.

"Let me go." I toss everything I can grab at him and attempt to push myself up to reach my boot for my blade, but it's impossible. He yanks me so fast, I have leaves and twigs rushing up on the inside of my top.

I keep thrashing and wriggling against him, screaming out while two of the enemy wolves follow close behind. When he finally drops my legs, I can't see my Alphas or the battle.

I reach for the knife in my boot as wolves snarl in my ear and the guy in front of me unbuckles his belt.

"I smell your slick," he mutters, and suddenly, I'm going to be sick.

Darkness spirals around me, and bile hits the back of my throat. My fingers grasp the knife.

I'm shaking horrendously, because if we lose this fight, I'll slice my own throat before I let these monsters touch me.

Before he can even push his pants down, I lunge at him, blade poised. The asshole pivots out of my path, lashing out and grabbing my blade-wielding hand, squeezing until I cry with pain.

The weapon drops from my grasp and he snatches my throat. "You will be fun to break, wild bitch."

"Fuck you." I spit in his face.

He raises a hand and strikes me hard across the cheek, the pain reverberating up the side of my skull. White stars dance behind my eyes as the world tilts on its axis.

One second he's there, the next he's ripped away, and I'm stumbling to catch my balance.

Growls and shouts deafen me. Panic crashes into me as I rub my eyes to see clearly again. Air buffets against me from the commotion. The wolves behind me whimper, and they're gone in seconds. I lower my hand from my face where it still burns, and in front of me stands Dušan in wolf form, blood dripping from his mouth. At his feet lies the bearded man, unmoving, with a gaping hole in his chest, like Dušan has broken right through his ribs to tear out his heart.

The bloody image should terrify me, but I've never felt so protected in my life. To see him go to such extremes toward anyone who hurt me makes my stomach flutter.

He's transforming, and within moments he stands before me as a man, his body cut and bleeding. But I rush into his arms, regardless.

Around my Alphas, I feel at home. I can't even make sense of that thought, but it's the truth.

I finally pull away as Lucien joins us, naked and battered, but smirking. "Well, that was fun." He laughs and wipes at the bleeding cut on his lip.

A shadow of a wolf darts amid the trees in the distance, chased by another. A strangled cry of pain floods the woods.

"What's going on? Is Bardhyl all right?"

As if answering my call, he races across the woods directly past us, his white fur matted and stained with blood. He's bigger than I remember him, teeth bared, and there isn't a hint of humanity in his eyes. He vanishes into the shadows, and another scream rings in the air.

"Bardhyl lost himself to the fight, so we're letting him clean up the rest so his Berserker can get it out of his system."

I blink in the direction he vanished, and I won't deny that seeing him that way scares me. He's taking down the rest of the pack on his own? "How often does he get like this?"

"When he's so angry, he can't hold back," Lucien answers.

"What do we do?" I ask. "And what about Evan?"

"Evan will never hurt anyone again, babe. Now we sit and wait for Bardhyl to finish off the pack. Then we try to calm him down."

That part sounds terrifying. I don't know how much time passes before Bardhyl reappears, still in his wolf form. He's breathing heavily, blood splashed over his long, pointy nose. His chest heaves in and out, his lips peeling back, his ears flat to his head.

A shiver races up my spine and buckles my knees. He's staring straight at me, and behind those eyes, there's no sign of Bardhyl. "Umm, guys, what is he doing?"

Then he lunges at us.

CHAPTER 15

MEIRA

I'm lost to fear, staring at the white wolf lunging right at me.

My legs won't move. My scream wedges in my throat.

There's no sign of Bardhyl in those deep, green eyes. Just his wild animal side.

Lucien drives a hand across my stomach and shoves me behind him, while he and Dušan intercept.

They leap at the wolf, each colliding into Bardhyl.

I retreat, my heart about to give out as the three of them land in a great heap. An explosion of growls pierces the air, the wolf's teeth snapping, his lips peeled back.

Bardhyl growls, and he never once takes his eyes off me—like I'm his meal and he'll kill anything in his path to reach me. Dušan locks an arm around his neck, while Lucien throws himself on top of him.

This isn't Bardhyl. Not my Bardhyl… the man who drove me crazy in the cave, who made me fall for him. How can he be my fated mate when he looks ready to kill me?

He's a monster.

Uncontrollable.

Savage.

Dušan and Lucien have him pinned to the ground, while a thunderous threat snarls through him.

"Meira!" Dušan yells. "Come over here."

I scoff and recoil further. "That's never going to happen. Look at him."

"*Meira*," he growls. "He seeks a connection with you to calm him and push back the wolf."

I blink hard at both of them straining to hold down the wild wolf. He wants me to *pat* him? "He's going to bite my arm off, isn't he?"

"We won't let that happen, but hurry the hell up."

Lucien glances up at me, his jawline tight, fighting with all his might to keep Bardhyl down. "He needs you."

Oh, geez, I'm doing this, aren't I? I step forward and lick my dried lips, my arms stiff by my side. The closer I get, the fiercer Bardhyl thrashes and growls. Does he know what we're doing, or will that come after he eats me?

I sidestep around them, giving Bardhyl's head a wide berth. His eyes follow me as I reach his side. My arms shake as I stretch them out and run my fingers through his thick, lush fur. It's knotted with blood, and his body is vibrating and scorching hot.

He thrusts, and with the touch comes an electric zap that jolts up my arms.

I flinch back just as Bardhyl bucks the other Alphas off him. A split second is all it takes for him to bite me.

I scream, my body numbing, and all I see is my end.

His head strikes my chest, bowling me over, and I yell from the pain. Then the ass leaps over me and into the woods. I cry out, clutching a hand to where he knocked into me.

I tilt my head back all the way to watch him vanishing into the shadows.

Dušan grabs my arms and has me on my feet in moments. He holds me close with one hand, pulling twigs out of my hair with the other.

"What the hell was that?" I snap. "You said you had a hold of him."

"Once you touched him, he wasn't going to hurt you," Dušan explains while Lucien joins us, dusting himself off.

"You could have said that earlier, you know. I'm pretty sure I just had my first heart attack."

Lucien smirks at me. "You're so dramatic. We had him under control. You think we haven't dealt with him like this before?"

"Well, *I* haven't." I pull myself out of Dušan's hold, breathing slowly to calm my pulse and chase away the fear strangling me. "So where is he now? Will he come back as himself?"

"He needs time to recover," Dušan explains. "He's a Berserker at heart, Meira. Something horrible happened to him and his pack back in Denmark, and the scar of the atrocity turned his wolf into a wild creature that even he sometimes struggles to control."

I swallow past the boulder in my throat. What have I gotten myself into? "Will he be okay out there alone?" I ask. I'd be lying if I said I'm not intimidated or a bit frightened by him, but what blossomed between us last night pulses just as hard in my chest now.

The crunch of foliage has me lifting my head as Lucien returns, dressed and holding clothes that he hands over to his Alpha. With everything happening, it's only now that I really full paid attention Dušan's nudity. The strong expanse of his muscles cut sharply across his chest, abs, and arms. Messy, dark hair hangs over his shoulders and face as he bends forward to step into his pants. I can't stop my eyes from looking at his cock, how perfect it is, how I remember him claiming me, knotting inside me. Everything about him—about all my Alphas—is beyond sexy. They're achingly beautiful, these men who have monsters living inside them... as do I, if we can ever manage to bring her out.

When Dušan catches me staring, the corners of his mouth quirk in a devilish grin, his eyes holding a silent promise of what's to come. "Let's move. We'll spend the night in the cottage by the river." He presses his lips together and glances over to Lucien. Without words, Lucien nods and goes in the opposite direction.

"Where's he going?" I look out after him.

"To find food. We won't make it back home by dark, and I want to wait for Bardhyl."

Warmth curls in my belly. Dušan cares for those close to him, and that I admire about him. In this world, no one gives a shit about others. Maybe that's why he has such a large pack, why they stay and fight for him. I reach up and pull a leaf out of his hair. He grabs my hand and brings it to his mouth. The kiss sends small sparks up my arm and through my body. Something in his blue eyes flickers, like he feels the sensation as well.

"Are you hurt?" he asks as he draws me toward him, holding me so near, I feel his erection. Hell, that is fast.

His fingers carefully comb through my messy hair. His scent, masculine and dark, is savage and washes over my senses. Shudders travel through me as his other hand crawls under my top and cups a breast, his fingers pinching my nipple.

I cry out with desire.

"Never run away from me again. We are one. And you are mine."

My panties melt in moments, and my body has no control when it comes to these wolves. His dominance is an aphrodisiac.

I pant against him, staring at his full lips, picturing them dragging down my body, pressed against my slit. One minute I'm scared for my life, the next I want to jump Dušan. That seems to be normal for me around these Alphas.

"I will never lose you again," he snarls and swallows loudly, the tendons in his throat moving as he speaks. "I will go into the afterlife itself to collect you if you die on me."

Dušan

er gaze widens.

I mean every damn word. These past few days have been torture. When I look into her pale, bronze eyes now, I see a woman who no longer resembles the lost girl I first found in the woods. She's changed, grown braver, started to find herself.

I lower my head and take a whiff of her sweet scent of cherries, her ruby lips parting expectantly. I squeeze her breast, her nipple pebbled tightly... so damn perfect. My cock twitches in my pants, hardening. Does she even realize what impact she has on me... on all of us? I never truly understood the connection between fated mates, even when Lucien explained it and I witnessed his excruciating agony. Nothing prepared me for the force that now wreaks havoc on my heart.

She looks up at me, her fingers curling around the fabric of my long-sleeved tee, and grinds her body against me. Our lips melt together. Heat and sweetness fill me when her tongue curls with mine. I draw her closer and kiss her back deeply, drowning in her growing slick scent that has my groin pulsing. I drive my hardness against her, and she moans in my mouth. My heart pounds faster.

Fuck, I've missed her. All I can picture is stripping her and taking her against a tree. Before I can stop myself, I walk her back, pinning her against a trunk, and plaster myself against her small form.

I was hers first, and she will always be mine. Gorgeous and fiery. But fucking her now isn't going to work. We're out in the open and in dangerous territory.

"You do such things to me," she breathes. "My body responds in ways I can't understand." She kisses me again, thrusting her breasts against my chest. Then her hand lowers and slides into the front of my pants. She grasps my cock, and I hiss with desperate need.

"Take me," she begs, and it drives me wild. Her mouth is on mine again, and she's biting my lips, her scent engulfing me, drowning me.

I tear my mouth from hers with all the inner strength I have. "Not here, Meira. When I fuck you, I will take my time, make you scream."

She protests with a groan that drives me insane, then she falls to her knees before me. Her hunger shudders me to the core as I struggle to hold mine back. I shouldn't have started this, because one touch awakens the savage essence that brings an Omega and Alpha together. Her need grows.

Her fingers pull at my pants, unbuttoning them, and my cock springs out, so fucking erect it aches.

I should say *no*, but the irresistible desire pushes and pushes me.

Those gorgeous, sexy lips slide down over the tip of my cock, and I'm gone. Her warm mouth is like wildfire and her tongue flicks me, licking me, sucking me harder.

I growl, my wolf roaring within me. I plant a hand on the tree behind her as she draws me deeper and hold my other hand to the back of her head, guiding her.

I twitch under her mercy, my gaze trained on her as she glances up at me with intensity in her eyes, as her mouth glides back and forth over me. Just seeing her claiming me has blood rushing to my dick.

Deep down, sizzling sparks mingle with my lust.

Tonight, I will fuck her... and that's if I can make it to the cottage without plunging my cock into her sweet, tight pussy first.

She sucks me harder and I howl, the pleasure thrumming over me with the ferocity of a storm. Thank the universe, wolves' cocks only knot when fucking, not during blow jobs, because I'd be pissed as hell if I couldn't enjoy this.

I groan louder and I want this to last... which is a problem out here. We're sitting targets while I get off.

Goddammit.

I slip out of her gorgeous mouth, and she stares up at me with pleading eyes.

"Don't look at me that way. I'm barely holding on." I collect her hand and help her to her feet, then button myself up. My cock is a fucking anaconda and barely fits in my pants in its current state.

"Please, Dušan."

I cup her cheeks and kiss her sweet lips. "That was sexy as hell, but we must get to safety first. Dusk is approaching, and we need to find shelter."

I glance over my shoulder. It's too quiet. Nerves crawl up my spine as I picture the undead coming at us.

She gives me a single nod, and the lust claiming both of us eases with the cold breeze washing past.

I lead her through the woods and to the old cottage by the river, picking up sticks on the way in the hopes that Lucien brings back an abundant catch.

"I missed you," Meira murmurs.

I squeeze her hand in mine gently and glance over to her as she smiles at me. She may not say it, but this is the closest I will get to her apologizing for running away. And I am okay with that.

CHAPTER 16

MEIRA

The door to the small cottage creaks as Dušan pushes it open. A stale, musty odor greets us. I cringe and stare into the darkness inside. Dušan enters first, the wooden floorboards groaning under each step he takes. He walks to the fireplace and dumps the armful of wood he collected. I grip my bundle, waiting at the doorway. As he vanishes into a corridor, I glance behind us. There's no sign of Lucien, who's hunting for food, and I have no idea where Bardhyl went.

Returning moments later, Dušan waves me in. "All safe."

Then he throws open the ancient yellow curtains decorated with small red chilis and creates a plume of dust in the air.

I cough. "This place has mountains of dirt."

I head inside, set my collection of timber near the fireplace, and help him open the windows to freshen up the air. The main room has one long couch positioned in front of an oversized, old-style fireplace housing a cauldron hanging from a metal hook. Several chairs are on their side in a corner, and that's it. No other furniture. The place seems lonely, barren, and sad. Walls are bare of images or any sign of the family who once lived here. Whoever they were, they had time to pack and leave after the curse took hold. I find a broom and start sweeping the floor clean of dust so I don't sneeze all night. Plus, once night falls, we'll need to close the windows and curtains to avoid getting the undead's attention from a distance with flickering light.

Dušan enters the room with his arms full of blankets and towels. "Look what I found in the closet. They'll keep us warm." He heaps them onto the couch, and I quickly grab the one that looks to be the largest and cover the couch with it.

He heads outside and returns with a bucket of water. "Sit down. Let me clean your bite mark."

"It should heal quick enough on its own," I say, but I still sit down on the couch.

He flops down next to me with a wet rag as I drag my top down over my shoulder to reveal the wound. Blood smudges my skin and sticks to the fabric. Gently, he wipes the blood away, focusing intently on what he's doing.

"Thanks for coming for me, for protecting me, for tending to me. I'm not really used to someone being so..." I can't think of the right word.

"Loving, caring, incredibly amazing?" he jokes.

I mean to laugh, but the rawness of the mark stings and I wince instead. Looking over to my shoulder, I see there are four clear punctures and several smaller teeth indentations. A perfect bite mark.

"Does it hurt a lot?" he asks.

"It's not the first time I've been bitten. Won't be the last, I'm sure."

He wipes the bubbling drop of blood and places the fabric against the injury, applying pressure until the blood coagulates. "From now on, the only bites you'll receive are from us three." There's burning fire behind his gaze, and my mind goes back to the woods when I took him into my mouth. I've never done that before, but it felt natural, and the hunger inside me for him was unlike anything I'd experienced. It's stronger than before. Just the thought of it has a pulse dancing between my thighs.

As if sensing the sexual craving growing inside me, Dušan's eyes widen, and I catch the skip of his breath. He's on his feet in moments. "Let me get the fire started. Go and see what you can find in the other rooms that we can use."

When he pulls away, my fingers tingle to reach over and draw him to my side. A burning intoxication crawls over me, and maybe he's right. I ought to distract myself with something else before we end up rutting and Lucien returns with our meal to find we've done nothing else.

Dušan wastes no time and kneels in front of the fireplace, getting set to light it.

Up on my feet, I lick my lips and ignore the growing itch to kiss him, then head into the kitchen. The cupboards are empty. There are only a handful of plates, some cutlery and even some candles scattered in the drawers. No oven. I wander down the dark hallway and into a gritty bathroom. The stink makes me gag when I spot the dead rat in the shower, so I shut the door quickly. The next room has a single wire bed, no mattress, with rags and paper tossed about on the floor.

The last room offers a large bed and even a standalone wardrobe. I peel back the curtains and cough from the dust it stirs in the air. Outside is a perfect view of the river about twenty feet away, water splashing against the rocks along the bank, and beyond that lies the forest. It almost looks tranquil, which is completely deceitful.

Hastily, I check the wardrobe that smells like mothballs. No clothes or shoes, but at the base I find more blankets. They're blue, my favorite color, so I snatch them up and spread one out on the bed. Then I throw myself into it and smile.

For years, I slept on the wooden floor of my treehouse, or on branches in trees, so this is utter heaven just as it had been on the beds in the Ash Wolves compound.

The mattress indents near my legs. My heart skips a beat, and I jerk around, only to come face-to-face with Dušan.

Prowling, he crawls over me while I remain on my stomach, his blue gaze finding mine. This Alpha is a warrior, a leader, a survivor. He has so many following him, in awe of his beliefs, and I admire that about him. It seems impossible that such a man would be here with me now, looking at me like I'm already naked and he's not releasing me until he stakes his claim.

He's on all fours over me, and his fingers scrape over my neck as he brushes my hair aside. Hot lips find the tenderness of my neck, his breath on fire, while his erection settles against the curve of my ass.

"For days, I've been thinking about fucking you," he whispers in my ear, leaving me shaking with arousal.

It doesn't take much for him to turn me on. A kiss, a touch, a few words, and I'm putty in his hands.

"Would you like that?" His weight lifts off me, and his hands are on the band of my pants. He rips them off me instantly, jerking my whole body from his aggressiveness. A hard slap connects with my ass.

I wince and glance over my shoulder at him. But his eyes are glued to my ass, his hands on his belt, pulling at the buckle.

He rewards me with a sinful grin filled with his intentions. A simple look and I'm shivering with the excitement building within me.

"Back in the woods, you undid me," he says, lifting his gaze to mine. "You make me feel things no one ever has."

His words are fierce and strong. Our first time together, he was gentler with me, more patient, but the man before me is too far gone to do anything but rut me. And I find it sexy as hell that I make him lose control.

"Up on your hands and knees," he orders. He captures my hips and lifts them.

I obey him as his hand slides between my thighs to part my legs. Greedy fingers slip over the seam of my pussy, soft at first, then with two fingers, he pries apart my lips, his touch grazing over swollen, tender flesh.

I still, my heart racing as I draw in a rushed breath.

His touch comes again, sliding across my slick heat that coats the inside of my thighs. He consumes me with his mere presence. He pushes two fingers into me, thrusting hard and urgently. I arch my back, loving the euphoria, and buck back against him. Then he draws them out and climbs off the bed.

I wrench my head around, but he shakes his finger at me. "I never said you could move. Stay right there where I can see your juicy offering waiting for me."

My core clenches at hearing his words, and he laughs like he sees the impact he has on me.

He strips off his pants and shirt, standing at the foot of the bed, naked and captivating.

"Your pussy is sexy as fuck."

Those have to be the most beautiful words in the English language.

He is mine and I am his... Those are the words going through my mind as my body burns for him. He's back, kneeling behind me, his fingers slipping up my back and twisting my hair around his hand. Gently, he tugs my head back as the tip of his cock nudges at my entrance.

He growls savagely, and my body responds, pulsing with adrenaline, my inner walls already sucking onto his dick.

My heart racing, I moan as he pushes into me, one hand pulling on my hair, the other grasping my hip. He drives deep, powerful and dominating.

I cry out with the arousal flaring over me, tearing through me with unbearable need. He fucks me hard, and I rock my pelvis back and forth to meet his. The bedsprings creak, the metal headboard hitting the wall.

He claims me, reminding us both of what he's missed, what he thought he lost.

My moans of pleasure escape as he thrusts deeper, his own growls thunderous. Letting go of my hair, he grips my hips, fingers digging into flesh, and he pumps, losing himself in me.

Fiery desire and sexual lust burn between us. His strength overpowers me, and I let him take me, opening myself up, wanting my wolf to connect with his. We are steeped in sex and fear that what we have will be ripped from us.

His cock grows within me, the tip swelling as he ruts me.

It's the perfect way he fucks me. I've wanted to hide from him from the beginning, to run away, but I've been wrong. He's the answer to everything I never knew I wanted.

"Don't you leave again…" he murmurs, the sound barely audible, but I hear it along with agony in his voice. It's why he's taking me so roughly, why he's on the edge of losing himself. This is his punishment to me for making him suffer. I get it, and I should be pissed, but all I see is a man who's struggling with unfamiliar emotions.

I moan with each thrust, my hands clutching the blanket, my toes curling. Rapture soars so fast across me that the room starts spinning. My nipples are so tight, they ache. He reaches around my waist and dips down to my clit, rubbing it. Arousal ignites as if it'd been waiting there for the trigger, and fuck… I scream with the orgasm tearing through me, shaking me, hurling me into the heavens and making me forget everything.

The climax makes me clench down on everything.

Dušan growls as I tighten around his cock, and he thrusts faster.

Suddenly, he stills as he roars, spilling his seed inside me. There's so much of it. I feel its warmth, crave it, need it. I gasp for air when my body finally buckles with exhaustion, and I drop face-first, flat on the bed with Dušan on top of me. Both of us are gasping for air, our bodies sweaty and hearts racing. He reaches down over my chin, forcing me to face him, then his mouth claims mine in a scorching kiss.

He's buried deep inside me, locked within me with his cock knotted.

It's everything I crave. Part of me keeps thinking that he, Lucien, and Bardhyl don't deserve a complication like me. That I will only bring sorrow to their lives. But I remind myself it's much too late now. Those thoughts are from the past me. We've come so far, our connection solidifying with every passing second we spend together. The new me wants to embrace change, to recognize that being on my own is no longer an option.

Dušan breaks our kiss and rolls us onto our sides, his arms wrapped around the front of my shoulders and stomach.

Our breaths ease, and I melt back against his chest, his passion pulling at my emotions for him.

"Don't you leave again."

His words sing over my mind. It never occurred to me that my absence would affect the Alphas this much.

His lips brush my ear. "I couldn't resist when I saw you lying on the bed."

"I craved that release," I admit. After the pent-up desire in the woods, I needed this more than I even realized.

He holds me and I close my eyes, letting myself pretend we're safe in his compound. A gentle heat spreads over my chest in his presence, and I sense my wolf stirring there, like she's trapped inside and doesn't know how to come out. Well, that makes two of us.

"Can you feel your wolf?" he asks me, placing a palm flat against my chest. "I sensed her trying to come out when we were as one."

"Yeah, for the first time, I really do. Like she's humming just below the surface, but she feels lost."

"I remember her trying to reach out to my wolf. That's progress, Meira. I never felt her like this the first time we were together."

I smile and grasp onto his strong arm around me, believing that there may be hope enough for me to somehow come out of all this surviving. It's odd after all this time I've longed to not be found, for others to leave me alone, for the world to take me if it wished. Loneliness does strange things to one's mind. But now, all I wish for is to not lose my life. And it has everything to do with what my three Alphas are offering me.

They are mine. I claimed them as much as they did me, and the universe can go fuck itself if it thinks it will get in our way. Though the trepidation doesn't leave me entirely. It's there at the back of my mind, constantly reminding me of my terminal sickness and the fear that if I do finally shift, my wolf will go mad and kill me and those I love.

Lucien

Night has begun to steal the day by the time I head down the hill to the dilapidated cottage near the water. I found it earlier, the hut having doors and windows intact, so I'm hopeful that no one will come crashing in here while we sleep. After the attack from that dickhead Evan, I contemplated the idea of us traveling through the night to get home already. But it's better we rest for the night and leave first thing in the morning. My stomach clenches at the memory of the fight. I wanted to be the one to rip Evan's head off, but Dušan finishing him off felt just as damn good.

Now, I head back to cottage with two rabbits and one pheasant that took longer than I anticipated to catch, as animals aren't so readily available these days. But they'll feed us, and I'd bet one of my legs that Bardhyl has already gorged on whatever he tracked in the woods to exhaust his wolf's adrenaline. More rabbit for me. I pick at my teeth, trying to remove the bit of fur still wedged in them from when I chased these critters in wolf form. One or two might have accidentally been eaten raw.

I stroll over to the single-story house. The weathered wooden walls have splinters of wood peeling away from the surface, the roof is rusty, and wild grass and weeds suffocate the landscape. Smoke curls out of the chimney, so that means Dušan and Meira are already here and ready for a meal.

The reality that we finally found Meira and she's ours still has my stomach bursting with excitement. I don't know what I would have done if we'd lost her in the woods.

I glance over my shoulder and find no undead following. Good. There's an old bench by the side of the house, where I dump the kills. Then I grab a wooden bucket and I fill it with water from the river. When I return and take a seat, I skin the rabbits and prepare them for roasting.

The front door creaks open, and Meira peers around the corner, staring at me in surprise. Her hair is wet and her cheeks rosy, like she's gone for a dip in the river. "Thought I heard the sound of the gruesome act of skinning." She smirks at her own sarcasm, and I adore that she can still make jokes after everything we've gone through today.

"Make yourself useful." I reach over and hand her the pheasant.

She sits on the opposite end of the bench, barely an arm's length away. She takes the animal into her lap and without hesitation begins plucking it. I notice the slight droop in one of her shoulders from where she was bitten by that asswipe Evan. It's creeps like that who have ruined our world.

"Dušan's preparing a spit, and there's a cauldron in the fireplace. He's making a soup with wild onions and mushrooms he found, and he's just waiting for the meat." She pauses for a moment, focusing on cleaning the bird. "You think witches once lived here?" There's mirth in her voice. "I mean, who uses a cauldron for cooking, right?" She snickers to herself, and there's a new energy around her, like she's slept and woken up rejuvenated.

And just as I have the thought, the answer comes to me. She's high on adrenaline, and when the breeze brushes past me, I inhale her scent, her heat...and also Dušan's. Whatever happened between them has taken the edge off her.

That's the thing... an Alpha's influence over an Omega is more than just satisfaction of a sexual craving for breeding. It helps stabilize emotions, which many Omegas don't realize.

"The last thing we want in this world are powerful witches who can turn us all into frogs." I laugh at the image in my mind.

"Maybe having witches in charge wouldn't be so bad. The undead would be dealt with, for one thing." She plucks at the feathers and throws them on the grass, making the place look like a chicken slaughterhouse.

"So you think the biggest problem in this world is the undead?" I ask.

Her head tilts to look over at me. "Well, yeah, you don't agree? The virus destroyed the world, and now it's unsafe to go anywhere."

"There are worse things out there than the undead, gorgeous. Alphas who slay anyone in sight, who imprison women for breeding... those kinds of wolves are multiplying, and *they* are the real plague making this world worse. Eradicate the warlords and we stand a chance to bring back some sense of community and humanity to our world."

"Wow, that's kind of deep." She twists toward me, drawing a bent knee up on the bench between us. "You, Dušan, and Bardhyl aren't like other men I've encountered. Why?"

I rip the last bit of fur off the rabbit's leg with a tug. "Dušan's belief that we can change the world for the better has rubbed off on us."

"You trust him with your life, don't you?"

I nod. "Of course. He saved me from the undead when I was young, and I pledged myself to him ever since. There hasn't been a day where I regretted that decision."

She goes quiet for a moment and keeps plucking the pheasant until it's almost clean of feathers, except for the head. "I'm sorry about what happened with your first mate." She looks down at the plucked bird. "Since all this, the feelings I have are so overwhelming that they seem to control me. So I can only imagine how it must have felt when you lost your fated partner."

"It's okay. Life takes and it gives again. I accept that," I answer almost immediately. I've had many people ask me this question, and my response comes out automated. "But I think I refused to let myself get over her... and used that as a reason to not be with anyone else on a serious level. I mean, wolves can be together even if not fated mates, but it always felt like I'd be cheating on her."

Meira places her clean bird next to my two skinned rabbits. "Lucien, I don't..." She licks her lips and looks at me like she's trying to find her words. "I don't want to be the next reason you don't want to find love again."

It takes me a split second to work out she's referring to dying from her sickness. The thought turns my stomach sour, the feeling pouring through my veins at what I've been through once already.

"I refuse to think of the worst-case scenario, Meira. Otherwise, I'd never get out of bed most mornings. We found each other for a reason, and I sure as fuck am not going to sit around and just lose you. Once we get back home, we'll talk to our medics and work this out." Threads of desperation seep into my voice, and I hate sounding weak.

She reaches over, her small fingers curling over mine. "I ran away from you all because I would rather have you hate me for leaving than have you feel guilty when you couldn't save me. Or be responsible for your deaths if my wolf rips out and slaughters you." Her eyes glisten, and fuck, my chest tightens. She did it for us, and it's in this moment that I see how deeply she has fallen for us as well. Even if she keeps fighting us, I know that comes from fear, not hate. Fear for our safety. Fear of what we could have. Fear of what we could lose.

"Meira, I'd rather have a few weeks with you than none at all."

Her chin suddenly trembles, and tears drench her cheeks. *Shit.* I'm on my feet and I draw her into my arms. "Don't cry. We'll find a cure, I promise you."

She glances up, and I wipe away a loose tear. "It's not me I'm crying for, but the pain I'll cause you three if I can't get my wolf out."

"There's only one solution then." I tuck a bent finger under her chin. "We get that goddamn wolf to come out, even if we have to lock ourselves in a bedroom for the next few weeks."

She laughs and I embrace her, my heart squeezing at the trepidation hanging over us at the thought that she might not heal. Fuck, I hate those thoughts.

She draws back and smiles, her eyes glinting in the descending sun. Her irises seem to almost glow in the reddish light, and her cheery smile desperately tugs at my heart. I reach over and twirl a finger in her dark hair.

"If you keep looking at me that way, we'll never make it inside," she teases, a tiny dimple appearing when she smiles so deeply.

"And that's a bad thing, why?"

She raises her shoulders. "Never said it was bad, just that we'd never make it inside."

Dušan steps around the corner of the house, carrying a bucket, and pauses when he finds us. "Hell, I'm starving. Bring those inside," he growls and tosses me the wooden pail. "Make yourself handy and bring in more water for the soup and tea. We can make some with the mint I found."

I laugh and stroll down to the river. When I glance back, Dušan leans a shoulder against the wall of the house, studying Meira as she collects the rabbits and pheasant. He's completely lost, as much as me, when it comes to her.

After losing Cataline, my heartbreaking agony left me useless and shattered. So gods help the whole pack if Meira doesn't survive, because Dušan won't know what will have hit him. Her survival has become about so much more than just her and us now…

If Dušan goes down, so will the pack.

CHAPTER 17

MEIRA

I can't remember the last time I felt so sated, so warm, so content. Lucien lounges on the floor in front of the fire like he's a cat all stretched out with his belly full of food, while Dušan sits near me on the couch, my feet in his lap and his magical fingers pressing in all the right spots on my soles.

"If you just gave me this massage the first time we met in the woods, Dušan, I would never have run away." I giggle at my silliness, and Lucien looks over at us, rolling his eyes.

"If only it were that easy, my little hellcat," Dušan says, laughing.

Lucien just looks at me with mischief.

The fire's blaze is a blanket around me, and it has me ready to sleep out here rather than back in the bedroom. I look toward the door, then turn to Dušan. "Do you think Bardhyl is okay out there alone?"

"In his current state he is, and there's nothing we can do for him until he calms down."

Lucien lies on his back on the blanket spread over the wooden floorboards to resemble a rug in front of the fire. "Last year, he was gone for three days and came back completely shaved, head and body."

"What happened?"

Lucien pushes himself to his ass and turns to us, already laughing. Dušan starts chuckling at whatever memory they've both recalled.

"It's only funny if you share it with me too," I explain, my gaze flipping from one guy to the other.

"Well, he slipped and fell down a gorge and landed in a patch of poison ivy," Lucien begins. "He itched like crazy, so much so that he ended up passing out right outside a small gated community for humans." He breaks out into hysterical laughter, while I'm still waiting for the punchline.

Dušan takes over. "Two girls, who were seventeen or eighteen, according to Bardhyl, found him naked in human form and red from itching. They thought he was a human like them and had been attacked, so they dragged him into their home and shaved his whole body, including his head, insisting he had fleas and they couldn't let them infest their house."

My mouth drops open. "They shaved him *everywhere?*" I emphasize the last word.

Lucien howls with laughter, happy tears dripping from his eyes. "Get this. They carved a heart in his pubes."

I can't hold back this time as I picture this powerful, Viking wolf completely bald and shaved, except for the heart over his groin. My stomach hurts from laughing so much, as I can just imagine how mad he must have been.

When I can't laugh anymore because it hurts too much, I slouch on the couch and wipe away my tears. "Oh my god, that is hilarious. He would have been so pissed off."

"He woke up and startled the girls, who screamed that he was a fleabag, then he bolted out of there, realizing he'd been shaved. We never let him live it down. It took him a long time to grow his hair back," Lucien says.

"And it's why he vows to never cut it again," Dušan murmurs.

"Poor guy. But I bet those girls had fun shaving a huge hunk of a man, and they would have *so* touched his large cock."

I smirk at the image in my head because I probably would have, too, out of curiosity.

Both men look at me strangely then. "What?"

"He was probably flaccid," Lucien points out, and I arch a brow. *This* is the part they're hung up on? Really?

"If it makes you feel better, I think you're all damn large," I say. "I've only seen a few here and there, and well, you three are packing incredible weapons."

Lucien gets to his knees and pulls at his buckle. "I think she wants us to compare for her. What do you say, Dušan?"

"No, that's not what I said. Geez, keep it in your pants." I roll my eyes hard at them, but it suddenly feels like an inferno in the cabin.

Dušan chuckles at us, and I am convinced my cheeks are burning up bright red.

"Fine. When Bardhyl returns, we'll line up for you. Then you'll see I'm the winner," Lucien says.

Dušan clears his throat.

I push up and off of the couch. "I'll leave it to you two to sort it out, and maybe you can get me a hot cup of tea while you're at it."

While my first option is to head outside to go to the toilet, I have second thoughts and instead head to the rat-stinky one in the house. I sure as hell don't want to be surprised out there while peeing, and more than likely, Dušan or Lucien would insist on joining me and probably watching.

The bathroom reeks so bad, stinging my nostrils with the pungent smell like spoiled eggs, and it really couldn't be from one rat, but for all I know there are half a dozen more in the walls. A small candle I found earlier in a kitchen drawer now sits on the dirty sink, the flame flickering and throwing shadows over the walls.

I stare down at the filthy toilet bowl. I doubt the flush is working, but I only need to pee, so that will be fine. Quickly, I get it over and done with, the whole time my gaze hovering on the rat. What killed him anyway? Starvation? There are no flies buzzing around, so it probably died a while ago.

In no time, I'm finished and out of the room, spotting Dušan and Lucien laughing as they head out the front door. "Fuck, I need to piss so much," Lucien mutters.

I roll my eyes and head into the main bedroom to grab another blanket, as it's getting cold, even with the fire.

Back in the main room, I stroll toward the couch when movement in a shadow by the door startles me, and I jump in my skin. A small squeal escapes my lips. "I swear to god, Lucien, if that's you, I'm going to skin you alive for scaring me."

My blade is in my boots near the fireplace, and I frantically scan for a weapon within reach when the figure steps forward into the fire's light.

Bardhyl.

He's naked.

Has a feral expression on his face.

His green eyes are locked on me.

On the bright side, he's no longer in his wolf form, though he still seems dangerous, even if alluring. My feelings are at war with my desire for him.

"Oh! When did you get back?" I glance over to the door, figuring I can make a run for it—or, better yet, scream—if Bardhyl makes a move.

He tilts his head to the side just like an animal might do, and this time, the fright crawls up my spine.

"We left you food."

He looks over to the cauldron. Okay, so he understands my words.

"Bardhyl, you're scaring me," I admit.

He comes to me with such speed, I don't have time to react. He drives into me, my back hitting the wall, his mouth on mine, stealing my scream.

Still on edge, I'm trying to make sense of which Bardhyl this is… the crazed wolf or the dominant one.

But as much as my own arousal flares in response and turns to liquid between my thighs, I don't want to become his prey. What if he can't tell the difference between sex and a meal?

I break from his kiss. "Bardhyl, stop." I stomp my heel on his foot.

He hisses, giving me enough space to slip out from him and rush down the corridor. Fuck, of course I'd go the wrong way. I dart into the bedroom.

Bardhyl charges in after me, clenching his jaw. The candle perched up on the cupboard illuminates him and reveals the hunger in his eyes for me.

My body betrays me, craving him and thrumming, which is so wrong. He's an animal, I see it in his eyes, and I'm struggling between going to him to calm him down and jumping out the window.

"Meira," he growls, so dark and heavy, and my body responds with a fluttering in my stomach. Really, wolf, you want him while he's in crazy Berserker mode?

"Bardhyl… this isn't you. Let's talk about it a bit first."

He shakes his head and is on me in seconds, pinning me to the wall. His mouth is on my neck, and he licks me from my collarbone to my earlobe.

I shouldn't find this arousing when I'm shaking with fear, but the more he licks me, the hotter I burn. Callused fingers graze under my top, and he rips it up and over my head, my arms forced up as he strips me with ease.

Fuck. I'm breathing heavily, my clit throbbing as he shoves my pants down my legs. By the time he's bent over and has pulled them off my ankles, I've collected myself and knee him in the chin. He stumbles, groaning as I leap past him, sprinting toward the door.

Strong hands snatch my wrist. I spin around to face one of my fated mates, the wolf who loves to toy around and do deals so he wins, who flirts with me and now looks ready to mount me. I'm battling between *fuck yeah* and *this is moving too fast* after seeing him lose himself in the woods.

Our bodies collide, and his large hand scoops me up by my ass, the tips of his fingers reaching the heat of my pussy. I moan from the touch almost instantly, like I'm programmed to respond to him. As though control is a thing of the past when it comes to me and these Alphas.

"Bardhyl, please, let's just take it slow." Not that it's what my body wants, but I'm not too sure what will happen if I just let him take the lead.

He looks at me, licking his lips, then shoves me onto the bed.

I land on my back and bounce, the springs groaning beneath me. Swiftly, he snatches me by the back of my knees, draws me to the edge of the bed, and spreads my legs. I push forward and shove my hand against his head while trying to shuffle away.

"Be still," he snarls, and his mouth assaults my pussy. He dives in and latches on to my lips, taking all of me.

A shudder races up my spine, and if I thought I was aroused before, now I'm a puddle, melting before him.

He frantically licks me, and god, he has a wide and long tongue. The moment he plunges it into my slit, I arch my back and scream with desire. He shoves my legs wider, eating me savagely. The wet, slurping sounds he makes should be illegal.

I writhe beneath him, drowning in pleasure, when I should be using the moment to get away from him. Though now I'm more torn about why I wanted to get away from him in the first place. My thoughts spin while I cry out from him tugging on my burning lips, the sensation driving me insane. My eyes are shut, and I can't think straight or even care right now that Bardhyl's beast side is claiming me.

I reach down and fist his hair, pushing his face on my pussy as I grind against him. His fingers dig into my inner thighs. He's loving every moment.

"Fuck me!" Lucien snarls.

My eyes flip open to find him and Dušan there, both of them with their hands on their cocks, watching Bardhyl go to town on me. Where the hell have they been… or have they been watching this the whole time?

He releases me and I collapse on my back, shyly pressing my knees together, which is crazy.

"How long have you two been watching?" I ask as I shuffle farther up on the bed, drawing my knees to my chest, the pillow at my back. I'm humming with an orgasm just under the surface. My arousal coats the inside of my thighs, and I'm close to drooling.

"Long enough," Dušan answers, his voice raspy, his eyes already glazed over with lust.

"And you were okay with him attacking me while being controlled by his wolf?"

Lucien shrugs. "You seemed to be having fun." He turns to Bardhyl. "When'd you get back, man?"

"Earlier. Popped in to find the house empty at first."

Rage rises through me. "What the hell? So you're not out of control?"

Bardhyl glances over and winks at me. "Oh, cupcake, it's just a little payback for tying me up in the cave."

My mouth drops open at the revelation that he did all that as revenge. I snatch the pillow at my back and toss it at him, hitting him square in the chest. "You bastard."

"And you, my sweet cherry pie, are a horny little girl with the most perfect and sweetest pussy in the world."

I'm lost for words, not sure what to say. I throw him a frown, because now I'm left unsatisfied, and I sure as hell am not showing Bardhyl that I need him. He can suffer for all I care.

But before I can get off the bed, Dušan closes the distance, peeling off his shirt. "You're not finished, gorgeous."

His words send a shiver down my spine, and my clit twitches as if it might bring me to orgasm the moment they touch me.

"Agreed." Lucien is next to him, taking off his pants and shirt, his cock erect. I can't stop staring. In seconds, all three are standing over me, naked and palming their cocks. Holy crap… How exactly is this going to work?

"Maybe we should make a bet?" Bardhyl starts, eyeing me. "Let's see if you can resist not coming tonight?"

"Shut up with your stupid bets," I state. "They somehow always lead to you winning."

He winks and smiles coyly. Right now I'm in bed naked, surrounded by sex-starved wolves, and my libido is craving them. And Bardhyl is back to his usual self.

Dušan climbs onto the bed with me, prowling closer, and in a flash, I forget everything. I shudder from the shiver racing over my slick heat.

Guess it's too late to turn back now, isn't it? This has to be the wildest thing I've ever done, and I'm freaking excited at the prospect of what's about to happen.

I chew on my lower lip, and Dušan is on me in seconds, his mouth on mine. He kisses me with aggression, taking what he wants. I make a strange sound in my throat as I slip under his spell. His body against mine is sizzling. His hand cups my breast, and I moan, pushing my chest toward him. His touch, his kiss, his voice pull at my nerve endings.

Heat flares between my thighs. I'm so horny from what Bardhyl started earlier, and Dušan ignites it back up to another level. His fingers slide down my stomach, over the small mound of hair. I widen my legs, needing him as he shifts to position himself between them.

Lucien and Bardhyl watch like this is a show for them… but they know they're waiting for their turns. And I can't believe I'm so turned on by this. A finger slides into me, then another, and every nerve ending in my body crackles.

I throw my head back, falling onto my back on the bed. My heart pounding, I moan as Dušan fingers me and takes a nipple into his mouth, sucking, gnawing.

Blood rushes south, and I'm so near to bursting from arousal, I don't think I can hold on for much longer. I rock my hips back and forth when Dušan suddenly stops and draws his fingers out.

I protest with a groan as he pulls back and sits on his heels on the bed, eating me with his gaze. His cock is so erect and large, the bulbous tip coated in pre-cum.

"What's going on?" I ask. "Why did you stop?"

He takes my hand and draws me to sit upright. He lies on his back across the bed and tucks his hands behind his head. "You're too close," he tells me.

"And? What's wrong with that?" I purse my lips. He's not resistant to the allure we have, the invisible chemistry that hums between us, the one that makes us fated mates.

"Tonight is for so much more. Tell me what you want me to do," he commands.

"I want you to make me come, to make me scream, to ease the growing ache in my body from how much I need you all."

"Then tell me to fuck you."

I kind of like his dominance more than I ever thought I would.

"Will you fuck me?" I ask, my voice soft and shaky. I want this, need this. So I don't hesitate to place one leg over his lap and straddle him, his erection grazing across my entrance. He's so smooth and hot, and he reaches up to grab my breasts. It's easy to push myself over his erection. I'm so wet that I slide over him, my walls clenching around him as I lower myself.

As his eyes roll back and a delicious groan builds in his throat, I find my bravery to really do this to my satisfaction. As I inch him into me, I feel myself stretch. I shake while he grasps my waist and bucks his hips up, driving himself further inside.

I cry out with strokes of pain and pleasure. But he can't stop himself, pumping into me, and then I'm riding him, Lucien and Bardhyl staring at my bouncing breasts.

Goosebumps flare over my skin, the friction Dušan generates burning me up from the inside out.

"This is so fucking hot." Lucien growls.

Bardhyl moves to stand at the end of the bed, right alongside us, and he palms his cock.

I angle myself forward, one hand perched on the mattress, the other reaching for Bardhyl's cock. Steel covered in silk, he's so hard and thick. I shift my head toward him, and he steps closer for easier access. He guides his dick into my mouth, tasting salty and strangely sweet. I have half a mind to prank him right now.

But Dušan is pounding into me so hard that I can't think of anything beyond our crazy sex act.

Bardhyl pushes deeper into my mouth and I suck on him. That's when hands clasp my ass, and it takes me a second to realize Lucien is now behind me. I know exactly where this is going.

Dušan slows as Lucien's fingers glide over my ass, using my juices to coat me.

"Babe, you're so wet and ready for me." He glides a finger into my ass and my muscles clench. "So tight. Just let me in, okay?"

I don't answer because I'm sucking on Bardhyl. But when I feel Lucien's tip edging into my puckered ass, I stiffen.

Dušan stokes my breasts, pinching my nipples. An electric buzz runs down my back.

Lucien pushes into me slowly, working his way in without any rush, and I appreciate that so much.

They're so tender with me when needed, and they know just how much pressure to apply when they're savage.

When all three men completely fill me, moisture floods me. They start grinding into me, all of us in a rhythm. I'm throbbing and aching with desire. They hold me up and fuck me while I dig my hands into the blanket, fire flaring on my skin. I've never felt so fulfilled, so right, so wanted.

"You're beautiful," Dušan groans, his hips pounding me, his cock pushing in and out past my pussy's lips.

Lucien's fingers massage my ass cheeks as he takes me from behind. The friction he ignites brings on a different level of exhilaration. Bardhyl's cock fills my mouth, his large hand on my back.

A moan rolls in my throat, and a trembling starts deep within me. Then I explode with an orgasm that slams into me like the most powerful storm. It rips through and takes everything before I even know what's hit me. I convulse, and my body clenches. The men growl and hiss.

Even as I float on my climax, their own happy endings burst forward, flooding me with their seed, the tips of their cocks swelling, knotting and locking in place. Dušan's and Lucien's cocks press against my inner walls, snug and tight in there.

Bardhyl howls, and warmth spills into my mouth as he comes. I swallow him, accept him into me, loving how in this one perfect moment, we are one. And a bit of each of them is now a part of me.

Heat flares over me as the guys' muscles tense. My sex squeezes as I float down from heaven.

Bardhyl pulls out and drops to his knees alongside us, his eyes glazed over as he roars with the explosive arousal. "Oh, cupcake, your mouth is wicked and delicious." His lips are on my shoulder, licking me, nibbling on my flesh, his hand finding a breast.

A sudden, eruptive power comes out of nowhere and sweeps over my body. A dark, all-consuming wolf energy I've never felt before. It crashes through me, punching forward. The combination of my body vibrating and the men filling me, does something to me. My wolf rubs within me, and her sweet smell engulfs me. It's overbearing, to the point where I no longer smell my Alphas.

An ache burrows through me.

The men remain glued beside me. But I'm changing, and a sliver of panic arises in that moment. Will I change while two knotted cocks are wedged inside me?

I whimper with the fear that I can't do this, that my wolf will overpower me and kill all of us in this perfect moment of ecstasy.

The images of all of us dead haunt me while energy bubbles and slithers down my spine, crawling through me from my head to my toes and everywhere else in between.

Dušan hisses with pleasure beneath me while Lucien's hand grips my ass, but it's only Bardhyl who doesn't make a sound. When I look at him, I see the whiteness of his cheeks. He feels it too…

He starts to stand when Dušan snarls. "Don't fucking break our connection." His voice deepens, and of course, he's sensed the energy between us. How could he not?

Is this the moment I shift? When everything can come to a halting end or a new beginning?

CHAPTER 18

MEIRA

Bardhyl finds my mouth, and he kisses me deeply. Goosebumps spread over my skin as flashes of fiery energy pop over my vision and in my mind.

It escalates quicker. A heat consumes us, and for those few moments, I feel like I'm floating amid the stars with my men, in a place where no one but us exists. But I can't shake the trepidation tensing my muscles that this might be the moment I shift.

My Alphas growl, as if their wolves are responding to my power. Maybe they are. My heart pounds savagely and heat burns me up. Sweat rolls down my spine, and suddenly, the pressure from their knots inside me ease. Yet Bardhyl's tongue continues to tangle with mine, and our kiss is hypnotic.

I inhale all their scents. I feel them... but what's between us is so much more than physical. There's the faintest stroke of fur against me, as if they are right beside me in their wolf forms. I flip open my eyelids. All three are still human.

Bright light blinks behind my eyes.

In a heartbeat, something snaps inside me.

Crack.

It sounds like bones breaking, but there's no pain, only that constant, annoying light behind my eyes that blinds me. It reminds me in a strange way of the moon...

My wolf rolls around within me, more active than she's ever been. She spreads through me, consuming me.

I open myself to her.

You're safe to come out. Join us.

A swift, sharp pain slashes across my chest, and I shatter. I scream, the pain swelling like someone is pouring acid over my skin.

I cry out, then pass out.

Coldness washes over my brow, and it takes me a few seconds to come to my senses and recall everything.

The Alphas.

Insanely delicious sex.

And something changing in me.

My wolf.

I snap open my eyes and shoot upright, finding myself sitting in bed. Dušan sits next to me, holding a damp towel. Lucien lies at my feet, while Bardhyl is on my other side. They all stare at me with shock in their faces.

I wrench my gaze to a blanket covering me to my waist, but I'm human, and there's no fur in sight.

"What's going on?" I ask, blurry on what happened right at the end of our groups sex.

"You passed out, cupcake."

I look over to Bardhyl, who stays close, still naked, as are the others. He reaches over and pushes away the sweaty hair stuck to the side of my face. His touch is tender and warm, luring me to lean closer and shut my eyes again.

But I shake away the urge, needing to understand.

"Did I change? It felt like maybe I did?"

No one responds at first, and when I meet Dušan's gaze, he shakes his head. "You're a goddess, Meira. The energy your body expelled sent unimaginable strength into our bodies. Your wolf lingered just below the surface. I felt her, called to her. But she never came."

I don't know how to feel. Sorrowful. Disappointed. Scared. Confusion crawls through me as I attempt to piece it all together, chasing away the other emotions.

"The moon," I state and quickly shuffle from the bed, pushing past the guys, the blanket sliding down from around my body. Naked, I hurry to the window and push aside the heavy curtain to stare outside. The first threads of sunlight spear upward from the horizon, staining the sky in oranges and reds. Shadows claim the woodland in the distance.

I scan the heavens for the moon.

"Did you hear something?" Dušan whispers behind me, the heat from his body spreading over me.

"It's only half a moon," I say. "It was so weird. One moment we are all together in bed, then a strange power swept over me, like my wolf would come out. I swore she would, and I sensed the moon calling to me. What went wrong?"

His large hands fall to my hips, drawing me away from the window. He turns me to face him. "A wolf's power comes from the moon, but it doesn't have to be full to affect us. Legend says the first wolf was born during a hunters' moon. A pack of normal wolves savagely attacked a human. She barely clung on to life after the brutal assault. But the only way to save her was with the blessing from the moon. Her energies blended with the energies of the wolves, from their saliva and blood that had seeped into her body. On the next full moon, she changed for the first time into what we are today. She is the first of our kind. Stories say she bore children to nine different men, and they all spread out across the world to populate the land."

I blink at him. "Is that a true story?"

He shrugs. "It's an origin myth, but while the details are sketchy, we do grow stronger on full moons and become more animalistic. Any wounds we have heal instantly on those nights. But our transformations aren't influenced by the moon's phases."

"Then why didn't my change work?" I breathe the words, barely a whisper. My throat thickens, feeling like I'm always fighting to barely keep my head above the waves. Nothing I do gives me a fucking break.

Dušan slides a hand to the side of my face, drawing me closer. "We are so close, gorgeous. Tomorrow we will all bond again, building the energy between us. And we'll do it again and again until she comes out. Together we'll guide your wolf to emerge safely."

Doubt dances around in my mind as I recall the sharp pain that sliced through me when I thought she was coming out. Something held her back. "What if—"

"No," Dušan insists. "I could practically touch her. In the next week, you are transforming."

His confidence is heartwarming, and I desperately want to believe he's right. I sweep my focus to Lucien and Bardhyl, who stand by the bed, looking at us, expecting something I can't give. I feel like I've let them down, yet Dušan has so much hope in his eyes that I remain quiet.

His slow, circular movements on my back ease the worry for now. "Come. We'll all get dressed and leave. We'll arrive home soon, and everything will be good once more."

Either he's convinced himself that I'm already saved, or he's doing an amazing job of sounding like he carries no doubts.

My heart thunders in my ears while coldness drops through me. But I don't voice my fears. Instead, I respond with a forced smile.

On the inside, my thoughts chant, *Please let my wolf come. Let her not kill me in the process.*

Dušan

The midday sun blares down on us. We've been walking since dawn. We come across no rogue wolves or packs, and the few undead we encountered werc too far away to catch up to us.

"When we get back, I vote for us all having a group bath in our pool," Lucien suggests, his gaze all for Meira.

She's beautiful, captivating, and scared as hell. She smiles cheerfully, but it's all pretend. I see it in the tightness around her mouth, I smell it in the perspiration that's heavier than it'd normally be at our walking pace. Her chest rises and falls like the rush of the rampant river.

"Agreed. So it shall be," Bardhyl replies. "Meira, I will teach you to duck swim. Even if you don't know how to swim, this will help."

Meira cuts him a confused look and her light laugh is genuine. She truly adores the men, and they bring out a playful side in her, which I love.

"I'm not picturing this duck swim," she answers. "Don't they just float on top of the water and kick their legs underneath?"

"Lucien taught it to me once."

Lucien chuckles, slapping a hand to Bardhyl's back. "It's not a fucking duck. I told you that before, man. It's called butterfly breast-stroking, and it's one of the most difficult styles to learn and master."

Bardhyl scoffs, but he claims he can do anything before he's tried it.

"Do butterflies even swim?" Meira asks, her brow arching.

"It's just the technique, the arm movements in the water depict their wings," I explain. "But I do agree, swimming might help strengthen and build endurance for when your wolf comes out."

She drags her gaze from Lucien and Bardhyl to me. "I agree to a pool party, and I'm sure I will pick up this swimming technique easily." Her eyes challenge Bardhyl.

The three of them break into chatter, but I'm struggling to focus on anything but last night's events.

Her hope was shattered when she discovered she hadn't trans-formed. It'd been heartbreaking to watch her expression crumble. I won't deny I had my hopes up that she would experience her first shift last night. The energy lifted all the hairs on my body; my wolf bounced inside me frantically for her release.

But she never did… Why the fuck not?

I say nothing about my worries. Not until I have time to look into her blood results and understand what piece of the puzzle I'm missing.

We aren't far from the compound, and these woods are familiar now. I couldn't be happier to be surrounded by my pack and the safety of our walls. I'll deal with Mad and his bullshit after I heal Meira. That's my priority.

I listen to them ramble about swimming, and I realize that maybe sharing her with my two closest pack members and friends will work out better than I expected. Though there will be some nights I'll want her completely for myself and no damn sharing will be happening.

The trees thin the closer we get to the compound, and already I can see the top of the old fortress in the distance. I can't keep the smile off my face. I never thought I'd be so happy to be home.

A sudden, heavy scent of wet dog fur and freshly turned soil, finds me on the breeze that whistles past us. My hackles bristle. Wolves.

Bardhyl and Lucien ease back, Meira between them.

Dead silence floods the woods.

I cut my men a look of concern. "Keep her close."

I smell it again, and I sniff the air, confirming it's Ash Wolves. Before I can respond, movement from my right draws my attention.

"Dušan," a male commands, the voice familiar. When the stranger emerges from the shadows of the forest, it's Danu, a Beta I recognize. I've spoken to him maybe once or twice before. My pack grows weekly, and I try to do the rounds to familiarize myself with everyone, but he's a recent recruit. He stands twenty feet away, tall and lanky with short, golden hair. He stares at us like a stunned deer.

"Did something happen to you?" I ask, closing the distance between us.

He doesn't respond but looks scared, his shoulders drooping forward, panic flashing in his gaze.

A low snarl reverberates in my head that something is wrong.

An unexpected explosion of thunderous footsteps drum behind me like a storm.

I pivot around to discover a dozen Ash Wolves in human form charging at us from all around. Members I've enjoyed a meal with, shared a beer with... Now anger warps their expressions toward us. I'm fucking confused about what is going on, and I react too slowly.

Bardhyl whips around, but one Beta has jumped onto his back, the other kicking his legs out from under him. He snarls, his arms flying as he loses his balance and hits the ground on his knees. The Beta on his back injects a syringe into his neck. The Viking pushes them aside with a wild swing of his arm, sending them off their feet. He clutches the side of his neck and stumbles before falling to his knees and flat on his face.

Fuck!

I lunge toward them, roaring, my pulse on overdrive, while Lucien drags Meira to safety. She's stumbling to get away, her eyes wide at the unwarranted attack.

But it's too late. Others crash-tackle Lucien and shove her to the ground. He attacks one of them, but three more jump on him. Meira frantically scrambles to her feet and picks up a branch as a weapon.

I charge and whip my arm around Meira's waist, wrenching her to my side.

"What the hell is going on?" she murmurs.

I back away from the dozen Ash Wolves, members who are supposed to be loyal to me. Lucien lies on the ground, buried under three men, Bardhyl passed out from whatever drugs they injected him with.

Ice fills my veins.

"You will pay with your life for this deceit." I growl, fully aware that we've been ambushed. How long have they waited out here for our return?

Meira is tucked against my side. I'll rip apart every one of these fuckers if they touch her.

I scan their faces, memorizing each one for when I come for them. Rein meets my gaze... a younger man whom I saved from the undead and brought into our compound. He'd lost his family to the creatures. His attention flicks from me to the woods at my side.

I jerk around and my throat closes.

Mad.

My fucking stepbrother emerges from the shadowy woodlands. His ice blue eyes pierce into me, white-blond hair fluttering in the breeze. He's dressed immaculately in pressed pants, boots, and... is that my white button-up shirt? Rage echoes through me.

"What the fuck have you done?" I nudge Meira behind me and lift my chin, my hands curling into fists. I want to rip the smirk off his face.

I should have killed him the moment he returned to the compound. Should have known he'd have allies. Should have been smarter, but finding my fated mate was my priority. It was also a deadly distraction.

"Brother, you took your time returning. Glad you brought the bitch back."

I spit on the ground between us. "I'll tear your spine out if you touch her."

Except it's too late. I see our fate in his hateful smirk, in us being trapped by wolves who've betrayed me. My stomach twists in on itself at the thought of what Mad must have offered them to convert to his side. The promise of immunity against the undead?

Meira is suddenly wrenched from my grasp, her cries ringing in the air.

I spin and lunge after the two men seizing her from me. She screams, one of her arms flinging free from her captors and reaching for me. The dread on her face will stay with me for eternity.

My wolf claws for release to destroy them. All I see is red and their deaths as I run to her, barely inches from claiming her back.

"Dušan!" Meira calls to me, her gaze on something behind me.

In that moment, a hard punch connects with the middle of my back, sending me sprawling forward on hands and knees. I try to get up, but Mad locks an iron arm around my neck, keeping me down.

"She's no longer yours," he whispers in my ear, his voice gravelly and flooded with wry mirth.

Murder plays on my mind. How much I will enjoy taking his life. I tremble with fury and thrust against him. But everything dissolves when I watch Rein jab a needle into the side of Meira's neck.

Her cries cut me.

I explode, my wolf pushing to tear out of me.

The sharp prick of a needle jammed into my neck comes fast, as do the tingles that rush through my limbs. Then the numbness hits.

Mad drives a fist into my shoulder, just as I'd done to him back at the pack house fortress. I collapse forward. My heart beats hysterically as I crash to the ground, devastation fueling my rage.

The world sits sideways in my view as I lie on the ground. Meira is on hands and knees, gasping for air like she's choking.

My mouth opens, but only a gurgled sound comes out.

She's screaming with agony, her back arching. Skin splitting and fur spilling out, her bones stretching, her jaw elongating.

The change has come now.

Oh, shit!

Straining, I shove myself up to my feet. The world spins and I can't even feel my body. Adrenaline owns me, and I grasp onto those moments. I need to get to her. Connect with her energy to help her shift.

Meira!

Her gaze finds me, and behind those wolf eyes lies my little gorgeous girl. Her panic calls to me, fueling the fear that curls around my heart that she won't survive the change, that the wolf will kill her.

Growling under my breath, I push my numb legs to move forward so I can see her through her first transformation. One step and someone strikes me in the back of my head. My vision dances with stars.

I roar and slam to the ground like a sack. I'm fucking useless, and it's killing me to hear her screams.

Shadows feather the edges of my vision. Darkness comes for me, but I fight whatever Mad injected into me. I tense up and push harder against the toxin in my veins.

I hold on to Meira's gaze, though my muscles refuse to respond, to help me get up again.

She thrusts and fights the change. Mad and his minions are standing around, watching her. She's mid-transformation, her cries like blades to my throat. First changes are gruesome and fucking excruciating. All I want is to take her into my arms as she shifts. To help her through this.

The fire inside me grows uncontrollably. Everything we've done to help her has been for nothing.

Her shredded clothes lay by her feet and she shakes herself, dragging herself up in her wolf form… a tawny, reddish pelt, round ears darker in color. She's not a huge wolf, but she's spectacular. Her eyes are pale with only a tinge of bronze, except I no longer see any sign of my Meira behind them.

My heart cracks in half, the agony slicing my insides, and all I can think about is her smile, her laughter, her body against mine. The joy she brought me will ruin me. I can't go on without her by my side.

Please don't let the wolf have killed my sweet Meira.

Seconds is all it takes for her to scan her surroundings and sniff the air.

A fraction of time for her to snarl at the two men lunging for her.

Lips peeled back, she growls with immense fierceness and turns on them with a aggression only comparable to Bardhyl's. She is nothing like Meira.

The wolf tears right into Rein and rips out half his stomach with one vicious bite.

A split second later, and she's on the rampage for the others.

Screams and a wild battle begins.

If the wolf has completely taken her over and she's gone, she will kill us all. If I manage to somehow survive this, I swear on my life that I will destroy every last fucking asshole who stood against us on this day.

For you Meira, I will burn down this world.

SHADOWLANDS SECTOR

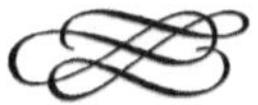

THREE

BOOK THREE

There is no more running...
    ...this time, I'm willing to fight to the death. Mine and theirs.

Because of me, my three mates have been captured by our enemy, and once again I am all alone.

But I can't let the enemy's treachery be their fate. Not for me, not for the future we thought we had.

My only option is to take this fight to him. Let embrace the monster inside me I have feared my whole life.

The enemy thinks I'm the key to his biggest problem...

The undead.

I can't be that key. I must return. I must save my men. No matter the cost.

I'm running out of time. My life for the alphas.

I have one choice. That's an easy decision. And my monster agrees. We're out for blood, and this time I'm not leaving until the enemy pays.

CHAPTER 1

MEIRA

Fear strangles my chest.

I step back, using all four paws easily, which is strange in itself.

I'm a freaking wolf with tawny, reddish fur. No longer the girl I was a year ago… or even the girl I was yesterday. We live in a brutal world and it changes you. Both mentally and physically in my case.

My gaze whips to my three men, three Alphas… three mates who've claimed me. And it kills me to see them lying on the ground, knocked out by Mad's men to get to me. And all I can remember is them being attacked, the terror in Dušan's eyes as he fell. Then I transformed.

These men who've attacked us inch toward me, a semi-circle of half a dozen.

I want them to pay with every fibre of my being, but I'm not even sure how to control my new wolf body.

My wolf is her own entity and it's like there's two of us in my body fighting for dominance. Is that how the other wolves feel?

She shoves against my insides, and I stumble on my feet to grasp onto any semblance of normality.

Involuntarily tilting my head back, I raise my chin and unleash a shattering howl.

A shiver flares over me, my mind fluttering between sanity and the savagery of my wolf. She's so strong I can barely hold her back.

Hunger and revenge course through me, the emotions rip at me. She craves death, unlike anything I've ever imagined.

Pure addictive ferocity, and I'm salivating at the thought. Except that's not me, is it?

Mad and his assholes approach me in slow motion in a semi-circle to trap me. Still, fear swims in their gazes and I smell it in their air like sour perspiration.

The syringe draws my attention to Mad's fist.

A tall brute lunges toward me, roaring more like a bear than a wolf. Something flashes over my thoughts, like a spark of energy.

Next thing, I'm darting toward the man threatening me, my head in two places at once. I scream on the inside as I crash into his middle, and bring him down fast. While my wolf snarls with satisfaction, panic frantically chills my bones that she has control over me. That I am the one in the backseat of this relationship.

Faster than lightning, she snaps back to his face, teeth sinking into his neck. She rips out his throat so fast, the man has no chance to scream.

Terror latches onto me, and I'm backpedaling, grappling to draw her back. My mind drowns in images of her completely dominating me.

I cling onto that semblance of control as she pulls against me.

If I truly let go and my wolf were to take charge, will I ever find myself again?

Mad smirks, not even caring that his man is gurgling on his own blood at his feet.

I growl, lips peeled back, the back of my neck bristling with fur. The white haired Alpha had captured me in the woods so long ago to trade me. He's going to pay for ambushing his true Alpha, Dušan, and betraying him.

One of his fighters, a barrel of a man, comes at me, a snarl on his lips. Another charges my way too, already in animal form. A gray wolf with a huge head.

Instinct jolts through me, and my wolf snaps into action, taking charge. Except, I hold on and am there with her, both of us pressed together in the driver's seat. Shoulder to shoulder, we shove each other while battling the real enemy outside.

I leap at the first man, suddenly feeling like I'm flying from the strength in my body. I crash into him, headfirst into his gut. He groans, but still lands a punch to my back. My knees wobble, but I never cower away.

My body tingles, and I pivot around and lunge up to bite deep into his shoulder, ripping away flesh to the bone, blood gushing free, splattering the dead leaves around us. The coppery taste is like dirt across my tongue, my body trembling with uncontrollable fury. The need to rip them all apart soars through me.

Something white flashes behind my eyes, an unsatisfiable rage, blinding me.

Another attacker smacks into my side hard, throwing me off my feet and to the ground with a thud. I'm shaking violently, my head still spinning.

His weight presses down on me, and footfalls close in around me.

But I won't be caught, not ever again.

I fucking won't.

I buck against the idiot and snap my head around, ripping my teeth into his arm. Tearing away with skin and fabric, I don't relent as he cries out.

Heat lashes over me, and I scramble to my feet, growling. I recoil from the four approaching monsters. Mad strides forward, his white hair blown off his face from the wind, the bastard looking older, more exhausted than when I last saw him. But a fuckhead is still a fuckhead. His twisted expression is one of a man who is disgusted by what he sees; me standing up for myself.

I can't look away from the syringe he grasps. They already jabbed me once in the neck, and it forced me into a transformation. I somehow doubt that was their intention, or that they expected me to put up such a battle.

My legs tremble beneath me, and adrenaline pumps through my veins, keeping me going. Except, my wolf suddenly drives me aside, and I refuse to stop her. I'm stumbling on my feet, snarling at myself until I crash into a tree.

"What the fuck's wrong with her?" someone asks.

"Stop fighting," Mad's voice cuts through the madness in my head. "I can take care of you. Protect you."

I growl in response. Liar!

"Your choice, Meira." He lifts the syringe. "Come with us calmly and I promise to release my stepbrother and his two men. Keep fighting and we'll take you by force. And with that, I can guarantee I will kill them."

He suddenly pauses as do his men, each of them glaring at me like I'm nothing but a means to an end. I know exactly what he wants from me… my blood. They think I am the cure to a zombie infection. Sad fucks have no idea how wrong they are.

My heart pounds in my ears, my wolf growling in my chest shuddering with violent need, but it's four against one. Even I'm not that foolish to believe I'll win. Another reason I need to pull back my wolf. Especially now that a wounded wolf is climbing to his feet.

I swallow hard as my breaths speed up.

Mad's expression darkens, and underneath the storm in his eyes, there is desperation—one I've seen on power-hungry Alphas before. He'll do anything, kill anyone to get what he wants.

Really, I have one option: get to Mad first and tear him apart while not losing myself to my wolf.

Easier said than done.

Electricity hums over my skin just as it had when my wolf first pushed out of me. She had my skin ripping, forcing herself to come out. The pain is gone now, knitting my wolf and me as one soul, one being, yet she fights me. This can't be right.

I recoil, my sight never leaving Mad's. This isn't the time to stumble. I step back, bumping into a tree, and I shudder.

My wolf growls her threat at me. She doesn't back away… well I fucking do.

They close in. All five of them. Three are in human form, and two have taken wolf form.

Dread taps fast in my chest. I frantically look around for a way out, for anything. Looking down to my men, they don't stir, and worry sinks through me. What had been in the injections to knock them out so fast?

Tension leaks in the air, while rage bubbles to the surface inside me, bringing with it a lick of fire down my back.

I loathe Mad. Wrath rises through me at what these men deserve.

But pain stings my side from where the bastard slammed into me earlier, pulsing across my ribs.

"Get her!" Mad bellows, and my gut reaction kicks in this time.

I twist and lunge away, ignoring the sensation like I'm trying to turn back around. My wolf's betraying me. Running isn't a sign of weakness, it's knowing when you're outnumbered and working out a way to take out the leader.

I dodge trees and dart deeper into the dense forest, scrambling for escape. Shadows seem brighter now, my vision sharper and crisper. Glancing over my shoulder, the five of them give chase. But it's Mad I need to get… chop off the head and the monster dies.

Swinging forward, I charge when an army of shadows emerge from the woods ahead of me.

Fear rattles me instantly. Have more Alphas surrounded me? I startle and skid to a stop by a massive pine tree, stiffening and swing my head in every direction for a way out.

A raspy groan comes from the woods, followed by more noises, and the clatter of teeth or bones follows.

My skin crawls as the first zombie emerges from the darkness.

I recoil. Will they attack me now that I've transformed? I step against the tree and glance back to the wolves' fear-stricken expressions at seeing who's arrived.

The zombie leading the charge has one missing ear and only a thin layer of hair over a spotty, pale head. Torn clothes hang off his bony frame. Another that comes forward has a mangled arm, others broken limbs.

Then the mass follows like a broken dam. They spill out from the woods, staggering, lurching, groaning. Others are licking the air as if already tasting the blood from the earlier wolves I've bitten and killed. That's what drew them here.

Even more undead stumble out of the woods. There has to be close to thirty.

The leader snaps its jaws and reels forward.

I hastily turn, needing to get out, except… fuck!

Dušan, Lucien, and Bardhyl are still on the ground, lying, waiting to be eaten. Are they covered in blood? I don't remember. Wracking my brain, I can't think straight when the undead approaches.

I dive away to escape, unsure if I'm their food or not.

Leukemia had made me immune to the zombies. A fact I learned recently, and everyone knows when a wolf transforms, all human illnesses heal. That means, I would be a meal for the undead now.

I sprint after Mad and his men who dart out of here, my wolf salivating as she thinks this is a chase. They are already so much farther ahead than me, having taken off the second they saw the Shadow Monsters.

Two more creatures suddenly appear at my right, so fast and unexpected, I do a double-take. My paw hooks under a tree root, and I'm tumbling forward and over my head before I can make sense of what just happened. I smack the ground hard and scramble to my feet.

Panic slams into me, feeling vulnerable and open.

Shadows crowd in around me, seeming to come from every direction.

Teeth gnashing, they close in, and I shuffle backward, ice filling my lungs that they're coming for me.

The creatures stumble forward, and I shudder. But then they dart right past me without pause.

Startled, I can't believe my eyes at first, and I study them flowing right past me. They don't notice or touch me!

It takes me moments to come to terms that I'm safe… and it's my wolf that takes charge and growls, warning them.

With their sloppy gait, they approach regardless.

One of them brushes right past me, and I flinch away. But they don't stop. Moaning, they stumble after Mad and his men. These monsters that should attack me don't. Skin peeling away, jaws dislocated, dried blood around their faces, they don't see me.

I'm invisible to them.

My head spins at first, trying to make sense of why they didn't attack me.

Am I still sick? I blink, watching them move away.

But reality catches up with me too, and I need to get my men to safety. I throw myself into the herd and shove them aside to get ahead.

Leaping over logs and dodging zombies, I burst out in front and into the small clearing where Mad and his men ambushed us.

Except, no one's there.

Not the wolves. Not Mad. And not my men.

Sickness churns in my gut that I'm too late. The bastard took them. I should be happy he saved them from the undead, but it doesn't make my men safe for long.

I'm also livid that he took them from me to ensure he has a bargaining tool to get what he wants. Snarls roll over my chest, and I unleash a pent up howl, desperate to chase them down and take back my wolves.

Seething, I catapult toward the Ash Wolves pack compound to catch up to them. To stop them.

The Shadow Monsters hurry to the spots on the ground where the bloody corpses of my victims lie. Falling to their hands and knees, the disgusting things lick up the remains.

My stomach turns.

I keep going, only trees in my view, as Dušan had said earlier we weren't far from his pack home.

It isn't long before I spot figures ahead, darting deeper in the forest, and a few look like they are carrying someone over their shoulders.

My pulse spikes, and I dart forward when a cry draws my attention to my left. My wolf seems to have pulled back. Did I just have to take control of her? Is that all it took?

I stop running and get a better look. A girl is tied to a tree, a gag over her mouth and she's thrashing for escape.

Jae!

What the heck is she doing here? I bumped into her in the woods days ago when she was like now, tied to a tree by a psycho Alpha. Perhaps Mad and his wolves caught her while they searched for us.

I glance back to Mad and his crew, almost vanishing in the woods from sight. My gut tightens.

Groans grow louder behind me, and I whip around.

Crap! Those damn zombies are making their way toward Jae.

Her eyes widen with fear and she cries frantically, writhing against the bonds keeping her tied to the tree. Mad and the others are moving further ahead, but how the hell am I meant to follow them now? If I do, I'm sending Jae to her death.

Frustration worms through me. But I can't waste time, so I throw myself toward her, scampering over the dried foliage and evergreens covering the land. Trampling anything in my way.

She squirms and draws away from me as much as she can, but I growl at her, then I swing to move behind the tree. Biting into the rope securing her to the trunk, I gnaw on them, tugging, and chewing.

I hear Jae sniffing the air then she glances back over her shoulder, down at me. "Meira is that you?"

My snarl is the only response as I wrestle with the rope.

"Please hurry, they're really close," she cries, making whimpering sounds. I inhale her perspiration and fear.

I wrench at the rope and my teeth bite right through it, releasing it.

She's quick to pull free and toss the bonds aside, then swings toward me. "Let's get out of here!"

And I freeze at first, unsure where to take her. Behind her, half a dozen zombies have noticed the commotion and are coming over.

It doesn't take long for the bastards. They are like the sharks of the land. Smell of blood or any sound that sounds like trouble and they appear to investigate. Just in case it's a meal.

"Meira," Jae calls out and is running in the opposite direction to the compound and away from the zombies.

I want to scream after her that we must get closer to the pack. There are snipers on the gate that will shoot the creatures on site. But all that comes out is a guttural growl.

Because I'm a wolf, and it's only now that it hits me, I don't know how to transform back into a human.

A Shadow Monster slips right past me and runs after Jae.

I lunge after the fiend, crash tackling it, bringing it to the ground. It bucks against me, not staying still, never staying down. Fury billows inside me as three others already pass me.

Jae is bouncing deeper into the woods.

Having had enough, I bite down into the back of its neck. It has a massive, healed scar across his bald head which looks painful, if this man was alive. Something suddenly cracks in its body. Please let that slow it down. I don't wait to find out and sprint after the girl.

Putrid blood taints my tongue, and panic flares that I'd made a terrible mistake. Taking their blood into my body might tip me into becoming one of them or… I don't really know because these creatures ignore me like I am still immune. But the notion still freaks me out. Nothing about what's going on with me follows any rules.

Seconds pass and nothing happens to me. No change or urgent need to kill the living. But I don't have time for this. Not now.

I'm running after Jae, attacking the next three zombies, biting deep into their sides and legs to cause damage, to toss them aside. Anything to slow them down. They don't even react, it's as if I'm invisible to them.

I lose sight of Jae, and I look left and right, I sniff the air to catch her faint scent—powdery and earthy.

In seconds, I am on her heels again. She screams at my approach, until she looks back to see it's only me. "I really hope that is Meira inside there," she says nervously.

Glancing behind me, she realizes we've left the creatures way behind us.

She pauses, resting against a tree, breathing fast.

I inhale raspy breaths, then my tongue dangles out, and more than anything, I need to transform back. Looking up at Jae, she stares at me, tilting her head.

Making a whiny sound, I sit in front of her, unsure how to communicate that I'm stuck.

"Why aren't you changing?" she asks, worry coating her words. "I don't really know this area too well, but there are caves farther up the hill behind me I passed days ago. We can go hide there?" She's breathing heavy and talking quickly.

I nudge my head against her thigh, then start moving toward the mountain so she knows I agree with her plan. Another glance behind us and no sign of the undead following. My attention sweeps over in the direction of the compound, where I want to be heading, not away from it.

But first, I need to get Jae out of harm's way.

She steps up alongside me and we're marching through the shadowy woods. She's talking, but I'm not listening at first. Instead, I scan the woods, smell scents, listen for sounds. Then I look up at Jae.

"Meira, please don't tell me you don't know how to change back from wolf form. I once heard of a wolf who got trapped and stayed in her animal form her whole life."

My heart jackhammers at her words. Is she serious? I don't hear another word she says when panic replaces everything else I feel with a dreadful sinking feeling.

I can't be stuck in my wolf form. Please, no!

CHAPTER 2

DUŠAN

$\mathcal{A}$ hard fist connects to my back, driving me into the dingy prison cell. Fire burns through my veins as I whip back around to the door made of iron bars slamming shut with a thunderous clang, locking me inside.

The whole room feels like it tilts on its axis, the dark stone walls, the floor covered in dirt and stinking of urine, and I stumble, crashing into the wall, losing my balance. Whatever the fuck they injected into me knocked me out cold. Even when I came to, moments before reaching the cell, I could barely stand, let alone think straight.

I shake my head to clear the fog in my mind. When I glance up, I meet Mad's gaze. He leans against the wall outside my cell in a wide stance, hands deep in his pockets. Shadows gather under his eyes and his mouth splits into a smirk, revealing yellowed teeth.

There's no sign of Lucien or Bardhyl, and only when I look around do I note I'm in the deepest prison, my underground prison. I have two floors of cells since I also use them to help Ash Wolves struggling on full moons. I once put Mad in here when his wolf had lost control on a blue moon. And now the bastard stuck me in here as a lesson, as torment, I have no doubt.

"You asshole!" A growl rolls over my throat as I push myself to stand upright. Every inch of me hurts while my thoughts lock on Meira and the last time I saw her. Mad's wolves injected her, then she experienced her first transformation. My fists curl and I want to slam Mad's head into the wall for touching her. I don't even know if she survived the change, and the thought brings a stabbing pain deep in my chest. I might have lost her.

I have to believe she's alive, or why else would my asshole step-brother be in here alone? Hell, he'd bring her carcass to haunt me if she were dead. My pulse ices over at the thought.

I promised to be there for Meira, but I let her down at the one time she needed me the most. All because of the weasel I'm going to murder. He betrayed me, and I should never have left him alone in the prison. Of course, he had allies to break him out… I fucking hate hindsight, but would I change things if I had my time over? Not if it meant not finding Meira.

Rage collides into me, and I roar more like a lion than a wolf at how fucked-up everything turned out.

I lunge forward, shaking the bars. "Let me the hell out!" I bellow.

"Brother, why would I do that?"

I spit on the floor between us. "You are not my real brother, but you are everything like your father."

His expression twists in a flash from a calm demeanor to a raging bull. He bursts toward me, nostrils flaring. His ice-blue eyes narrow, while his white hair sits wildly around his face. I want him fuming so he makes a mistake, comes in for me. Desperation for a savage fight rattles through me, and my sights are set on the wolf I should have eliminated long ago. I should have listened to Lucien and Bardhyl. But that's not a miscalculation I'll make again.

Mad stops just out of reach from me, strangely in control for someone who rarely thought before he acted. His entire body trembles, and he inhales heavily, the struggle to hold back clear. He stands as broad as me, but runs from most fights. So I poke the bear.

"Father betrayed us, hated us, beat us. You loathed him for what he did, and yet you became the monster you feared as a child."

"You're a fucking weak leader," he spits. "Father was right about that, it seems." He cracks his neck and lifts his chin. "Your pack is crying out for a solution to the undead, but instead, you play trading games with a damn Alpha who has a cure for his members. You're a laughing stock, and I'm no longer sitting back and letting you kill everyone here as those abominations break into my compound again."

I clench my teeth, grinding my back molars, but I refuse to let him get to me. He's a liar. The relations I have with other Alphas like Ander in X-Clan is the way of the future. Not stealing or bringing war to our doorstep from deceit.

"You're a fool." I growl. "Ander's serum is not a solution for us. It's tailormade for *their* race of wolves. You risked everything by—"

"And I'd risk it all again to save this pack!" he shouts.

I huff. "You mean to save yourself."

A guttural snarl reverberates from his chest. "Your time is over, brother. I've been your lackey long enough. Now it's time to show you how a real pack is run. And that little slut of yours will spread her legs for me, and her blood will help me bring immunity to the pack... *my* pack!" He slams a fist against his chest, his head high, so fucking proud of himself.

All I can think about is ripping out his throat, my hands curling into balls. If there's one bright light to come out of this asshole's mouth, it's his admittance that Meira is alive. That sliver of hope floods me with the determination to never stop fighting.

"So, you have what you want, what the fuck do you want with me?" I snap, needing to know his motivation and understand how long I have to escape before my time is up. Mad does everything for a reason that benefits him.

I'm under no illusion that Mad will finish me. He knows as well as I do that I will never just stand by and watch him take my pack from me.

He bursts into maniacal laughter and begins to stroll toward the exit door. "How else do you think I'm going to claim your wolf girl?"

Sonofabitch! I'm his bait.

Meira slipped away from him, and now he's hoping she will come back for me so he can trap her.

For the love of all things, I pray to the moon goddess that Meira runs as far from this place as possible. If I escape, I'll find her even if I have to search the entire world. For once, I hope she runs.

LUCIEN

"That fucktard, lying, wankface cockroach," Bardhyl murmurs under his breath as he paces back and forth in our small prison. Pale blond hair flutters over his broad shoulders, his vivid green eyes narrowing as he scowls. He's a damn huge bear of a wolf, a Viking who's eager to fight.

My head still hurts from whatever the hell was jammed into me with the syringe, and now we were brought back into the compound to be tossed in the dungeon.

Jolting, I sit upright, my head spinning, and I scan the filthy cell, the barred walls revealing that the other three prisons are empty. We're down here alone. "Where're Dušan and Meira?"

"No idea. But we're going to break out of here and find them." He pauses in front of me as I climb to my feet.

"It's close to impossible to get out of here. We made sure of that." The window isn't in our cell, and we've had these bars and locks secured to resist a wild werewolf's attack.

"We will with sheer brute force." Bardhyl growls with each rapid breath he takes, clearly not thinking straight.

I rub the side of my neck, where I feel the lump from the injection. Mad's ambush came so fast… the bastards must have seen us coming and we walked right into their ambush. *Fuck!* I cross the prison, a mere three paces, and stare out into the dark hallway, finding the door into this basement shut. There's no sign of a guard watching us, and keys are never kept down here for obvious safety reasons.

"With brute force! Didn't you hear me?" Bardhyl stomps toward me.

"No need to repeat yourself. I ignored you just fine the first time. You know as well as I do these dungeons are unbreakable."

He snarls, and I glance over to him as he punches the brick wall. The dull thump that comes with it must hurt, but it doesn't stop him.

"Hold on to your anger. Maybe there *is* a way to break out."

Bardhyl snaps his attention my way. "I'm listening."

"The door hinges on the prison cell are the weakest point. When we had these made, we had several that kept easily snapping off. So if we're lucky, maybe one of these has a weak point."

Bardhyl huffs, squaring his shoulders. "Well, this I can do. I'm the master at breaking things." He marches over to the door, and I track alongside him.

Unease simmers in my gut about where exactly Meira is. I keep telling myself she's with Dušan, but something tells me that's too easy and we need to find her urgently. When Mad is involved, the worst-case scenario is most likely.

I curl my hands into fists at the possibility of what he'd do to her and shake my head, my muscles tense. I already lost my first mate… And I never imagined finding someone else to love, to connect with my wolf, but Meira is that and so much more. My heart squeezes as my throat thickens.

She can't be dead. I'll die before I go through losing her.

CHAPTER 3

MEIRA

I straddle two worlds. The human side that comes from my father, and the wolf from my mama. I grew up being told I'd never truly belong anywhere as long as my wolf refused to show. But now that she has, I don't know how to return to my human form, so what am I supposed to do now? Go hang around in the wilderness with actual wild wolves? I half-sob, half-snicker at the notion.

How in the world am I meant to be with Dušan, Lucien, and Bardhyl? I've been a human for so long that it's all I know, and I kinda liked it. Now, I pace back and forth in the cave up in the mountain, my paws moving swiftly over the stone floor. In a strange way, it almost feels like I'm flying at how fast and easy the movement comes.

A hawk screeches in the distance, and I turn my attention out of the cave's entrance where storm clouds roll over the sky, and a rumble bellows somewhere over the land. Miles of treetops swing back and forth in the rising wind. Dušan's compound lies behind this mountain, and my insides churn every time I think about him and my other two captured men. I want to believe Mad won't hurt them, but I don't trust a single thing about the bastard. I want to rip him to shreds.

"Come over here," Jae says in her soft voice, pulling me from my thoughts. I find her kneeling by the small fire. "I'm going to help you change. You saved me. Now it's my turn to repay the favor."

I startle, staring at this young girl, maybe thirteen or fourteen years old, taking the lead to save me. Her round face glows red from the fire and she has lots of freckles over her nose and cheeks. Her short, dark hair sits messily, and everything about her looks adorable. Even the jeans two sizes too big for her and cinched in by a belt, not to mention her T-shirt with a penguin riding a sleigh on it.

I trot over and flop down on my belly, legs bent under me, but it feels uncomfortable, so I shift and awkwardly stretch my front legs out in front of me. Ah, that's slightly better. Heat from the flames embrace me, and a wave of exhaustion comes over me.

"Relax," Jae says to me. "My sister, Narah, taught me how to change back when I first transformed a couple of years ago. It's as easy as exhaling, but you need to be calm."

Speaking and doing are two very different things. I look up at her and groan with a rushed breath.

She reaches over and strokes the top of my head with her small hand. The impression snakes down my back with the most soothing sensation I've ever experienced, and my eyelids are fluttering with the need to close them.

"There are places in this world that are riddled with secrets and danger," she explains. "But one thing for certain is that our wolves will always be there, and that we have control of our animal side. Think of all the things you experienced in your life up till now, and how afterward, you became a slightly different person. Every day changes you."

I study Jae, who now sits with her legs crossed in front of me. Her words are profound and deep for someone so young, and I'm guessing she is parroting what her sister told her. Maybe one day I'll get to meet her sibling, as she sounds wise.

Jae's fingers scratch over my ears delicately, and my eyes close. "You are in control. Call your wolf inside you."

A gentle ripple skims through me, the warmth from the fire soothing me with its sputtering sounds, and I'm half-falling asleep from Jae's soft petting. A single thought of my wolf retreating crosses my mind, and a sudden sweep of fur brushing against my insides begins.

My mind turns over to memories of going apple picking with Mama as a child, my breaths heavy. And then darkness sweeps over me.

"*M*eira, are you hungry?" a soft female voice asks, then someone shakes me harshly by the shoulder.

In a heartbeat, my memories roll over me like a truck, and I flip open my eyes to Jae's face. She's looking down at me, chewing on something, and the smell of grilled meat has me salivating.

"What are you eating?" I say, the words out loud. I'm human. With a gasp, I lift my hands to see they are in fact hands. No fur or claws or anything animal-like. "Oh, hell yes, I'm back to being me." I get up quickly, staring down at my naked body, cut and bruised, but I changed. It didn't seem too hard to do, though it put me to sleep, so hopefully, that's not a common side effect.

"Thank you so much." I glance over to Jae as she bites into the small drumstick, her chin greasy from the meal. The fire spits and crackles from the two rabbit rotisseries sitting over the flame, and I'm starving.

But my thoughts swivel to my three mates captured by Mad. Behind me, rain drizzles over the land, the sunlight cowering behind the heavy clouds staining the sky.

"I have clothes for you. Come eat before rushing out there," Jae says, smacking her lips.

I follow her pointed finger to the wall across from the fire, where a pile of clothes waits for me. "Where did you find them?"

"At the back of the cave. Told you I was here before, and one thing my eldest sister taught me was that everywhere I stay, I leave a small survival pack."

Dragging on the baggy pants, I pull at the corded string so they don't fall off me, then reach for the black T-shirt. "She sounds smart. You never know when you might be back at a cave. Case in point here."

"Oh, it's not just for me, but for any woman in trouble and needing clothes, fire supplies, and a warm blanket."

I'm partly gobsmacked by her admittance. Why has her idea never crossed my mind before? I was so busy surviving, keeping away from everyone, that helping others who are just trying to live never occurred to me once. And now, I make a note in my mind that it's something I intend to start doing.

I stroll over to the fire and plonk myself down on my heels, already reaching over for a piece of rabbit.

"You were busy while I fell asleep, and I would love to meet your sisters one day." I rip free a drumstick and sit back, eating. The meat is a bit tough, but it's hot and fatty, making it everything I need.

She shrugs, gnawing on a bone before going in for another helping. "I never made it to our spot." Her voice grows faint and she stares into the flames, the blaze dancing in her eyes.

"So tell me, what happened after you ran away from me?" I ask, trying to distract her a bit from the obvious pain of not reaching her sisters. Jae told me last time that they'd gotten separated, but they had a meeting point if that ever happened. Smart. I've heard of people spending weeks trying to cross paths with someone.

"I didn't want you to try stopping me, so I took off to meet with my sisters. One person on her own is easier to slide through the woods unnoticed than two, especially from the undead." She holds herself strong and her fighting spirit reminds me so much of me.

Most likely, I would have done the same in her position.

She swallows the mouthful and wipes her mouth with the back of her hand. "I didn't hear the Alphas sneak up on me. I should have been more careful, and now I'm even farther away from the meeting zone."

"Your sisters will wait for you," I urged.

"I know they will," she answered adamantly. "She made me agree that we'd meet there even if it took years."

The hope in her voice tears through me. I used to believe in so many things before I watched the Shadow Monsters kill my mama. After that, I lost my hope in this wretched world we live in that eats and spits you out daily if you let it. The only way I survived was to become selfish, to accept that no one would come rescue me. I spent many nights crying myself to sleep, and it doesn't get easier being alone. But how can I say those things to Jae when she holds on to that thread of possibility like a lifeline?

"How about we make an agreement?" I suggest. "You don't run away anymore, and I will help you track down your sisters with the Ash Wolves."

Her eyes widen with shock. "Are you mad? No Alphas help Omegas, don't you know that? And I don't intend to be captured."

"You won't be. I have three mates, all Ash Wolves, and well, I need to rescue them from the assholes who tried to kidnap you. Then they will help you get back to the waiting spot, I give you my word." There was no doubt in my mind that they would help.

Jae shakes her head. "You worry about what you need to do, but I don't need your help."

"We all need help sometimes. Like when I rescued you from that rogue Alpha in the woods over a week ago, plus today."

She stiffens, her shoulders squaring. "And I saved you and got you to shift back into your human body. We're even."

I laugh and collect the rest of what's left of the half-eaten rabbit. "I just want to help you, Jae. You leave items in a cave in case other females are in trouble because you want to help too. It's okay to accept assistance."

Her brow furrows instead of fighting back.

Only the crackling fire floods the silence as we eat.

"Why don't you come with me?" she finally says. "Narah will welcome you to stay with us. There will be no Alphas to command or try to rut you." She snarls after saying the words.

And I realize then, she doesn't quite understand the concept of meeting a mate. But I understand. I spent so long hating males, seeing them as nothing more than wanting me as their slave. And some of them are that way, but not all of them. The connection with a fated mate is unbreakable and captivating and alluring. I want to scream that I'm away from mine while they remain in danger. At the back of my mind, I keep wondering if I still have leukemia, seeing as how the Shadow Monsters are keeping their distance from me. But I push those thoughts aside. I can't think about that when I have Alphas to save.

The ache in my chest burns for them, but I'm also not an idiot to know Mad would have wolves out there searching for me. The pouring rain outside is my savior, concealing our scents and that of the cooking rabbit.

That's why this is the time for me to check the perimeter of the compound to see how the hell I'm going to break in to help them.

"My place is here," I answer, something I never thought I'd ever say. For all my life, I've run away.

Except that stops now. The time has come for me to claim what is mine and fight for my three wolves.

I discard the rabbit bones into the fire and wipe my hands down my pants, then get up.

"Where are you going?" Jae asks, a quaver threading through her voice.

"To scope out the Ash Wolves' compound. I need to break in."

She trembles, as if the mere thought terrifies her. "That place is filled with Alphas. Are you sure you don't want to come with me and leave this war zone behind?"

"I've never been more certain in my life about anything. But I hope you change your mind and don't go anywhere," I plead, though based on her past behavior, I doubt she'll listen to me. "Whatever you decide, stay safe."

"You too." She returns to eating, while I head out of the cave and into the tragic weather. It may be wet and cold, but it'll conceal me from the monsters out here.

I have no idea how I'm meant to save them, but I guess I'll come up with something once I reach the pack home.

"Good luck," Jae murmurs behind me.

Yeah, I'll need it.

CHAPTER 4

MEIRA

Rain drenches everything, slips under my clothes, and I'm soaked to the bone. But I welcome the wild weather to keep away the Alphas searching for me, no matter how much I'm trembling with the cold.

The canopy of leaves overhead mostly protect me as I press up against a wide fir tree where only the occasional heavy drops fall onto my head. From my location, I get a clear view of the Ash Wolves' compound.

Thunder roars and the ground trembles, sending the branches into a tremble, throwing more water onto me. But I don't move, even as an icy drop slides down my spine.

A metal fence, about fifteen feet tall, closes in around the settlement. Left and right, it stretches outward. I've circled the perimeter from within the woods already to scope out my potential entry points. There are three into the place.

First, the main entrance gate with two snipers sitting up on the stone posts. There's another on the opposite end from me with one guard, and a third gate to my left at the rear of the settlement. And I remember the guard on the back door. He stood outside my room when I was first brought into this pack, and he always smiled at me. Plus, I've seen him talking to Dušan a few times, and you can always tell a lot about a person by the way they treat others, especially prisoners. I don't even know the man's name, but there was awe in his gaze when he spoke with his Alpha. Perhaps it had to do with him being older than the other guards, so if I trust any of them, it would be him.

Yeah, it's a risk, but what else can I do? I need a way in. Scaling the fence is close to impossible, and breaking it down will bring all sorts of attention. My plan is to sneak in as undetected as possible.

I chew on my lower lip, my stomach churning as I'm standing out here as an easy target should anyone come in from behind me. I keep looking over my shoulder, but with the heavy rain, I can't detect anyone.

The more I stare at the brick fortress beyond the lofty fence, the more I'm reminded of Dušan and the first time he brought me here. Terrified, I would have done anything to escape capture, and ironically, now I'll do anything to get inside.

Steadfast stone walls, the pointy towers, the crenellations across the top. I can't stop thinking about the time Lucien took me up on the top balcony for breakfast, and we shared our first kiss. Later when I escaped my room, the Viking beast, Bardhyl, tracked and dragged me back inside. My heart clenches at the memories, and an urgency drums through me to get to my men faster. Every second that passes, I drown farther in thoughts that I'll lose them. But I can't allow my worries to pull me under. Not until I do everything I can to rescue them. So I need to cause a distraction at the opposite end of the enclosure. Then, I can finally slip into the compound.

I scan the open land and find no sign of anyone, so with my head low, I push out from behind the tree and hurry through the woods. Running, I remain in the shadows and follow the downward sloping land toward the front gates.

While scouting the entry gates to work out which guard looked easiest to convince, I discovered a recently dead deer carcass down in this area that I intend to use for the interference. Now, my heart beating frantically, my lungs burning, and I'm mentally gathering my energy to triumph.

Cause a disturbance.

Then bolt back up to the rear entrance.

Beg the guard to let me in. It's a long shot, but I'll try anything right now.

Rain pelts down on me, the sky growling, and I rush forward when the ground suddenly slips out from under my feet and I fall on my ass. "Argh," I moan from the sharp pain of landing on a branch. Mud coats my pants and hands. "Crap." I get back up, taking the hill slower this time.

Dead ahead, I come around a cluster of trees where the terrain flattens, and where I last saw the dead animal. Except now two Shadow Monsters are hunched over the thing, gorging, their slurpy sounds sickening me.

"Okay, maybe this will work even better," I whisper, meaning I won't have to lure them to me. I skid to a halt several feet away, and that's when I catch movement deeper in the woods, more undead coming to the scent of blood. At least a dozen of them lurch amid the trees.

"Oh, shit." They'll make this harder if I don't move now.

Sucking in a deep breath, I throw myself forward, cringing on the inside that I'm actually going to do this. Reaching the rump of the deer, I grab its hind legs. They are cold and damp to the touch. Thank goodness it's not a huge animal.

Then I haul the thing, directly out of the undead's reach. The creatures don't seem to even notice me but lurch after their meal with outstretched hands and gaping mouths dripping with blood.

Groans from the woods draw my attention to the other monsters coming this way.

So I move with speed, shuffling backward, tugging this half-eaten carcass and doing my best not to look at its open ribcage or I'll be sick.

One zombie latches on and bites down on its neck. As I drag the deer, the undead loses its balance and falls, still attached on with teeth and fingers. Their weight resists me now, and I swear under my breath at the fucking thing.

My heart pounds in my chest, and the rain is unrelenting, soaking me. It drips down my face and into my eyes and mouth.

Glancing behind me, I approach the edge of the woods, and behind that is a clearing between me and the fence of at least twenty feet.

I scan the area and find no one there, so I move fast with the deer and creatures.

Emerging from the woods, the sheet of rain pours buckets over me, slamming into me ferociously. I slide the deer over the muddy ground, one zombie still clinging on to its neck, eating, while the other staggers after us.

Fear pummels into me now. Those guards in the compound shoot on site, and I'm in open territory with their enemy.

My arms tremble with exhaustion, but I keep wrenching the damn deer over the bumpy ground and shrubs. I pivot and tow the meal closer to the edge of the settlement. Farther around the corner stands the main entrance, and well, I need to create a big enough diversion that draws attention to this end of the settlement.

After the last break-in Mad caused, I'm guessing most of the pack members will be hypersensitive to uncover a horde of zombies clustered together near their home.

On cue, the dozen monsters emerge from the woods, so now I have little time to waste.

Gritting my teeth, I fight the dead weight and two damn creatures eating the deer. I want to scream but keep my mouth shut. Those in the mob chasing after us are moaning enough to make a racket.

A shiver races down my spine, my body shaking over the thought that I'll get caught.

My back hits the wall and I dump the animal to the ground, my muscles screaming with pain, my legs straining, and I wipe my hands down my soaking pants. Scraping the rain from my face, I peer around the corner. No trees or people. There's a driveway at least fifteen feet away, leading to the main front gates. Peering up, I can't make out anyone, but I know the guards are there.

Growls rise behind me, and I snap around, my pulse racing. The other zombies have arrived and all are pushing over one another to get to the carcass.

Goddammit.

Two Shadow Monsters are in a tug-o-war with part of the deer they tore free. I don't even try to make sense of what part of the body they're fighting over.

Instinct kicks in, and I lunge toward them. Like a crazy person, I snatch the long bone, still covered in meat and fur, and wrestle it away from the zombies.

They are so slow to react at first that they snap toward me with savagery. A shiver races down my spine at the hunger in their eyes, but I remind myself it's the food they want, not me. They would have attacked me by now already if that were the case. The idea that I am still sick flutters over my mind, but I don't have time for that.

I pivot and rush around the others in a wide sweep, carrying a damn deer leg, and now that I look down at the hoof, bile hits the back of my throat.

The moment I reach the corner of the fence, I hurl the leg as far toward the front gate as possible.

The thing lands with a thump about seven feet away, then rolls a few more, landing in a small puddle that splashes.

Undead shove past me, moaning, pushing me aside. At least half a dozen of them take the bait. I swing back around the corner and avoid being seen.

My heart booms in my chest, and I bolt toward the woods. This is my moment to escape and head up the hill.

But farther up the slope, four large gray wolves approach. I startle, tripping over my feet as my stomach drops through me. They are Ash Wolves, most likely Mad's search party for me. *Fuck. Fuck. Fuck.*

I throw myself to the ground where the undead roam to reach their meal. The bastards walk over me, bony feet against my back and head. I wince at something kicking into my side, then a Shadow Monster trips over me. The shrubs around me whip wildly in the weather, rain battering into my back.

In the distance behind me, gunfire pops. I flinch. The guards are taking out the zombies. How long before they come to investigate this side where I'm hiding from the wolves?

Terror seizes me, and I don't know what to do.

My hand flies forward and parts the greenery for a view. The wolves are running this way already, and I'm trembling. Have they seen me?

I shudder, and adrenaline shoves into me. My mind screams to run. Fucking run!

But I don't move. Not an inch. My brain is on overdrive, sparking and every nerve snapping. I'm no stranger to danger, but this is me cornered with no way out.

Bang. Bang.

The shots come again, louder, closer. I jump in my skin with each shot.

I won't allow myself to be caught.

When a feeding undead suddenly lurches upward from the deer in front of me, I jump into action.

Scrambling to my feet, I dart behind the creature, lowering my head to hide, fisting the torn shirt it wears. I stay close behind the putrid thing that has me gagging from the stench of rotting flesh.

I shove him sideways, shuffling to remain hidden. It moans, stumbling on its feet as it fights the direction I'm forcing it to go away from its meal and into the woods so I can hide from the wolves.

I keep looking over to the wall, expecting to find the guards popping up on the fence any second now. I suck in every rapid breath, terror raising the hair on my arms.

Peering over the shoulder of the undead man in my grasp, I see the wolves charging down the hill.

A whimper slips past my throat. I need to get into the woods. The high pitched howl pierces my ears. It sounds close and comes from somewhere back in the compound.

Panic buttons have been pressed and my distraction worked to get their attention, but I'm not meant to still be caught in the chaos.

A blinding light flashes over the land, followed by an earth-shattering boom of thunder. I shudder as the sound shakes me to the core. And as if it weren't raining hard enough before, now the heavens split open and fall unrelentingly heavy, blurring my vision. Rain drums incessantly on the trees and grounds, dinging furiously as it hits the metal fence behind me.

I push the damn zombie to get moving as it attempts to turn around, but I won't let go of him. Pushing my shoulder into his back, I drive him toward the woods as I keep concealing myself from the wolves, praying they haven't seen me. Its moans of protest are lost beneath the storm ripping away all noises.

Suddenly, the stupid zombie trips and falls sideways, taking me with it. I cry out and fall.

I'm soaking, and the wolves are almost upon me, leaping down the hill, one of them sliding over and crashing into a tree. I'd love to laugh, but I'm too busy trying not to die. I clamber to my feet and dart right the last couple of steps into the woods just as a wall of Shadow Monsters emerge. There are dozens of them, careening right for the dead deer, some already reeling to where I tossed the leg. They hustle against me, driving me back at first.

Hell! I burst into the mass, fighting their shoving and shoulders knocking into me or them stamping on my feet. But I push my hands against them and carve a path for my escape.

I stumble into the woods from where more emerge, and I want to kiss them for just saving my ass.

All right, that's a bit much. I will never lay my lips on these disgusting things. Freeing myself from the tangle of putrid bodies, elbowing and thrusting past me, I search for the wolves.

Growls flitter somewhere in the distance. I start making my way up the hill from within the woods. The back entry into the settlement is my goal.

A bloodcurdling cry shatters the silence, and I quiver, missing a step.

I keep going up the hill but can't stop looking back to where a wolf is engulfed by the creatures, while the three other wolves lunge at the monsters.

Bang. Bang.

The shots start again, and the war I've unleashed is in full throttle.

I can't think about anything but using this time to get inside the compound. I planned a distraction, and fuck, I got one hell of a commotion.

Running up the hill, my thighs ache, as do my lungs. I grab on to low-hanging trees to pull myself up over the steeper sections. My feet keep slipping out from under me, and my heart beats like it's intending to burst out of my ribcage.

I look back and catch enough of a glimpse of the battle, but if the wolves survived, it's too difficult to tell.

Farther behind me, there are three or four Shadow Monsters following me… hard to tell how many in truth with the shadows and rain. They aren't moving in a mad rush for food at me, either, which makes me think they are confused. The rain washes away scents easily, I guess.

The battle grows in the background as I make my way swiftly to the rear of the compound.

I stop for a moment and steady my racing heart as I suck in shaky breaths.

Thunder cracks overhead, the trees whipping in every direction around me, the wind pushing against me when I finally emerge from the woods into a clearing at the back of the settlement. I'm huffing and puffing. I need a few seconds to just calm down or speaking with the guard will be impossible when I attempt to convince him to let me in.

The mental pictures of my three wolves hurt and on death's door pushes me to keep going. Chills flare over my skin while bile rises in my throat that I might lose any of them. I almost want to laugh at how easily I call them 'my wolves' when there is still so much I want to learn about them.

But it sure as hell isn't going to happen if I'm daydreaming about them, either.

I race alongside the fence, for any kind of protection from the ravenous weather beating into me. Ten feet away, the narrow gate comes into view, and when I look up, the guard from earlier is gone.

Crap. I run my hand over my face in the rain, but it's useless as more water is coating me, yet I can't stop doing it.

Standing around won't help me get this done fast.

I hurry toward the gate, my gaze constantly drifting higher along the fence in case a guard pops up and mistakes me for an undead. Panic makes anyone trigger happy.

The gate is made of solid metal with no windows, and I knock on it, then instantly feel stupid. I doubt anyone can hear it, so I call out, "Hello!"

Again nothing.

Have the guards all gone to the other side? Which is a good thing, right? So I press down on the handle of the door, which of course doesn't open. I frantically glance around for a solution, for anything, when I find an oversized fallen branch as thick as my leg.

Looking back up, I see there are still no guards on the stone posts along the metal fence.

Desperately, I lunge toward the branch and haul it closer. There's a wooden platform over the gate entrance where I saw the soldiers stand guard earlier, so I need to get up there.

With quivering arms, I lift one end of my new ladder and carry it closer, then drop it up against the wall. It comes to about chest height. It needs to be higher, so I leave it there and rush to the other end.

I might end up pulling a muscle, but I don't care right now. I crouch down and lift the thick branch and shove it forward, inching forward with my steps. The tip slides up against the wall until it hits the lip of the fence across the top. Rain pelts down, stray leaves thrown into me, and this timber is unsteady as hell. But I have to make it work.

Searching around me, I find several rocks about the size of a huddled fox, and I collect one. Tucking it at the base of the branch to keep it wedged in, I'm partly terrified of my contraption.

But the wood is thick enough and damn heavy, so I put my foot on it, bouncing it. Suddenly, the tip slips sideways from the pressure, making a scratching sound against the metal. Hell, this is going to fail miserably. Stepping back, I take in a deep breath, shake my arms, and just run. No overthinking this.

My first step is solid, my balance strong, and I press forward, my arms jutted out on either side of me in my crazed climb.

The branch suddenly dips out from under me, throwing me sideways and to the ground. I swallow my scream as my stomach lurches and I hit the ground hard with my hip and shoulder. Muddy water splashes me, and I groan from the dull ache pulsing down my back.

Sonofabitch.

Getting back up, I study the branch, which is wedged in where the door and frame marry. At least it's held in place. Up on my feet, I try again and again, and by the fourth time, bruised and battered from falling, I'm burning up with fury that this damn thing won't work.

I rush at it once more, reaching halfway up, farther than I'd achieved previously when the flex in the branch starts to bend from my weight. Adrenaline driven, on my next step, I throw myself forward and madly snatch the top of the fence. Gasping for air, I dangle from there for a few moments.

My entire body shakes, muscles screaming with pain.

I need to get over the damn thing, I have to. I lever one leg up against the branch and push myself up. Then I throw a leg over the top of the lofty fence, straining to pull my body to follow, my heart pounding from exhaustion. I roll onto the wooden platform and lie there for two seconds to just breathe because I can't believe I made it. I want to laugh at the craziness I've just gone through, but that will have to wait.

Getting back up, I find I'm definitely alone. Finally, something is going right for me.

Several howls come from much farther away, and from my vantage point over the tops of the trees, the whole territory comes into view. The land sloping downward to the castle-like structure, the pack members running down to the front gate, the houses where pack members live.

Hurrying, I rush toward the wooden ladder leaning against the platform and scurry down. At the base, I search for anyone, but it's quiet.

So I slip right into the cluster of trees and sprint to the castle, my feet slapping the wet ground with each hurried step.

There's movement to my right, and before I even look around, I dive behind a tree, then look out. A man is marching to the rear gate I just climbed over. Adrenaline rises faster and my brain is firing off panic like a shotgun. That I'll be caught, that I'll cause my Alphas' death, that this was the wrong move.

I wait. *Just calm the shit down. I've got this.*

My skin feels like it's on fire even when I'm being rained on. I shake like a leaf as I glance out from my hiding location to where the figure disappears somewhere near the back fence.

Then reality punches me in the gut. The branch I used to climb over the fence! *Shit!* I left it propped up against the door. *Idiot!*

Terror seems to swell in every cell in my body as dread grips me. So I do the only thing I can… I lunge toward the Alphas' home.

The woods blur past me, and I follow the path Lucien showed me last time he and I were up here. We had sex, mind you, out in public, and it was ridiculously alluring. A moment forever imprinted on my mind. One of the many times that Lucien made me fall for him and so hard. Just thinking about him has my heart clenching. And this is why I'm running and need to save him and the others before it's too late.

Reaching the side entrance to the castle, I press my back to the stone wall, frantically looking in every direction. Just then, someone bursts out of the doorway and looks in the opposite direction from me, missing me completely just standing feet from him. He bursts into a sprint toward the front gates.

I'm plastered to the wall, petrified he'll turn around, but he never does as he vanishes around the building.

Gunshots ring in the air, popping, one after another. Someone's shouting; others are yelling. Must be from the guards.

A dinging bell rings from the direction of the back fence. I cringe. The guard must have discovered my branch. Well, that didn't take long.

Quickly, I slide into the building and pray with everything I have that I don't bump into anyone. I recall someone mentioning prisons in this building, and from what I've read, cells are always in the basement of castles.

No time to waste, I hurry down a quiet corridor with dark stone walls and the torches on the walls flickering. The wind howls savagely in here, my skin suddenly icy cold. I'm heading to the large set of stairs

I remember in this fortress going underground. My head swims with so many doubts that every move I make might be wrong and my undoing.

Voices come from up ahead, and I shudder. Terrified, I lash out toward the first door I find and shove it open. I dart inside, my pulse banging in my ears. It's someone's chamber, judging by the messy bed and table with a jug and cups. I also spot a blade inside a sheath on a belt, so I sprint over and snatch the weapon, just in case.

Back at the entrance, I press my ear against the wooden door and listen as I wrap the belt around my waist, the blade at my hip. It's super large and even in the final belt hole, there's a bit of wiggle room, but it will have to do. For those few moments, I try to calm my raging pulse. I've been going non-stop and I might pass out. I remind myself I can't afford to make any mistakes.

Loud footfalls pass like whoever's out there is running, and I don't leave the room until I'm certain they are definitely gone.

Stepping into the corridor, I swing my gaze left and right, and with no one there, I move with haste to the stairwell farther ahead. The hairs on my nape shift, and my brain is on overdrive.

I rush downstairs and arrive at a door. The stairs curve around and lead farther down. Is this the basement? Because it smells rank enough that it could be? Then what is on the next floor down. I'm chewing on my lower lip over what to do but find myself drifting to the door and listening for any sounds.

Quietly, I open it and in front of me are a set of prison cells. Both are empty, so I stick my head inside to check out the rest of the room.

"What are you doing here?!" a male's voice snaps behind me.

I flinch around, my nerves shot.

A huge guard with wet hair and clothes clinging to him like he's just run in from outside is thundering down the steps toward me. He has a hooked nose, and I've seen him amid the wolves fighting alongside Mad in the woods. Fuck, why did it have to be him of all people coming down here?

His eyes grow as he really sees me... recognizes me.

Shaking, I stumble backward into the nearest cell and trip over my feet, falling over. I recoil on my ass as he marches right up to me, hands curling into fists, his jawline clenching.

"Meira!" a familiar voice calls me from within the room, and I swing my head to the left and lay eyes on Lucien and Bardhyl inside the cell at the end of the row. They're gripping the metal bars, appearing just as shocked as I feel. Sweet hell, they were in here!

I hurry to get up when the back of the guard's hand collides with my face. Pain explodes down my cheek, and I'm reeling, my back smacking the floor. I'm crying out with excruciating pain, clasping the side of my face.

"Got you, you little bitch!" he snarls.

CHAPTER 5

DUŠAN

I close my eyes, my back against the ice-cold wall, and I'm drowning in fury. Spiraling, falling so damn fast, I'm losing control.

Meira.

She floats in my mind as I slip in and out of panicked thoughts and fucking blind anger at Mad.

I always gave him everything, made him my second-in-command, permitted him free rein in my pack. But it wasn't enough for the greedy sonofabitch.

I assumed I'd handled his demands and outbursts well but still gave him enough leniency so he didn't feel any less important. The Ash Wolves' pack came from his father, and I claimed it by fighting almost to my death to stake my claim from other Alphas. Mad never helped and always ran from danger.

He's gutless, a terrified asshole who would rather sit back than battle in the way of the wolves. Instead, he manipulates and steals.

A nerve pulses in my neck each time I think of incident after incident where the clues were right in my damn face, but I overlooked it again and again because I considered him family.

I pitied the fool, remembered the shit we both went through as kids, how I covered for him so I got the beatings from my step-father, not him.

Maybe that's the problem. I've protected him for so long, he's become complacent, arrogant, entitled.

No fucking respect for anything I've done for him, or for the pack, and he only sees his own selfish desires.

My foolish oversight will never happen again.

A groan sounds from up ahead, and I slide open my eyes to the guard leaning against the wall outside my cell, ordered to watch over me. Most likely in case Meira finds her way to me, which I want to laugh at. She doesn't even know we have dungeons in the basement, and I'm hoping she's smart enough to keep her distance from this place.

I climb to my feet, stretching my back, gaining his attention.

Nico watches me, and I know him well, so to see him betray me like this sits like barbed wire in my gut.

"I saved you years ago." I groan, then clear my throat.

"That you did," he answers, his voice strong, as though ready for this conversation.

"And yet you so easily break your loyalty and change allegiance."

His mouth thins and he folds his arms over his chest. "It's about survival, Dušan, you know this best. It's why you created our pack home. But times change, and there is no shame in admitting your ways are not going to ensure we remain safe. We live surrounded by fucking zombies." His voice climbs, his arms falling by his side.

"What has Mad promised you? Immunity from the undead? He's wrong. There is no such thing. We all carry the virus in our veins already. We die and we become one of them. We get bitten by a zombie and we're the undead. He's making empty promises. The serum he stole from our partnered packs is made for the X-Clan race of wolves, and it won't work for us." I suck in a sharp breath. "His action could bring that pack to our doorstep to annihilate us. So now you have two enemies outside your home." I'm partially lying, as I promised Ander the serum Mad stole back, and I intend to keep my promise, even if I have to pry it out of Mad's cold, dead hands.

Nostrils flaring, he growls under his breath. "The bitch is immune. Everyone saw her walk right through the mass of zombies unscathed. She isn't X-clan. Mad told us how you intended to keep her for yourself, to protect yourself while letting us live in fear so we followed you."

I'm seething. "A fucking lie."

"He promised everyone who showed him loyalty that they will receive the antidote once he caught her. We all live in fear, especially after they broke into the compound through the fence so easily. If you were smart, you'd stop fighting against your brother and help him find the cure for us all."

"That's where you're wrong," I answer with a growl in my voice. "Meira's sick and dying and that's why the undead leave her alone. Not because she's a cure." I need to get through to him so he sees the truth. My whole pack's future is at stake.

Nico blinks at me, thinking through my words, and about fucking time. "So she's immune, which means something in her blood or sickness may hold the key for all of us. Why can't you see this and do something to help all of us instead of insisting there is no way to help us? It's why so many have turned their loyalty to Mad." His face contorts in disgust.

"That's not how this works. Open your eyes. Our wolves abolish all illnesses, and she is half-human, half-wolf. What works for her will be killed off in our blood system."

He snorts and turns away, refusing to hear the truth.

My hands fist, my nails digging into the palm of my hand until it hurts so much, I can't think. I'm burning up with rage at how Mad planned everything out to undermine me all these weeks, maybe months ago. And these fools... *Fuck!* They're all scared, which was Mad's intention all along. Terrify the pack into submission with his fake promises. Sad thing is he believes Meira is the cure. Transformations eliminate all human illnesses, so when Mad discovers Meira is no longer immune to the zombies herself...

All fuck's going to hit the fan, isn't it?

BARDHYL

*M*eira's cries shatter through me like shards of glass.

"Leave her the fuck alone," I bellow from the cell I'm locked in with Lucien. My knuckles are white from how tightly I strangle the metal bars, throttling them.

Lucien is rattling the door with fury.

My eyes are locked on Meira. Always on Meira.

She cries and kicks and scratches the brute daring to lay a hand on her. I'm trembling, my wolf surging through me, my skin pricking with the change.

In my mind, I'm already ripping his throat out. I always push back the hunger from my wolf, try to tame him before I lose all control.

But not anymore… My heart is pounding, fists by my side.

"Bardhyl, I need your help to get this damn door down."

I whip my gaze in Lucien's direction as he kicks his boot into the bottom hinge of our prison.

The guard snaps his attention our way, snarling and twisting to come over, when Meira jumps onto his back, slamming a fist into his head.

Damn fucking brute swings around and throws her off with ease.

Her scream as she hits the floor burns in me like scalding acid. She's mine… my mate, and I am livid with the hunger to kill the guard for defying our Alpha, for ambushing us, but most of all, I'm going to rip his head off for daring to touch what belongs to me.

"Get the fuck over here!" Lucien shouts, and I march over to the door as he backs away.

I kick my heel with all my strength into the bottom hinge. The door shudders, the metallic groan echoing across the room.

I don't relent, don't feel anything but madness in my veins.

Meira's in the bastard's clutches. He holds her by her throat, lifting her off her feet. Lucien is yelling at them, and I'm barely holding back my wolf, except there's no use letting him free until I'm out of this cell. The more I watch her hurt, the more my head spins, and I'm breaking on the inside. It kills me to hear her cries, to do nothing.

I slam my heel again and again into the hinge, when finally, it gives a loud, metallic crack.

"Finish it!" Lucien commands.

I kick ferociously, my hands balled into fists and a growl in my throat as I put everything behind the thrust.

Metal warps, the bottom half of the door near the hinge buckles and snaps away from the bar.

Lucien lunges forward, shoving a shoulder into the door so it pushes away, offering a slight gap. I'm right there and shove my hands into the side of the door, pushing with all my might. Together, we bend the bar upward just enough for escape.

That's all we fucking need.

Lucien slides out of the prison cell first.

But before he can pull the metal back, the guard appears suddenly from where he was beating up Meira at the other end of the room. He now crash-tackles Lucien to the ground. I didn't even see him rush this way, too caught up in getting free. Lucien kicks him in the gut and scrambles back up while lunging at the bastard.

My gaze swings to Meira, who lies on the ground in a heap, blood on her face, nose, and jawline. On the ground near her lies a blade, and my heart plunges to my feet.

Did the asshole stab her?

Rage engulfs me, and I shove my shoulder into the bent door and squeeze out, bursting free. My wolf erupts out of me as I snatch the back of the guard's neck, dragging him away from Lucien and hurling him into the wall.

I roar, my body pulsing, aching, burning with the change. Clothes rip off me, falling away in shreds. Seconds is all it takes, and I'm on all fours, covered in white fur, leaping at the man. His head twists around to see me charging.

His mouth falls open in a silent scream, and his fear taints the air. He took too long fighting to bother changing. Too late.

My wolf is right there, nudging me while the corners of my vision blur in blinding rage. All I can see is red, and this fuckwit is going to pay.

MEIRA

*A*n agonizing sting flares along the side of my face. I groan, scrunching up the eye where I was hit and push myself to sit upright.

The prison cells surround me, metal bars, a terrible stench. But my attention swings to the explosion of growls and blood and cries from the opposite end of the room.

It takes me several seconds to clear my vision and work out what in the world is going on.

White fur, and the guard on the ground standing no chance, while Lucien stands in his path to ensure the asshole doesn't go anywhere.

The growls, the shouts bounce off the walls, and when I push to my feet, the room tilts.

Then Bardhyl in his animal form charges. The guard screams, and I turn away, not wanting to see this attack. He deserves to pay, but right now from the way he hit me, nausea washes through me. It takes everything in me to not throw up. I'm aching all over from being the prick's punching bag.

I hold on to the metal bars, taking deep breaths, while the savagery of growls and ripping and bellowing floods my ears.

"Hey, gorgeous, I got you." Lucien is by my side, his arms looping around me, and I sweep around to face him. We're pressed together, and I cling on to his shirt, needing closeness, needing him.

"I missed you," I murmur, then glance over to the bloody assault, which will be over in seconds now. I'd seen the way Bardhyl fought back in the woods, remembered what I'd been told about his wild wolf. So I doubt this one guard stands any chance against him.

Lucien's hand slides under my chin and turns my head toward him. "Focus on me, beautiful." He leans in and steals a light kiss. It's short and closed-mouthed, but the fire he ignites inside me awakens a storm of emotions. Desire. Sorrow. Anger. And a desperation to never lose what is mine ever again.

"I wasn't sure if I'd see you again," he whispers against my lips. "It would have killed me."

His words pierce right through my heart. He mirrors my feelings exactly, and as ridiculous as it sounds, tears prick my eyes. There's an asshole having the shit beat out of him, and I'm drowning in fear of losing my mates. I've never once imagined that finding my soulmate came with a savage torment if I lost them.

All I can think about is Lucien's first soulmate dying, and I can't even begin to understand how he survived such a loss.

"You really think I'd let Mad get the better of me?" I answer as I press myself to Lucien's chest, his heart pounding in my ear. I don't want him to see the tears or how easily I fall apart because of them. He holds me tightly and kisses the top of my head.

Mama always told me life is hard. Don't expect anything to be easy. You've got no one to count on but yourself. And those words kept me alive for so long. I am convinced they are the only reason I survived living in the woods. They helped numb the darkness in the hardest of times when I swore I was going mad.

That's how fucked-up I was. Looking back, it's so clear. But at the time, I held it together by holding on to my hardened life. Maybe I've softened since first coming into Dušan's compound, or I found a new reason to fight for my life. More specifically three reasons.

I've searched for a purpose to life, and with the overwhelming sensation slamming into me at how much my soulmates mean to me, I feel weird. Though I know the truth. I finally fit in somewhere... with someone.

"Bardhyl, end this," Lucien suddenly commands, then he lowers his hand to my cheek and his thumb wipes away my tears.

He doesn't say anything, simply holds me. I glance up and look into those spectacular steel gray eyes, the smile on his lips, and my words tumble past my lips. "I think I love you."

The moment they leave, my cheeks heat. What is wrong with me? Is this the place to confess to such feelings? In a prison?

"Baby girl." He breathes heavily, his smile contagious and in every way captivating. "You are everything to me. My life. My future. My sun. I love you too."

His kiss comes swift and covers me in goosebumps. More than anything, I want to be away from danger for a change. For so long, I've been running from everything and everyone.

And now for the first time, that is no longer me. A guttural growl has us pulling apart, and we both glance across the room.

The guard whimpers, curling in on himself, bleeding and battered. It surprises me that he still lives. Bardhyl stands near him in wolf form. He looks at us, a gleeful expression sweeping behind his eyes just as he lifts his back leg over the man and pees on him.

"For fuck's sake, Bardhyl!" Lucien turns away from him, shaking his head.

I laugh, but it hurts my jawline from where I was punched. In fact, I want to cry out with excitement. I finally found Lucien and Bardhyl.

"Where did they take Dušan?" I ask.

"We don't know. He wasn't with us when we ended up here." Lucien's arm around my waist squeezes like he's afraid I might go too far from him.

Bardhyl trots over and nudges his head into my side. I reach out, looping an arm over the back of his neck, drawing him to me. He's burning hot against me, his fur splattered with blood.

Lucien pulls away first, breaking our embrace, and as much as I want to protest, I know we're in danger the longer we remain here. "We need to go now," he says.

Time with them is always too short, and my gut churns with concern. "We need to find Dušan first."

"Down in the dungeon below us. Bet that prick Mad tossed him in there." Lucien takes my hand and leads me to the door, Bardhyl at my back, and I take one last glance at the guard at the end of the room. He's slumped against the wall, not making a sound, but his huge eyes are staring at us, his empty gaze haunting and terrified.

Bardhyl left him alive on purpose because he had to have known these Ash Wolves made a massive mistake in betraying Dušan, yet he believed this man could repent.

Fear makes people desperate, and that's when shit goes sideways. But everyone fucks up sometimes. I misjudged all Alphas for so long, while Bardhyl lives with the agony of those he killed back in his home town in Denmark.

I glance back at my Viking mate still in wolf form, following close on my heels, and while everyone might see him as a terrifying warrior, I see someone else.

Someone who might be trying to atone for his past mistakes.

We all step out of the prison, my heartbeat quickly rising. Just as we swing toward the descending curving steps, a loud thud comes from down below.

Footfalls slap the stone floor, and panic races down my spine.

Lucien's hold around my hand tightens, and he's flying up the stairs, me in tow, and Bardhyl alongside us. He growls low to himself.

As we run away before detection, Dušan floods my mind, and I can't stop the images of him lying down there being tortured from playing in my mind. And I hate myself for leaving him behind.

CHAPTER 6

LUCIEN

We force ourselves to run faster, me pulling Meira by the hand to keep up, while Bardhyl takes the lead. He sniffs the air to prevent us from running into anyone, taking us left and right down corridors. He knows this place inside out.

Voices and shouting booms from outside the building, coupled with the distant popping sound of guns going off. I don't know what's going on, but it sounds chaotic. Better for us to slip out of here undetected. Though leaving behind Dušan is a punch to the gut, and there's only one place I can think of to hide to get my thoughts together on what to do next, which is where Bardhyl is headed. We discussed our escape plan to get out and go find Meira. Seems the little fox discovered us first.

When I glance over, there's an innocence behind her pale bronze eyes, coupled with fierceness. She doesn't whimper despite the guard having attacked her but steels herself against me as if ready to confront whatever danger emerges.

I fucking adore everything about her, and my heart clenches as her words back in the prison float in my head.

I love you.

Three words I never expected to ever hear again, and it plays heavily on my mind. I accepted my loss long ago, and that my future would be filled with women in my bed, not my heart. Until Meira. Except this isn't the place to fall apart and get all mushy. I need to get my shit together.

We sprint down an empty corridor, my heart in my throat at the thought of being found, so I keep looking behind us.

Bardhyl careens left around a corner. He's going for the side exit from the building and into the settlement grounds. Perfect.

"Quickly," I whisper to Meira, who's huffing but still keeping up with me.

My thoughts ping-pong in every direction. I will fight to the death to protect my soulmate. To defend our home. To safeguard those we consider family, currently living in fear within the pack. And then there's Mad, the fucking prick. He is a certified psycho, and I told Dušan this long ago. But you can't reason when it comes to family. I know this, but it doesn't change my mind.

It sucks we had to devolve to this chaotic disaster for Dušan to finally open his eyes to who his stepbrother is: one twisted sonofabitch.

Everything about him is screwed, always has been. From the times I caught him assaulting two newly arrived Omegas in our woods, feigning he was helping them. To his constant goddamn spying on everyone. No one does that unless they are up to shit.

Meira's hand slips in mine, but I hold on to her tighter as we dart down the darkened hallway. There are doors on either side of us. These are the staff quarters and our kitchen. Beyond lies a door leading outside, always locked from the inside.

Bardhyl skids to a halt at our exit. Letting go of Meira, I shuffle past Bardhyl's big ass and find no key. I try the handle. Locked.

"Stand back." I kick the damn lock. A clang sounds.

"Wait." Meira interrupts, and we both turn to her. "I entered the settlement from the rear fence, and they already know I've probably broken in, so there might be guards out there. I caused a diversion at the front gate, but I don't know how long it will hold. Is there anywhere else we can go without going outside?" She glances back down the corridor. "Maybe we should return and find Dušan."

"Hold on," I start, trying to process everything she told me. "How did you escape Mad's men in the woods?"

Even Bardhyl makes a rumbling sound in his chest.

She's still breathing heavily. "Everything happened so fast, but I had my first transformation after they attacked and you two were knocked out."

"Holy fuck!" I drag her into my arms. "You had your first shift… Hell, this is massive." I look her over, and she's not harmed. "You survived." My heart beats so hard. Gone is the worry of how we were going to find a way to fix her. This is the best news, especially considering everything else is falling apart.

Bardhyl is right there, rubbing himself against Meira's legs, letting her know he's there for her.

She gives a small laugh as she pets Bardhyl behind the ears. "When they injected me, it must have triggered something in me and I changed." A frown creases her perfect forehead. "It freaking hurts to transform."

I chuckle and embrace her before lowering my face to her and kiss that sweet mouth. Short and sweet, and now I desperately long for time with her alone.

"So you ran from them?"

"Yes, and then let's just say, the horde of zombies who showed up suddenly saved my ass."

"You were damn lucky those things didn't get you too." She must have been fast in her wolf form.

She blinks at me, her mouth parting, like she's going to say something, but she nods. Something swims behind her gaze, an unease, but we don't have time for this now. She'll tell me later what happened in the woods after I was knocked out.

Bardhyl groans and headbutts my leg, then looks at the exit. Yes, we need to get the hell out of here.

I turn to the door and steel my shoulder, then ram it into the wooden surface. It groans and splinters in response, rushing open in a wide swing.

A burst of rain and wind slams into me, blustering wildly, snatching at my clothes and hair, howling.

The storm booms overhead, darkening the world, as though night has arrived early to claim the land.

A small clearing of grass stands between us and the array of homes surrounding the large cobblestone courtyard where most of the pack lives.

Bardhyl growls and shoves past me, leaping into the field, sprinting toward the rear of the homes that back onto the woods. Exactly where we need to go.

Meira's hand glides into mine. "Let's go," she says, determination fierce on her gorgeous face. Blood and dirt stain her cheeks and chin, her dark hair a mess, but to me, she is still beyond perfect.

We both rush outside into the wild weather battering into us, rains drenching us in seconds, icy cold against my skin. There's no one around, the commotion from earlier coming from the front of the compound. As much as I want to explore and find out what the heck Meira did, I can't risk being seen.

Gravel crunches under our feet as we hurry past the first few small houses and follow the narrow trail behind the homes to our right. Meira keeps up, her gaze sweeping over the woods to our left.

The alarm bell from the rear of the settlement is going off, and my skin crawls. They will definitely be scouring the area, and they aren't stupid, so they'll know it's Meira. My mind strays to leaving Dušan behind, except I can't risk Meira's life.

Get her to safety, then I'll return and find my Alpha.

Running, Bardhyl takes a sudden swing right into a small backyard with a tiny vegetable garden, and he charges up to the back door, where he turns. He waits for us, his ears pressed to his head with impatience.

"Is this Kinley's place?" Meira asks. "Why are we here? We can't endanger her. We can't be here."

"Trust me, gorgeous, Kinley's got the best way out of here and only we know about it."

She looks worried, but I don't have time to explain this out here.

I step past Bardhyl and open the door. Kinley's house is rarely locked.

We rush inside, where there's heat in the house, coupled with a fire stove burning in the kitchen we just stepped into. I lock the door behind us.

"Who's there?" Kinley's soft voice calls out from the main room, and I go in first, scanning the dimly lit living room to ensure she's alone, which she is. Curtains cover the windows, the small fireplace spitting embers against the metal grill in the fireplace. Kinley sits in her chair by a small table piled high with books, her teapot, and cup. She wears her hair short for convenience. She's paralyzed from the legs down. Like Meira, she's also half-human, half-wolf. A rogue wolf attacked her during her first change, and it was her fated mate's wolf energy that saved her from dying when her own wolf broke out of her. The rogue wolf severed her nerves and she lost the feeling in her legs. It's a fucking tragic story, but she's alive and we're grateful we still have her.

"It's me, Lucien. I've got Bardhyl and Meira with me," I say in a lowered voice, moving forward to collect several logs from the basket and toss them onto the dwindling flames.

"Why are you all here?" Her voice cracks and worry taints her words. She blinks over at Bardhyl and Meira as they enter the room, and a smile splits her mouth. "Everyone's looking for you, girl."

Smiling, Meira makes her way across the room and kneels next to her, taking her hand. "Someone had to save these Alphas."

Kinley laughs, and she pats Meira's hand.

Bardhyl is pacing back and forth near the door, keeping guard. Being here is risky… Anywhere in the settlement is with Mad in charge.

"I experienced my first change," Meira tells Kinley, who gasps with startled excitement, then scans my gorgeous babe head to toe.

"And everything's all right?"

"Yes. I think. I'm not too sure yet, but I'm not dead, so that's a bonus."

I trace the curve of Meira's body, searching for anything to show she's not fully recovered after her first transformation. The way she talks is like she's not convinced yet she's healed. A chill slides down my back at the thought that she hasn't told us everything yet.

Bardhyl gives a short growl, grabbing my attention while the two women talk. I head over to him just as electricity skips down my arm. His body begins contorting, stretching, growing. The familiar sound of bones cracking and skin popping fills the room. Before I step back, he's standing in his human form, naked as a doorknob. There's way too much cock on show for my liking.

"Put it the hell away," I snap as I turn my back to him, smirking because I love getting him all riled up.

"Bardhyl," Kinley says. "In my bedroom, I have spare clothes in the cupboard. Always have spares."

He doesn't say anything but marches across the room and vanishes into the hallway. I don't miss Meira staring at the big guy, at his nakedness on display, or the way her eyes glint at seeing him exposed.

I have no doubt she'd stare at me with the same desire if I stripped right now. Though with the way Kinley is looking my way with amusement it's as though she can read my thoughts, I walk away and close the distance to the window. Pulling back the curtain an inch, I scan the grounds outside.

The rain is coming down in sheets, puddles covering the courtyard, and figures are darting about. But how much longer before they start searching houses? The gates out of the fortress grounds would be heavily manned, so using those to exit are out of the question.

I turn to Kinley, who's still chatting with Meira, but she lifts her gaze on my approach. "You know why we're here," I say.

She nods.

"Why is that?" Meira lifts to her feet as Bardhyl returns, and I look over as he strolls into the room, carrying a pair of black sneakers, too small for him.

The dark pants he wears are plastered to his thick legs, the fabric appearing thin, and it leaves nothing to the imagination. His black, long-sleeved top has a V-neckline and pulls taut across his chest. He pulls at the material, and if there's one thing I know about Bardhyl, it's that he loathes constricting clothes and prefers to be in his wolf form. Sure, those were two facts, but it's like he chose those pants on purpose to display his wares.

I turn back around to Kinley, noting Meira doing a double-take of Bardhyl. I roll my eyes. "Okay, focus." I grab everyone's attention, all three staring strangely at me. Hello, who's wearing tights clinging to his cock? It isn't me!

"So, are we hiding out here until we go rescue Dušan?" Meira's voice is full of hope, then she smiles wildly as Bardhyl hands her the sneakers. She's been running around barefoot, and the big guy is soft when it comes to Meira.

"Thank you." She wraps herself around him, hugging him, then peers up at him. He leans down and kisses her quickly. My heart beats faster and it has zero to do with jealousy, but everything to do with admiration at how much Meira has tamed the beast in him.

I hate to be the bearer of bad news, but… "We're getting out of the settlement now. Homes will be searched soon, and we'll be no help if we're imprisoned again."

The lovebirds pull apart and Meira's expression falls. "Wait, we can't leave without Dušan. Can't we stay here and go back for him later?" She puts her shoes on, tying up the laces.

"I wish we could, but we can't risk you getting caught. We'll be back for him, I promise," I explain.

Begrudgingly, she nods, her mouth tight.

"I have a bag under the sink filled with blankets and water," Kinley says to Bardhyl. "Go fill it with food from the pantry. Meira, help him. There's also a fire starter kit and dry kindling and wood to take."

"What's going on?" Meira asks.

"We have another way out," I say. "Go help Bardhyl before we end up with only salt." He coats it on everything he eats.

I face Kinley as the other two hurry into the kitchen. "You are a blessing."

"What I am is prepared. Just like you and Bardhyl have been in case a day like today happened." She smiles, but there's concern behind her eyes. She knows as well as I do that danger comes in many forms and our Alpha only really trusted a handful of Ash Wolves. He may have given his stepbrother lenience, but he didn't trust him. Which is why Mad has no clue of our backup escape plan right here under his nose.

"Go quickly before it's too late," Kinley says.

I lean in and hug her. I've always seen Kinley as my older sister who looked out for me, who told me stories and helped me get through the devastating sorrow after losing my soulmate. "Be careful," I whisper.

A sudden burst of voices comes from somewhere outside. I break free from Kinley and dart across the room to peel back the curtain a bit. In the courtyard, at least a dozen pack members stand guard as Mad marches toward them. The sight of him makes me curl my hands into fists, fury bleeding through my veins. I shudder with anger and urgency to rush out there and make the asshole pay for what he's done.

I can't hear his words, but his arms are waving about, all while it's pouring rain out there. I'm under no illusion that he won't be sending out a search party through the settlement to look everywhere. It's what I would do.

I whip around and say in a quiet voice, "We leave now!"

Darting into the middle of the living room, I roll back the rug spreading over the floorboards and reveal a trap door I'm way too familiar with. I reach down and drag the metal latch free, then wrench up the door.

The gaping mouth of darkness greets me, bringing with it a cold chill. There's a ladder that goes down into old tunnels that crisscross under this land from ancient times. Dušan had Bardhyl and me work to secure the passage from here and right out into a secret spot in the caves in the woods. Years is what it took, sweat and fucking aching muscles to unblock cave-ins, and now it's worth all the damn time we spent on it.

"Whoa!" Meira states as she emerges from the kitchen, Bardhyl behind her, a large bag swung over his shoulder. "Is this our way out?" She sounds almost scared.

"Yes, and we need to go now! Hurry up." Voices from outside escalate as though they're moving closer.

"The torch," Kinley reminds me, rolling her wheeled chair forward, ready to drag the rug back over the trap door once we're gone.

I take a thick, wooden stick hidden near her fireplace and plunge one end covered in cloth and oil into the fire. It takes instantly, an orange blaze flickering and coming to life.

Bardhyl has already jumped into the tunnel, and Meira is on her way down the ladder, and she looks at me with uncertainty, but there are no complaints.

"I'm right behind you, gorgeous," I assure her.

Though, in truth, I wish I could fly her out of here so she didn't have to run and hide, but I can't, so I'll do the next best thing. Protect her from the fucking demented wolf on our doorstep.

CHAPTER 7

MEIRA

"Hey, you okay, angel legs?" Bardhyl asks, slowing his relentless marching through the tunnel and turning his head toward Lucien and me. Flames flicker from the torch he grasps, tossing shadows across the tunnel walls.

In reality, it's more of a sauna as I'm sweating like a beast. The rains aboveground seem to have made this place a sweltering and stuffy cocoon. Each breath gasps as I draw it in. Luckily, a light breeze brushes past every now and then, and I crave more before I pass out.

I wipe the perspiration from my brow and push away the hair stuck to the sides of my face. "How much longer?" Compact earth covers the walls of the tunnels, wooden arched beams keeping the place from caving in. "Feels like we've been walking for half a day. I really don't like being closed in here." Pain coils in my chest at not seeing a way out. We've passed several passages spiking in different directions, but the men insist this is the right path. But what if it's not and we get lost underground, going in circles?

My pulse races and I'm frantically looking behind and forward to where only darkness awaits.

Shadows dance under Bardhyl's eyes, the pitch-black snatching away everything else in its grasp. "Not long now. I'd offer to carry you on my shoulders, but…" He glances up to the low ceiling.

"I want to get out of here." My voice wavers and more sweat drips down the side of my face.

Lucien reaches into the bag he's carrying over his shoulder. He pulls out a bottle with water. Yanking the cork top, he offers it to me. "This should help."

I swallow past my dry throat and greedily accept the bottle with two hands. Pressing the opening to my mouth, I tilt it back and gulp down several mouthfuls. Cool water runs down my throat, chasing away the heat and dryness clinging to my insides.

"We spent many weeks working down here, fixing these old tunnels," Lucien assures me. "We are very close to reaching the end. Just a bit longer, beautiful. All right?"

I nod and wipe my mouth as I hand back the bottle. He takes a drink then passes it to Bardhyl. Soon enough, we are on the move again.

"What were these tunnels used for before?" I ask, needing a distraction from the sensation of the walls closing in around me. I've never felt so claustrophobic before. Then again, I've never been in such tight confines with no way out. I think that's the problem… a lack of escape and feeling trapped.

"This is Râșnov Fortress built by Knights to protect local villages against invasion from other countries," Lucien explains. "Afterward, the Hungarians and Saxons expanded the location, so it could have been any of them. But most likely, it was used as a way to defend their land, using these passages to surprise invaders."

"Remember those two skeletons we found down here?" Bardhyl asks.

Lucien starts laughing, leaning against the wall alongside me. "I swear they died while having sex. It was vanilla sex, but still freaky to see them in the position. Now *that* is a good way to go."

"Really?" I butt in, trying to hold back my laughter at what they remember from this tunnel.

Bardhyl smirks. "There are only two ways I want to go. Either in battle, or buried deep in…" He pauses, looks at me shaking my head, and shuts his mouth. But the rest of the conversation dissolves and the flame on his torch flicks wildly to the point of going out.

"Well, hopefully, that never happens to us," I respond, rubbing the goosebumps out of my arms. "And for the sake of all things, don't let the light go out." A small whimper escapes past my lips.

"It'll be fine. We won't let anything happen to you," Bardhyl says. "Even if the flame goes out, I can get us out."

"That doesn't reassure me." I wrap my arms around myself, hating how this confined space is affecting me so much. "Does it feel like the tunnel is getting smaller?"

Lucien pipes in. "Two of us can stand side by side, babe. It's not narrowing. But I agree, it's not a big deal if the flames go. Means we no longer have to stare at the sausage in Bardhyl's pants."

"What?" Bardhyl and I say in unison, turning to Lucien.

He sighs and blows a long breath out. "I wasn't going to say anything, but fuck, bruh, why did you select those pants? Your plums and cucumber are sticking out like a damn sore thumb. I mean, you almost made poor Kinley faint back in her house when you came out with your bed snake on show."

Bardhyl glances down, lowering the torch, and I can't stop myself but follow his gaze. The fabric clings to his cock, which sits at an angle, and hell, he is a huge boy even when not turned on. I must agree that when I first saw him in those pants, I almost choked on my breath because the material concealed nothing, curving over his ridge and bump. The saying about guys having three legs is not wasted on Bardhyl, and my skin heats at the image.

"Why are we talking about this now?" I ask, unsure of Lucien's point, except that it comes from a place of jealousy, and I don't want Bardhyl to feel bad if those pants were all that fit him.

"It looks incredible, right?" Bardhyl answers, and it's not the response I expect.

"Told you, he wore them on purpose to fling his pecker around. There was a reason Kinley sent you quickly to get dressed. Then you came out like this." Lucien flings his hand at him.

Bardhyl laughs and is already walking away. We are hurrying up behind him, and I'm just shaking my head that this topic is even being discussed.

"There was another pair. If I knew you'd be this jealous, I'd have brought them out for you."

Lucien scoffs and reaches down to grope himself. "What I'm packing leaves Meira gasping, but I don't wear fancy pants to draw attention to my ammunition."

"Hmm, don't bring me into this," I murmur as we walk faster.

"Babe, you are completely in the middle of this sandwich," Lucien answers.

While Bardhyl still laughs, he glances over his shoulder. "Later, you can try on my pants and then we can let Meira judge who looks best in them."

"Um, no," I respond.

"Deal!" Lucien answers.

I roll my eyes. "Seriously, I'm not sure why guys are so obsessed with the size of their penises. You don't see females going around flashing their… their flowers for comparison."

"There'd be nothing wrong if they did," Bardhyl responds. "I wish you would."

"Yes, finally we both agree," Lucien adds.

I glare at Lucien, who winks at me, and while the discussion is absurd, my knees wobble slightly at how easily he affects me.

The path curves to the left and only once we clear it does a small light come into view from up ahead. I'm suddenly bouncing on my toes. "A way out!"

A whistling wind curls around us, and relief washes over me. "We've reached the end. That's the best sight in the world."

I'm moving faster, the men right there alongside me.

"Feeling better?" Lucien murmurs.

I turn toward his smiling face, and it takes me a few moments to really understand what he's talking about. Then it collides into me like an avalanche. "You orchestrated that whole conversation about Bardhyl's pants to distract me, didn't you?"

He blows me a kiss while Bardhyl faces us, and those delicious eyes narrow seductively.

"You bastards," I tease. "Here I thought you both had major jealousy issues. Though I will admit, those pants are super tight." This time, it's me who laughs about the fact that they so easily fooled me. "Thanks." I move to hug them both, and for a few moments, we hold each other. How in the world did I get so lucky to score these smartasses as my mates?

Finally, we take a step out of a gaping hole and into an oversized cave, with its opening at least twenty feet away. I hurry forward, never wanting to be in another tunnel ever again.

The sight of the woods stretching out before us, the fresh smell of pines and rain fills the air… I missed it. I can't see exactly where we are, but we are definitely outside the compound.

"It wasn't that terrifying," Lucien murmurs as he pushes the strap of the backpack higher up his shoulder.

Bardhyl walks toward us, his nostrils flaring as he takes in a deep inhale, his chest rising. "Do we remain here until the right moment to sneak back for Dušan?" he asks.

"No. I mean, yes to finding Dušan, but we can't stay here," I answer before Lucien gets a chance. "There's a cave up on a hill near the settlement and my friend Jae is waiting for me, I hope. It faces away from the compound. With the rain, we shouldn't be detected. I just don't know how to get there from here." I'm speed-talking, wanting to get away from here, as I hate the open tunnel. Mad and his men could be barreling after us right now.

"What side of the settlement is your cave?" Bardhyl asks.

"The same side where we were attacked by Mad."

Lucien pulls out a blade from his boot and winks. "So we've got a bit of walking to do. Let's join your friend while we wait then."

Bardhyl straightens his posture before offering me his hand. "You run with me and lead the way once I get us to that side."

"Okay. I'm ready."

His hand grips mine and we hurry into the pounding rain. Its coldness leaves my skin covered in goosebumps, and I duck my head as we dart into the forest.

I'm freezing and my heart beats overtime that we might bump into Mad's men. Or Shadow Monsters. It's not me I worry about, but my two wolves, and I just pray we make it safely.

Rain assaults the forest around us, thunder growling in the sky, and we don't stop. I'm pretty sure if I do, I'll fall asleep in seconds. Though I'm also starving. My thoughts keep going to the cheeses and dried meat and bread we took from Kinley. I can't even remember the last time I ate. Starvation drives me to run faster.

I don't know how long we've been running for, but when we pause, I'm out of breath and lean against Bardhyl, who holds me, gasping for air himself.

"Hell, please tell me we're near the hill." Lucien drops the bag to the ground, hands on his knees, sucking in rushed breaths.

For a long moment, no one says anything, but we all breathe heavily.

Drenched, we look like drowned rats, and I might have laughed if I weren't so exhausted.

I glance around us and know exactly where we are now... in the woods at the rear of the settlement where I scaled the fence. And farther to my right, the mountain rises like a giant. "Up there." I point, and Lucien groans. "We're close."

"Fuck. When you said *hill*, I assumed a small hill, not a freaking monstrous mountain to scale." He huffs and picks up his bag.

Bardhyl stiffens, his eyes locked on something behind me, and suddenly, he shoves me to stand behind him.

I stumble to catch my balance, terror strangling my lungs. Have we been discovered? I step out from behind him, my muscles bunched along the length of my back.

Farther ahead near a cluster of trees stand three Shadow Monsters. They don't charge us in a mad rush to attack. Instead, they watch us like the ones I saw on my run toward the back of the compound. I assumed they were lost from the herd, and technically, they wouldn't have been drawn to me. But why aren't they coming for Lucien and Bardhyl?

"What's wrong with them?" the men ask in unison.

"I don't know, but the more I look at them, the more I recognize them. Not only did these three follow me in the woods before I came to rescue your asses, but they were part of the horde that attacked right after I ran away from Mad and his men gave chase."

All three of us just stare at them for a few moments, but they're too far for me to make out clearly if they're the same Shadow Monsters or different ones. They look so similar.

"We move and keep an eye on them." Lucien has already drawn his blade, and I take the lead toward the mountain.

Every few steps, I look back to the undead following. They aren't running and keeping a fair distance.

"Something's up. Since when don't those fuckers attack?"

Lucien has a point and I don't know the answer, though could it be related somehow to me still being immune? I don't see how.

"I should probably mention," I start and then my voice fades as worry creeps over my thoughts at what I'm about to reveal to them. Do I really want to tell them about my immunity and have them jump to the conclusion that I'm still sick? I've never felt stronger than when I transformed, but I also want to stop hiding secrets.

"What is it?" Lucien asks as he starts our ascent, moving quickly, the rain slowing to a trickle. Sticking to the paths with less foliage and more trees to grab on to helps us travel faster.

"Somehow, I'm still invisible to the undead. I don't know how, but—"

"You're still sick?" Bardhyl pauses and steps in my path. "You said you transformed."

Lucien takes my hand in his. "How can this happen?"

I shrug, and I want to hide from them, instantly regretting I said anything. I hate the pity in their voices, the strain in their eyes. That was the old me... the reject no one wanted, and I thought once I changed, I'd become someone new. Someone who fit.

"Not sure how or why. I don't know if I'm still sick or maybe the injection Mad jabbed into me made me temporarily immune."

I glance over my shoulder to confirm the zombies have stopped at the base of the mountain just staring at us. So, what is the deal with them then?

Little makes sense. "Please, can we keep going and not stand around here," I say.

"Tell us everything," Lucien insists, so I do just that, keeping my voice low. I summarize what happened from the moment they were knocked out by Mad's men to when I found them in prison. I explain it all, including my distraction and the zombies.

"Fuck that!" Lucien growls. "You can't be sick. Your wolf side heals everything."

I'm not quite sure whom he's trying to convince then. Himself or me.

"We need to have her blood tested again," Bardhyl states.

"That's not happening while Mad's taken over," Lucien corrects him in a distressed voice, then he lifts my hand to his mouth, where he kisses my knuckles. "Even more reason to destroy him and claim back our home."

I melt on the inside to hear his devotion, to watch it slide over Bardhyl's face. They both keep looking over their shoulders, and I nudge them to continue climbing. The quicker we are in hiding, the more we can relax and talk about everything.

"I've never felt better," I tell them as they keep stealing glances my way. "The sickness I experienced before is no longer there. Maybe the zombies not sensing me now that I've had my first transformation is a temporary thing."

"I'm thinking the same," Bardhyl says.

The rest of the way, we travel in silence, and only the rain hitting trees echoes around us. Each time I check the path behind us, the undead follow, and I'm terrified they'll suddenly snap into their frenzied forms and attack my men. Or are they scouts for other zombies? Ridiculous. They're undead and don't have any brain capacity to work as a team in such a manner.

I swing back as they approach, frustration building in my chest, as I don't want those things scaring Jae.

"Get lost," I call out as softly as possible, flicking my hand at them to leave. "Go away!"

They freeze and just stare at me with empty, dead eyes. Who were these three in their previous lives? Humans? Wolf members?

My men stand on either side of me as the Shadow Monsters slowly turn around and start trekking back down the mountain.

I'm gobsmacked, completely and utterly convinced that didn't just happen.

"Are you kidding? Did they just listen to your command like you're their queen?" Lucien gasps.

"I-I t-think so! No, this can't be right. How?"

"You've become the Zombie Queen," Bardhyl says almost in awe, like he's proud for me to carry such a title.

I cut him a sharp glare. "Don't even joke about that. Seriously, that is not a thing, right?"

"We need to keep moving," Lucien says, taking my hand to join him, but my gaze remains locked on the three Shadow Monsters lurching away from us at my command.

This must be a mistake, a coincidence because they must have smelled blood somewhere close.

My stomach rolls in on itself, and I can't even convince myself I commanded the Shadow Monsters.

And Bardhyl's words float over my thoughts, refusing to leave me.

Zombie Queen.

That's ridiculous. There's no such thing.

CHAPTER 8

MEIRA

We stumble into the cave at the top of the hill, the trees behind us swishing, and coupled with the drumming rain, I can barely hear myself think. So I step deeper inside, scanning the enclosure for Jae.

Lucien and Bardhyl stand alongside me, dripping, their bodies almost blocking out all the light from outside. I move to allow a little illumination to spill into the cave.

Rain drips down my body, leaving small puddles around my feet, and unease settles in my gut.

"Jae!" I call out, even if the cave is small enough that she can't be hiding anywhere. All I see is the burned-out fire, a small pile of blankets and clothes in the back, and an old glass bottle. She left… again, and I want to scream at her for not waiting for us. Why would she go out in the rain?

"She's long gone." Bardhyl states the obvious as he studies the fire. But it's not him I'm angry at… Maybe *anger* is the wrong word here. I'm disappointed with Jae.

That's what floods my veins. I want to protect and help her. I know how hard it is to live alone in the woods. And she doesn't even have the immunity against the Shadow Monsters like I do.

I look over my shoulder to the heightening storm, the spray of water coming in and coating my face.

"You're not going out there to search for your friend," Lucien says, like he can read my mind. Though he's right, and I tense at the realization. All I can think about is rushing out there to find her.

Foolish. She could be miles away, and I have no clue which direction she headed. I can hazard a guess, but what about Dušan? I won't abandon him, distracted by something else.

He is what matters right now, his survival, or I may lose him forever.

I sigh and turn away from the entrance, moving deeper into the cave. I ignore my churning gut and decide that I will search for Jae once we rescue Dušan.

"Fire, shelter, and food," Lucien says, dumping his bag on the stone floor at his feet. "We have it all, so we need to prepare and find something to block out some of the cold wind coming in during the night." He and Bardhyl get to working on the fire first.

I march to the rear of the cave and paw through the clothes. We're soaked to the bone and something dry and warm would be perfect. I also grab all the blankets I find, then begin laying them behind the kindled fire. Bardhyl finds broken tree branches in the cave that just keeps on giving and throws them onto the blaze.

I finish laying the third, large blanket over the other two for as much insulation as possible from the freezing stone floor. There should be another blanket in Lucien's bag, and I have every intention of snuggling up to the men to steal their warmth tonight.

"What's our plan for rescuing Dušan?" I ask, though I keep speaking, not giving them a chance to respond. "Do we break in at night and go search for him in the dungeon?"

"Something like that," Lucien answers, while Bardhyl focuses on stacking more wood on the fire.

I blink, staring at both men, knowing them well enough to understand when they are placating me. They never accept things so cavalierly. "I hope you're not thinking of ditching me and going back on your own?"

They both raise their gazes toward me, revealing their true intentions.

Bastards.

"We are not splitting up. I almost lost you once—not again. I'm tired of being alone and losing everyone I care for. I won't let you do that to me." I don't even know where this came from, but something stings in my chest at how fast I get worked up.

Bardhyl closes the distance between us in two long strides, lays his hand on my cheek, and lifts my head to meet his gaze—beautiful green eyes that appear paler tonight. "We will fight to escape hell itself if it means coming back to you, but we are petrified of something happening to you. Can you understand why we make the decisions we do?"

He leans in closer and whispers, "Losing you will destroy me. And being away from you is the hardest thing. But we won't put you in danger." His lips brush against mine, stealing my chance to respond.

I ought to push him away, but instead, I melt against him, cupping his face, and kiss him back. Since Mad attacked us, it's been a relentless rush to escape, to find my men, to survive. Now, I let myself slow down and pitch closer, our bodies pressed together, our clothes soggy. I don't care about anything but being with Bardhyl and Lucien. I've missed them terribly.

My other man clears his throat near the fire and we pull apart, then glance at Lucien's unimpressed expression. "While I'd love to join you two, we should find a way to block out some of the wind from the entrance. The cold spilling in here is hellish. Then Meira won't be so cold when we strip her down." He raises his eyebrows in my direction and gives me a small nod to indicate it's happening. His gaze sweeps over me and pauses on my lips before rising back up to my eyes.

The mischief in his gaze is ravenous, and how can I feel anything but pure rapture when a gorgeous man says such things? I lick my lips, swallowing the lump in my throat.

Bardhyl looks at me, nodding. "Be back soon, beautiful."

Then he whips around and heads right out of the cave with Lucien, both turning left where there had been a cluster of trees, with large branch potential for covering the entrance.

A coldness sweeps inside, sending the fire into a wild flicker, while my skin shivers. I'm soaking wet and I need to get changed before I die from the cold.

Rushing over to the pile of clothes Jae had left in the cave, I grab a small pair of black leggings that have a hole across the knee, and a baggy sweatshirt, both too small to fit the guys. Quickly, I peel my shirt off, the fabric stuck to my skin, so I wrench it off me. The wind coming from behind me sweeps over my bare back, and I tremble. Damn, it's icy to the touch and my teeth are chattering. Just as fast, I pull down my pants, dropping them in a wet mess with my top.

With shaky hands, I grab a fluffy jacket that looks way too small to even fit me and frantically wipe the water from my body. Rapidly, I collect the leggings from the pile and step into them. Dragging them up my legs is a nightmare. They're tight and the fabric glues to my skin from not drying myself enough.

Fighting the damn thing, I get it halfway up my thighs, when the snap of wood has me twisting my head around.

In the doorway, Bardhyl and Lucien are caught frozen, the wind whipping against them, blowing their hair over their faces. They're holding large branches covered in leaves, seeming to have forgotten they're getting wet as they stare at me.

"Hurry up," I tell them as I wrestle to heave the pants up and over my ass.

Hastily, I pull the tee over my head and down my arms, then I tug it down over my stomach and turn around.

"You didn't need to rush for us," Lucien adds as he and Bardhyl layer the cave opening with half a dozen branches in a crisscross fashion from inside the cave. They've also managed to bring in several large rocks for use at the base of their structure. Branches are sticking against the narrow sides of the enclosure, bent and shoved into place.

There are still some gaps here and there in the layers of branches, but instantly, I feel the change in the fading cold. With the fire crackling, this cave will be cozy soon enough.

"And we left a small opening here," Bardhyl states, pointing to the base of the structure near the edge of the exit. "For toilet breaks."

Speaking of which, I step forward for just that. "This looks great. Thanks. I have some dry clothes for you in the back to change into." I peer outside through the holes in the covering to where night falls over the landscape and the rain has eased to trickling.

"I'll be right back. Toilet break." I rush outside and don't steer too far, but it's freezing out here, and the rain catches me just as I push back inside through the gap.

"It's going to be a chilly night," I say as I straighten, but my voice flatlines.

My eyes land on both men standing on either side of the fire, butt naked, glancing my way with smirks.

"Careful. Before you burn something precious," I tease as I wander closer to chase away the cold clinging to me.

Neither of them move from the blaze, and I join them, stretching my hands out to warm them up. "So, what's the plan?" I ask, fighting the urge to lower my gaze over both of them. "Food."

"Getting stripped firstly," Lucien answers swiftly, grinning at me, and I feel Bardhyl's gaze on me, both like wolves in waiting for the perfect moment to strike their prey.

I laugh, mostly for show. "So you saw a bit of ass and that's got you both hot and bothered already?"

"Do you need any other reason?" Bardhyl asks, and he's being serious.

I roll my eyes at them, even if on the inside, I'm extremely impressed and slightly turned on by their eagerness. "Let's eat. I'm starving."

They don't even hesitate and jump into getting dressed, both of them in loose shorts, and shirts a size too small. "Fine, food first, then stripping," Lucien reiterates.

Bardhyl is bringing out food from the bag. The white tee he wears forms across all those hard planes and muscles. Damn, he is toned. Lucien strolls over to me as he tugs on a long-sleeved tee the color of a sunset. The fabric is tight and also hugs every contour. He stands over me and pushes loose dark strands of hair off my face, while I can only think of how gorgeous he looks. Clearly, I'm unable to form thoughts that don't concern me picturing them naked again, muscles flexing, and me all over them.

"Sounds like a plan," Bardhyl begins. "Food first. Take a seat and we'll join you."

I eye him as he blows me a kiss and goes to assist Bardhyl. I'm beyond exhausted, and I might fall asleep while eating.

Soon enough, I find myself sitting cross-legged on the blanket, the fire warming me up, and my two men joining me. We're having a mini picnic of crackers, cheese, and dried meat, served with fruit chutney. The small salad of tomatoes and cucumbers I roughly chopped at Kinley's is on offer, along with a large slice of fruit cake. This is the biggest feast I've ever had while on the run... which has been most of my life.

"Enjoy," Lucien says as he reaches for a piece of the meat. "It's no roast pig, but it will do. And it's more than what Dušan will have to eat tonight."

I lower my head and send my thoughts to Dušan, praying that he's safe and we'll save him hopefully tomorrow. Glancing at Bardhyl and

Lucien, all three of us sitting in a semi-circle around the food, I notice they also have their heads low, praying for their Alpha.

When we start eating, no one says a word, and my reason has to do with the sheer hunger I'm drowning under. I help myself to everything, except for the cake. I rarely get to taste such a delicacy, so I'm saving it for dessert.

"After I kill that fucking asshole, Mad," Bardhyl starts with a mouthful, then he swallows it, "I am cooking up my famous Viking stew for you. Three kinds of meat, potatoes and carrots, plus spices that will warm your insides. You will love my cooking."

"You're making me hungry while I'm eating. Is it a family recipe?" I create a stack of cheese, meat, and cucumber slices in my hand.

"A dish my father made for us growing up. I loved his saying that it made even the Berserkers stronger in battle. So of course, I'd insist on having three bowlfuls."

Lucien pushes a large slice of tomato into his mouth. "When I grew up, my dad would always tell me to love without strings attached. He helped around the house, always went out on hunts, so he didn't quite say those words, but rather showed it in his actions. In the way he aided others in need, how he worshipped the ground my mother walked on."

"He sounds like a romantic," I muse, unable to pause my thoughts drifting to the father who bailed out on Mama and me, who was too afraid to stay behind and look after us.

I can't protect either of you, he'd shout. *Meira is weak because of me. She'll always be an outcast.* He's human and couldn't live with himself, so it was easier to be gutless and run away than stay with us to make it work. I clench my teeth. Even after all these years, I struggle to forgive him, and part of me blames him for Mama's death. If he'd stayed and helped, maybe we would have been staying somewhere else and the Shadow Monsters would never have killed her.

My eyes prick, and I hate how quickly he still affects me, but it's not him I've cried for. It's losing Mama. I lower my head, pretending to stare at the spread of food as I blink away the tears. *Don't live with the past,* my mother said to me. *Always look forward.*

"That he was." Lucien nods, breaking my concentration, and it takes me moments to remember what he is referring to.

I breathe heavily and push aside the thoughts of my past as I can't do anything about what's happened, but I *can* control my steps forward. I found three men I will never abandon no matter what.

We eat with only the company of the crackling fire. It's only when I look up at each of the men that I recognize the expressions they wear as their thoughts drift miles away. Lost in their past. After all, it's all we all have left in this broken world that takes and takes from us. Luckily I have them in my life now, which wasn't always the case. Those are memories no one can erase, so what we have left, we cherish.

Exhaustion must have taken its toll, because after finishing the cake and licking every sweet crumb off my fingers, everyone settles into their own routines. Bardhyl packs up the leftover food into the bag, while Lucien stands and wanders over to check the barrier over the cave entrance.

I collect the crackers in a small plastic bag and fold it closed before handing it to Bardhyl. Our hands graze, and I soften at how warm he feels.

"You all right?" he asks, but I can't stop looking over at Lucien, about ten feet away, his back to us. It's clear he needs time alone with his thoughts.

"Is he okay?" I whisper behind the snapping sounds of the blaze.

Bardhyl nods. "Losing his parents so long ago to a rival pack still affects him. Just give him a bit of time. He always bounces back."

"I lost my dad when I was really young, and then my mama, so I know the feeling." Leaning over the blanket, I use my hand to dust away the crumbs from our meal. "But I don't want him to hurt over what we can't change." The words spill from my lips, and I feel hypocritical, seeing as how I can't even get over the loss of my mama.

Zipping up the bag and pushing it aside, Bardhyl comes and sits next to me, his arms draped over his bent knees. "You care for him a lot, don't you?"

I nudge him with my shoulder, but he doesn't budge because he's a rock. "If you haven't noticed, I care about all three of you... a heck of a lot more than I ever thought I would. I mean, I accepted long ago that I wasn't intended to find my fated mate. But look how that's turned out."

The look he cuts me, those sexy eyes narrowing, makes me smile and forget everything else. This is one of his magic tricks I notice, and one of the many reasons I've fallen so deep for him.

He takes my hand and kisses each fingertip. "Once in a lifetime, everyone should meet someone special, maybe even three of them at once. Someone who ignites their world, who changes everything."

His words are the most beautiful things I've ever heard, earnest and passionate. Since meeting him, it took me a while to understand Bardhyl was so much more than a powerful Viking warrior with a berserker wolf. Beneath the layers is a man who suffers, who carries darkness from his past. But most of all, he is an Alpha who wants to be loved. I see it in the attention he gives me, the tenderness in how he holds me, the words he shares. Everything from when his hypnotic gaze meets mine to when he fucks me like a man driven mad by emotions he can't control.

"Do you think Lucien still misses his first mate?" I whisper, almost regretting at once that I asked such an intimate question.

His hand slides across my back and curls around my waist, drawing me against him, chasing away any space between us.

"Soulmates exist," Bardhyl assures me. "There is no such thing as an accidental meeting of souls. It was all meant to be." He glances over to Lucien, who stands at the mouth of the cave, staring into the downpour outside through the gaps, the sound of rain hitting the mountain hypnotic. "Just like you've given your heart to the three of us, Lucien will always hold on to a piece for Cataline. It doesn't mean he loves you any less."

"I know," I say, and part of me wonders if the ache I feel in my chest has more to do with feeling his sorrow of losing his first partner, rather than jealousy. "You know, I never used to believe in soulmates—well, until I met you three. Heck, after watching the undead kill my mother when I was fourteen, I stopped believing in anything but survival, including my own happiness."

He leans in close and kisses the side of my head. "Which is why I will hug you tightly every chance I get so all your pieces can fit back together. Until you remember how incredible you are and find that happiness you lost so long ago."

I tilt my head up and look him in the eyes. He has green eyes like the forest, and I fall deep into them, offering myself to this Ash Wolf. "You three are the part of me I always needed and never knew until you found me."

"No matter what happens, I want you to know that to me, what we will face, whatever the outcome, it is worth it. Being with you is everything, loving you, claiming you. Everything is worth it."

My heart flutters at his devotion, his words imprint on my mind so I never forget them. He shifts toward me, and I twist around too as his hand glides through my hair. I adore the way he looks at me, how when

I'm in his arms I feel incredible, free, and safe. Add to that my body buzzing with an electrifying arousal. In any of their company, a single touch ignites my desires for them, entices me to their sides.

His eyes are deep and penetrating as he looks at me. His heartfelt musings have gone, a mischievous sexy expression now replacing it. We are stuck in the cave while the storm wreaks havoc outside, and all I can think about is how much I thought I'd lose my three wolves, how I want to crawl into their arms and remain there.

"I missed you," I murmur.

A delicious smile crawls over Mr. Gorgeous Warrior's lips, and my toes curl in response.

We come together, a slight pressure on the back of my head where he holds me just as he wants me, and he says, "Remember what happened last time we were in a cave together?"

My heart thunders behind my ribcage, and heat pools instantly between my legs because I will never forget. Clasping on to my confidence, I hold his gaze. "I learned my lesson already," I tease. "I'm never doing deals with you again."

He laughs, the sound like honey… sweet and addictive. And I don't wait another second. I close in and press my lips to his.

Seconds is all it takes for his fingers to curl over the elastic of my leggings, and I push a hand against his chest. "Um… what are you doing?" I have no plans on playing easy after his games the last time we spent together in a cave.

"Oh, you thought we were joking earlier?" Lucien's breath washes over my neck. I flinch at his sudden appearance and turn to face him as he gives me a sinfully sexy smile. He's back to his flirtatious self.

He leans in, kissing my lips over my shoulder. Like the storm raging outside, our mouths clash, even our teeth clinging together. And he's tugging down on my pants while Bardhyl wrenches up my top.

And I let myself fall into their arms and into this sexy fairy tale I've missed so much.

CHAPTER 9

LUCIEN

arder. Faster. Insatiable.

That's how my little beauty kisses me, twisting her body toward me as we remain seated by the fire, holding my face in case I plan to get away. I'm close to bursting with desire at her passion, at how much affection comes from her when she's with me. We get lost in each other's company as I push down on the tight pants she wears, needing more.

They need to go.

Bardhyl is at her back, leaving kisses along her neck.

Meira is everything I want, every soft curve, every delicious taste, every tempting morsel that I'm craving. She's glorious and perfect.

She reaches between us, her hand gently clasping around my erection through my shorts, palming my cock. I'm so fucking hard, and I hiss at her teasing touch.

Bardhyl drags her top up and over her head, breaking apart our kiss. I use that moment to rip those pants off as she lifts her butt off the floor. Her body shudders in the speed and force at which I strip her. My gaze sweeps over her jiggling breasts and straight down to the small mound of dark hair between her legs.

My cock twitches as I catch a glimpse of her lips glistening from arousal before she clenches her legs, hiding from me what's mine.

As Bardhyl slides his arms around her waist, embracing her from behind, his large hands glide up and cup her perky breasts.

I use that moment to stand and lower my shorts. I step out of them, kicking them aside as I pull my T-shirt off, also tossing it behind me. Meira has the back of her head nestled against Bardhyl's shoulder, moaning as he pinches her nipples between his fingers, tugging them.

Dropping onto my knees in front of my queen, I watch this gorgeous woman who is our soulmate, whom we almost lost. I'll do anything to keep her safe and by our sides because losing one fated mate in a lifetime is more than I can survive. So I made the decision when Meira ran from us that I'll give her everything I have. To remind myself this was my second chance. I put my sanity on the line, my future, my heart… and I don't regret a thing.

I reach over and clasp her bent knees, running the tips of my fingers up to her hips, rousing her from her elation with Bardhyl. Sweeping my touch back down to her knees, I try to pry them apart, but the little minx resists me. She looks at me with a dirty little smile, and I lick my lips as Bardhyl laughs.

"You're going to play hard to get?" I say, flicking Bardhyl a knowing look as my hands grab her hips.

In one quick movement, he shuffles back on his knees, his hands tucked under her armpits, holding her up as I swiftly lift her ass up and off the blanket.

The shock has her shifting to escape us, her breath hitching, and in her mistake, her locked knees fall apart. "Hey, two against one is no fair."

"Who said anything about fairness?" Bardhyl murmurs, mirth in his voice, and he's enjoying the show just as much as I am.

My pulse pumps harder, faster through my veins as her sweet, wet pussy reveals itself to me, her pink folds needing attention. Hands sliding under her asscheeks, I nudge my shoulder forward to spread her legs wider, which dangle over my shoulders now, and position myself right between her thighs, eye level with what's mine.

She bucks for escape while she's in the air, both of us kneeling, holding her. Despite her actions, she laughs. "Put me down."

One swipe of my tongue over her sex, and her protest turns into a surrendering quiver. I inhale her perfumed scent that goes straight to my cock, my balls tightening, and I seal my mouth around her juicy offering and suck. She tastes sweet and so aroused, that I can't stop from eating her like I'm devouring a peach.

Memories flood my brain of all the times I've claimed her, how they were too few and infrequent. What we shared is not enough and I have every intention of rectifying that. But the more I lick and drown in her pussy, the more all those thoughts fly out of my mind.

Bardhyl groans with his own growing arousal, mingling with Meira's cries of pleasure. He gently lowers her shoulders and head to the blankets, while I grip her hips, latched on to her, holding her pussy nice and high. Her ass rests against my chest, so I take her weight.

He makes quick work of stripping, and his cock springs out of his shorts.

Meira reaches out for him. She sucks on her lower lip, then murmurs, "Come to me."

I continue to lick and nibble on her inner lips. My tongue strokes her all the way down to her entrance, where I plunge into her.

She writhes beneath me, her legs quivering with the approaching climax. I feel it in her taste, in the swelling of her lips. Everything about her consumes me, while my need to release thunders through me.

Her body shudders as I slowly pull on her clit, and the image of her squirming and moaning undoes me. I invade every inch of her with my tongue, flicking with speed.

Her pelvis rocks against me with her mounting need.

She reaches over and palms Bardhyl's thick shaft, pumping him back and forth. He roars, while I'm floating in my own fantasy. I can't get enough of being buried face deep in her radiant throbbing core. This is everything I dream of. That saying about guys being an ass or tit lover... I'm a pussy man through and through.

The three of us bond in carnal desires, needing this pure connection after almost losing her. Unable to stop watching her, all I want is to hold her in my arms, never let go. She's so beautiful, so innocent, so captivating.

Meira looks up at me, her expression overflowing with desire and confidence. She is no longer the scared girl whom Dušan brought to us from the woods, the girl who escaped Mad's capture, the girl who kept running from us.

She is a goddess.

Her body quivers harder, her moans louder.

"Meira! Not yet. Don't you think about cumming," I command as I lick her sweet candy juice from my lips and chin. With her weight on me and holding her with one hand, I run two fingers across her spread offering. She's velvety to the touch and so wet.

She turns over to look at me as she slips her lips over Bardhyl's cock, taking him deep into that gorgeous mouth. Her fiery eyes drown on the edge of her orgasm. I see it in her eyes, how close she is.

Bardhyl pushes in and out of her mouth, and I sweep my touch down her slickness and press them into her opening. Her eyes widen as her inner walls clench around me, squeezing, and she moans from what's coming.

"Not yet, Meira," I remind her and I pull free just as Bardhyl slips out of her mouth.

MEIRA

The way Lucien says my name melts me, my whole body tightening. Those big, strong hands grasp my ass, his face buried between my thighs. My attention is glued on these two men's bodies... powerful as steel, biceps bulging. There is something primal that makes the feminine side of me go crazy with lust over these men.

I try to respond, but only a faint moan slips over my throat as Lucien lowers my hips back to the blankets, and I want to scream. The ache deep inside me pulsing, and I'm out of my mind with holding on as they pause.

"That's totally not fair," I protest through gritted teeth, drawing my legs together to bring forward that exhilarating promise of pleasure.

"Not happening." Lucien nudges my legs back open, holding them wide.

"I think she needs a bit more encouragement." Bardhyl growls, a deep sound growing in his chest, one that reminds me of hunger.

"I'm ready to burst like a volcano."

They exchange glances and smirk in a way that slightly scares me as to what they could be up to.

Lucien lowers his body over mine, and I arch my back in anticipation, then rock my pelvis upward to meet him.

"Please," I whisper.

His mouth claims mine, kissing with an aching desire, and I return the favor, needing him so badly. The tip of his cock glides over my entrance. I must have him in me.

He lets out a delicious groan, and a flush of heat washes over me, a desperate yearning. Balancing on the fringe of a climax, he teases and teases, never fully giving me what I want.

"Lucien," I beg into his gorgeous lips, tired of waiting.

He laughs, then pulls back.

I sit up, but before I can protest, Bardhyl reaches down and collects my hand. "Come to me," he assures me.

He's standing, his cock stiff and glistening from my mouth, and I can still taste his salty deliciousness.

Once I stand to face him, he makes little effort of leaning in and grasping the back of my thighs. In seconds, I'm up in his arms, my legs wrapping around his waist. I shift my pelvis back and forth, rubbing myself over the tip of his hardness.

I grip his round, iron shoulders as he closes in, our foreheads touching. "You've been away from me too long, sweet cheeks."

Unceremoniously, he slides into me, his grasp on my hips pulling me down. That earlier ache intensifies as he goes deeper, stretching me. I cry out at first from his sheer size, and the pain turns into exhilaration.

"Take all of me," he murmurs, the corded muscles in his neck twitching. He's fighting the urge to just fuck me like a wild animal.

Buried in there, he kisses me, then draws out halfway, and slams back into me. The rhythm escalates, intensifying.

My arousal billows within me to the point of explosion... I'm chasing the climax, desperate for release.

Lucien's strong hands clasp my waist from behind, and his chin props on my shoulder. "Are you ready for both of us, beautiful?"

I'm not exactly in a state to think straight, as I'm floating on clouds, and right now I want more. So much more.

"Yes," I purr, remembering the last time I was taken from the rear and how incredible it felt once I got over the initial shock.

Bardhyl pauses his thrusting and steals my mouth with his as his hands part my ass cheeks.

Lucien wastes no time. His fingers glide over the wetness, over my rear, and I'm already so turned on, so wet, I'm ready to go. Positioning the tip of his dick at my entrance, he takes his time and presses into me.

I stiffen, but I'm in good hands. His mouth is on my shoulder, leaving a trail of pecks as he slowly nudges into me, widening me.

Right now, I'm filled to the max with two huge cocks, and while the thought might have had terrified me months ago, now it's everything I lust after.

The three of us gradually fall into a rhythm of both men gliding in and out, alternatively, igniting an overwhelming friction. There's fire between us, burning us up.

I'm sandwiched between my two men, holding me in place as they fuck me.

My body shudders, the sensation sending me into the clouds. I cry out with each thrust, my breaths racing.

They gasp for air and groan their own pleasures, the three of us lost in the pleasure that our bodies tangled together to create.

I ride the two cocks, bouncing on them, my whole body contracting as my orgasm slams into me.

I scream, my body convulsing, and everything goes white for a few moments. In that same moment, Bardhyl stiffens and growls, shoved deep inside me, and I feel the end of his cock knotting, growing within me, filling me, locking in place.

Two pumps later, and Lucien's fingers digs into my waist, bursting with his own pleasure. I don't know how he fits, but his knot also swells. It's strange, but the pressure of them growing inside me triggers a deeper level of satisfaction, like somehow my body makes it clear I belong to them. They've staked their claim and I'm theirs.

The three of us moan, and I'm floating as they fill me with their seed. I feel it pulsing out, its warmth flooding me.

For years, I've struggled to find my place and home. I told myself things were perfect, but they weren't.

It's clearer now than ever that life back then was never simple, but a disaster waiting to happen.

"Wow," I exhale deeply. Swallowing hard, I chase my breath.

"You deserve everything," Lucien says, while Bardhyl sucks in a small inhale as though he's still going, pumping his seed inside me.

Seeing his handsome face lost in lust reinforces all my desires and how fast I've fallen for them.

It isn't long before the haze behind his eyes clears and he smiles wide. "Fuck! I need more of that."

I lean forward and rest my head on Bardhyl's chest, feeling more at home now than I ever have. It's not about the location, but the people I'm with that makes me feel that way.

Bardhyl and Lucien lower themselves to the ground, me still pinned between them, still joined.

Before I know it, we're lying on the blanket on our sides, near the flames. I doubt I'll get cold tonight. Bardhyl offers me his bicep to lay my head on, while Lucien presses his chest against my back and runs his fingers gently through my hair.

A slow smile creeps over Bardhyl's mouth.

"What's funny?" I ask, exhaustion quickly replacing the earlier adrenaline. Snuggled between my men, there is nowhere else I'd rather be.

"I'm seeing a pattern with us and caves." He laughs, the sound like warmth wrapping around my heart.

"Sure, but not all caves will mean sex."

Lucien slides hair off the side of my face. "I'm with Bardhyl on this one. All caves we stay in must come with sex."

Bardhyl chuckles and he nods his approval to Lucien.

I roll my eyes even if I can't stop smiling, but as I rest, worry creeps into my thoughts. How I may be enjoying a moment of perfection now, but we're not even close to being out of the woods.

Especially when Mad will be expecting us to come for Dušan.

CHAPTER 10

DUŠAN

The punch to the gut sends me to the floor, blood coating my mouth. I suck in each raspy breath, clutching my middle, curling in on myself. *Goddamn idiots.* When this is all over, they'll be on the chopping block along with this fucker, Mad.

I'm furious that men who once were loyal to me have betrayed me. Now, they don't even look me in the face, ashamed of what they've become, but it didn't stop them from changing allegiances. They believe this liar glaring at me will be their salvation. Well, they can all go down with Mad.

I cough, spitting blood on the stone floor, looking out at the two guards.

But it's Mad's twisted smirk I zero in on. He's standing outside my prison cell having the time of his life seeing me at my lowest.

Fucking sonofabitch, I want to rip his spine out. Our pack was a family, a home… Now, it's as broken as the rest of the world.

I wipe my bloody mouth with the back of my hand, sitting upright and slumping against the back wall of my cell, bruised and strained from the beatings. But Mad needs me alive and I can play this long term. My healing will thread me back together soon enough. Even if the frigid chill from the constant rain all night and day licks over my bones, and my sides burn from the kicks I received.

"Tell me," I start, my voice croaky, and I spit more blood onto the floor. "Is this everything you'd hoped it'd be? You getting a big fat erection over claiming the pack and being the big chief? But we both know you're still a coward." *Fighting* for dominance with honor is the way, not the trickery bullshit he's pulled.

I am way past caring about not antagonizing Mad.

He snarls, the hatred palpable on his face, and I can't help but smile.

"You're living on borrowed time, brother. Make the most of it, because your wolf girl will be mine by the end of today. Then..." He shoves away from the wall and stands tall, running his hand through his white hair. "I will no longer have a need for you. No one will." He strides toward the exit, but I'm not finished with him.

Mad's a fool and lets his anger rule him.

"Word has it that the smaller rogue packs up north are uniting and have their eyes on this land." I hate giving him any insight, except my intention is to make him realize the situation is much more than about him taking leadership or an antidote for the zombies. "You will have the X-Clan pack coming for revenge for stealing their serum, along with the northern barbarian pack. How many of the pack do you think will remain loyal by your side when your promise of freedom proves to be a hoax?"

He jerks his head to look at me over his shoulder with a wry expression.

I've touched a raw nerve and he knows it... Maybe he never thought this through, but that path he's taking will be a wretched one.

"Is that your attempt to plead for your life? Ain't working."

I half-chuckle. "You think this has anything to do with me? Unlike you, I care for this pack's members. They are my family, but to you, they are your servants." I shrug, cutting a glance to the two guards listening in. They lower their heads and don't meet my gaze. "Just pointing out a massive flaw in your plan."

"This has nothing to do with you any longer, brother." He growls. "You are my pawn until I get the girl. That's all you are, and I don't take advice from pawns." A snarl hangs off his last word, and I smirk at the thought that I've pissed him off.

Good. Maybe my point will get through to try to save the pack from slaughter from the oncoming dangers. Except with my brother, nothing is predictable.

He charges out of the prison with the guards. I sigh and draw my bent knees to my chest, hugging my legs, wincing as the ache flares through me like someone is holding a flame to my insides.

I have every faith in the world that Bardhyl and Lucien will escape their capture. Seeing as they are not with me, I can only assume Mad has them in the other prison cells, which aren't built as strong as this one.

Mad doesn't really care about them… it's me he wants to torture. Whether it's sooner rather than later is another story. Yet Mad's words swirl on my mind about him having Meira by the end of the day.

What does he have planned?

An urgent need grips me to break out and find her first. The desperation squeezes my lungs, hurting more than the strikes to my ribs.

I glance up at the door to the dungeon, the only way out of here. I'm too deep underground for a window escape, and I ease up to my feet. Every inch of me screams with pain. The guards left me alone down here with the other two empty cells and a rancid smell of wet earth, with the trickle of water coming through the walls from the wet ground outside. It's been thundering endlessly since yesterday, and I grasp on to hope that this is not where it will end for me. I'll fight to get out. Still, that thread of doubt lingers.

The main door to the dungeon room swings open, and I lift my gaze to the guards dragging someone unconscious by their arms. The man has pale blond hair, is built like a bull, and is wearing black jeans and a fitted leather jacket. They toss him into the farthest cell from me. My first thoughts leap to Bardhyl, except this man has short hair, and it has been a long time since I have seen anyone wear a leather jacket. Mostly because they're hard to come by.

Slamming the cell door, the guards march out, and I turn my attention to the newcomer. He lies on his side, curled, unmoving.

"Hey," I call out, but he gives no response. He's been knocked out.

Taking a deep inhale, I sniff the guy's scent to place him.

Strong wolf musk, perspiration, and beneath that lies his unique smell, akin to a saltiness in the sea. Who exactly is this stranger and what is he doing on our land?

What is going on out there?

I stumble toward my cell door and turn to study the main door of the room, listening for any faint voices from the guards.

Silence.

Mad is long gone, and his plan worries me.

A shiver tracks down my spine and it has nothing to do with my demise, but Meira's safety if Mad captures her. I return to my neighbor and will work on waking him to find out what's going on.

BARDHYL

"**G**et the hell up. We need to leave now!" Lucien's voice rips right through my sleep and tears me awake.

I snap upright, my heart thundering, and I half expect attackers in our cave. Scrambling to my feet, Meira's eyes flip open and she groans with confusion.

"What is going on?" I bark at Lucien who's gasping for air like he's been running.

"Mad's men are coming up this hill. Saw them when I went out for a piss. We transform into our wolves and run from here."

"Run where?" Meira climbs to her feet, clutching the blanket she's wrapped around herself, her eyes darting to the cave entrance and back.

"Somewhere safe," Lucien says, the energy in the air thickening with the electricity of his teetering change.

I'm shaking my head, panic coiling in my gut. "If they're out here searching for us, then this is our chance to retrieve Dušan."

"Yes." Meira is nodding her head, stepping forward. "No more running because you two are not safe out there with the undead. So we do this now. But how far are the wolves from us?"

"At the base of the hill," Lucien answers.

I adore my angel's resolve, and I wrap an arm around her shoulder and drag her against me.

She glances up, her smile tight and eyes filled with trepidation, still she pushes herself up on her tippy toes and steals a quick kiss. The softness of her lips cushion against mine, but she draws away just as I turn to take her fully into my arms.

"We don't have time for this," Lucien reminds us, his foot tapping the stone floor.

"I know," Meira says, her voice shaky, and she throws her arms around him, kissing him on the lips just like she had with me. "We go after Dušan," she reiterates.

Begrudgingly, Lucien nods. "Fine, I'm outnumbered in votes, but we leave now."

"Let's do it." My skin already pricks as I call my wolf forward and unleash him. He shoves past my barriers and spills out. It's always a race for him, needing freedom, to chase, to take control. But not yet, boy.

Serrated pain carves through me as bones crack, skin splits, and I growl from the deepening ache. Just as quickly as my transformation had hit, it vanishes. I drop to the floor on all fours. Colors morph into muted hues, the world is sharper, crisper, the scent of the pines outside fresh and ripe.

A deep rumbling snarl reverberates through my chest, and I shake myself, my thick pelt fluttering. I never feel as free and ready as when I'm in my wolf body.

I twist my head toward the other two remaining in human form, chatting quietly, Lucien holding Meira around the waist.

I trot closer, feeling like I've missed something.

"Close your eyes," Lucien says. "And only think of your wolf easing forward. Call her to you."

A shiver clings to my heart. This is only her second shift, and not once had it occurred to me that she'd struggle to change. Guilt strikes me in the gut, but it's done now, so I leap toward the cave opening to check on the intruders.

Sunlight beams brightly today, and it's way past morning, so how long had we slept in for?

Silently, I sneak into the shadows of the woods, sliding from one tree to the next down along the sloping terrain.

I sniff the air, catching the wet fur and wolf scents on the upwind. I pause near a rock ledge on the side of the hill with a deadly sharp decline. At the base, three wolves search the area. The rain should have covered my scent, but Lucien is right. We can't risk it.

Gradually, I ease backward, stepping out of sight before I turn and make my way back to the cave. I rush past lofty trees and jump over shrubs. My heart beats faster that we had let our guard down by sleeping in so long. Low branches swipe over me, droplets from the storm splash across my face.

A sudden howl shatters the peace. The echo of paws pounding the ground fills the air, growing stronger the more I listen.

They've picked up on my scent.

Fuck!

I throw myself forward faster, the cave coming into view and still no sign of Lucien and Meira.

A growl thunders past my throat, a warning to Lucien, and I pray he helped Meira transform.

We've just run out of time.

CHAPTER 11

MEIRA

My wolf rips through me so fast and sudden, that panic grips me. I shuffle about, wincing, needing to somehow stop the pain burning over my body. It didn't work. I'm still human, and part of me is freaking out that she'll fully take control of me this time.

"Relax. Don't be afraid of it," Lucien's voice floats around me, while my heartbeat thunders in my ears. I'm trying to concentrate on his voice and don't seem to be doing a great job.

Sharpness digs through every inch of my body. My body heats up, almost as if I'm on fire and about to explode. It's not different from the first time… transformations are damn painful, and my wolf is coming out harder than the first time.

"Meira, stop fighting it."

I take in a sharp breath and thrash wildly, my clawed feet scratching the stone ground. I twitch all over and suddenly collapse on all fours, shuddering. My vision blurs back and forth from present to dark spots. Just as it had on my first transformation.

Seconds later, and I'm inhaling deeply, my pulse on fire, no longer in my human form. Now, I stand on four paws as my wolf, and I lift my head, sniffing the acrid smell of the burned-out fire, the muddy earth outside, the delicious scent that is all Lucien. There's something freeing about being this way, except just as I have that thought, my wolf rises through me like a shadow. She's always there, always pushing and pushing me aside.

I twist my head toward Lucien, and his approving smile is all I need to calm down.

He runs a hand down my back, the touch like the most incredible massage in the world, and I soften against him.

A sudden growl from outside the cave has us both snapping our attention to the opening, my pulse spiking at the threat of danger.

"They're coming," Lucien announces, and a spark of energy abruptly flares over me. His body shifts from man to beast in seconds, so effortlessly while mine felt achingly painful and slow. He meets my gaze, and I stare into familiar pale steel-gray eyes that don't change in color from when he's in his human form. Thick brown fur covers him, his long ears swivelling, taking in all sounds.

The air thickens, and a chill grips my spine. Gone is the peace with my wolf. Something different overcomes me—the heightened awareness of every sound, every movement, of survival.

Lucien pivots and darts out of the cave.

I scramble after him, desperate to keep up, my wolf pressing forward, steering me toward the enemy. Panic burns me, and with every inch of willpower I steer myself back around and chase after Lucien. Tensing, I concentrate on every step, every move, and part of me is convinced my wolf feels stronger.

Coldness wraps around me.

Around me, the earlier smells are now tenfold, smothering me. From the muddy soil the rain has stirred, the pine trees, the smell of fire smoke in the distance I assume is coming from the Ash Wolves' compound.

I sprint right after Lucien, who swings left from the cave and we're bolting down the slope between the trees.

I see Bardhyl running with us, his white pelt like a blur amid the shadows, leaping over shrubs, his frantic movements belonging to someone fearful. He's an Alpha where little scares him, so his reaction terrifies me.

Our pursuers are close.

He swings toward us, glancing at me for a split second, a powerful energy swirling behind his gaze. The three of us in wolf forms leap down the hill, cutting our escape with extraordinary speed. It startles me how fast I move, not too different to flying, I like to think as my paws barely touch the ground as I lunge downward.

We pick up our pace and sprint over a rushing creek when I spot the same Shadow Monsters lingering not too far from where I'd sent them to leave me alone. And I clearly see there are four of them. Like before, they don't make a motion to chase after us. The more I look at them, the more I can't help but feel like I remember the one with the massive scar on the side of its bald head. Then the memory comes to me like a storm. It tried to attack Jae after I untied her from a tree. It's the same damn Shadow Monster I fought and bit. Why is it acting this way now?

An ear-shattering howl from somewhere behind us shatters the silence in the woods, and I twist my head around.

Two figures charge after us. They have our scent and their call would alert others. How long before the place crawls with Mad's followers?

Lucien doesn't pause, and I rush to keep up with him. Bardhyl has fallen behind me, keeping me always in view. I can't ignore how protective they are and how much I love that about them.

Ears alert, I listen for anyone sneaking up on us, for sounds, but the farther we race, the more my lungs tighten. But I don't mind constantly moving. It keeps my wolf occupied.

I don't know how long we've been running. Lucien never slows, and only when movement at the edge of my vision grabs my attention do I look around at the surrounding woods.

Shadow Monsters push through the forest, streaming forward from our right. Lucien lurches away abruptly at having noticed them too.

Crap! Terror floats on the back of my mind that we've ended up in a swarm of them. Maybe this isn't the best path to run.

When I look behind me, Bardhyl is practically on my heels, our trackers closing in, except there are now close to a dozen in their wolf forms charging this way.

My chest clenches at the sight.

I tip my chin toward the horde of undead noticing our commotion, and I pray we are quick enough to escape them while the Ash Wolves at our rear are taken out.

Abruptly, the mass of undead on our right pour toward us with such speed that it takes me aback at first, my heart galloping. They're coming for my two men.

Lucien swings a sharp left and right to where the forest is less dense, where he has more of a chance to escape. Bardhyl does the same, nudging me with his head to follow.

I swing my attention to the Shadow Monsters, to the Ash Wolves, to my two men darting away, and it's all happening too quickly.

Slivers of seconds to make a decision.

Bardhyl looks back at me as I pivot in the opposite direction to him and lunge at the undead that move fast. I want these creatures to focus on our enemies instead.

I slam into a dead man, bringing us both to the ground. He reeks of death and putrid things. Brittle bones snap beneath my weight on his chest cavity, but it makes no difference to these creatures. He's already rolling to get up, groaning. I scramble forward and tear down the next monster, and another. Sure, they keep returning, but I'm slowing them long enough for my wolves to escape.

In a chaotic dance of leaping and tearing them off their feet and shredding clothes, I stop as many as I can. Already, half a dozen swing toward the wolves careening toward my men.

When I stare out that way, Bardhyl and Lucien stand by a twisted grand old tree, farther away, barely a shadow, but I know it's them.

Frantically I study how nimble the Ash Pack moves toward my men while curving away from the encroaching zombies. The members don't see me, not while I'm surrounded by the undead.

Problem is that the moment I step out to join my lovers, I will reveal myself. Instead, I recoil deeper into the river of undead emerging from the woods.

Desperately, I stare at my men, imploring them to get the hell out of here, hoping they understand. I will find them. Our only saving grace is starting to see some of the zombies chasing after the Ash Wolves.

When I swing my attention back to Bardhyl and Lucien, they're gone.

My heart twists and hurts, but it's for the best. With the Ash Wolves out, better for me to remain near the undead for now... at least until I can make a clean break.

Jittery nerves rush through my veins and I jostle about following the flow of zombies heading after the Ash Wolves. They shove past me, moaning, flooding the air with their reek. I may hate them, but they have saved my ass a few times. Beggars can't be choosers.

When I can no longer see the Ash Wolves in the woods up ahead, I start to pull away from the undead and decide to keep going in the direction Lucien had been taking us initially, away from where the Ash Wolves and zombies headed. I pray that once they shake off the Ash Wolves, they'll resume their course in this direction too.

Woods blurred, closing in around me, this part of the forest is tightly packed with trees, and sunlight barely pierces the canopy overhead.

Shivers of panic blaze over me. The farther I travel and keep looking over my shoulder, my stomach hurts. Maybe I should have tracked after my men being chased by the Ash Wolves but kept my distance? Did I make a mistake?

Pausing for a moment to catch my breath and slow my drumming heart, I wrack my mind for what to do next.

There's no one following me that I can see when a twig snaps behind me.

I whip around, teeth bared, my rage unleashing. My thoughts fly to the Ash Wolves, except my gaze lands on Jae and the three huge men by her side. They are dressed in clothes too clean, too perfect to be from anywhere in this place. Pants, boots, long black coats, and wild hair. Brutality gleams in their eyes. The sight of them scares me and reminds me in many ways of three bears rearing up on hind legs before they attack.

With their sheer sizes, these large men standing at least six-foot-five or higher look like beasts to me. They aren't from around here, so where the hell did they come from?

"Meira," Jae says at first, stepping closer, her hand stretching out to me. "Don't be afraid."

The man with honeyed hair, cropped short, snatches her arm to hold her by their side.

Yeah, right, don't be afraid, she says.

Jae frowns and glares up at her captor, then shakes her hand free. "She's not a danger, but an Ash Wolf. She saved me from the zombies and from the rogue wolves. She is with me."

I tilt my head to stare at how confident Jae sounds, and I'm proud of her in that moment, but these three men she keeps company are nothing but danger. Does she know what she's doing?

The man who took Jae by the arm steps forward, which tells me he is the leader of these Alphas. I can smell it on all of them in fact, feel the Alpha heat that radiates from them like fire. Just as Omegas like me give off a certain scent, so do these men.

But I'm no fool... Alphas search for two things when they hunt in the woods.

Food.

And women to claim. To trade. To rut.

I sure as hell didn't come this far to end up back in square one.

I recoil from them, Jae's mouth dropping slightly as she sees me retreat. I am not a match for three men. I know my limits, but none have made a fast grab for me either.

"Meira, please," she pleads. "They aren't rogue. They arrived here from the north, and they'll help me find my sisters."

North... my mind swirls with the rogues who live there, how there are only small pockets of wild Alphas working together. Fear climbs through me.

"Your friend tells the truth," the leader assures me, his voice deep and husky.

Three pairs of pale eyes study me, their expressions not concealing their intentions if given the chance. To me, there is nothing alluring about them and only fear collects in my chest for me and Jae. "Change and we can talk, Ash Wolf."

I want to laugh as I will not take his word, but Jae's I will. And for all I know, this could be her code to help her... yet again.

"Please," she insists. "Change so we can talk properly. They just want to know about the Ash Wolves."

The fur on my back bristles. What do they need to know? Their weak points so they can attack while chaos reigns over the pack? Though this also gives me the chance to mislead them and uncover their true intentions. We are already dealing with a demon, and we don't need the devil sneaking up on the compound to take over.

The leader unbuttons his coat, which falls to his hips and shoulders the fabric down his arms, before handing it to Jae. She dutifully takes it and holds it out like a curtain to cover me from these three men who leer at me. Her eyes plead with me, and she truly believes they will not harm me.

My skin crawls because I don't need to be dealing with this right now. But I can't walk away if new predators stalk these woods either.

As Lucien had taught me, I exhale slowly and call back my wolf, her attention on the newcomers. With a growl in my chest, a protesting sound at these enemies, she slides into me, the pain slithering over me, making me tighten. I won't show these men any weakness.

In moments, I'm standing naked. Quickly I take the coat from Jae and turn my back on the audience to thread my arms into the too-long sleeves. The strong musky male and perspiration scent from the fabric floods me, doing nothing but raising my hackles. Though I appreciate them giving me something to wear, where many males wouldn't. I button up the coat that looks more like a dress on me when it falls to my knees. But it covers everything I need.

I swing around just as the leader grabs my arm, squeezing, and growls. "Let's walk. We need your help, Ash Wolf."

CHAPTER 12

LUCIEN

skid to a stop near a gurgling creek, my lungs furiously pumping for air, and whip back around. Bardhyl leaps right over the water before he pauses.

Behind us, there are no signs of the Ash Wolves. No sounds, either. The same can be said for the undead. We've lost them.

All I can think about is Meira and how she saved us by turning the zombies toward the wolves coming for us. Normally, I'd stay and fight, especially as I vowed to never lose her again, but I ran. And I hated myself for that, yet to remain meant our certain death among that swarm. Running is not a weakness, even if guilt now twists my insides into a knot so tight, I feel sick.

A sudden spark of electricity blazes down my arms, my hairs lifting. I turn to find Bardhyl pulling himself to his feet, in his human form, the last layers of fur vanishing into his skin.

He cracks his neck, his wry expression bursting with fury.

"Fuck!" is all he says.

Exactly my sentiment. I take his lead and summon my wolf back, my transformation clawing through me. I welcome the pain, the agony, anything's better than the feeling of my heart rupturing.

"We need to find her." I growl, pulling myself up. "She either chased after us or continued in the direction I was taking us up north to the mountains that neared the Savage Sector. It's where Dušan told us to go and hide if things ever got really bad." Wolves rarely visit the area and I figured it might be a good spot to lie low to shake off the Ash Wolves.

"I don't know if she'd go in that direction. She doesn't know that's a hiding spot. We retrace our steps carefully and try to find her here," Bardhyl says, sounding more like he's reassuring himself.

"Fine, but if we find no sign of her, then we can split up between the north and the direction heading back to the compound. Whether she's caught or of her own volition, she will go there eventually, right?"

Bardhyl's response comes in the form of a growl. I sniff the air and don't sense her. "We just need to find her scent."

For the most part, she might be anywhere in the woods, but I'm trying to think like Meira. She saved us from the cell in the settlement, which means she won't steer far and come to track us down.

I glance the way we came, part of me desperate to see her silhouette appear out of the shadows, to know she's safe, but she never comes. I know it deep in my heart that she didn't follow us.

"The woods are teeming with undead and Ash Wolves who've turned against us," I say.

"If fortune is upon us, we will find her in the woods."

"I hope you're right, my friend." Trepidation worms through me at the thought that it won't be that easy.

MEIRA

"Let me go!" I wrench my hand from the brute, except his grip might as well be an unbreakable stone.

"You will help us," is all he keeps demanding, walking us quickly back the way I just ran, dragging me alongside him. This Alpha with the palest green eyes makes no effort to slow down.

If luck shone on me, we'd cross paths with the undead, giving me the ideal chance to escape. Worse, we'd bump into the Ash Wolves searching for me. Well, maybe these northern brutes might finish them off for me. Again, offering me plenty of time to run away with Jae.

I glance back over my shoulder to where she speed-walks between the two other Alphas, though neither of them are holding on to her.

"Nikos," she calls out. "Please. You're hurting Meira."

The man hauling me pauses, turning slowly toward us, his grasp on my wrist constricting. "There is no time to waste." His attention falls to me, his features tightening.

Up close, there are flecks of gold in his eyes, and a fresh scar across an eyebrow still blushing pink. He has thick, long, chestnut hair on the top and back of his head, which is shaved at the sides. It's easy to see him as a wild man, but I remind myself he hasn't hurt me yet, which means he can be reasoned with.

"Just tell me what you want?" I ask, holding his attention. "You want my help, then talk."

The sound of the other two men breathing heavily tells me these Alphas aren't used to females talking to them in such a way.

Nikos, as Jae called him, smiles. "The Ash Wolves have something of mine and you will help us retrieve it." There's no patience in his voice.

"What is it?" I ask immediately.

"That's none of your business, Omega. You will aid us or I will feed you to my two men." His head juts up before I can respond. "Jae, if you want us to take you back to Narah, you will shut the fuck up."

Unease curls in my chest, and I twist to look at Jae, at how white her face has turned. Her shoulders curl forward, like she's trying to make herself smaller, to vanish, but her gaze never leaves mine. Behind her eyes, there's a battle between forsaking me to reach her family, or give that up to assist me.

"You give your word you will not hurt my friend? Narah, hired you to find and keep me safe, but I ask you to do the same with Meira," she finally says.

These men have been contracted by Jae's sister? Hired to find her? Who exactly is her sister to have goods to trade or power to hire such powerful Alphas?

Nikos thumps a fist to his chest fiercely. "My word is yours. We will not harm the woman if she helps us."

Jae nods, and Nikos turns to pull me back into his fast walk, but I yank against him. "Wait. So you want me to get you inside the settlement? Is that all?" My skin crawls at the way he stares at me, but I can't hate Jae for not begging them to release me. We all do anything we can for survival, for our family. I've spent enough time with Jae to know she's true of heart in her intentions, wanting nothing more than to get home and feel safe. We all deserve that, so any anger I feel is for these men who, like the rest, take what they want for greedy reasons.

"Yes," Jae whispers in response instead as she looks away.

Nikos drags me back into our rushed pace. My head swims back and forth to make sense of everything. What did the Ash Wolves take from these Alphas?

In truth, I don't know enough about the wolf packs around Shadowlands Sector, even whom Dušan has dealings with. For all I know, these are disgruntled Alphas coming for retribution against him while they are in the vicinity, and they want me to open the front door for them.

Still, even that theory doesn't sit right with me. Eradicating the top leader of any pack is not an easy feat. Is it a job for just three men? Maybe. Well, I sure as hell will not be handing over my mate to these monsters.

We move faster now, the ground rushing under my feet. Nikos keeps holding my arm, carrying some of my weight so I keep up with his long strides.

Much to my disappointment, there are no Shadow Monsters on our path.

"If you tell me what you're looking for, it will be easier," I break the silence. "I'll know where to sneak you in from. I mean, I assume you want to be snuck in, or why else drag me there like a madman?"

He doesn't make a sound or even glance my way, but we rush over terrain covered in dead leaves and twigs. Our approach is easily heard by anyone nearby, though it doesn't seem to faze him.

Behind me, Jae and the other two men remain close. Any attempt to escape won't get me far. I can tell this by the size of these men alone. Three against one, basically.

"Meira." He snarls, somehow making my name sound dirty. He leans in closely. "Listen carefully. These men have been starved of a good rut for weeks since our departure." He grabs me by the chin, hurting me. "Keep pushing me, and I'll gladly watch them take their turn with you. After that, you will still help me collect what's mine. The decision is yours."

I freeze as my panic flares. But I don't flinch or dare show him how furious he makes me. In my mind, I want to make him suffer, to hurt, to cry with pain. Jerks like him get off on seeing the terrified impact they have on others.

"Please, Meira, just do as they say," Jae pleads, and I hear the quiver in her voice. Despite these Alphas coming to collect her, they still scare her. That much is obvious.

But I hold Nikos' stare. He's trying to get under my skin. "Fine, we'll do this your way," I finally say.

He lets me go and snatches my arm. "We always do."

We're off again.

I exhale hard. I'm seething on the inside, shaking, but I shouldn't expect anything different. My whole life I steered away from males for this reason. Most Alphas rarely relent and never see Omegas as anything but their slaves.

His threat haunts me with every step. I lift my head and we move swiftly through the woods, while the whole time, I keep wishing the undead would find us. Then, when they eat these assholes, I'll not feel a morsel of guilt.

My legs ache from the pace we maintain and how we've been moving nonstop for what feels like forever.

The firs and the hills in the distance are starting to look familiar. We're nearing the compound, and nerves bunch up under my skin, as I have no idea what to expect. I'm stuck between a mountain and a hard place with two adversaries after me.

Please let Bardhyl and Lucien at least be somewhere safe.

We stop abruptly and even before I can make sense of what's going on, I smell Ash Wolves on the cold breeze, but not my men. Shadows rise ahead of us alongside the trees. A dozen of them approach in animal form, snarling.

A shiver worms down my spine. "We need to leave," I whisper to Nikos. "Before it's too late."

"I never run!" he bellows, his gaze jerking toward the encroaching danger.

He leans in and whispers, "Answer everything I ask you truthfully and I promise to release you." He steps forward, hauling me alongside him by my arm.

I have no clue what he's talking about. Fear grips me, and I slide in close to him, wanting the ground to open up and swallow me. If Mad gets me, he'll never let me go. He'll torture me, and eventually kill me when he finds I am not the answer to his demands for immunity. I'm no fool and know exactly what he wants, how terribly this will play out for me and my wolves.

"I want to speak to your Alpha!" Nikos shouts, loud enough for everyone to hear.

There's no response at first, and I curse my grasp on his arm. Does this crazy northern wolf know what he's getting himself into? That he is literally exposing me to a den of starved wolves?

His fingers around my wrist never loosen. His hold is cruel, and I don't know whom to be more afraid of. I make no move to fight, only watch as a man steps out of the woods up ahead.

Wolves scour the land around us and with each passing second, the chance to escape fades on the wicked wind tugging at my coat.

The man has short hair. He's someone I remember seeing in the compound a few times. He would definitely recognize me, and I slide farther into Nikos' shadow.

"You called for me," the stranger responds, his chin high, his shoulders broad. Except I'm confused, as this man is not Mad, so whoever he is, he's faking. Or is Mad somewhere around us in wolf form, watching?

Nikos leans toward me and whispers, "Does he speak the truth?"

"He's not the leader," I answer softly.

"Who is he?"

I shake my head. "I think a guard."

Nikos bristles, clears his throat, and turns back to the imposter.

"Your men took someone who belongs to us. I am willing to overlook it as an accident, but I am here to get him back. Bring him to me now, or your blood will spill."

I glance up at Nikos, half-impressed by his cockiness, considering there are only three of them against a dozen Ash Wolves. Either he's the best fighter in the world, or he's bluffing. But whom exactly did Mad kidnap from this man anyway?

The imposter spits on the ground between us, his face twisting into fury. "You trespass on my land and dare threaten me?"

He flicks a hand at his wolves, and before I take a breath, we're being attacked. I jerk backward, but Nikos holds on to me like a freaking lunatic.

"We need to run." I gasp.

Half the wolves charge at us, their teeth exposed, their ears flat against their heads.

Nikos skims his hand up my arm, and to the back of my neck, pulling me closer to his side. "Hold still."

A swish of wind suddenly rushes past me, a blur moving so fast, I flinch and bump into Nikos. My initial mistake is thinking an Ash Wolf attacked from the side, except it's the two northern wolves at my back leaping forward into battle.

White as the snow, these creatures in animal form are bigger than any wolves I've ever seen, even larger than Bardhyl, and he is massive. These northerners could easily stand as tall as me at eye level.

Shivers crawl up my arms, but I can't look away from how swiftly these two monsters pounce on the other wolves. One bite and bones crack. Whimpers and terrified Ash Wolves dart to escape. Whimpers flood the air, it's a bloodbath, the tangle of fur and fangs and dust.

Who the hell are these Alphas?

I glance back to Jae, who is close to us now, her head low, hugging herself, not watching the assault. I want to tell her she will be safe, but there's no way I can make such a promise for either of us.

"These damn fools. Don't they know we'll kill them all?" Nikos murmurs to himself.

It all happens so fast, and before us lie dead bodies, bloodied and broken, transformed back into human form. I scan them all for Mad's face or anyone I recognize. Nothing on both accounts from my vantage point.

The imposter falls to his knees before Nikos, the monstrous wolves on either side of him, filling the air with their growls. Red stains their white fur, mouths dripping with blood. The sight alone leaves me trembling. An absolute massacre surrounds me, and it hardly took any effort.

In the distance, more Ash Wolves appear, which isn't missed by Nikos' wandering gaze. He might have fighting machines under him, but even he would have to realize he will fall against a full pack.

"I will ask one last time," Nikos states. "I don't want war between us, but I will destroy every last one of you. Bring me who you stole now!" he bellows. "And to show you I am a fair man, I will give you back one of yours."

He whispers in my ear, "Change of plans." His large hand shoves me in the back, and I'm stumbling forward before I can stop myself.

My heart pounds in my chest frantically, and suddenly, I'm backpedaling. That idiot just threw me into the lion's mouth.

I glance back to him, to Jae. "Please no. Don't let him do this."

"Deal!" a dark voice responds as strong fingers clasp around my wrist.

I snap around and come face to face with the imposter standing inches from me, sneering. "Got you," he mouths.

I pause and try to still my shudders, then look back to Nikos one more time. "Please. They'll kill me."

Jae's tugging on his arm, fear twisting her expression. "Don't let them take her. She needs to come with us."

"We made a deal," the ass holding on to me snarls. "She's ours, and I will have my men fetch your man."

No, no, no! Rage fills my veins. I haven't come this far to be caught. I swing around, my fist flying, and I clip the asshole Ash Wolf right in the face.

His grip loosens as he groans, clutching his bloody nose.

I rip free and whip out of there.

He suddenly grabs me by the hair and wrenches me backward. I stumble, my feet buckling out from under me, and I hit the ground on my ass. I cry out, holding on to my hair to stop the excruciating pain.

Jae is screaming and running to me, but Nikos snatches her by the arm. "No, this is not our fight."

"Bastard!" I bellow at Nikos. I've been right all along about these Alphas never seeing females as anything but commodities. And this prick has just sold me out.

CHAPTER 13

DUŠAN

"Get the fuck up!" The growl rips me abruptly from my sleep. I jerk upright in seconds, my heart jolting into a race, only to find there's no one in my cell barking orders at me.

Movement from my right draws my attention to the farthest cell, where the other prisoner lays. Alen, a guard I recognize with a scar down the side of his neck, stands above the prisoner, kicking him in the leg. Two more guards wait outside the cell.

I tried talking to the prisoner earlier when we were alone in here, but he was knocked out, which I can only assume came in the form of the same injection Mad jammed into me. Though I didn't need to speak to him to identify his Alpha scent. With it came the acknowledgement that I don't recognize him. A rogue? Maybe. Or even someone from a nearby pack surrounding Shadowlands Sector. There are many I haven't had the chance to meet yet, but then again, I'm selective when it comes to whom I'll consider working with.

"Did you hear me?" Alen bellows.

The stranger groans awake, the side of his face red from where he was sleeping on the stone floor.

Leaning over him, Alen snatches him by the hair and yanks him upward. I hear the low rumbling threat rolling through the stranger's chest.

"Leave him the fuck alone," I command.

Alen's head twists in my direction, his lips warping into a wry grin. "Don't fret. Your time is coming."

"And *you* have forgotten your place. Something I will be certain to remind you of when I claim back my pack."

He barks a laugh, though I hear the unease threading through the sound. Yeah, he *better* be scared. Sitting here alone has given me a lot of time to think about how I will run my pack from now on. At first, I accepted that these traitors were frightened and that meant they were doing anything to save their own hides. And while that is still true, there's a vast difference between those who bow down to Mad to show allegiance out of fear and those who happily carry out his dirty work. The latter is whom I will never forgive for their betrayal.

I refocus on the newcomer, who's on his feet, and a lot taller and broader than I first realized. Dark hair sits cropped short around the edges and back, while longer along the front.

Alen reaches for him, but this man is fast and snatches his arm, twisting it around his back in seconds. He shoves the guard face-first into the metal bars.

I can't stop laughing. "Make it hurt," I sneer.

The other guards rush in just as the Alpha slams his foot into the back of the open door, which goes swinging into their faces.

I'm howling with laughter at the incompetence of these men Mad entrusts. I know each of these Ash Wolves and there is a reason they never gained a high position in my team of warriors.

When it comes to this stranger, he is something else and might make a good addition to my team.

He cuts me a look, a slight nod of acknowledgement that we aren't enemies here.

The other guards finally make their way back into the prison as the Alpha pulls back, hands in the air. They lay into him, punching him until his knees hit the ground and he curls in on himself.

"Fuck him up." Alen wrenches away from the bars, his nose bleeding. He wipes the mess with the back of his hand, dragging a line of blood across his cheek.

I curl my hands into fists. "He's had enough!" I yell.

The other two stand over the prisoner as Alen shoves past and delivers a fist right to that prisoner's face, sending him flat on his back.

"Take him. Looks like today's apparently his lucky day after all."

I stiffen, unsure what's going on, suddenly taken aback as they grab the prisoner's legs and drag him out of the dungeon.

I pace up and down my prison cell for movement to stretch my legs. Annoyance burns through me at the thought that I'm still stuck in here and have no damn clue what's going on outside.

I don't remember how long I wear a path into the floor when the main door opens with a creak.

My head jerks up and settles on Meira stumbling into the dungeon, Alen shoving a hand into her back.

Devastation sinks through me to see they caught her. Bile swirls in my gut.

"Meira," I call out, rushing to the corner of my cell, closest to her. Mad implied she'd escaped from him, but the bastard must have found her. To see her is like someone let the sun into the room. Her head turns in my direction, her eyes huge with the realization of finding me.

"Dušan." Her soft voice cracks with emotion, her arm reaching out for me when she's ripped away and forced into the last enclosure. The door shuts, and the guards leave us alone in the room.

I clench my jaw and focus on Meira stumbling to catch her balance.

My little wolf pauses and swings to the side of her cell facing me. She grips the metal bars, her knuckles white, her dark hair messy around her shoulders, dirt streaking her cheek like war paint. It suits her.

"Dušan," she repeats. "We tried to come back to get you, but it's madness out there."

"Are you hurt?" I ask, scanning the long, black coat she wears. It's two sizes too big for her. Her bare feet are filthy, and she reminds me so much of the wild girl I picked up in the woods when we first met. The only difference is that there is no hatred in her eyes when she stares at me, only painful longing. "You changed into your wolf."

She nods enthusiastically, her smile forced at a time I would have thought she would be cheering.

"Something's bothering you?" I ask, waiting for her to answer.

She pushes loose strands of hair from her face. "Despite transforming into my wolf, it seems I'm still invisible to the undead. I don't understand what that means. Am I still sick?" Her tone softens, like it hurts her to admit that out loud.

"Are you vomiting blood like before?" My voice thickens at the notion. She was supposed to heal once she shifted, but if she still suffers from leukemia, does that mean the disease will take her from us? This isn't what I want to hear when everything else is fucked-up.

She shakes her head. "I feel strong and like nothing can touch me."

I huff and lick my dry lips, attempting to make sense of why she's still immune. Was I wrong this whole time and maybe Mad is correct—she holds the key to our salvation? I seethe at the thought that he might be correct about anything. Just because immunity is in her blood doesn't mean it's a solution for the rest of us.

"I will do everything in my power to get you out of here so we can work out why you're still resistant." The swell of overwhelming admiration in my chest threatens to suffocate me at the thought of how much she's grown on me, how much a part of me she has become, how I can't bear to lose her. She looks at me, giving me that gorgeous, lopsided grin, and I want to bellow with frustration and rage.

There's an empty cell between us, and more than anything, I wish I could hold her, kiss her, and tell her we will get out of this somehow. She breaks our gaze and lowers herself onto the cold floor, tucking her legs in beside her. It doesn't take her long to get as comfortable as she can, while every fiber in my body is close to the breaking point at being so far from her.

She wipes at her glistening eyes. "I'm so angry. We ran from the Ash Wolves, and I got split up from Bardhyl and Lucien. Then I bumped into the girl I told you I met in the woods last time, Jae, except she was in the company of three northern Alphas. I've never seen anyone transform into such monstrous wolves before. Dušan, they were like Bardhyl, but bigger and scarier."

My mind whirls with what she tells me, with the stranger who occupied her enclosure not long ago. Up north, there are many rogue wolves and packs, more akin to barbarians in their behavior. But that Alpha I saw today appeared calculating and not a rogue. Could he be from up in the Savage Sector?

"That northern asshole traded me for someone else Mad had kidnapped. And the worst part is that Jae is with them. Whoever they are, apparently, her sister hired these goons to come find her."

That tells me Mad's men intercepted the outsider pack and must have taken one of their own. That's who the Alpha in here was before.

I grind my jaw at hearing how my fated mate has been used as a trading pawn. Fury bleeds through me that anyone dared lay a hand on her in the first place.

"Guards are all over the woods," she says. "I just hope Bardhyl and Lucien are safe."

With the Ash Wolves tracking the surrounding forest, my Second and Third will lie low until they get the chance to come in here through the tunnels. Unless the location has been compromised.

"What else is going on out there?" I ask. "Is Mad part of the search too?"

She leans in closer, pressing her face between two metal bars, and it kills me that there is an empty prison between us and I can't hold her or brush away the terror painted on her face. "The man who negotiated with the northern wolf declared himself the Alpha of this sector. But he's just a guard. And if Mad had been there at the time, he'd have rushed out the moment he saw me."

I nod. "You're right, which means he doesn't yet know you're in here or he'd be here in a flash."

My chest tightens, but I refuse to voice my concerns to Meira. Mad's plans are straightforward. Now that he has Meira captured, there's no more need for me. My end is near. Sweat rolls down my spine, and I ought to be fearful, but what I worry about more is what the lunatic will do to my beautiful mate if I'm not here to stop him.

Lucien and Bardhyl are my last hope.

"We'll get out of this," she assures me, most likely picking up on the deepening of my concern.

I've fought my whole life for a better place for our pack. And the one person I protected all his life will now be my undoing.

I glance over to the door, my racing heartbeat sounding like a countdown until my stepbrother marches in here for Meira. I swallow the bile at the back of my throat. Anger echoes in the confines of my head, and I try to push away the mounting dread. I comb a hand through my hair, needing to shake the nerves away.

"Dušan, are you all right?" Meira interrupts my thoughts, and her singsong voice draws my attention to her. Her beautiful eyes study my every move, every reaction.

My mouth curls into a smile, but on the inside, I break, my emotions spilling free. To never look on her face again, to never feel her warmth, to never hear her laugh destroys me. And in its place, fury builds over me, swallowing me. I ball my hands at the thought that Mad will do everything to take her away from me.

"I refuse to believe we won't make it out," Meira says, and it takes me a few moments to roll the word *believe* over in my mind for it to finally settle into my thoughts. For so long, I'd been that person that convinced the pack members we were safe in this compound. To have faith in me and believe their future is secure from the zombies. But little did I know, the true enemy was in my ranks this whole time.

I shift my gaze to Meira's beautiful face, which I've memorized, every line, every curve, every color. She's a painting in my mind I will never forget. "You're right, gorgeous. We will get out of this."

I take a seat and listen to her as she tells me about her rescuing Lucien and Bardhyl, her diversion with the undead, and even some strange zombies that seem to follow her. Which is unusual in and of itself, but I can only imagine it has something to do with her still being immune to the undead.

Her voice calms the beast inside me bursting to go ballistic at being locked up.

Everything about her is addictive. She smells so good, like the fresh meadow on a spring morning. I crave to feel her body pressed against me, her soft breasts, her long legs wrapped around me, the fire between her thighs. I miss her terribly. We may share the same room, but she's too far away.

I want out of his fucking prison now!

When I meet her gaze, an ache reflects inside them. She senses my agony and suffers herself from the hellhole we've all fallen into since Mad started playing his games.

This will end with blood. His and mine. I won't go down without taking him with me.

CHAPTER 14

MEIRA

click from the door into the dungeon wrenches my attention away from Dušan. With it, I stiffen, grasping on to the metal bars, straining to see who's entering.

Mad storms inside, his gaze sweeping from Dušan to me, then he lets out a loud exhale. His smirk infuriates me. "My men told me they caught you, but I didn't believe them. I had to come and see you for myself." The tight curl of his mouth covers me in goosebumps—and not the good kind.

I shuffle backward in my cell, terrified of what this crazy man has in store for me. The look in his eyes belongs to someone who cares about only one thing: himself. And I am merely a stepping stone to him, a way to get an upper hand in this twisted world.

"You're a fucking monster," I cry out. "Let us go!"

He ignores me and steers over to stand outside Dušan's prison, three guards following closely.

As one of them opens his prison door, a flare of panic spikes through me like razor blades. I suck in each racing breath and drag myself to my feet.

I stare at them, my eyes pricking, because I'm not stupid and know exactly what's happening here.

Mad has me, so what need does he have of Dušan? Leaving the

Alpha alive is a danger that will have Mad looking over his shoulder for the rest of his life.

Two guards approach my soulmate and take an arm each. Dušan doesn't fight them... four against one, he won't win. So he willingly stands up, holding his chin high, his lips tight.

I choke on a desperate breath, drawing their attention. But I only have time for Dušan. I look into his eyes, trying to remember how to speak while terror climbs through me, building slowly like a tempest. It comes faster and faster, my chin trembling. All I see in return is a man swallowed up by a destiny forced upon him. The struggle on his face to be brave for me shatters me.

Now I see why he doesn't put up a fight. So the last thing I see of him isn't a panicked man, but the fated mate I fell in love with.

Someone strong.

Confident.

Stubborn.

But beneath the layers is a man who's dying to keep it together.

A tear slides down my cheek. "You can't do this." I gasp each word, glaring at Mad.

"And why is that?" Mad asks, like he has every intention of giving me a chance to convince him to save my soulmate. But he's placating me, humiliating me.

I wipe the shedding tears with the heel of my hands and square my shoulders. "Because you are a piece of shit, and you'll never be anything else compared to Dušan. You use bribery and fear. You're weak, and I will murder you the second I get a chance."

Rage bubbles through me. My wolf sits in my chest, pushing and pushing for release. But not yet. When the time is right, I will slaughter him.

Mad rolls his eyes at me, half-chortling. "Big words from someone who will soon be nothing but a rat in an experiment."

I shudder at the thought, at the inferno burning through my veins at this asshole who doesn't deserve to live.

"It'll be all right," Dušan reassures me. He always puts me first. Except today, that's the last thing I want.

Death has walked into his cell to collect him, and all he cares about is my wellbeing. "Mad," he says. "If you still retain a thread of brotherly love for me, then you will promise me to not hurt Meira. Give me that as my last wish."

My knees buckle under me, my chest cleaving in half. This can't be happening.

Mad responds to Dušan with a threatening growl. "Did you show me mercy when you tossed me into the dungeon, when you stripped my title in front of others? You deserve death, and I'm going to make sure you suffer while I watch. And as you take your last dying breath, it will be my face you see smiling."

Dušan's expression darkens, his shoulders curving forward, and his wolf growls through his chest.

"You fucking asshole!" I cry out.

Mad simply laughs, and he makes me so mad, I want to scream. Fury battles inside me, an explosion of heartache and frustration at the thought of being stuck in here.

They shove Dušan toward the door, and I rush to the front of my prison, sticking my arm out. "Please, don't do this! I'll do anything you want, Mad. I beg you."

It's Dušan who still looks at me, holding my gaze while my tears run rampant down my face.

He smiles, and I'm crying, unable to stop. "Our souls will always be united. I promise this won't be the last time you see me. I love you, Meira."

He's forced out of the prison, with the guards and Mad following him. Before the main door is barely closed, Dušan turns ferociously onto two of the guards. Brutally, he slams into them, bringing them down to the ground.

The door claps shut.

I freeze.

I can't breathe.

I'm falling apart.

Growls and thuds erupt, the banging and shuffling escalating. *Kill them, Dušan.*

I wait breathlessly for him to return. To find out that he finished them off. To take me away from here.

It takes moments for the blast of noises to flatline. Silence.

Anticipation coils around me, suffocating me.

The longer I wait, the more I deflate, and my insides incinerate with anguish.

Never had I dreamed that I'd fall in love, let alone with three men.

But to have one ripped from me is like tearing my heart physically out of my chest.

I collapse to my knees, crying loudly in my hands, hissing my anger through clenched teeth.

Seconds pass.

Minutes.

He doesn't come.

Dušan never returns.

He's gone.

My world breaks into pieces that will never be put together again.

In my mind, all I see are his wolf-blue eyes, the softness of his lips cushioning against mine, the soft whispers in my ear of what he promised me. Everything we shared had been taken from me and I can't bear to fathom a future without him.

A sob breaks through me.

Those memories sit inside me like horrible, jagged shards of glass.

Tearing me.

Shattering me.

Killing me.

Selfishly, all I can think is that I wish I'd never fallen in love with anyone.

BARDHYL

"Hurry the hell up," I bark as Lucien lags behind me.

"Hold your fucking horses."

Frustration crashes through me that we haven't found Meira anywhere in the woods.

When we started to go north, we finally caught her scent. But it brought us right to the back entrance to the settlement. And that meant one thing.

She's been captured. There's little other reason she'd be using that entry when the woods are crawling with Ash Wolves.

I wipe the trickling blood from my busted lip with the back of my hand. Lucien and I took out a small group of Ash Wolves we found searching the woods, and in all honesty, we couldn't resist. The idiots were men we knew. Lowest of the scum in our pack, easily manipulated into being loyal to that traitor, so that small service to clean out our tribe was the least we could do.

Now we burst through the tunnels in human form. We wedged several boulders at the cave's entrance leading to these tunnels, just in case anyone finds it.

I glance back. Lucien finally catches up, bouncing in the dark. He's a shadow I easily discern with my wolf eyes… Partial transformation has its benefits.

"Had to make sure it was securely in place," he murmurs.

Both of us frantically bound forward in the narrow tunnel, darkness chasing after us, and all I can think of is Meira.

"We rescue Dušan first, then the three of us bombard Mad. I'm tearing his head off." I growl.

"Fine, I'm laying a claim on ripping out his spine. But on one condition." Lucien doesn't wait for me to respond. "He's alive so he can feel pain. I want him to fucking hurt so much, it burns inside me with urgency."

"That assmuncher is going down," I bark. "Then I'm dancing on his grave. Well, actually, you can do it with your cowboy boots, seeing as how he hated them."

His brow bunches up, eyes widening. "What the fuck? He hated my boots?"

"Bruh, he laughed about you to others. When I heard him doing it, I hit him so hard, I knocked one of his back teeth out. Never heard a word after that about your boots."

"You're a good friend, you know that? If there's anyone I'd share my soulmate with, it's you and Dušan."

"Don't get all soppy on me."

Lucien laughs and pats my shoulder as he shoves himself past me, nudging me into the wall on purpose. "Hurry the hell up," he mocks, but he keeps laughing softly.

I burst after him. We both know these tunnels like the back of our hands, every turn and every dip.

Once we reach the end of our passage, we enter the small makeshift area with a ladder leading up to Kinley's place.

Wasting no time, I race up the steps and pause just below the closed trap door.

Placing my ear as close as possible to the wooden panel, I listen.

Nothing. Not even vibrations to imply Kinley has visitors and they're walking around.

When I'm confident we're clear, I bang my knuckles twice on the horizontal door.

I glance back down to Lucien and he just stares at me, shrugging. Kinley rarely goes out, and I doubt she would with the chaos in the settlement.

Unease hardens in my gut at the idea that something happened to her. I can easily break through, except I want to make sure before I destroy this entrance.

Swinging back to the wooden panel, I take hold of the metal latch, ready to rattle it in case Kinley has fallen asleep.

The creak of wood echoes down here, and I release the latch, rushing back down, just in case it's someone else up there. Another creak.

Lucien and I slide into the shadows around us when a female voice calls out, "It's unlocked."

Kinley. Relief washes over me.

I dart up the ladder and push open the panel.

In moments, Lucien and I are in her room, the trap door shut and covered by the rug. I search the whole house to make sure we're alone.

Lucien is by Kinley's side, giving her an update on what's been going on. He's always been great at making connections with others, much more than me, so I leave it up to him.

"Have you heard anything?" he asks her.

She shakes her head. "Everyone is scared and most families are staying hidden in their homes. No one wants Mad in charge." Her words quaver

Lucien holds her hand and reassures her. "He's going down," Lucien assures her, and when she glances over to me, I nod. Suddenly, I feel awkward just standing there.

"We need to go," Lucien explains. "Keep the doors locked until we return, all right?"

"Of course. But put some clothes on or you'll stand out in the crowd."

She's right. Here we are naked. Most in the settlement hold their human forms and rarely walk around in the nude. Well, except old Rog, the oldest member in the tribe, who sometimes forgets where he is.

"I'll get us some clothes," I offer, well aware of where Kinley keeps her stash.

The backroom is small and filled with shelves of folded clothes, a variety she collects for anyone in need. Problem is that most are smaller sizes.

Footsteps close in behind me, and I twist around to find Lucien right behind me.

"You think I was going to trust you to get me something to wear?" He grins, and I sneer back at him.

"You're worried I would get you tights? Don't worry. No one expects you to look as good in them as I did."

He grabs folded blue pants and tosses them at me. I snatch the jeans that appear close to my size.

"What the hell? She had proper clothes in the drawer?" I ask.

Lucien chuckles to himself. "Only *you* wouldn't check in there, right, tights boy?"

I don't care what he calls me. I get dressed, tuck myself in there comfortably, and zip up.

When I lift my head, another piece of clothing hits me in the face. "Goddammit."

He hasn't stopped laughing to himself as he pulls on a slate gray knitted top, already dressed in a pair of black jeans.

I drag on the long-sleeved deep-green hoodie.

Somewhere in the supplies, Lucien has found us boots. "Try these."

Taking them, I waste no time and put on the ankle-high black boots with thick soles. "They're good."

"Let's go do this."

Out in the main room, Kinley greets us with a smile. Despite the fear behind her eyes, she doesn't voice her concerns. Like the rest of us, she knows that the only way to eliminate a tyrant is to stand up to him. And while that is fraught with danger, it's the only way to stop him.

One must fight for what one believes in, my father would always say.

"Stay safe," Kinley says.

In a hurry, we sneak out of her home. The courtyard in front of her house reveals several guards strolling about. No one from neighboring homes has emerged.

I flick a hand at Lucien to follow me as I dart alongside Kinley's home and down the side to her vegetable garden. Back here, a passage runs the length of all the homes, and across from us stands the settlement woods.

A quick check, and finding no signs of anyone, we both sprint left.

The fortress rises before us, steadfast stone walls, towers... No longer the place I called home, but a danger.

Voices come abruptly from the woods to my right. I pause, frantically looking for where to hide.

Lucien snatches the sleeve of my top and hauls me back behind several wooden barrels in someone's backyard. Behind us are fig trees and a small hut-like house made of gray stone. As long as no one looks out the window, we should be fine.

Crouched low, Lucien huddles close. "Did you even look before you ran out so quickly?" he whispers harshly under his breath.

I cut him a glare. "Of course I did."

Tempers are high, but I shake it off. It's not him I'm frustrated with, but what Mad has taken from us all.

Peering through the gap between two barrels, I watch two Beta males talk in hushed voices and head down the path this way.

I tense. I exchange glances with Lucien, who's pointing at them from the back of our hiding spot. He's seen them. If there's one benefit of so many pack members living in the compound, it's that all our scents are so heavily mingled in the air that I pray to the moon and back that they won't pick up our wolves.

While we have no idea whose side they're on, we can't take the risk.

Huddling near Lucien, I watch them with intensity, but in my head, I have it all played out. The moment I sense a whisper of being detected, I will take them both down.

Moments later, they stroll past us, and behind the frantic beating of my heart, all I can make out of their whispers are four words. "He's doing it now."

My mind catapults to Mad, and all I can picture is him hurting Meira. He's got her and is going to cut her up, take her blood, take everything.

Electricity jolts through me at the thought, and a desperate urgency flares over me. I'm on my feet, charging after those bastards to make them talk.

Strong hands snatch the back of my hoodie and wrench me backward.

I stumble, my heel catching on a broken stone in the garden. My stomach lurches as I fall onto my ass hard near the row of spinach. I growl under my breath when Lucien gets in my face.

"The fuck, man?"

I shove him off me. "They know something about Meira."

"You don't know that. We can't reveal ourselves."

Heat pulses in my temples as I twist my head to find the two Betas are long gone.

"Shit." I'm on my feet. "We go now!"

Lucien's lip curls upward. "Keep it the hell together. We stick to the plan. Get Dušan, and then we'll be stronger to take on Mad."

Fury knots in my chest, but I swallow back the anger. "Let's do this then."

Checking the perimeter and finding it clear, we run straight for the fortress and to the side door, where I broke the lock last time we were here.

We burst into the hallway. Shadows cling to the walls.

There's not a soul in sight and the deeper we travel through the compound, the more my stomach knots. It's never this quiet here. Ever!

Lucien sprints down the stairs silently, and I lunge after him, ever vigilant. We go all the way down to the base dungeon, convinced that if Mad put our Alpha anywhere, it's down there.

We curve around the stone steps, suddenly face to face with a guard.

I stiffen.

Lucien stops.

The man is as startled as us at first, frozen on the spot, his eyes practically bulging out of his sockets. I've seen him several times before. Jarrod. A Beta with more muscle than brains.

I clench my fists, but Lucien lunges at him, stealing my fight from me. "You think you can laugh at my cowboy boots?" He growls as they both hit the floor hard.

I roll my eyes and charge right into the dungeon. We have no time to waste.

My sights scan the area for guards, and the cells for Dušan, but I come up short on both fronts.

Instead, my gaze settles on a small bundle at the back of a cell, her heartbreaking cries filling the room.

I stumble forward, my throat thickening. "Meira!"

CHAPTER 15

MEIRA

My head jolts up at the sound of my name, at the familiar voice, with hope threading through my chest.

Bardhyl stands outside my cell, gripping the bars. At first, I can't believe my eyes, but I'm scrambling to my feet and rushing over to him. I crash into the bar door, my arms threading through the gaps to reach him.

He came for me!

Tears never stop falling, while my heart bangs loudly into my ribcage.

"Angel legs," he coos.

"Dušan! They have Dušan!" I blurt out, just as Lucien bursts into the room, his gaze sweeping wide until it lands on us.

"I've got keys," he declares.

Bardhyl and I step back, and in moments, Lucien has the door to my cell swinging open.

I throw myself at my men, all three of us in a tight hug. I can't stop trembling. I want to remain here and never leave their sides, but we are nowhere near safe. Our fight has only just started.

"Dušan," I breathe as I untangle from them. "Mad took him and he's going to kill him. We have to find him."

Lucien's mouth drops open while the corded muscles in Bardhyl's neck twitch.

"Where would he go?" I ask, desperation raking through my chest.

No one responds at first and that tells me they don't hold the answer. I'll scour the whole settlement to find him.

"He'd do it with an audience," Lucien finally answers, and there's trepidation behind his voice. I hate hearing him scared because that skyrockets my own anxiety.

"It'll be either in the courtyard or out in the field."

"We follow the crowds," I squeak, panic sinking in. Terror strangles me.

Bardhyl nods, then takes the lead and wrenches open the main door, while Lucien grabs my hand and we rush out of the dungeon.

"I'm sorry," Lucien says, his face pale as fear swirls behind his gaze. "I promised to look after you, and I lost you again."

"That doesn't matter," I say. "I would do anything to protect you—like you would me. And right now, we need to get to Dušan."

An ache flares in my chest each time I remember the way Mad hauled him out of the prison. My insides shatter at the look on his face.

Dušan's last words linger with me, refusing to leave me. Already, I know that if we don't get to him in time, that memory will destroy me.

Rip me to shreds.

I can't live a life without all three of them with me.

And I can't even begin to imagine how I am meant to go on again. I glance over to Lucien, remembering how he lost his first fated mate. He is braver than I can ever be. Tears well in my eyes each time I think of losing Dušan.

But in my head, it's clear that whatever happens, I will kill Mad.

I will burn down everything. My only salvation is Bardhyl and Lucien, but I'm not a fool. This will destroy them too.

Nothing will ever be the same again.

I feel it in my bones.

Distraught, I gasp for air and race up the stairs with my men.

We sprint out into an empty hallway. There is no pause. We swing right and frantically run to the side door we last used. The answer lies outdoors. I check the corridor behind us as Bardhyl sticks his head outside. With a wave of his hand at us, we hurry into a yard devoid of people.

In that same moment, an ear-piercing siren rings through the air, stealing the earlier silence.

I shudder in my skin, spinning on my heels, half-expecting an army of Ash Wolves to charge down on us.

"Fuck, fuck!" Lucien's hand in mine shakes.

Bardhyl charges to the right and vanishes around the edge of the stronghold building.

"What the hell is going on?" I cry out.

"That siren goes off only when the undead have breached the settlement."

My head spins. "Zombies have barged in here?"

Lucien draws me closer; the color from his face is mostly gone. "I suspect there's something else going on."

Moments later, Bardhyl careens around the far corner of the building farther away and bolts toward us like the devil himself chases him.

Fear twists his expression, and I feel sick to my stomach. Bile rushes to the back of my throat as anxiety strangles me.

I suck in each shaky breath as the ringing continues.

"I think Mad's sacrificing Dušan to the zombies just outside the compound." He gasps. "The siren must be to call the undead to him."

A shiver grips my spine, and my knees buckle under me.

"I can stop it." Before either of them respond, I rip my hand free from Lucien's grasp and sprint to the edge of the fortress.

"Meira!" he calls after me. "Don't go there!"

But nothing will stop me. My hands curl into fists, feet shoving against the ground, running like nothing else in the world matters.

And it doesn't.

I curve around the corner of the fortress, my heart in my throat, but I skid to a stop as fear ices me all over.

Before me, hundreds of Ash pack members scramble toward the wall of the compound. Many are climbing the ladders, others hurrying to find a way to get up there and see what's going on. Cheers come from a lofty pedestal where I spot Mad laughing. He's drinking a glass of wine or something while enjoying staring out beyond the fence. He has guards surrounding him. They are everywhere. There is no way we can even try to attack him. We're outnumbered, and my priority is finding Dušan first. I can only assume he's what everyone is looking at over the wall.

More Ash Wolf members appear and join the others.

But I can't see Dušan from down here.

Bardhyl and Lucien are at my side in moments, heaving for breath. "Don't run off like that," Lucien reprimands me.

"I-I c-can't see him. Maybe it's not him." Tears roll down my face because even as I say the words, I know the truth.

This is exactly how Mad would dish out punishment. Make Dušan's death a spectacle.

My stomach drops right through me and a scream surges through me at the injustice, at how fucking wrong this is.

"We need to get to him." I scan the area when a group of pack members dart right alongside us. Five of them, but they don't even pay us any attention when they're running to witness the show.

Lucien shoves me between him and Bardhyl as more people move in a hurry. "We can't be spotted."

"There's no way out that way," Bardhyl whispers. "We go through the tunnels."

"No. It'll take too long. The back entry," I say, pointing to the way I first entered the settlement. "If there are guards, we'll deal with them and get over the fence. We have to get to Dušan quickly."

They both nod in unison.

Checking the grounds, we make a break for it and sprint across the lawn toward the explosion of trees higher up on the rising landscape.

I keep glancing over to the spectators. No one pays attention to us, but the guards are definitely staying close to Mad. Some cheer, but many cry out from what I assume is fear at seeing their Alpha being offered up as a sacrifice.

My heart bleeds for all of us. For the devastation Mad is about to unleash once he gets rid of Dušan. He'll treat everyone like a slave and punish anyone for not obeying him.

Please, let Dušan be alive by the time we arrive there. Don't let there be too many guards at the rear door. I push myself to go faster to reach my Alpha.

Swift and silent
Swift and silent.
Swift and silent.

Dušan

*T*he rope burns into my wrists and around my chest, my shoulders screaming as my arms remain pulled taut around the pole at my back. I thrash and wrestle against my restraints, attempting to find some movement in the pole. But Mad made sure his guards dug it deep into the ground, and any chance of me knocking it over or wrenching it out is impossible.

Fury lashes over me and I jerk my attention over to the asshole. He stands on a platform behind the wall within the safety of the compound, while I'm left outside. An offering to the starved zombies.

And the siren wails around us like a roaring demon. There is no zombie breach in the pack grounds, but a calling for them to come outside the settlement and find me.

This is his final gift to me after everything we've gone through together. Growing up with his abusive father, when I took most of the beatings so he wouldn't have to. I guarded him in the pack, gave him a high ranking position. But nothing was good enough. I should have seen this coming, should have fucking seen it.

Dozens and dozens of faces are climbing up the fence to gawk at me, and I meet every one of their gazes. Dread twists in my chest, but I want them to watch me fight to the end against a tyrant.

Fear fills most of their eyes. All part of Mad's plan... Show them what happens when someone crosses him, and no one will stand up against him. I ache for these Ash Wolves who are left behind under the control of a monster.

But the depth of my pain surges for Meira.

For the agonizing heartache he will bring her. I fight against my restraints to escape and seek my retribution against my stepbrother. The whispers in my mind repeat, *Break free and kill him. Every fucking flying, deceitful, arrogant inch of him.*

I want blood.

Revenge.

Death for Mad.

He barks a laugh, standing up there, making sure no one misses the joy this brings him.

The crowd gathers behind the fence, climbing up to watch me, and they murmur their own whispers.

I seethe on the inside, my wolf crashing into me for escape, but changing will still leave me tied up, my back plastered to the pole just the same. Tugging against the pole, I won't stop. Not even as the hollow ache in my chest spreads through me, swallowing me with the threat that maybe it's too late for me.

Time drags too slow, and I suck in a hot breath beneath the scorching heat. Dread crawls through me as I keep picturing my death. Breathing heavily, I struggle to focus on nothing else but breaking the restraints holding me in place.

"How does it feel, to be on the receiving end, brother? If only you had trusted me instead of turning against your own family." Mad's words are like a whip, lashing over me.

"Fuck off! You are not my brother." My response seems to echo. I have no time for his gloating. I'm barely keeping it together and not losing my shit. *I'll get out of this. I will.*

And still the siren rings.

Then instead of his mocking voice, which I expect, comes a deep moaning sound that sends shivers down my spine.

Someone screams, and I twist my head toward the woods at my back.

Mad declares, "They're here."

The asshole grins deviously, while my gut twists on itself.

Trying my best not to tremble, I fail miserably. Silhouettes lurch out of the shadows, lanky things with torn clothes and gaunt faces. Missing eyes and limbs. Nothing stops the cursed.

Fighting harder, I yank on the ropes, the burn on my wrists digging deep, ripping at skin. Panic slices through me because this isn't where I'm meant to die. Not like this. Not like fucking this.

More keep shambling out of the forest and the sight shudders me to the core. It's a kick to the gut that despite everything I did, this is where I ended up.

"Beg me," Mad demands.

I'd rather die than grovel to him. Nothing I say will make him change his mind. I've seen the darkness in his eyes, the hatred, the retaliation he thinks I deserve.

I straighten my spine, staring back around to the encroaching monsters. Moving ever closer. Darkening shadows blot the forest. These aren't just a few zombies… but a whole herd.

A tremor jerks through me. Tugging for freedom, I never give up while trepidation claws at my insides. Gone is my calm demeanor as the sound of shuffling feet draws nearer.

A sudden lick of electricity hums along my skin, like it always does when a wolf shifts. Who is it? There's nothing behind me but zombies staggering closer. The crowd on the fence isn't changing but rather crying in panicked gasps. No one dares demand my release and I can't blame them. Not when that's all the push Mad needs to shove them over the fence and at the mercy of the undead.

Frantically, I tug on the rope, a tornado whipping in my chest with adrenaline and the terror coming for me.

A deafening growl slices through the air and it comes from deep in the woods, away from the settlement.

My heart soars. I pray it's Bardhyl and Lucien. I crane my neck to look back. My men better be damn quick because the horde in the distance grows denser. And I hear the terror in people's voices from the wall, their panicked words. *They'll be too close... There're too many... like last time.*

Such a cluster of the undead can have bigger consequences than the pack losing me, if they crash into the compound with so many spectators just out of reach. For the innocents trapped in there, I worry, but for Mad, it's everything he deserves.

Someone screams, and I flinch at the reaction as the ground beneath me shudders like a small quake.

I wrench my head around as a huge white blur charges toward me.

So fast, so large, I can't make it out at first.

"Bardhyl," I murmur to myself, but the scent is all wrong. It's no one I recognize, yet it belongs to an Alpha. My thoughts fly to the man sharing the dungeon with me. Except Meira insisted they negotiated her for him... so why are these trespassers still here?

The sudden swish of air across my back leaves me hardening my spine. I twist my head to the encroaching zombies.

Nothing is stopping the river from coming this way, and I desperately pull for escape.

Four Ash Wolf guards drop from the fence on either side of me. Seconds is all it takes for them to transform into their wolves. Clothes are torn, skin popping as it splits and bones elongate. Trotting closer, they linger around me in a protective circle... This has nothing to do with them keeping me safe from the zombies, but everything to do with stopping the newcomer wolf from freeing me.

Mad is so paranoid I'll escape, he risks his own men to ensure I am torn apart by the undead, even if he loses a few of his own followers.

Except for all I know, whoever these wolves are, they might want me dead as much as they do Mad.

Sadistic asshole.

Tension thickens the air.

I lift my gaze to Mad glaring at me, his lips thinning. I never lower my gaze from his, and for as long as I breathe, I will challenge him.

A howl pierces the air somewhere behind me, and I stiffen against the pole. Seconds later, the pounding of paws hitting the ground booms, coming right up behind me.

My heart pummels against my ribcage. I swivel my head as the four Ash Wolves dart toward the white blurs that burst out of the nearby woods with extraordinary agility. They clash tremendously and all chaos breaks loose.

The crowd is screaming and cheering, while Mad's bellowing commands fall on deaf ears.

And if there was ever a time for me to break free, this is it.

Wriggling my hands in the rope proves harder than I hoped. Fighting the tightness, I struggle to curl my hands enough to fit through the knotted binds.

Frustration suffocates me, and I growl under my breath, rage flaring through me. But I won't stop.

Anger and retaliation float to the surface. I draw on those to fight the ties. I glance up to the spectators watching me from the fence, and it must be clear what I'm doing, but no one says a word. They cheer me on with their gazes, their desperation painted on their faces like war paint.

I suck in each rapid breath, sweat dripping down the side of my face. Every few seconds, I check on the undead. They are mostly out of the shadows now, but more seem to be swaying deeper into the woods coming this way, no doubt drawn by the booming sounds.

My arms tremble, every part of me aching.

Whimpers and cries pierce the air behind me to a resolute ending that one side has lost.

Suddenly, a burst of gasps and *oohs* rise out of the crowd. I strain to look around, but barely a second later, there's a flush of cool air against my back.

The cords instantly slacken and fall away from my wrists and ankles. I stumble free from the pole, rubbing the red marks from where my skin is rubbed raw. I shake the rest of the ropes from my ankles and pivot to find four massive white wolves roaming impatiently at the clearing farther up the hill, staring at me. Blood stains their faces, lips peeling back over razor-sharp teeth stained in blood. Ash Wolves lie torn apart near the woods, their bodies already shifting back to their human forms.

The first few zombies are already throwing themselves at the corpses, gorging on their bodies.

The crowds are screaming for me to run away, and I don't need to be told twice.

Mad is shouting orders at his guards, who are pulling away from him, stricken with fear. My idiot stepbrother shoves one man down off the fence, then another.

"Get the fuck down there and finish them!"

Except his followers are backing away.

I whip around, my heart banging in my chest, when several feet away, the first undead lurches my way.

A phantom hand squeezes my lungs to the point where I can't breathe.

There's no time to wait or think, but I run up in the same direction my saviors dart to save myself.

They aren't stupid and they run.

Behind me, there is shouting, including Mad calling for the guns. And that right there is what is wrong with him. He never thinks anything through. He attracted zombies close to the compound but didn't arrange to have the snipers ready just in case.

Yet I know the bastard. He would have rushed to tie me up right after discovering he had Meira. No thought process, just hurry and move on. This is why everything he's ever touched went to shit, why so many times I've had to cover for him.

A mistake I will never make again.

Thundering as fast as possible before the bullets start flying, I glance back to the masses of zombies piling over the two men Mad pushed off the fence.

The screams ring through the air while the sirens flatline.

But escape is all I care for now... along with darting back into the compound to rescue Meira.

Up ahead near the edge of the compound, the white wolves pause. They all snap in unison to something out of my view and growl, then lunge to attack whatever it is.

More zombies or Ash Wolves waiting in ambush? My skin crawls. I'm surrounded by enemies already.

Running, I finally careen around the far corner of the fence and slow down, having no intention of barging into something blindly.

Except tremors wrack my body at the sight before me.

Four white wolves in attack pose, low, fur bristled, are facing Bardhyl and Lucien in wolf form.

But between them stands Meira, her arms out wide, as if her mere presence is stopping these two powerhouses from colliding and ripping each other apart.

A deep guttural growl tears from my throat and I charge, ready to battle to the end to protect my family.

CHAPTER 16

MEIRA

"Stop! Neither of you are the enemy." My voice streams over the guttural growls, slicing through the thick air filled with Alpha testosterone and dominance.

I remain trapped between two opposing parties, arms stretched toward each to stand in their way of colliding into a bloody battle. Four monstrous white wolves from the northern regions snarl from my right and two men who own my heart on my left. Lucien and Bardhyl. Yet my pulse rages desperately in my veins. The moment we jumped over the fence, we encountered these damn northerners instead of darting around the corner to rescue Dušan. And time is running away from us.

Tick.

Tick.

Tick.

A growl spills from my throat. "Enough of this. We don't have time to waste."

Gunshots and screams sound in the distance. I flinch with each pop, my nerves like shattered glass.

Frantically, I scan the lofty fence farther in the distance to my left. When we'd climbed earlier we found no guards… but how long before they return?

And where the hell is Jae?

I want to scream and shake sense into all these males. Tremors wrack my body, every inch of me clenching.

The threatening growls from each party send out alarm bells in my head, a warning that I'll just get crushed once they attack one another. Except there're two against four, and I've seen the way these northerners fight in the woods. It's terrifying, and I can't bear to have my two wolves taken out. One on one, I have no doubt they'd be equal opponents, but this match is just unfair.

Agony hits me square in the chest when I think of the massacre this can lead to. Desperation clings to me.

"Jae!" I shout. "If you're nearby, get your freaking butt out here now!" I figure if I have someone else at my back, it might help diffuse this situation quicker. I turn to the northern wolves. "Please, Nikos, stand down. These are my pack members and they won't harm you."

Bardhyl's and Lucien's threatening snarls fuel the tension, not helping my cause. But turning my back to the northerners is asking for peril. I may have spent most of my life hidden in the woods, but even I know to never look away from danger.

The scents of sweat and aggression taste sour on the back of my throat.

A sudden figure emerges from around the corner of the lofty fence.

I jerk my head in that direction, and my mind races, initially picturing a Shadow Monster, but it isn't long before my eyes make sense of who's joining us, sprinting across the open ground.

"Dušan," I bellow, all the anguish and dread melting. *He's alive!* The earlier darkness crowding around me softens. Exhilaration floods me as I realize that somehow he escaped Mad's clutches before we got to him. Whatever is responsible for the miracle, I thank with every fiber of my being.

I grab on to him once he reaches my side. "How did you get free?" I keep looking over his shoulder, half-expecting Ash Wolves and the undead to come running after him.

"These wolves freed me," he announces, his chin pointing to the northerners.

He steps in front of me and faces the biggest of the intruders, the one with the gray streak under his throat.

The wolf steps forward, his pack remaining ever vigilant in their attack poses, their heads low, fur bristled, ears flat against their heads.

He's large and is easily Dušan's height. But my Alpha doesn't back down. He stands tall, faces the enemy bravely.

My skin crawls. I clench my fists, and dread grips my heart when the first pricks of energy dance down my skin. With it comes the white wolves' transformation.

Moments later, four men stand before Dušan. Muscular, tall, and unbelievably handsome. Nikos and his two men, then the Alpha that Nikos must have exchanged with me when we crossed paths during the trade.

Bardhyl and Lucien step up next to us, and I'm terrified we're sitting targets here. "We should get out of here," I whisper to Dušan.

Gunfire pops in the distance, and I jump in my skin.

"She's right," Dušan states, breaking the silence. "You barely knew me, but you saved me. But before we can discuss why, we need to move deeper into the woods—and quickly."

No one protests against the suggestion, and we move with haste until we reach a denser part of the forest where I can no longer see the compound, where the shots being fired are faint now.

Dušan doesn't miss a beat and continues his conversation. "You saved me, so I will do anything in my power to permit you safe passage through my sector for now."

The man who steps forward has the gray streak and it isn't Nikos, which surprises me, as I assumed he was the Alpha of this pack.

Their leader is a ferocious-looking man. Short dark hair around the edges and the back, while long across the top. He has small metal rings tied into his hair, adding to the whole wild appearance. I am tiny in comparison to him, and while I search his face for cruelty, all I find is tolerance.

Captivated, I stand close to my men, watching the newcomers, and while I come to terms with realizing the northern wolves might have been the miracle who saved Dušan, I have another thought.

All the naked men.

All the carved muscles.

Heat creeps up the back of my neck, and I shake it off. Keeping my head high, I remind myself this is a tense moment, not a gawk fest. Still, what is it with most Alphas being so well-endowed? Is that something in their genes to aid with the process of knotting?

My gaze slides over to Nikos, who eyes me like he's been watching me as I check out everyone's packages. I grit my teeth and refuse to show him I care. If they're hanging out, hell, I will *inspect the merchandise*, as I once heard a woman say long ago. I never understood it at the time, but boy, have I understood it more recently. The size of the ammunition an Alpha carries ensures a higher chance of procreation, since he can penetrate a female deeper. It's why women want a partner with a long handle.

"I am Ragnar, Alpha of the Savage Sector," the northern Alpha announces, his chin high, chest sticking out. He speaks with a guttural, authoritative voice. His dark green eyes are filled with sincerity. Earnestness that tells me to believe him. As strange as that sounds, I can't help but sense he wears his heart on his sleeve.

He continues. "My men messed up by trading your Omega's life for mine in prison." He glances down at me, his eyes roaming down my body, making me feel as though I'm naked. I refuse to lower my gaze from his.

He clears his throat and keeps going. "I follow a strict code of honor, where no innocents will ever be killed for me or under my ruling. So the woman had her life swapped for me wrongly"—he glares at Nikos—"and as a result, I owed you. But now my debt has been paid to you by saving you from your fate."

Everyone's fallen quiet, and I'm not surprised. It's rare to meet another Alpha with such honorable integrity.

"I am thankful for your honesty and aid when I needed it most," Dušan answers. "If our sector were in better circumstances, I would welcome you into my home for rest and a meal."

Ragnar's gaze sweeps over us. "I have no doubt. You have a lot to clean up and wolves to slay." His voice darkens. "What promise I will make is that I will return to your land with my warriors. If you are not in charge upon my arrival, and this mess hasn't been swept away, I will wipe out all the males on this land, claim the females, and take ownership."

I swallow hard, a shiver crawling up my spine. Though in a roundabout way, he's showing Dušan respect. I wonder how different his view would be if he had his whole army with him right now. Would he take advantage of the situation and claim Shadowlands Sector as his own without giving Dušan a chance to win the pack back?

The thought has me tensing my muscles. I don't know these wolves and while they're granting Dušan respect now, that doesn't mean they're always trustworthy.

Neither Lucien nor Bardhyl comment or disapprove. While the thickness in the air remains, I suspect this is normal behavior among pack leaders.

"If I do not reclaim my sector by the next blue moon, I will not stand in your way," Dušan answers. "But when we do meet again, I propose we make arrangements for our packs to work together."

His response startles me. But I also understand its true meaning. If he's not Alpha of this sector, it'll be because he is dead. A shiver snakes up the back of my legs at the thought because he will fight to the very end before letting Mad steal his pack. Even if we are outnumbered.

Ragnar gives a slight nod, his upper lip curling slightly, then he turns to Nikos. "Get the girl, and we leave."

The earlier darkness grows closer, and Ragnar's gaze lashes over us with his promise.

I don't dare say a word as Nikos marches into the nearby woods. I glance in the direction of the compound, unable to see it, but I still worry about Mad's men finding us. I'm jittery and ready to get a move on.

Bardhyl steps toward the Alpha and starts talking to him in another language... which I can only assume is Danish. When the man responds, Bardhyl breaks into laughter.

I exchange a look with Lucien, who shrugs.

"Meira!" a female voice suddenly cries out. I turn to see Jae running toward me. She crashes into me with a strong embrace, taking me by surprise. "I'm so sorry," she says, taking my hands in hers. "I tried to stop them from exchanging you, but they didn't listen to me. I was worried sick for you." She throws her arms around me once more, hugging me so tightly, I can barely breathe.

"I'm all right." I break free and grasp her hands in mine. "Are these Alphas trustworthy? You're sure they'll take you to your sisters?"

She's nodding before I finish talking and sticks her hand into the pocket of her pants. When she pulls it out, she unfurls her fingers and reveals a gold bird-shaped brooch with a large emerald right in the middle. It's beautiful, and I don't remember the last time I saw jewelry.

"It belongs to my sister, Narah. When they found me, they gave me the brooch as proof." She leans in closer and whispers, "I have to believe my sister hired them." Her lower lip trembles as she offers me a lopsided grin. This means everything to her. Since first meeting her in the woods, she's had one mission: find her sisters. I pray to the moon that she will find her family and these wolves are indeed honorable.

"I really hope so."

"We're leaving," Ragnar announces.

I hug Jae one more time. "I hope we can see each other again."

"Me too." Her voice cracks, and she clears her throat as she pulls back. "Take care, Meira, and I'll miss you saving my ass all the time."

I laugh as she turns and walks toward the four powerful northerners waiting for her.

They quickly vanish into the shadows. *I'll miss you too, Jae.*

Strong hands clasp my waist and suddenly, I'm lifted off the ground as a hot breath washes over my neck. "Hey, beautiful. I missed the hell out of you."

My heart bursts with joy at having Dušan back with us. When my feet touch the ground once more, I twist in his embrace and loop my arms around his neck.

We kiss, our bodies pressed so close and tight, it feels impossible to ever separate again.

"I love you all so much," I murmur. "Let's never be apart again, please."

"Beautiful, you are mine, and I love you." His words touch me in ways I never could have imagined.

Lucien and Bardhyl join us, both on either side of me, embracing me, ensuring they press themselves against me, especially their cocks, like dogs humping a leg. I want to laugh because they're so much more similar than they'd both ever admit.

"I love you, angel legs," Bardhyl murmurs.

"You are my everything, and I love the hell out of you," Lucien adds.

Everything feels surreal and incredible at the same time. I'm falling harder and harder for my men, loving deeper than I ever thought possible. They care for me so much, and I never thought I'd be so lucky. But in no way has this union been easy. The shit we've gone through is crazy.

"We need to get going." Dušan finally pulls back, as do the other two. I remain in the circle of my three men.

"Where to?" I ask. "We can't leave Kinley and all the others in there under Mad's leadership."

"I want to destroy Mad." Bardhyl growls.

"Then we go into the tunnels," Lucien adds.

"My thoughts exactly," Dušan admits. "We just need to lie low to catch our breaths and work out our plan to take back the settlement and Ash Wolves."

I absolutely agree with him, yet a small part of me can't help but feel scared. We barely escaped, barely survived, barely came back together. But as exhausted as I am, I've been frightened my whole life. Hiding. Running.

This time, I'm embracing the fear, the darkness ahead of us, and will walk as far away from the safety of light as I can to make things right. The final battle isn't just about saving a pack… I am fighting to hold on to the one thing I've been missing since losing my mama.

Love.

CHAPTER 17

LUCIEN

"We use the old tunnel room," I suggest, to which Bardhyl scrunches his nose.

"That dump. I hate it there."

I roll my eyes at him as we rush over the slope of the mountain to the blocked-up cave leading into the tunnels. Dušan and Meira rush ahead of us, hand in hand, whispering to each other. She's missed him so much, worried for him. All I want is to wrap up Meira in silk and keep her safe from the world. It's ridiculous and even she'll fight me if I pulled such a stunt. But my wolf burns at the notion of us not keeping her protected.

I cut Bardhyl a stare as he hurries alongside me, constantly looking over his shoulder for signs of pursuit. Then he meets my gaze. "We just stay low in the cave," he says.

"It's too open, and we can't exactly have a fire, with smoke coming out of the cave."

"I agree with Lucien," Dušan throws over his shoulder. "We stay in the room."

Bardhyl grumbles under his breath, glaring at me.

"What can I say? When I'm right, I'm right," I gloat.

"I accept no responsibility if we all catch fleas," he responds.

Meira looks back at us, her eyes wide. "Fleas?"

I shake my head at how dramatic the guy can be. "There are no fleas." I scowl at Bardhyl. "Why are you making up shit?"

He eyes me. "So the family of raccoons who moved in while we used the room during our tunnel building doesn't count?"

I want to laugh out loud at him, but I keep my voice low and whisper, "Big bad wolf is afraid of raccoons."

"Fuck you, Lucien. I woke up with one chewing on my ear."

Dušan pauses at the entrance where two boulders cover the entrance into the tunnel. This place is our saving grace. No one knows about it aside from us four and Kinley. Dušan was right to have kept this little project from his brother and it's serving us well.

Without a word, the three of us head to the barrier, while Meira steps aside, studying us. Hands pressed up against the side of one stone, the three of us make quick work to slide it over the stone ground until a gap appears into the tunnel. It's big enough if we slide in sideways.

Bardhyl goes in first, shuffling, and gets jammed halfway, catching around his chest. That time, I can't help but laugh, but I drive my hands into his sides, shoving him through. "Your fat ass won't fit." I groan.

He pops out on the other side and stumbles. "Hell, that was a tight squeeze."

Meira is giggling to herself as she easily steps inside. Dušan is next, then I follow.

We emerge in complete darkness, but the small room we made during our reconstruction of this tunnel isn't too far and it's easy to find. I take the lead. "Follow me."

The darkness is a welcome friend. I spent weeks... *months* here during construction. A task Dušan gave me when I newly arrived in his pack, and while I didn't realize it until later, he used this to help me deal with the loss of my first soulmate.

I came to Ash Wolves a broken man but ended up as my Alpha's right-hand man. I found a family and future I thought I'd never have again.

Back then, I made friends with the dark, the shadows hiding the heartache ripping me in half. Once more, this familiar place resurrects hard memories, but in my mind, it will always be where I found solace and purpose. It's why I sometimes stay alone in the room we're heading to, so I can remember what I've lost and how I found reconciliation when my memories threaten to swallow me.

Coming here now with Meira brings it to a roundabout closure. I first came here with a shattered heart. Now I return with love flooding every pore in my body.

Footfalls echo from the three following me, and their presence alone confirms that I'll fight for the three of them. For our futures to the end.

"Hey, Bardhyl, what did you and the northern Alpha talk about back in the woods? You were talking in Danish, right? It's like you made a joke or something," Meira asks.

I glance over my shoulder to see Bardhyl smirk to himself. Even Dušan, who remains in the rear just in case anyone sneaks up on us, leans in, curious to hear the conversation.

"He asked me what region I came from, and when I told him, he said he thought I looked familiar, then made a joke that one of my distant relatives is marrying someone in his pack, and she's just as big as me. Her fated mate is not. But you know what this means? I have some blood family alive." He chuckles to himself, and it warms my heart to hear Bardhyl found a connection back to his roots. After his past, he accepted that he'd lost his blood family, so to know there are some family members remaining must be a godsend for him.

"That's amazing," Meira says. "If you go back, I want to join you and meet your relatives. I've always wanted to travel and visit other countries."

Bardhyl chuckles before saying, "If I do go, you're all coming with me. But let's see how things turn out."

"You haven't returned since leaving?" Meira asks.

"No." Bardhyl swallows loudly because what he went through when he lost control of his wolf is a hard burden for anyone to carry. Even for a huge bear like him. I shake my head. I fucking love him as a brother and this is fantastic news.

Dušan doesn't say anything, but what we all need now is rest after everything we've gone through. And thankfully, I stock up on supplies in this room regularly.

Rounding a corner deep in the tunnels where it smells heavily of earth, I reach out and my fingers graze a wooden door, just as I expected. Lowering my hand to the metal handle, I swing open the door.

A sliver of light comes from thin cracks in the ceiling.

I scope out the small room, taking it in one sweep of the empty space. It's safe.

The place is just as I left it. Two medium beds against the back wall, a table near the slits of light coming in, and a cupboard in the far corner. I plastered the walls with wooden panels long ago, and now they've faded to a pale brown. Simple, but what else is needed?

"Whoa. This is so cozy." Meira steps inside, as do the other two, and I shut the door, locking it behind them. Just in case anyone tries to sneak in.

Meira darts around the room, inspecting the beds, and the pantry cupboard filled with food.

Her smile brightens any day.

The feeling never gets old. Floating on her joy is a thing of amazement and it helps me deal with the shitty situation we've found ourselves in.

"We stay here for the night, rest, and then take the next steps," I suggest as Bardhyl moves over to the cupboard. He grabs blankets, while I take the bottle of water and metal containers I've filled with dried food. Then I begin to make a small feast on the table.

Whispers draw my attention to Meira and Dušan making themselves comfortable on the bed, her curled in his arms. Bardhyl gives them space and sits at the table helping himself to dried meats, lost in his own thoughts. I unwrap a large piece of cheese and cut it into chunks with the knife. Down here, the temperature remains cool enough that food doesn't spoil quickly.

Before I know it, I'm joining Bardhyl, slumped in my seat, both of us still naked, eating cheese and meats on crackers. "Didn't realize how starved I was," I murmur.

"I could eat everything here and still be hungry." He smiles lopsidedly, and his gaze sails over to the pair on the bed. They need some alone time after everything.

"So, thoughts on how we destroy Mad?" I ask.

Bardhyl stuffs a big slice of cheese into his mouth before reaching for more crackers. When he swallows his food, he says, "Element of surprise. We need something he isn't expecting to give us time to reach him."

I scratch my head. "Great idea. We just don't *have* the element of surprise. Mad's surely expecting us."

His lips thin. "That's the part I haven't worked out yet."

MEIRA

. . .

*D*ušan wipes away the loose tear threading from the corner of my eye. "No more crying, gorgeous. We made it out alive and now we're the ones Mad should be scared of."

The determination in his voice, the belief he holds, is reason enough that I straighten my back and chase away the fear of what could have happened. I've always been one to put the past behind me and move forward. But with my growing feelings for these three Ash Wolves, something within me has shifted. A trepidation, a gut feeling weighing me down that I may lose them.

"You're right," I say. I wipe my cheeks clean as I pull a leg under me and twist to face Dušan on the bed. "I'm holding on to fear, and that's stupid."

He cradles the sides of my face with his large palms, and I beam under his gaze. He always makes me feel like nothing can touch me. "You are the strongest person I know. We are going to defeat Mad, and then the four of us can be together how we were meant to."

I try to ignore the shiver gripping my spine and avoid asking the obvious question of how in the world we're going to achieve that. This isn't the time for those thoughts. After being battered and deflated, this is a time to recharge.

"I'm ready to destroy Mad."

He laughs softly, and the way he looks at me, I almost expect him to say I'm not going to be facing Mad. But instead, his mouth suddenly grazes mine, gentle at first, then he kisses me intensely. It's scorching hot, thunderous. I melt against him. After everything, this is exactly what I desire. To have him against me, to hear the hunger in his growls, to feel his desperate arousal.

Whatever we have going is so much more than animal and physical attraction. This is a deep passion that sweeps through me like an inferno, and I stand no chance of driving it aside.

When he pushes his tongue past the seam of my lips, I moan with need, and I glide my hand along his rock-hard chest, my fingers pulling at his top. I draw him closer and kiss him with the built-up emotions that have me knotted up.

Eagerly, we kiss like chaotic teenagers, lips bruising, teeth clicking, and I want so much more. We may be in a small, icy cold grotto of a room that smells like stale bread, but a sense of comfort and safety encases me.

It's been too long since I had all my men with me, and now I intend to make the most of everything I've missed.

He groans against my mouth before dragging his lips over my chin and to the curve of my neck, where he nibbles on my skin. I tilt my head back, my eyes shut, and only focus on the heaviness of his breath, the warmth of his mouth, the hunger at which he takes mock bites out of my shoulder.

Greedy fingers tug on the sleeve of my coat, finding more skin to smother in kisses.

His hands fall between us and unbutton my coat hastily. He nudges the fabric open, exposing me completely naked underneath. Sliding the coat over my arms, he makes quick work of scrunching the material halfway down my arms. With my arms trapped in the sleeves, he tucks them behind my back.

"I'm caught," I whisper, breathing heavily, trying to pry free my arms.

His smile is devious and it sends shivers of exhilaration up my spine. "No, you are exactly where I want you. I've dreamed of you every moment we were apart, my wolf going mad with the need to connect. And I'm going to claim that sweet pussy I've missed so much."

Just hearing him talk this way has me practically on the edge of a climax. I suck in each breath, my hands tucked under my back.

Lucien and Bardhyl close in on either side of Dušan, their cocks erect as they have no doubt been watching us from across the room.

Dušan doesn't even seem to notice, but if he does, he doesn't bat an eye. His attention never leaves me as he slides his fingers over my knees and lower, then he grabs my ankles. He brings them up, my knees bending, as he props my heels up on the edge of the bed. With two hands, he pries them wide open.

There is no denial that having three men staring at my most intimate of places does something extraordinary to my confidence.

I feel like a queen, like someone so precious that everything I'd suffered in the past dissolves. And I adore that sensation so much.

"Cupcake, you are stunning," Bardhyl says in his deep voice, his hand on his large cock.

Lucien's eyes have already glazed over, lost in his thoughts.

Dušan strips down in seconds and before me stand my Alphas.

"Please…" I implore them.

That small demand has Dušan running his hands along the inside of my thighs, spreading me wider.

His thumb brushes over my clit so lightly, it sends me into small shudders.

"Is this what you want?" he asks.

"Fuck!" Lucien claims, his hand also palming his thick cock in slow strokes.

The edge of Dušan's erection dances over my entrance.

I'm drenched, and I crane my head forward to reach him, anything to make him take me.

Gripping the sides of my legs, he pushes into me. The other two watch like nothing in the world can rip them away from the sight.

I moan the deeper he plunges, spreading me, filling me. Energy skitters down my body as he thrusts so hard and fast, my whole body jerks on the bed.

I arch my back, crying out with the arousal burning through me. The sounds and the smells are hypnotic.

"Never stop," I murmur.

His fingers find my hardened nipples and he plucks them, flicks them, all while riding me. Our bodies grind together, his gaze never leaving mine. We stare into each other's eyes as he fucks me madly.

I belong to him, to Lucien, to Bardhyl. Months ago, I would have laughed hysterically at the thought of belonging to anyone, let alone three Alphas. Now I can't imagine my life without them.

And just as much I am theirs, they belong to me as well.

Dušan shoves into me, and my entire body jolts, my breasts bouncing. Lucien and Bardhyl stroke themselves quickly now, their gazes devouring me.

Adrenaline charges across my body, and already, there's the familiar sensation of Dušan swelling inside me. There's nothing that compares to the euphoria of him enlarging, his cock knotting. Pushing and nudging and hooking himself to remain locked within me.

Arousal rockets through me. Hastily, he loops an arm under my back and lifts me up and off the bed. I wrap my legs around his hips as he loosens my hands from the coat.

I throw my arms around his neck and bury my face against his chest as he ruts into me.

I'm gasping for air when my climax bursts from deep within me. I cry out, but he kisses me, stealing my scream as I convulse in his arms. My body is wracked with shudders.

"Fuck!" Lucien growls in the background.

Bardhyl snarls like a lion, while a primal animalistic roar rolls through Dušan's chest.

Nothing even comes close to the warmth pulsing through me, at my inner walls clenching Dušan's cock. I'm wrapped around him, and I feel his thickness thrumming within me. He grunts against my mouth suddenly, and that warmth spreading inside is him flooding me with his seed. He pumps into me, claiming me, laying his stake over me.

And it's everything I want.

We're both sweating, perspiration running down my back.

"That was fucking hot!" Lucien mumbles from the corner of the room, where he's grabbed tissues and is now cleaning himself up.

Bardhyl has his shirt pressed up against his erection, his eyes fluttering upward, as he's clearly still floating from his arousal.

When I meet Dušan's gaze, he kisses me once, gentler than before, and murmurs, "Now I feel like I'm at home."

CHAPTER 18

ARDHYL

I lie awake, on the floor on blankets while war plays on my mind, and my heart clenches at what is at risk. I consider the idea of us four just leaving everything behind, not endangering our lives. It won't be easy, but it's a direction forward. It's safer.

Except leaving behind the rest of the Ash Pack is not feasible option. We have friends we consider family, and there is no way Dušan will walk away. Which brings me back to how in the world we overcome Mad when we are outnumbered. Not to mention, Meira's at risk, and the woman is so stubborn, she won't remain behind if I command her,

I grind my teeth, exhaling loudly at the thought. No matter how I look at this, I don't know how to keep her safe. There are no guarantees we'll win this battle, but I can't bring her down with us. So, once Dušan wakes, he and I need to talk. We have a fucking problem and I need it to be resolved before we take on Mad.

"Can't sleep?" Meira's soft voice finds me in the early morning light barely illuminating the room.

I glance over at the bed, where she stares down at me, smiling. Sleep still clings to her eyes, her dark hair a mess, and she's yawning. When I look at her, I see everything I'm not, everything I wish I could be. I'm no fool. I lost my innocence long ago. Killing does that to you, but Meira is different. So how the fuck am I meant to risk her life?

"Not really," I answer.

Carefully, she climbs out of bed trying not to disturb the other two snoring away. She doesn't bother covering herself, coming to me naked, like a beautiful apparition. Those gorgeous curves undo me. *Shit!* My gaze trails over perfect tits, her tiny waist, the small thatch of hair between her legs. She's everything I desire in a woman… soft curves and swells, her scent intoxicating, and a damn temper to match my own. Everything about her is tempting. She's smart and quick-witted, rushes headfirst to protect those she's loyal to. I adore everything about her.

She kneels beside me.

With her naked and my erection hardening, the problem is keeping my head on straight. Last night after Dušan claimed her, she fell asleep in his arms from exhaustion. I finished off the food, by which time Lucien and Dušan had gone to bed with her.

Now, she leans in close and kisses me, the softness of her breasts on my chest. My breath catches in my throat. The enticement to lift her and place her over my hips suffocates the air out of my lungs. I long to bury myself deep inside her, to have her ride me.

I'm only a male, for fuck's sake. A horny bastard who can't get enough.

"Morning," she whispers, her breath warm on my ear, sending blood rushing down to my cock. "I need to go to the toilet," she says.

I almost burst out laughing. Here I am getting a hard-on, and my girl is bursting. "Of course, angel legs. Let's get dressed and I'll go outside with you. There are some old clothes in the cupboard."

What should have happened never does, though now I have more purpose to make this a quick trip and return to claim her while the other two remain asleep.

It doesn't take long before we're out in the tunnels. Meira's hand is in mine and my ears are alert, and even though I am still horny as hell, just being around her gives me a sense of peace.

It's deadly silent. Only the sound of wind whistling through the passage, and the scents reveal no intruders. By the time we reach the main tunnel, the faint trickle of light from the opening in the distance guides us forward.

"If you were a gambling man, what are our odds of defeating Mad?" Meira asks, which makes me wonder if I wasn't the only person unable to sleep last night.

"My confident self says there's no doubt we'll eradicate him."

"But..." She glances over at me, her hand stiffening in my grasp. She's worried, and how can I blame her when we still don't have a proper plan that goes beyond sneaking in and trying to get Mad alone? A plan riddled with holes that might get us killed.

"Nothing ever goes as smoothly," I admit. In truth, that's where my head is at, unable to see a clear path to end this quickly.

Meira takes my response as doom and gloom, and she looks ahead, shadows gathering under her worried gaze.

"Hey," I say, turning her to face me. "You will get out of this if I have anything to do with it."

"Just me?" She's quick to catch my mistake.

"I'm not going to mince my words, angel legs. I fear for your safety, and I would feel a damn lot more comfortable if I knew you were somewhere safe while the three of us went in for Mad."

She stares at me blankly, and I expect an explosion, but having her say nothing is worse. I can handle a verbal spar, but what do I do with silence? I know she'll keep her vow if I can get her to agree, but she's so stubborn.

"Say something," I prod.

She shrugs. "There's nothing to say. That's your opinion. It's not going to happen in this lifetime, but nice wish."

Her mocking tone... is more of what I expect. Still, I find myself grinding my teeth at her headstrong determination. The fault is mine in telling her about my thoughts, and now she'll suspect any plans I put into place will leave her behind.

"We'll see," I respond, guiding her back to the exit of the tunnel. Her hand tightens against mine, and she may infuriate me, but I don't expect anything less from her.

What I want is to claim her in every possible way right here, remind her I'm her Alpha, that she *is* staying behind. I want to protect her so nothing ever touches her again. I pray the moon goddess helps me, and I want to lock her up to know with confidence she will remain away from danger.

"What *is* the plan?" she asks.

"We need to work it out," I reply truthfully. "A big distraction might do the trick, though the hard part is how to get close enough to Mad without being attacked by his guards."

Her brows pull together, like she's pondering the answer. "Maybe we need to lure him out of the compound somehow?"

"Possibly." I squeeze out of the gap between the rocks blocking the entrance with a bit of grunting force. Surveying the forest for movement and sniff the air, I come back with the morning dew on the grass in my nostrils. It's clear.

When I turn to notify Meira, I practically step on her as she stands right behind me.

"All safe?" She arches an eyebrow.

"Let's make this quick," I say, my muscles clenching at how she puts herself in danger without thought.

Outside, the orange sun peeks over the horizon in the distance, tinting the woodlands in strokes of fiery colors. Meira hurries near the trees to my right, and I take the chance to relieve myself too on a huge shrub located in a spot that still lets me keep an eye on her.

A sudden snap of a twig has me stiffening, my feet glued to the ground. I jerk my head up in the direction of the sound from deeper in the woods.

The stale wind brings no scents. Panic rises through me, and I quickly tuck my cock in, retreating.

I give a thin whistle and glance over at Meira, who's standing, looking at me. She heard it too.

I point into the woods, in the direction the sound came from, then cock my head for her to join me.

Fast steps bring her to me just as the scent of death finds me, floods my nostrils, and stirs sickness in my gut. Undead have tracked us.

Before I step back into the cave, four shapes stumble out of the woods farther to my left, exactly where Meira stood barely moments ago.

She pauses, staring at them, while I snatch her arm to drag her inside. Once these fuckers get a whiff of me, they'll be crawling all over these woods.

"Wait." She bats my hand away and turns back toward the zombies.

"Meira, this isn't the time—" But my words flatline when I sweep my gaze over the deathly monsters.

Familiar faces I've seen before. "Hang on. Are they—"

"Yes. They followed us before and never attacked." She suddenly heads toward them and unease curls in my gut. I don't want to be anywhere near those filthy things.

They roam around her like she's a magnet and completely disregard the fact that I'm even standing here. She takes steps toward me, and the creatures lurch after her.

I back up, standing in the cave's entrance, as I'm too damn close to these things. One twitch, and they'll come at me.

"That's close enough," I command.

Meira stops about five feet away, and again, the zombies pause as well.

"Sit," she orders them.

Instantly, all four fall to the ground, sitting.

My mouth drops open with utter shock. "How the fuck are you doing that?"

Meira twists her head in my direction, smiling like she's just discovered a treasure chest. "I think I have an idea for how to take down Mad."

CHAPTER 19

MEIRA

I burst into the bunker, Bardhyl on my heels. "Wake up! I have incredible news!"

Just as the words leave my mouth, I notice they aren't needed. Both Lucien and Dušan are up and about, dressed and staring my way. Lucien lowers the bottle of water from his lips, while Dušan takes a bite from a large cracker.

"What's going on?" he asks, crumbs dusting down his top, a black sweater with a few tears around the neckline.

Bardhyl shuts the door behind us. "What I just saw outside might hold the answer to everything we need," he says, excitement teeming through his voice. "It seems our girl is a lot more special than we first thought."

"Out with it," Lucien insists, his attention completely on us.

"I think I can control those undead that have been following me around," I say in a strong voice. "I probably need to try again to make sure, but I just told them to sit and they obeyed me." Adrenaline zips through my veins, and I'm bouncing on my toes at what this means for us. "It just never occurred to me until now to understand why those four zombies followed me."

Dušan and Lucien blink at me like I've gone mad.

"She's telling the truth," Bardhyl adds. "If I hadn't seen it with my own eyes, I'd be as bug-eyed as you two are right now."

"You can control the four undead that were following you around?" Dušan repeats my words as though shocked, scratching his head. "What makes them so special? What about other zombies?"

I pinch my lips together, running through all my encounters with these specific Shadow Monsters, all the way back to when I first saw them. Then it hits me like a lightning bolt.

"I might know why. I don't understand the reason, but—"

"What is it?" Lucien asks, his voice taut and impatient.

"When I was helping Jae escape from Mad's attack in the woods, I fought several undead to stop them from reaching her. And the four outside, I think I bit during our scuffle."

Bardhyl's gasp draws my attention. "You infected them?"

"I think… maybe I did." My voice comes out unsure. "Whatever makes me still immune to the undead seems to have the opposite effect on them."

"Sweet fuck!" Lucien runs his hand through his hair, pacing, his gaze miles away. "This changes so much. Here Mad thinks you are the key to immunity. Except you're a million times better." He pauses in front of me, taking my hands and kisses the back of them. "You, my little one, can whip the zombies to your command. They are your slaves. You could rule sectors with this ability alone."

"Let's not get ahead of ourselves." I almost choke on my response. His enthusiasm is a bit scary. Ruling over zombies has never been my lifelong ambition, and this is a means to the end to get rid of Mad and gain the Ash Pack back.

"I was right," Bardhyl declares, the corners of his mouth curling upward. "You are our gorgeous little Zombie Queen."

I cringe on the inside at the title, but it's not like I can even rebuke it now.

"The question is," Dušan, who's been quiet, says, "how do you get more zombies under your control so we have an army against Mad? Do you need to bite each one?"

"Most likely. But what if it was something else… Me giving them a scratch?" I don't know why I'm tossing out random ideas… Maybe it's the whole idea of me going around biting zombies for a living to convert them. Doesn't that make me one of them but in reverse? And it was disgusting the first time I tasted their blood… I sure as hell don't look forward to doing it again.

"Only one way to find out. We're going zombie hunting," Dušan commands.

My mouth is suddenly dry, but I'm nodding. As much as the notion is strange, he has a point. And if this is the way to eradicate the world of Mad, I'm ready. Not like I have much of a choice if I intend to help my men. I straighten my spine and summon my bravery. "Let's do this."

Lucien claps like an excited kid while Bardhyl grins, and Dušan draws me toward him. "Are you sure you're okay with doing this?"

"Not really, but what are our other options?" I hold on to his hands a bit too tightly.

"I can see the fear in your eyes." His expression softens, but there's strength behind his gaze, like he's ready to catch me if I fall from this mission. "What are you scared of?"

"That I'll fail and somehow this is a huge misunderstanding that will get you three killed." My arms tremble.

Concern worries his brow. "If you have several zombies out there following your lead, we're already one step ahead of Mad." His hands squeeze mine lightly as his words reassure me.

"What's the plan?" Lucien looks at me, wearing the same painted expression of dread. "We track down a zombie, then we stay close as you do your thing in case we need to come help you?"

As much as dread fills me, I know pulling back now isn't going to help us. I swallow my trepidation and suggest, "It's still morning, so hopefully Ash Wolves aren't roaming the woods. So we should do it now." I hate my suggestion, but it's for the best. This isn't about me, but the pack's safety.

"Agreed," the three of them say in unison, which should make me laugh, but I'm too worried about having missed anything in our plan that might come back to haunt us. Mostly, I need to calm my jumping nerves that I have to change into a wolf again, and I still struggle to control her.

We are heading down the tunnels in no time, and the thought that so much relies on me making this work strikes me. It's one thing to make the undead sit down, but I have no clue how I'm meant to get an army to attack just Mad without hurting innocents.

I push those doubts aside. For now, let's just make sure they listen to me. It isn't like we're swimming in easy options, so I need to make this work.

Once we're outside, my ears prick for sounds and my gaze falls on the four Shadow Monsters still sitting on the ground exactly where I left them. Each of them look my way, not seeming to notice my men.

"Well, fuck me!" Lucien growls. "Never thought I'd ever see anything like this."

Bardhyl stands close by my side, and Dušan steps closer to the undead. He pauses within arm's reach, but none of them even seem to observe him.

Bardhyl murmurs, "I can hardly believe this. It's like they're hypnotized or under a spell of something. They're loyal to you, listening to your orders and all but completely ignoring us. This is insane."

"I want to get this done," I say, cracking my knuckles. The moment I emerge from the cave's entrance, I say, "Stand." The undead climb to their feet.

Dušan retreats instantly in panic, as do the other two men.

"I don't think they're going to attack you," I say. The four creatures stand there, staring at me. "Maybe it's best I do this alone."

When I meet my men's gazes, their eyes fill with the fire to argue, but I don't give them the chance. "I'm quieter on my own. The zombies can't trap me, and I can be faster this way."

"I said, *no more separation*." Dušan raises his voice, and it takes me off guard.

He comes from a place of caring, but my hackles rise too. "I'm doing this my way, and you know it makes sense. It's not like I'm going to go far."

He's shaking his head. "I'm going with you, and as soon as we find zombies, I'll retreat."

It's not something I want to keep arguing over when I know he won't back down.

"Fine." I unbutton the shirt and pull down my pants, then step out of them.

Their eyes are on me… I feel them like a lover's caress. The cool morning breeze curls around my body, rousing goosebumps over my skin. My heart bangs in my chest as I remember Lucien's instructions to bring out my wolf. I can do this.

It still terrifies me how much she fights against me when I'm in wolf form, so what happens that one day when I lose control of her? What then? She'll kill everyone in sight?

As if sensing my uncertainty, Dušan whispers, "Deep breaths in and out, then let her flow out of you."

If only it were that simple.

Swallowing hard, I close my eyes and fill my lungs with oxygen. On my exhale, I call my wolf.

This time, she spills forward and out of me fast, like rushing water. I tense all over as I groan and fall to my knees, the stinging like the pain of a hundred blades slashing across my body.

Moments later, I'm breathing heavily, standing there as a wolf in my tawny red fur, the agony melting away. I embrace the sharpness of sights, the crispness of pine smells. And even before I take a step from where I am, the pungent scent of undead finds me from up ahead in the woods.

She half-howls, half-growls. The buzz of adrenaline soars through me as my wolf shoves me forward. I mentally push her aside, so it's not just her in the driver's seat.

Energy flares down my body and I teeter on the spot.

"You okay, angel legs?" Bardhyl asks.

The four undead watch me, waiting for a command, while my men stand alongside me. I suddenly burst into the woods, the fresh air splashing through my fur.

A quick glance back shows Dušan trailing behind, but so are the four undead.

I dart forward, past trees and over logs, when two silhouettes linger straight ahead.

But I keep running, my wolf refusing to pause. The inner battle inside me is like two animals fighting for control. Next thing I know, I'm veering directly into a pine tree, bumping into it. I can't even walk straight with both of us fighting for control.

My wolf silences, and I use that moment to sniff the air. The pungent reek confirms the creatures are Shadow Monsters.

Ruffling myself, savagery plays through my veins, and I lunge toward the newcomers.

Foliage crunches under the feet of two undead lurching forward, their heads suddenly jerking upward like something's caught their attention. Something behind me.

Dušan.

My heart pounds just as my wolf unleashes a dangerous snarl.

I fly past a dense bank of trees and charge for the first creature. Crashing into it, I bring it down with a thud to the ground. The sharp snap of my teeth crunching bones in its shoulder cuts through the silent woods. Tainted, stale, putrid blood coats my tongue, and I release my grip. Even my wolf agrees and backs off.

The breeze whips around me, and I coil around, throwing myself into a sprint after the second Shadow Monster.

I glance at the four other undead standing in the woods, watching like spectators at an arena.

I close the distance between me and the new fiend, then I slam into its back, flattening it in a heartbeat. I lash out, sinking my teeth into the back of its neck. I'm certain biting them will be more reliable than scratching. His flesh is tight and hard. Like before, I lurch off him right afterward, and shake my head to get the taste out of my mouth.

Wrenching my gaze over my shoulder, I watch the first Shadow Monster stagger to its feet. The shoulder I've bitten into slopes lower than the other, dark blood oozing from the wound down its gaunt, bare chest.

I've done my deed, and while my wolf is still coping with the putrid taste in our mouth, I shove her deep within me. The flare of energy clamps around me, and I suck in rapid breaths, calling to my human side.

Darkness rises in my mind as she fights the transformation, her hunger spilling through me like a river breaking its banks. Panic grips me, but I won't give in, won't let her take control, won't let her win.

The air pulses. I clench my whole body and shove her aside.

A warning growl cracks past my throat, shuddering me right to my bones.

No, you don't. I stiffen, holding myself strong... She is mine and I won't let an animal take me. I shove her energy as far as possible within me. Grasping that moment of reprieve, I fling myself out.

My change tears through me. I wince at the agony, at the drumming of my heart. I stumble upright on two feet, falling into the arms of a tree.

That was too damn close. She's getting harder and harder to control.

I turn to the encroaching undead, watching everything, waiting to see its behavior.

The second one is climbing to its feet as well.

There's no sign of Dušan, but if the Shadow Monsters gained his scent earlier, they'll keep following him.

"Please stop," I whisper. Holding myself tightly, I glance from one fiend to the next.

In unison, they both come to an abrupt halt a couple of feet in front of me. They stare at me with blank, dead eyes.

A hulking outline emerges from the shadows from the direction of the cave. Dušan steps forward, and his eyes are wide, shock palpable on his face. What is he thinking? What a freak I am?

"Fuck, you did it!" he says, and his words soften the hardness in my chest.

"Where there were four, now we have six." I grin at him.

He closes in to my side, and none of the monsters are going for him. They literally don't sense him. "This is incredible."

I look over and search his eyes. "Maybe this is going to work. I think six will be plenty. Easy for me to command and we can go do this now. Sneak into the compound. Right?"

The corner of his mouth twitches with tightness. "We only get one chance to take him by surprise with the zombies. So we need more of them, as Mad's guards know how to take out the undead."

I take a step backward. "I think we're fine like this," I answer.

He studies me for a long pause. "What's going on, Meira?" he asks.

I shake my head and look away from him, studying the undead watching us. Like statues, they stand as still as the trunks surrounding us. Getting more of them to follow me isn't the problem. It's the process of me doing it and not losing control of my wolf. Each time I transform, I worry this will be the last time before she claims me completely.

"Let's go see what the others think about how many undead we need," I suggest and I turn to move, but Dušan steps in my path.

"Meira." His stern voice carves through me.

"It's nothing." Just when I think I finally succeeded by transforming, by keeping my men, the universe refuses to give me a clean break. Not only am I still immune to the zombies, which makes me worry that I'm still sick, but my wolf refuses to kneel.

"Talk to me," he persists, his eyes narrowing. "Something's wrong, isn't it?"

His question wrenches me from my thoughts, and I blink at Dušan. There's a silence between us, and I don't know why I struggle to tell him about this. Or why it scares me to reveal the truth with the others too.

"We can help," he suggests, his concern swimming behind his eyes.

"I-I d-don't think I'm fully healed," I admit, my voice low. It's only when I see the reaction flaring over his face that I realize why I kept from talking to my men about this. His lips tighten and the color in his face drops a few shades. Fear darkens his gaze. That terror right there is like a knife in my gut, twisting and twisting.

"Because you're still immune to the undead? We're going to fix this, Meira, as soon as we deal with Mad. I promise."

"No, it's not just that." My arms shake by my side. I lick my lips and let the words roll free. "I can't control my wolf. When I change, she tries to take over, every single time. All she wants is to attack and hunt."

He takes my hands into his. "Oh, Meira, that's normal. The first time I shifted, my wolf took over and ate all the neighbor's chickens."

"And what about your next change and the one after?"

"It gets easier once you assert your dominance. You don't need to worry about this."

"No." I push his hands away. "You don't get it. It's not getting easier. Each time I've shifted, my wolf is stronger. It takes everything to fight her back."

I hug my middle and glance over to the undead, who haven't moved, just watching. I doubt they really understand what's going on. They resemble something robotic needing activation.

Dušan reaches over and takes my arm, holding me firmly. His finger brushes the inside of my arm, the touch coaxing a calmness racing up my arm. "Have you allowed your wolf to be in control at least once during your transformations?"

"Of course not. Are you crazy? If I do that, what if I never gain command over it again?"

"You will," he says sternly.

"You don't know that. Something is wrong with me and the normal wolf rules don't apply here, Dušan. You're not listening to me. What if when I let her have free rein, she becomes the monster you feared would tear out of me all along? What if I'm then forever lost while she goes on a rampage and kills everyone? What if she comes for you?" I'm shaking my head, my chin quivering at the thought.

Dušan drags me into his arms and holds me in his strong embrace. I sense the quickening of his heartbeat, and there's no denial I've touched a nerve.

"You're letting fear control you," he explains.

His words infuriate me because he's not listening to me. "That's not true." I shove my hand against his chest to get away from him, but his arms are like iron and he holds me in place.

"Listen to me," he says in a deep, authoritative voice. "Our wolves are part of us. They are our other halves. And I know it's terrifying, but to complete your connection with her, you need to let go of the reins on at least one transformation."

He's insane! The thought alone terrifies me.

Unease twinges in my gut. How can he think I can ever do this? I tense up just thinking about it, let alone going through with it.

"I can't," I say, shaking my head again.

"You have no choice. The only way your wolf will become submissive to you is by showing her how much you trust her."

I wrinkle my nose with confusion. "That makes no sense."

"Yes, it does. And we're going to do it this morning, as soon as we find a big enough herd of zombies."

Fury blinds me, and I wrench free from his grip. "Don't tell me what to do!" I stand toe to toe with him, a cocktail of dread and anger coiling in my chest until I can't breathe.

His jawline clenches, and I expect him to lash out to grab me, force me into this. But that never comes. Only words. "We get one chance at the element of surprise. To save the families and innocents like Kinley and help them escape the shackles my stepbrother will impose on them. A few zombies will be taken out quickly against a pack. We need an army of them. I'm sorry you don't like having the responsibility placed on your shoulders. Fuck, if I could, I'd take it from you in a heartbeat and bear it myself." He leans in closer, still not touching me. "But I offer you the next best thing. Me by your side every step of the way."

Hurt rages to the surface of my thoughts. What he says is true, but worse yet, I can't shake the guilt that I'm too terrified to give my wolf full control.

A drop of sweat runs down my spine.

"You know I'm right," he reminds me.

"Yeah, but that doesn't mean I like it."

He laughs, and I hate how easily he breaks through my barriers. My insides are a battleground, emotions rising in me like a storm.

"Shall we do this?" He stretches out his hand, palm side up.

I huff, exasperated. "I'll try."

"That's all I ask." He grabs my wrists and yanks me to his side. Before I can protest, his lips are on mine, and he whisks me away to another world, where I forget my worries.

It's so unfair that he affects me this easily. I cling to him, loving the feeling that I can't escape. Fire ignites between us when he whispers against my mouth, "Never stop believing in yourself."

DUŠAN

$\mathcal{M}$y heart hurts.

Meira is terrified, and it kills me to push her so hard. In truth, unleashing control of our wolf happens naturally when we transform the first time. But Meira isn't exactly a role model for following the normal wolf rules. She has a human parent. She has… or had leukemia. Her wolf refused to come out for most of her life. And then a damn tranquilizer from Mad forced her first change. Nothing here is normal.

My beautiful wolf needs to believe she can do this. And not just for the sake of the Ash Wolves pack, but for herself. If she doesn't relent power to her wolf soon, she will never gain its trust. So her whole life she'll battle for power during her changes rather than taking charge of her wild side.

She holds my hand as we traipse back to the cave, and I study the six undead wandering in our direction behind us. It's incredible to see the aggression in their eyes now replaced with a haziness.

I am beyond proud of Meira and what she's able to accomplish.

Once we emerge from the woods, Lucien and Bardhyl jerk their attention our way. They stand in the cave's entrance. Their attention flips to the small tribe behind us.

"Fuck yes, you did it!" Lucien cheers.

Bardhyl rushes down to take Meira in his arms, lifting her off the ground. Her laughs are a song of promise as she radiates the beauty of a warrior still yet to unleash her wings.

"What's next?" Lucien asks.

"We find a herd of undead," Meira answers as her feet touch the ground. She stands tall and glances over at me with determination and I couldn't be prouder of her at this moment.

Lucien rubs his hands together gleefully. "We're making a zombie army."

The three of us surround Meira. The wind blows her dark hair over her face and she struggles to push it behind her ears. She's naked and isn't shying away. Whether she knows it or not, she has come so much further than she realizes.

Bardhyl kisses the top of her head. "Are we all going?"

"Only if you promise me to stay in the trees when we find the herd so you don't get trapped by them," she says, her voice suddenly serious and stern.

"Agreed," I answer, followed by Bardhyl and Lucien doing the same.

She looks up at me, sincerity deep in her gaze, and her expression screams terror. It kills me to see her still scared, but if I don't push her, she'll lose that opportunity to bond with her wolf. She may hate me for it, though I would rather live with that than have her suffer her whole life.

She jerks away from me, her shoulders curving forward.

My fingers tingle with the urgency to reach over and tell her she isn't alone. But a surge of electricity dances down my arms. She groans with pain before falling to the ground, transforming.

We watch over her, and each one of us would do anything to keep her protected. She means everything to me, and if she's going to be what Bardhyl coined, the Zombie Queen, then I'll adore her even more.

Seconds later, she's in her stunning tawny fur, her ears pointy, and her long tail behind her. Pain rages behind those beautiful eyes, and I hope she listens to me and releases her wolf once we find the herd.

She lifts her head, inhaling the air, then she nudges past Lucien and trots into the woods.

"We stay close," I say, and we're off. Meira takes the lead, and we three watch her back. The six zombies trail behind us. I won't deny it still unnerves me to have them so close.

We travel deeper into the woods, farther from the Ash Wolves compound, which puts me at ease. This area is less likely to be occupied by wolves hunting us down. But it doesn't take us long before the moaning sound of the undead finds us.

Enormous fir and oak trees surround us, trees exploding with green leaves. The place would be beautiful, if it weren't for the lurching shadows amid the trees. Disfigured silhouettes in the distance are exactly what we're here for, yet a shiver crawls up my spine.

Meira hurries forward, and we're running to keep up.

When the first zombie emerges, a barrel of a man with a shirt hanging off his body and ripped jeans, his eyes lock on to us.

A guttural growl shatters the air, and suddenly, the thumping of feet on the ground grows louder… closer.

Meira wastes no time and jumps at the hulking man, taking him down quickly, tearing half his arm off. Blood gushes from the wound staining the Earth.

"We need to hide now," Lucien whispers, his hand on my back.

That's when I spot the wave of the soulless emerging from the shadows. Several dozen at least. Fright shakes me to the core to be out here with so many of them.

I turn and follow Lucien's choice of a tree with low-hanging branches. Bardhyl is already up there. I jump up and snatch one, then swing myself up. Hastily, I make my way to a thick, sturdy branch to easily take my weight. Close to fifteen feet off the ground, I sit close to the trunk with a clear vantage point of the grounds below.

Lucien is above me, while Bardhyl is on a branch facing me.

"If this works, how do we get all the zombies into the compound?" Bardhyl asks. "It's not like we can ask Kinley to not mind us while we drag dozens of zombies through her home. She'll die of fright."

"Plus," Lucien adds, "it might cause a bottleneck once others spot zombies coming out of her house and start shooting at them."

The thoughts plague my mind. "The only option I see is getting them through one of the main entries to the compound."

I turn my attention to Meira. She's already taken down three creatures, but as I watch her calculate every move on whom to attack next, worry creeps across my mind. She hesitates as she looks around, and I sigh. She's still holding on to her wolf, instead of giving it free rein. *Dammit, Meira.*

This makes her slower to kill these while battling her own chaotic war in her mind.

Coldness seeps into my bones at the thought that I didn't realize earlier how much she struggled with her wolf. She will forever lose the ability to control her wolf if she keeps pushing it away.

"I'm sure she'll be fine," Lucien tries to reassure me. "The zombies won't touch her."

"That's not what I'm worried about. It's her not relinquishing control of her wolf yet. She hasn't yet given her wolf full trust yet."

"Oh, fuck!"

I tense, fingers clenching the branch beneath me, and I pray to the moon the damage she's done to herself so far isn't too far gone.

But as those thoughts tumble through my mind, a tsunami of zombies breach the shadows of the forest.

Next thing I know, there are close to a hundred of them pouring out.

My heart slams into my ribcage as I wrench my gaze from them and to Meira, who leaves a bloody trail in her path.

Fuck! Please don't let me have made a mistake by letting her handle this alone.

CHAPTER 20

LUCIEN

"**G**o to the right," Dušan bellows in my direction. "She's coming your way." He's in human form, hoping Meira seeing him this way will help her fight harder and gain power over her wolf.

Bardhyl and I run in our wolf forms to cover ground faster.

My heart pounding wildly, I careen around a tree and pivot to go back the other way. We've been chasing down Meira for the last twenty minutes at least. Since she butchered every last zombie from the herd, she's gone wild. My chest squeezes to see her frantically darting right and left in the woods, lost and confused.

No matter what we do, we can't seem to catch a break. And more than anything, Meira is our priority.

Stop her, then bring her back.

My insides clench with dread that her wolf is too far gone to be controlled again. It tears me apart to know she'll live with that her entire life. I just pray by some miracle it's not too late.

I charge faster, leaping over logs, darting after her.

MEIRA

I'm falling.

That's how it feels. Darkness pounds across my mind while my wolf takes charge. She's running wildly, so out of control, I sense her fear, her confusion. I'd lost her with the attack on the Shadow Monsters, her hunger too hard to tame. Even now, I taste the putrid blood at the back of my throat, while my adrenaline is on fire.

I shake off the heaviness trying to drown me. Once again, I push up against her, to steal back control.

With every last reserve, I drive her aside. My paws hit the ground, and my men surround us.

Her panic is palpable, while I scream in my head to slow down so they can catch me. They'll find a way to help. They have to.

Because I can't live like this.

Trapped.

Forgotten.

Ruled by a wild creature.

She veers right, and kicks me out of her way, and darkness comes for me once more.

I scream.

LUCIEN

*B*ardhyl steamrolls up ahead of her, but she's too busy glancing back at me closing in, Dušan flanking in from the right.

She swings left, like I knew she would, and I leap diagonally to meet her, to cut her off.

Fast paws carry me over the ground, and I scramble toward her, spearing through the forest.

She lunges over a log as I reach her, and I use that moment to throw myself at her from the edge.

I crash my shoulder into her, knocking her over.

Her desperate snarls slice through the air. We both slam down to the foliage-covered ground. With the momentum, we roll, tangled together in a furious mess of growls and kicking up dirt.

My head spins. The ground is hard and unforgiving, but it's her I'm worried about.

The moment we come to a pause, I scramble up to my feet, as does Meira, a growl rolling over her throat.

She backs away from me, her lips peeled back, ears flat against her head. I search for my mate in her eyes, but all I see is a feral wolf.

A phantom hand grips my heart, squeezing it.

Bardhyl suddenly leaps out of the shadows. He's in his human form already. He lands on her other side.

She bolts from him, but I'm on her in seconds when Bardhyl runs and jumps across her back.

His weight brings her down fast. She growls a warning to back away, a desperate and terrified sound that rips me apart on the inside.

Bardhyl doesn't wait a second, still straddling her, grabbing hold of her head, pressing her cheek to the ground so she doesn't bite him.

I call to my swift change as Dušan bursts past the shrubs and joins us. He throws himself to his knees so she can see him. I'm at her rear in seconds, grabbing her kicking back legs, holding her down as Bardhyl shuffles to kneel behind her, his large hands pushing down on her torso.

As cruel as this seems, it's the only way. If she escapes, Meira will struggle to come out. And by the time her wolf is exhausted and she does emerge, who knows where her wolf will have taken her?

But the more I look at her body bucking, hearing her distress, the more my heart shatters at the thought that maybe we're too late to have saved her wolf. Her strength is extraordinary. She attacked over a hundred zombies and the three of us still wrestle to keep her down, but what good is that if she can't bond with her animal?

"Meira," Dušan begins. "Listen to my voice. Focus on me, and pull yourself out. You are in charge. You are the wolf." He never stops encouraging her, letting her hear his voice.

She's been alone so long in her life that it makes me wonder if her wolf has assumed a lone wolf approach. I've heard it said that while our wolves may not emerge until we hit puberty, they can sense and experience the emotions we do.

Meira bucks harder against us, and I glance up. "It's not working. You need to dominate her," I demand.

"He's right," Bardhyl adds. "It's the only way if she hasn't calmed down yet. Her wolf is too wild."

Dušan is grief-stricken, and I don't blame him. He pushed her to do this. But in truth, we're all just as responsible. Each one of us owes her for putting her in this position. Salvation of the pack drove her to the edge and never once did we ask if she was really ready.

I grind my back teeth, fury lashing through me.

Dušan gives a single nod, and instantly, a charge of electricity threads through the air with his change.

His thunderous growl rises through him and covers even me in goosebumps from the power he exudes. Some wolves are born to be leaders; their wolves carry tremendous power. Their presence alone can drive other wolves into submission, and Dušan is one such Alpha.

With a sudden shake of his head, his lips peel back, and he unleashes a deep, gravelly growl. The corded muscles in his neck flex, the sound earthy, carrying a deadly warning.

Meira falls still. Her chest rises and falls rapidly with her fear. Still, a rumble rolls past her throat.

Bardhyl half-grins, but I can tell it's a struggle. "She's a fighter, my angel legs."

Dušan suddenly jerks forward, his mouth and teeth instantly latching on to the side of Meira's neck. He bites down. Not to kill her, but to hold her to the ground of his own force. To assert dominance, to get the wolf to back the fuck down.

Bardhyl and I release her. This is something that is done by Alpha and Omega. If Meira can't control her wolf, then Dušan will take charge for now.

Threatening growls punch through the silence.

Meira doesn't move, her wolf well aware that such a bite could kill her, so she sits in silence.

And Dušan will force her down for as long as it takes for her to submit.

Bardhyl clenches his jaw, watching them.

Waiting.

Come on, little one. Just give in.

A brutal wind rushes past, rustling the branches, chilling my skin. All I can think about is the hardship Meira has been through her entire life. Losing her family. Surviving alone in the woods. Not understanding why she was different. And now to see her on her side on the ground like this makes me sick to my stomach.

I don't know how long we've waited, but when Meira finally quiets down, relief washes over me.

Moments later, her body morphs and stretches. Dušan pulls back, sitting on his heels.

Bardhyl and I approach her. All of us are on our knees around her as she transforms.

In a heartbeat, our soulmate lies on the ground between us, curled in on herself, naked, bruised from her earlier assault on the undead.

She cranes her head up and looks at each of us, the wolf still in her eyes.

I've never seen her this frightened, and her reaction carves through my heart.

"I-I t-thought, I'd never…" Her words fade and tears stream down her face. The terror of knowing she was stuck in the wolf would have been petrifying.

Dušan swoops her into his embrace, an arm cradled under her knees, the other at her back, and she curls against his chest. Her soft cries are blades to my throat.

"I'm so sorry," Dušan whispers to her.

I've never heard him apologize, but the heartbreak in his voice has me choking up.

Bardhyl is just as lost in his thoughts, in his misery of what we almost lost today.

On the way back to the cave leading to the tunnels, the herd of zombies from the earlier massacre wander through the woods. There are so many of them, it leaves me uneasy. My pulse spikes because in truth, I can't tell if they're under Meira's control or wild creatures.

Regardless, the four of us keep a quick pace to our cave without a sound. As we enter, I glance back.

At least three dozen zombies thread through the woods, trailing after us, moaning, lurching, leaving blood in their wake.

Bardhyl's face blanches. "You think they're the safe ones?"

"I fucking hope so," I reply. Then we waste no time rushing to the bunker in the tunnels.

MEIRA

arkness still clings to my mind like cobwebs. Even lying in bed in the underground room with my three wolves, I can't

shake off the sensation of being swallowed by the dark, falling deeper and deeper. That's how it felt being under my wolf's strength.

The terror rose through me so jagged and fast, I swore that would be the last of me. All I pictured was the wolf running into the woods and I'd forever be trapped in my own mind.

I shiver while Dušan wipes my brow with a damp cloth. He sits on the edge of the bed while Lucien covers me with a blanket and Bardhyl sticks another pillow at my back.

"I'm sorry," Dušan says.

It's strange to hear those words from a powerful Alpha. He forced my wolf into submission to help me emerge, and I owe him everything. But there's pain etched over his face, and he's thinking of our conversation in the woods before I transformed. It's in his eyes, the burden that carries the weight of the world. It's been on my mind, too.

I reach over and take his hand in mine, bringing it to my chest. "What happened is not on any of you."

He's shaking his head. "The blame is on no one but me, as I knew better." The grief in his voice splinters my resolve.

"You don't get to say that when everything is chaotic outside. When we barely get two moments to think things through." I lift his hand to my lips. "We can't succeed if you're going to start hating yourself."

Lucien and Bardhyl sit on the bed too, moving closer, but keeping quiet for now.

"Meira, do you understand what happened today?" Dušan explains, his voice thin.

I lick my dry lips and nod. "I have zero control over my wolf, basically." My voice cracks.

He leans in, sliding loose strands of hair from my brow. "When you push your wolf away too often without establishing trust, you lose the ability to control your animal forever."

I stare at him. "What do you mean by *forever*?" Already, my stomach twists in on itself. For so long, I craved to release my wolf, and now that I have, I'm about to lose her once again. All because of my fear.

My throat chokes.

The corners of his mouth pinch. "It means that you can shift of your own free will, but when you do, the wolf will control you in animal form. You will struggle to change back, just as you did today. I'm sorry." He pauses, breathing heavily. "In our eyes, you're still a wolf, still one of us."

I blink away the tears threatening to spill and glance from one Alpha to the next, each staring at me with pity. And I hate myself for wanting the world to open up so I can drown in my tears. I've always been strong, always come through any adversity.

I'm a survivor.

But no matter how many times I tell myself that, I can't stop the tears. Dušan reaches over and catches one as it rolls over my jaw.

"So I can't really transform again, can I?" I ask in a faint voice.

He lowers his gaze and nods. "It's safer if you don't."

"That's not great news," I croak, and my attempt at smiling to push away the dread feels forced and lopsided. Before I know it, I'm sobbing in my hands. Deep, heart-wrenching crying, like my chest is cracking wide open.

My three men close in around me, holding me while I cry for the loss of something I only gained recently. I feel stupid for letting this upset me so much when I grew up without my wolf. Except the first couple of times I did transform awakened something inside me. A primal side, and for the first time in my life, I felt complete. Now it's been ripped away, and what's left is me.

The broken girl with no wolf.

My sobs grow louder as reality settles in. I'll no longer be able to trust my wolf. And I loathe myself for making such a horrible mistake that has cost me so much. For letting fear restrain me.

I don't know how long we stay huddled close, but when I finally lift my head and wipe away the tears, I'm determined to make a difference with what I have.

Glancing up at my three Alphas, I say, "Let's focus on getting our pack back, then we can deal with all this crap. I didn't go through all that with my last transformation to have it wasted. There are over a hundred undead out there under my control. And I'm fucking angry, and I want to destroy something... or *someone* called Mad." My voice trembles.

"I'm ready," Lucien confirms, his hand on my leg squeezing. "I know how it feels to lose so much, but like Dušan helped me get back on my feet, we will be here for you. First, let's kick some ass."

Bardhyl is on my other side. "I should've known there was a reason I fell for you so fast. You're a survivor. We all are, and that makes us the most dangerous wolves out there." He steals a kiss, and I soften against him. "I'm ready to start ripping out spines."

During moments where so much goes to shit, having my three wolves by my side makes all the difference in the world.

Dušan sits back, smiling at me.

"What are you thinking about?" I ask.

"I'm ready to save my pack and finally give you the home where you'll always be loved and protected."

I want to cry all over again at all of their heartfelt words, but the time to shed tears is over.

Mad wants to fight. So I'll bring him a war.

"Is everyone ready?" Dušan asks, standing tall and strong. The wind rustles through his dark hair, a contrast to those hypnotizing blue eyes. They shine brightly today, more than they have before, and behind them is a warrior who's had enough of running.

"I'm ready," I answer, as do Lucien and Bardhyl, though both are preoccupied with staring at the army of Shadow Monsters fanning outward in the woods behind Dušan. The creatures look our way, and even I'll admit there's an eeriness in having so many of them peppering the woods. Each as gross as the next, they're just instruments, I tell myself. There's no soul inside them, no emotion. They're only empty shells carrying a virus.

"I still think one of us should join Meira," Lucien says, his voice clipped, and the way he looks at me, his hands sliding into mine, softens me. He's worried...hell, we all are. After what I just went through earlier today on top of all the other shit, I don't blame him.

"Agreed," Bardhyl states.

I swing my gaze over to him standing on my other side, and I lean against him so he knows how much he means to me. "You're all incredible, but we already agreed. You three are breaking into the compound through the tunnels and I'm waiting near the rear door with this mismatched group of undead, so you can open the back door."

"As much as I hate leaving her too, it makes sense," Dušan adds. "If she's surrounded by over a hundred zombies, no wolf will get close to her. Plus, she'll be waiting for us in the woods, up a tree, so even if the Ash guards are near, she won't be spotted. And if us three are together in the compound, it's easier to fight off anyone if we're found."

I nod. "It's the only way to get all of the creatures into the settlement. And if I can get close enough to Mad and get him and his loyal men away from the innocents, then I'll unleash the zombies on them." I'm hoping with every fiber of my being that the sight of the creatures alone will be Mad's undoing. His men will panic, and Dušan, Lucien, and Bardhyl can take him out.

Well, that's the plan, at least.

Lucien and Bardhyl's misgivings are written all over their faces. "Really hate splitting up again," Bardhyl says, with Lucien nodding.

"I know," I say, "but you may need more of you in there if guards find you."

"Let's move," Dušan commands. He glances at me as his hand reaches for mine. "We'll take you near the compound, then the three of us are heading into the tunnels."

Straightening my posture, I step forward, the harsh wind tugging at my black baggy pants and a T-shirt that hangs off my shoulder. I never pictured myself going to war dressed so casually, but armor is not easy to come by in the stash of clothes in an underground room. Plus, my protection comes from the dozens of undead bodies following me.

Slipping my hand in Dušan's, the four of us hurry into the woods. We maneuver around the standing dead, and it's hard not to know they're there. I can't shake the shivers snaking up my arms at how close the monsters are to my men. The moment we pass them, they turn and proceed to follow. Soon enough, we have a long tail in our wake, with Lucien and Bardhyl extremely close at our backs.

"This is kinda freaky," Lucien murmurs.

"If I ever come back as one of those things," Bardhyl says with a soft voice, "chop off my head. I don't want to lurch randomly searching for food like a creep."

"Bruh, you'll be dead and won't have a brain to think beyond eating."

"What if we've all been wrong this whole time about them? They clearly must have some ability. How else do they understand Meira's commands?"

I glance over my shoulder at them, the men's conversation making me curious about the answer. "Maybe it's just a muscle memory. A few words they recognize and their meaning? Whatever's in my blood that I infect them with has to connects us to an extent, so it could be a combo of things." I shrug, though the thought that my influence may not last forever does cross my mind.

"It's one theory," Lucien responds, while Bardhyl nods.

Dušan says, "What matters is that right now they want to do your bidding."

"Absolutely." I squeeze his hand lightly.

We remain silent for the rest of the trip through the woods, and soon slow down as we approach the rear of the settlement.

When the compound finally comes into view beyond the trees that surround us, my stomach clenches.

Shuffling feet on the ground closes in behind us, and most of the Shadow Monsters have paused, staring my way. Dense trees, and shadows, are the perfect place to hide.

"This spot should work," I say.

"And this is your tree, cupcake," Bardhyl says, standing near an enormous fir bursting with heavily ladened branches that span outward at the base and cinch in the higher it reaches for the sky. I can't help but be reminded of a Christmas tree. Something I've seen a few times in old books. A tradition humans used to celebrate. The reason for the festivities wasn't clear, but it clearly always involved lots of food, gifts, and a tree like this one decorated in the most spectacular colors. It must have been beautiful.

"This will do." Lucien heads over to the tree, dodging several zombies standing in his path, and we follow him.

Dušan's grip pulls me to him. "Stay hidden no matter what until we come for you. We'll be quick to open the rear door from the inside. Just remember how much I love you."

Before I can respond, his lips are on mine. I lean against him, my hands on his chest, and kiss him back, not ready to part ways. His arms let go of mine and they slide around my back. Breathless and hot, I fist his shirt, needing more of these soft, cushioned lips, and the way his tongue explores my mouth.

Someone clears his throat. "Careful you don't give the zombies any ideas." The mirth in Lucien's voice has us breaking apart, and I roll my eyes at him.

Lucien takes the chance to close the distance between us, drawing me by my waist to his body. His kiss is instant, those wicked lips rolling against mine, his grip digging into my hips with need.

Fingers crawl up my back, when I realize it's a third hand and not Lucien's. Breaking from our kiss, I whisper to him, "Please take care of them."

"Love you, babe. We got this."

When I turn to Bardhyl, he grabs my waist and has me off my feet in seconds. I gasp and grip his shoulders as I snap my legs around his hips. His lips are on fire. And we kiss like this is our last day on Earth, ravenous and desperate. I adore how he's always rougher with me, and I'm left with bruised lips afterward.

In moments, he pulls from my mouth, and with strong hands, he lifts me higher as he turns us toward the lowest-hanging branch. "Grab hold and I'll give you a boost."

I snatch a branch that is rough under my fingers.

Bardhyl's hands run down my legs and he grabs the back of my thighs, then pushes me higher.

In haste, I throw a leg over the branch and shuffle up until I'm sitting. I glance down and blow Bardhyl a kiss.

"Love you. Behave and stay up there," he commands.

"I promise," I say.

One last look my way with heartfelt smiles, and the three of them slide into the woods amid the undead, vanishing from view. The density of pine needles on this tree makes it difficult to see too much. Slowly, I get to my feet, grasping on to the trunk, reminded of my days living in trees. A time that feels so long ago.

I climb up to the next branch, which offers a better vantage point. And right there in the distance stands the lofty, metal fence of the compound with a small view of the back door. Nerves tangle inside me that Ash Wolves will ambush my men. I chew on my lower lip and just need to shove those thoughts aside or they will drive me crazy.

Settling down, I get comfortable and straddle the thick branch, my back to the trunk.

Now I stare out and wait, hoping that everything goes according to plan.

BARDHYL

$\mathcal{I}$ suck in every rapid breath, filling my lungs. We ran the whole fucking way back to the cave and through the tunnels. Now we're catching our breath inside Kinley's house at the back door.

Lucien peers out the window through a gap in the thick curtains, while Dušan has the door slightly ajar, staring out into the backyard that flows into the woodlands inside the settlement.

"Is it clear?" I ask, glancing back into the empty living room. We helped Kinley into her bedroom, and she shut the door, closing herself in to stay safe until this is over in case the fight breaks near her home. We told her the bare minimum but enough to know what's going to be happening outside.

Dušan's plan is simple, but the best ones usually are. Going for Mad directly exposes us easily to his guards. We'd be overpowered. So a massive breach in the settlement will make him less protected by his guards as panic spreads. And that is when we strike.

I've known the dickhead long enough to not expect Mad to get his hands dirty. He sends his men out to search for us in the woods while he sits back in the compound, taking it easy. *Sonofabitch.* His little rise to the top is going to be short-lived.

"Area's clear," Dušan whispers. "We make a break into the cluster of trees leading up to the rear entry of the compound. We'll be less likely to be spotted this way, then we can open the gate for Meira."

The door to the house swings open, and we're on the run.

A strong wind collides into us. My gut tightens and I hold my head low, stealing looks from either side of me. No one to see the three of us cut across the wide grounds and burst into the cluster of trees running along the edge of the settlement. It's not enough to conceal us completely, but the shadows are a cloak should anyone glance this way.

I can't stop thinking about Meira and praying she's safe. She's surrounded by zombies, but Ash Wolves are in the woods, and I hope to hell and back she remains up in that tree.

We pound the Earth, rushing up the slope, staying close to the trees. I remain behind Dušan and Lucien, and I keep checking over my shoulder. My skin crawls being out here; I feel damn exposed. I loathe how I feel anything but safe in my own home. And this is why I want to murder Mad slowly, make him squirm and cry. And, well, those worms who follow him blindly will also feel my wrath. I've taken down a mental list of names. None of them have escaped my attention. I don't forget.

Dušan glances back, and with two fingers, signals we're heading left and toward the rear door, where the woodland inside the compound spreads, offering us better coverage.

We move swiftly, and I scan the rolling landscape that leads back down to the fortress… the home we will reclaim.

About a dozen pack members roam near the back of the building, and I can only assume they're guards. Since Mad's forced takeover, most of the pack seem to remain hidden in their homes. It's better this way, as they'll stay out of danger.

Lucien swings right sharply, along with Dušan, just as the hairs on my nape start lifting. The air thickens, and I sense someone near. I snatch the back of Lucien's top, just as a group of figures emerge from up ahead where the woods are thicker, darker. Dušan pauses with us.

Guards, maybe twenty of them, come at us so suddenly, I retreat.

A hum carries on the wind, closely followed by thundering steps racing up behind us as well. My nerves wound tight, I snap around just as a fist crunches right in the middle of my face.

I groan, the pain zigzagging across the bridge of my nose, and stars dance in my vision. "The fuck?!"

Fury blasts through me, and I'm already lunging at the enemy before I can clearly see who it is. Who gives a fuck when I'm tearing him down?

Punch after punch, I finish him, my anger a blinding bull pushing and pushing me. If our war has begun, I won't back down.

Someone smashes into my side, throwing me to the ground. I roar and leap up to my feet when a wall of guards rush toward me. Lucien and Dušan are fighting their own battles, but they're outnumbered.

This isn't part of the plan… we made a grave mistake. We assumed that Mad would leave this entrance manned with the usual number of guards.

I recoil, my legs slipping out from under me down the slope. My wolf shoves forward when the siren abruptly goes off, right as more guards emerge from the direction of the back entrance. Except the alarm has nothing to do with a breach. It's to announce to Mad that we've been caught. This was a damn trap.

Fuck!

Lucien and Dušan both look at me, and dread sweeps over their eyes. With guards coming at us from every side, the realization that we've walked into a trap sinks in. There's no way we can fight our way out of this, and I see it painted over their faces as well. I grind my teeth, fury bleeding into every fibre of my being.

Two guards leap onto Lucien, and he tosses one aside, the other clipping his face with a swinging fist. Another three guards circle Dušan. I dart toward them when more men came at me, and I'm knocked backward from their sheer force. Fire lashes over my back from the hard, rocky ground while I lose sight of Lucien and Dušan.

Instinct has me scrambling back up, recoiling, searching for a rock or something as a weapon.

Sucking in hard breaths, I meet each of my attackers' eyes. Asshole Alphas and Betas at the bottom of the pack hierarchy. I will destroy every last one of them.

Then they charge toward me.

Fists, knees, knuckles. They find me. Pummel into me. I lash out as ferociously as possible, needing a few seconds to transform, but more pile on top.

I snatch one by the neck and squeeze, his lips curling upward with a snarl. All the while, I deliver a punch to someone else's face. A hard whack comes to the back of my head, and yellow stars glint in my vision.

I snap around, my stomach tightening from the pain spearing over my skull. Before I can even kick the shit out of the brute, two others slam into my back, shoving me the ground. Rage rises through me like an inferno.

I buck and throw myself against him, hissing each time they belt into me. More and more of them come, giving me no chance to even get to my feet.

Blood drips from my mouth and nose, and for the first time in too long, fear creeps over me at the realization that maybe we've chewed off more than we can handle.

CHAPTER 22

MEIRA

A sharp, siren wails through the air. Sudden and loud.

I flinch at first, not expecting it. *Please don't let that be about my men.* Last time I heard that sound, Dušan had been tied up outside the settlement and left as food for the undead.

Blinking toward the compound through the gaps in the tree I'm perched in, I don't notice any commotion. But beyond the fence might be a different story.

My fingers tremble as I grip on to the branch, and a deep pain bites into my chest.

What if they're caught? And I'm waiting for them and they'll never come?

I chew on my lower lip, gnawing it, unsure what to do. They said to remain up here, and I toy with the notion back and forth.

Stay.

Go and check on them.

Fuck!

The siren wears on me like a mosquito refusing to leave me alone. And well, this mosquito is screaming for me to run to the compound.

Determination flares over me. There is a growing need to find them, to help them.

I grasp the thick branch I'm straddling, fingers digging into the timber. Down below, there's no sign of anything but the undead, who are near the tree, waiting for me.

Urgency furiously clings to me. While my throat tightens at the thought that I'm sending my wolves to their deaths by doing nothing.

Darkness feathers at the edges of my mind, coming at me in waves.

I'm shaking, fidgeting, anxiety knotting in my gut.

Choking on my breaths, I start descending, unable to stop myself if I tried. I will never be able to live with myself if I don't check. And I have enough regrets to live with already.

I jump down and my feet kiss the ground.

The surrounding Shadow Monsters flick their heads up, eyes on me, suddenly attentive. Turning away from them, I sprint through the woods as quietly as possible in the direction of the compound, keeping to the shadows.

Please, let them be all right. Please.

Behind me, the undead move slowly, so I'm hoping if I'm quick enough, any guards at the gate won't see the hoard of zombies coming their way.

I remember there were several trees not too far from the fence. If I climb one of those, it should give me a better look into the compound. The farther I move, the more sparse the trees become.

My skin crawls with the thought of being so easily exposed, but I'm not going to sit back if my wolves are in danger. As Dušan said, we have one chance to create the element of surprise… and that comes down to me. If Mad did capture them, then our plans change.

I duck under a branch and swerve around a large fir when a shadow falls over me. A shudder races down to my bones.

I turn and come face to face with a huge brute, with close-cropped, shaved hair and a crooked nose. A Beta, by his bitter scent, and definitely belonging to Mad, seeing as he's this close to the settlement. Omegas and Betas aren't made for each other, so to me, they don't smell appealing.

Recoiling, I glance quickly to where the Shadow Monsters are… They're still just shadows in the distance in the woods, making their way too slowly.

Shit!

I throw my hands up as he approaches. He grins, covering me in shivers, then I kick him in the knee hard.

A split second is all he gives me, but it's enough. I whip around and jolt away, right for the edge of the woods. And my anxiety goes off… If there's one guard, there are more and me bursting into the clearing will grab their attention. I keep looking back and the undead are still too damn far away, blended in among the shadows in the woods.

I swerve left and right to ditch the dickhead coming for me now.

The siren ends abruptly, and a deafening silence settles over the land. My ears pulse, my heart banging loudly in them.

The bastard snatches my top and yanks me backward. I stumble on my heels and slam into his chest. Despair floods me, along with images of him beating me until I'm unconscious. Then I'm no use to anyone.

His hot breath brushes over my cheek. "You're not escaping this time, Omega bitch."

Rage burns me, and I slam my heel into his foot, shoving myself away from him. Iron fingers snap over my wrist too fast for me to escape. Panic swallows me.

I swing back around, my fist crashing into the side of his head. Just as he snarls and wrenches me closer, I drive my knee deep into his balls, loving every moment of his fallen expression.

"Don't fucking touch me!" I shove my fists into his chest and he falls over, curling in on himself, moaning.

I snap around to escape, but I charge right into someone solid. Bouncing back, I teeter to catch my balance.

The new asshole snatches my hair and yanks me to him, sneering. "You dare raise a hand to us, you pathetic, plague-ridden filth?"

Pain roars over my scalp, and tears fill my eyes. I'm scratching his hand to get him to release me. Every inch of me trembles.

I grind my jaw, refusing to give in to them.

He's suddenly hauling me by my hair across the land and right out of the woods. Desperately, I run to keep up with his long strides. I'm half-bent forward from his grip, so I can't even look back to see how far the undead are.

Hell, if there was ever a time I needed them by my side, it's freaking now.

The ass holding on to me pauses, growling. "Open the fucking door." He bangs a fist against the door, and I crane my head up to see there are no guards on patrol on the fence.

Though from inside, the faint sounds of shouting reaches us. My stomach locks at the thought that maybe I'd been right all along and my men are captured.

Loathing for Mad burns all the way down to my gut. I want to make him suffer so much.

When the man goes to bang on the door once more, I drive a fist into his ribs, then another.

He sneers, his grasp tightening, wrenching me by my hair.

I cry out and twist around just enough to glance behind us.

The undead are emerging from the woods like a great wave, and I've never been happier in my whole life to see them.

A creak sounds from the door to the compound opening, stealing my attention.

"Get the fuck in here," another guard bellows from inside. "We've got them."

I yell and punch my captor's arm, digging my heels in the ground to slow him. Anything.

I twist my head as the Shadow Monsters approach, closer and closer.

Just a bit more time.

"Well, look what I found." He wrenches me toward his friend, whose eyes bulge out of his head. His gaze is locked on something over my shoulder.

"Zombies!"

I feel the man holding me shake against me as he whips around.

"Goddammit, where'd they come from?" His voice trembles.

I'm kicking and shoving against him to escape as he drags me into the compound. I drop to my knees, and his grasp slackens.

In desperation, I scramble over and push myself off the ground.

Thick arms loop around my middle as he yanks me into his arms. "No, you don't."

I scream, my hands reaching out for the undead.

"Run to me!" I screech.

In seconds, they descend upon us like a storm, running awkwardly, lopsided, but they thunder onward regardless. Thin, ragged things that today have become my saviors.

Aggressively, the brute manhandles me, shoving me over his shoulder, and darts past the enormous metal door and into the settlement.

The guard from the door drives it shut, just as several undead slam into the entrance.

He growls, pushing his hands against the metal door, his feet pressing into the earth. "Help me!" he roars.

But there are no other guards in this area.

The man shoving a shoulder into the door is driven backward, his feet skidding over the soil. As I watch through the gap, wave after wave of them pushing to get to me. He stands no chance.

And then the sudden thumping against the nearby fence comes, over and over, I know exactly what's happening.

They're breaking it down.

I want them to tear it down and get in here.

The brute holding me shoves me to the ground as though I'm nothing but a sack. I collapse hard on my hip, but I scramble to my feet, when the back of his hand collides with the side of my face. His knuckles feel like I'd been whacked by a bag of rocks.

"Stay down!" he sneers.

Stars dance in my vision, and I fall flat onto my back. Fiery pain spears over my face. I cry out, clasping my cheek, as my head feels like it's cracking in half. *Damn idiot.*

Around me, the sounds of moaning escalate, and suddenly, the siren blares again.

This time, it's for a real breach.

My face throbs with a sharp ache. The world tilts for a few seconds, then settles.

I blink to clear my eyes as the two guards dart in my direction, panic-stricken. One bolts down the hill toward the fortress, while the other comes for me.

He goes to grab me, but I frantically roll away from him and rush to my feet.

He's too busy glancing over his shoulder when I quickly sidestep him to reach the creatures, but his hand seizes my arm. His grasp squeezes until it hurts.

I spin and bash my fist into his grip. "Leave me alone," I cry out.

His face is as white as a sheet, yet he still drags me behind him.

I lose my footing and drop to my knees as he lugs me by my arm.

The undead are upon us, careening right alongside us now.

The idiot holding me glances back. He does a double take, his eyes bulging out of his head at how close he is to them.

Then he does what any frightened person does... He releases me and runs like mad down the hill.

Shadow Monsters gather on either side of me, behind me, and with the siren blaring, I guess I've made one hell of an entrance that won't go unnoticed.

CHAPTER 23

LUCIEN

A kick to the back of my legs has my knees hitting the ground right near the fortress. My stomach lurches, and I tense with fury. Dušan and Bardhyl are on either side of me, their deep, guttural growls matching my own. Mad's men had ambushed us, and now, I burn to know that he fooled us.

Abruptly, the sirens of a breach screech through the air. I jerk my head toward the rear entrance. There, shadows flit about in the woodlands within the settlement, moving erratically. What the hell is that?

Did they find Meira?

I glance over to Dušan and Bardhyl, their gazes locked on the movement up on the hill.

My adrenaline spikes as I picture the guards tracking her down, dragging her in here. How did they find her? I grind my teeth, knowing for a fact she would have willingly gotten down from the tree.

"What the fuck is going on?" Mad roars, marching in front of us, staring up the huge hill at the frenzy of shadows amid the cluster of trees. All I can imagine is how easily I can attack him right now, kill him in a heartbeat. Well, easy if there weren't a gun muzzle pointed to the back of our heads.

"Jack," Mad barks. "Get up there now! Find out what's going on." Then he turns on us. "There was never any doubt you would end on your knees before me," he gloats.

There is something so repulsive about a man whose ego exudes from every pore in his body, and he's proud of it. His attention homes in on Dušan. "You're not so great now. Only two men follow you, while the rest stay loyal by my side." He pats his own chest, a sneer of arrogance on the corner of his lips.

I see it now… This petty man has spent his whole life trying to prove to others he's greater and better. His desperation to be praised and seen as successful in ascending to the pack leader position has been nagging him his whole life.

It's why he stares at Dušan with vicious hatred. Jealousy can make someone horrendously vile and vindictive.

"Stefan," Dušan snaps, using Mad's real name. Something I rarely hear him use, and the few times he has have been when he's fucking pissed at him. "This isn't who you are. Most of the pack are in their homes terrified. You can't rule a pack on fear alone. You know this. Your father told us this all the time."

Mad spits on the ground, inches from us. "Fuck you. Easy to say when you claimed what was rightfully mine. He was my father by blood, not yours, but you still forced yourself to be Alpha of the pack, didn't you?"

"Could have something to do with you being too weak-assed to fight the previous Alpha to claim the Ash Wolves," Bardhyl snarls. "So you take the pack like all gutless pigs. By cheating."

The guard behind him whacks him in the back of his head. The thump has me cringing as Bardhyl falls face-first to the ground from the impact. He groans but pushes himself to his knees. Blood drips down his neck from the hit.

I clench my fists. My blood races with vengeance. The need to destroy all these bastards swallows me. Staring past Mad, I see Jack and two others heading up the hill, and there's no sign of what's causing the commotion farther up there.

"Today will be my happiest day. To see you three finally fucking killed." Mad's upper lip curls.

He lifts his head to the guards behind us, looking ready to give the order.

I stiffen, bending my arms, prepared to attack the prick behind me first.

A sudden scream, dark and terrifying, definitely belonging to a man, spears through the air from nearby on the hill.

We all glance in that direction.

Two guards are sprinting down, Jack and his followers, suddenly doing the same, darting like death chases them.

Near the edge of the trees, a cluster of undead lurch forward, dozens of them pouring out of the shadows. Their moans are lost beneath the siren. I want to shout from the rooftops. *Fuck yes!* About damn time, and that's when I know it's Meira who must be there. I adore that little wolf.

"Who the fuck let them in?" Mad bellows. "Shoot them!" He's shuddering, his face red with rage.

My heart leaps, thundering as more of these filthy creatures that are the best sight in the world shuffle forward.

Someone stands from the ground in front of the zombies. Dark, long hair flowing over her shoulder, she's like a goddess rising out of the underworld with her followers crowding around her. As morbid as that sounds, there's something spectacular about seeing her wield such power.

"Meira," Bardhyl whispers, and Dušan's breath catches. While others fear her, we love her to hell and back.

The gun from the back of my head falls away, and panicked voices burst around us. I curl my fingers as Dušan climbs to his feet. Bardhyl and I follow suit.

Mad whips around to us, his eyes bulging. "Shoot these three now!" he shouts at the guards behind us.

My stomach tightens, squeezing the terror right up to my throat.

When I glance over my shoulder, the guards have recoiled, the guns in their hands trembling. It's one thing to shoot zombies from the safety of a fence, but to be in front of them brings out a raw, primal fear.

An explosive shot sounds, and my attention turns to a guard aiming for the monsters running down toward us.

Meira. I can't see her. Has she given the monsters a command? Where the hell is she if Mad's men are firing? The terror of something happening to her grips me.

The wave of undead is like a tsunami, relentless, and it sends a shudder down my back.

"We need to move and find her," I suggest. "We don't know what order she gave them."

Dušan swings around and runs up behind Mad, who's distracted.

Bardhyl charges toward a guard who has his back turned to him and takes him down.

And suddenly, the walls of chaos close in around us. All I can think about is finding Meira, then finishing Mad, and I pivot toward the undead.

A sudden slamming into my side so hard, it has me hissing, my spine arching inward.

I whip around to the guard pointing his gun directly at my chest, and a dull, cold ache fills me. My feet are glued to the ground while the commotion around me fades and only the pounding of my heart sounds that this is it.

BARDHYL

Zombies rush toward us while guards with weapons are running to stop them, shooting wildly.

Pop. Pop. Pop.

I frantically scan the area for Meira. One moment she stood at the top of the hill with the zombies, then she merged into their mass and vanished.

Fury skids across my mind as the siren in the distance howls like a wolf. Where the hell is she? With bullets flying, my insides clench at the thought that she'll get shot.

A hard punch comes to my shoulder "Get the fuck to the ground!"

I grunt with pain and swing around, my fist swinging. Clipping the bastard in the head, I follow his fall, delivering two more blows into his face.

Someone shoves a foot into my back, driving me flat on top of the guard. Rapidly, I roll off the first guy, seeing the other culprit stumbling to catch his step from being pushed by a zombie. But he's now lifting his gun toward me. So I kick out my leg, my heel striking him in the groin. He stumbles backward, crying like a baby, and I get up.

Several feet away, I spot Lucien iced over, looking at the man pointing a gun at his chest. I swallow hard.

Acid spills into my veins, scorching my insides. I don't even remember moving, but I sprint over to them, slamming into the guard, coming in from his side like an avalanche.

He hits the ground as his gun goes off, shooting into the air.

My ears ring with a tremendous buzz.

Frantically, I snatch the man's wrist and squeeze it until he drops the gun. I headbutt him in the face for good measure. My head spins, but it's damn worth it. He cries out, blood spilling from his nose.

Lucien is there in seconds, punching the shit out of him as I climb to my feet.

"Always saving your ass." I groan, smirking at my friend. He turns to me, a slash of blood across his cheek from the guy he just beat up. Looks like war paint, and it suits him.

"I had him right where I wanted him," he answers, but he smiles his thanks. "Where's Dušan? Last I saw, he was dashing for Mad."

I scan the yard.

There's madness all around, but there's no sign of him. Did Mad take him? "We gotta find them and Meira."

The zombies are closing in. They fan out, covering the slopes like locusts coming in for a feed. The three or so dozen guards don't even bother with us anymore, not when they're anticipating being eaten alive.

"Maybe it's not a bad idea to stay out of the zombies' way until we know they aren't going to eat us," I suggest. "And let's take out these disloyal motherfuckers working for Mad in the process."

"Hell yeah." Lucien rips his top up and over his head, undressing so fast, he's already half-transformed by the time his pants hit the ground. He bounds out as his gray wolf, and I call mine just as quickly, the sharp pain of transforming deep and agonizing, but I embrace it as I ready for war.

The moment I leap forward, the first wave of zombies reaches us. They scramble onward, not attacking, but slamming into whoever stands in their way.

Everyone is screaming as pandemonium strikes.

Lucien and I make a mad rush to the side and out of their way. From my perspective, not one undead has attacked anyone. They're stopping once they reach the fortress, so that must have been Meira's command.

Those terrified guards don't seem to notice and deliriously shout, shoving against the creatures spreading around the yard, shooting them. But there's no way they have enough ammunition for the whole herd.

And this is our moment. I exchange a glance with Lucien, then I crash into the masses, him doing the same. It's a strange feeling to be pressing against the undead… monsters I feared my whole life, and now look at me. Rubbing shoulders with them.

It's ridiculous.

But I also wonder if this is how Meira feels being immune around them.

Like she's untouchable.

A squeal comes from my left from a guy shuddering, trying to avoid touching the monsters all around him.

Darkness slips over me and I have no regrets. It's time to bring these dickheads their long overdue punishment.

CHAPTER 24

MEIRA

I sprint away from the zombies, cutting across the grounds and hurrying toward the side of the fortress. Moments ago, I rode the wave of the undead, using them as a shield against the bullets. My pulse is still in my throat. And now it beats frantically after I had spotted Dušan darting after Mad. They headed down this wide path between the building and lofty fence. Several of his guards followed, and that worries the hell out of me.

I desperately bolt after them because I want Mad dead, and I don't trust anything about him, let alone him not trapping Dušan.

The main yard is exploding with combat. There are so many Shadow Monsters that it's difficult to discern who is who down there. I instructed the undead to run down to the building, hoping that was enough to drive fear into the guards and get them to back away. It seems to have worked with them desperately trying to get away from the zombies.

My feet punch the ground, and with my head low, I sprint down the slope and toward the passage alongside the fortress.

Up ahead, two wolves are spiraling in a wild battle. Fur and fangs are all I see in the vicious fight. Dušan against Mad by his wolf size. Thunderous roars spill around us, primal and explosive. The way they tumble and bite into each other in violent motions has me shivering.

Two guards still in human form watch them, and I don't miss that one is holding a rifle.

Ice fills my veins.

Will he shoot Dušan?

My legs explode in rapid movement just as the gray wolf with black ears who has to be Mad is tossed aside from the fight. He rolls and lands on his side with a huff. Blood mats his fur, peppering his body, and he scrambles upright.

My Alpha stands tall, heaving for each breath, blood running down the side of his wolf face. But he remains strong, head high and a growl erupting from his throat, his teeth exposed. The image is terrifying. Yet seeing him this powerful, this brutal, warms my heart. I love every inch of him even more when he's this dominant.

I duck behind several trees against the fortress. Everyone is too occupied with the fight to notice me, and I don't intend to get shot, either.

Dušan doesn't spare Mad a second. He charges him, headbutting him in the side, throwing him off his paws. But in that same moment, the two guards snarl and drop to their hands and knees. A heartbeat is all it takes for their clothes to shred and fall away as their bodies enlarge, giving way to an explosion of charcoal fur. The snap of bones fills the air.

It happens so fast that terror sinks through me. My wolf rises in me at my heightened anxiety. She pushes to escape, to deal with this for me. Except that would be suicidal. If I let her loose, I can never shift back.

"Dušan, watch out!" I scream, throwing myself out from behind the tree.

The two guards are already on him, the fight suddenly three against one.

Anger flares over me, my body heating with the rage of them all turning on him. Of course they wouldn't make this a fair fight.

I rush toward them and snatch the first rock I lay my sights on, something the size of my fist, then I grab a short, thick branch.

My brain is numb from the horrendous, cruel sounds of their barbaric brawl. My head spins, but they all leap as one after another, taking bites at Dušan. They move with tremendous speed.

The sight of my soulmate butchered will haunt me forever. I suck in shaky breaths and with all my strength, I hurl a rock at one of the guard wolves.

Thump.

It smacks right into his head, just below his ear, hard enough that it knocks him off Dušan. He teeters on his feet, then shakes his head. But I don't waste a second and sprint toward him.

My knees tremble as I rush to him. Before he reacts, I jab the pointy end of my stick right at his ribs. With all my weight behind me, I drive the branch into him, piercing skin. It sinks deeper than I expect.

He yelps and flinches away from me, sucking the branch right out of my hands, still jabbed between his ribs. His cries add to the chaotic sounds flooding the air. He collapses and starts transforming back into his human form, already passed out.

I turn to the fight, where I notice now it's only Dušan on top of the guard, but Mad has slipped from the fight. My heart speeds up. Where the hell is he?

A sudden, loud whistle carves through the sounds. My head swings toward the back of the fortress.

Mad stands about fifteen feet away, naked, his body covered in bitemarks and bruises. He's now holding the rifle the other guard carried. The butt is tucked into the pocket against his shoulder, one hand gripping the stock, and the other on the trigger. He's aiming at Dušan.

Darkness sweeps over me, stealing all my thoughts… taking everything but the ringing of the gun firing.

I scream, catapulting myself toward Dušan. "Run!"

My heart thunders as my world dissolves and moves too fucking slow for me to ever reach him in time.

The bullet strikes Dušan right in the chest with such force, it throws him backward. He hits the ground with a heavy thump. The guard next to him throws himself to the ground, barely missed by the bullet.

My insides shatter like glass, and I'm at his side in a flash. Dropping to my knees, I cry out, "Dušan, please tell me you're okay! *Please.*"

So much blood pours from his chest where he got shot. I can't even see the bullet in the tangle of blood and fur.

His eyes are glassy and he's looking up at me.

Tears run down my cheeks. I'm breaking apart. "Y-You h-have to heal." I hiccup my breaths, hating the feeling coming over me. I'll lose him. And the emptiness I lived with all my life rushes forward.

The hurt, the agonizing despair, the constant battle to make it through another day. All those feelings are tangled in a knot, swelling inside me.

He's still breathing, drawing in rugged, hissing breaths.

I'm sobbing uncontrollably as his body changes back to his human form.

Lying before me is my Dušan, trembling, curled on his side. Deep gash wounds cover his body, just as they did on Mad. I press my hands to his chest to stop the bleeding. His mouth moves, but no words come out.

"Just hold on. You'll heal. It's what wolves do. Please don't leave me. Don't you dare, Dušan."

Blood seeps between my fingers, dribbling down my hand and splattering into the soil.

He needs help.

"Hold on." My pleading slips past my lips as more tears fall.

Suddenly, someone grabs my hair and yanks me backward.

I cry out, reaching back to free my hair, my feet moving with the motion, all the while, my heart thundering.

"It's over. He's dead and you are mine." Mad's hoarse words tear over me.

I can't breathe from the anger crashing into me. My lungs tighten, as do my muscles. And I can't stop looking at Dušan, but I don't know if his ability can heal a bullet wound. He's on the ground, in a pool of blood.

This is too fucking much. I scream and shake violently.

I've lost everything once already, and I won't let someone take it from me again. I thrust and buck against Mad, my hands clawing at his grip on my hair. But on the inside, I'm dying at Dušan being left to suffer.

My entire body pulses with adrenaline.

With it comes a hatred that rages inside me, beating through me.

I'm broken. I've always been this way, and there's only one way to really finish this.

My monster lingers just beneath the surface, nudging me to come out, to be free.

She is my salvation, always has been, I see this now. And without her, I can't stop Mad.

And in an abrupt moment of desperation, I open my floodgates to my wolf.

She doesn't need coaxing and rushes out of me, coming so fast, her brutal growl startles even me. She's a tempest of vengeance, and I set her free, well aware of the consequences she brings to me. And I don't have a single regret.

I can't live with myself if I don't do everything in my power to finish this fucking bastard who should have died long ago.

His grip slackens as my transformation rocks through me, ripping me apart like someone's taken a blade to my body, and then stitched me back together. The world sharpens, and for the first time, I ease my grasp over my wolf.

You are free, I tell her. *This is all you now.* I shudder, my thoughts constantly on Dušan. While the other half of me drowns in violent fury.

My wolf whips around without any encouragement from me.

Mad's raising his rifle, his lips twisted when he looks at me, but my wolf pounces on him, shoving him backward. The gun drops from his grip as he shouts for backup.

A large form slams into my side so abruptly, the world tilts around me.

With a snap, my wolf bites right into the side of the guard's face while bent over me. The ferociousness is stark and animalistic.

He screeches with terror, clutching the side of his head, batting me away with his other hand. I taste his blood, the metallic, coppery tang drowning me. My wolf spits out the man's ear on the ground, and that grosses me out.

As I get to my feet, a snarl soars from my mouth, and my wolf's bloodthirsty hunger floods me. For the first time, a new sense of confidence flares over me.

Lifting my gaze, I meet Mad's eyes.

He's backing away, his eyes locked on the rifle he had dropped several feet away.

And I dare him with my sneer alone to collect it.

My wolf freezes, watching him, my ears flat, breaths shallow.

Go for it, asshole.

He makes his call, and it's just as I hoped.

Mad scrambles desperately for the weapon.

My wolf takes off.

We crash into him before he takes another step. Adrenaline races through my veins. Sharp teeth bite into his neck, my wolf savagely shaking him, and she rips free with a chunk of him dangling from her mouth… my mouth. It's hard to tell when I feel and taste everything, like it's me moving.

There's no stopping her now. She goes back and rips him to shreds. Breaks bones, tears flesh. His terrifying gurgling sounds are too fast a death for him. Yet he doesn't deserve another moment to be alive. He's a pitiful excuse for a life.

After he took my Dušan, he needs to suffer.

My grip on my wolf hardens suddenly as blind fury burns me. And before I know it, it's me there with my wolf, greedily stealing Mad's last breaths away, stealing everything from him, as he's done to me and so many others.

Coppery blood fills my senses, and warm blood drips down my face.

Anger burns me. I'm screaming in my head for what I lost, for how hard I fought to finally have a fair life. Now it's gone.

I glance down at Mad. His eyes are wide and frozen with shock, staring into the sky. Gone from this world but not soon enough.

Stars dance in my vision, and I blink them away. Instead, my wolf presses forward once more and tilts her head up. She unleashes an ear-shattering howl.

Darkness comes at me, curling around me.

My wolf darts back toward Dušan, who hasn't moved. Then she recoils within me. I feel her pulling back until it's only me left.

The ache in my heart deepens to the point where it hurts like hell each time I stare down at him gasping for each breath. I need to get him help. It may not be too late.

I turn to fetch someone, when the agony, the exhaustion, the grief swallows me. My legs buckle out from under me, and I'm falling into a darkness that sweeps in and carries me away.

CHAPTER 25

DUŠAN

I startle awake, sitting upright so damn fast that the room spins. An excruciating ache burrows through my chest. I cry out with the pain and clutch my chest as I fall onto my back. Eyes shut, I inhale each deep breath, wading through the pain that comes and goes, but slowly, it eases.

Wait... Room?

I peel open one eye and then the other and stare up to a white ceiling with a single lightbulb. Turning my head, I take in the door and wardrobe in my bedroom.

Memories rush at me.

The zombies in the settlement.

Mad shooting me, and well, I'd have expected him to throw me into a prison if I'd survived. He sure as hell wouldn't take the time to try and fix me. I finger the bandages wrapped around my chest, confused as to how I survived that. When I really look at myself, I notice most of my bruises and bites from the fight have healed. But a bullet wound is something else.

And Meira's sweet face was the last thing I remember before... I thought I'd died.

Soft snoring sounds come from the end of my bed, and I wrinkle my brow, leaning forward, which only sends a shot of pain up my chest.

I clench my teeth, riding the wave of slashing pain, then I push my legs out of the bed. They touch the cold floorboards, and I get up, groaning. I don't remember the last time I ached so much.

With slow, agonizing steps, I come around the end of the bed to find a tawny red wolf fast asleep on the plush rug.

My heart twists with the sight of her in wolf form, curling in on herself, sleeping by my bed. And things are starting to make sense. She must have saved me by transforming and letting her wolf take care of Mad… but at what cost? To be forever locked in her wolf?

A pang of guilt seizes me. Because of me, she sacrificed everything. A desperate, ugly feeling grabs me, and my knees wobble.

What have I done?

Inch by inch, the cold, hard truth hits me over and over.

This was never the future I wanted for her. I'd give up mine instantly for her to have everything.

Never this.

I crumble and fall to my knees, the thumping sound rousing her awake. Her head jerks up, and she looks over at me with sleepy eyes, her fur all flat on the side she slept on.

My eyes prick as I stare into those beautiful pale bronze irises. I reach over and hug her as my throat thickens with an overwhelming emotion that chokes me. "Oh, Meira, what did you do? I'm not worth it."

I hold her, close my eyes, and pretend she's with me like before, where she laughs in a way that brightens my darkest days. To feel her lips against mine. I try not to overthink everything I'll miss because it will destroy me. She is still with me, but the sting in my heart hurts more than the bullet wound.

A sudden charge of electricity runs up my arms. I snap open my eyes just as Meira begins to tremble violently in my arms. Her body stretches, and she's literally morphing into her human form.

I have no words, because one moment my heart is ripping out, and now I'm bursting with an unfathomable joy.

It isn't long before I'm holding a gorgeous, naked Meira, who's grinning at me. "Are you really crying because you thought I'd be a wolf all my life? Lucien said you would, but Bardhyl bet you'd still love anyway."

I laugh that she's already making a joke. "Well, they'd be right on both fronts." I have so many questions, but the important thing is that we're still alive.

"How are you feeling?" she asks, glancing down at my bandage.

"Someone was looking out for you." She leans in and kisses my lips, my cheeks, my chin. "The bullet went right through your torso, missing all organs and arteries completely. Can you believe that? I think you have an angel caring for you."

The news floats in my mind that somehow I managed to survive such a shot.

"And what about you and your wolf?" I ask. "Seems we all have surprises."

She smiles widely and snuggles against my side, avoiding the injury. "I did what you told me to and gave my wolf full control, and it seems she rewarded me by submitting. I don't know why I was so afraid for so long to just give her control."

"After everything you went through, it's understandable. The important thing is that you are here and mine."

She pulls up and finds my lips again. We kiss softly, full of love. Everything I feared I would lose.

When she pulls back, her lips curl upward, and while I want to just drown in her gaze, my question escapes past my mouth.

"What happened to Mad?" It's not him I want to talk about while I hold my soulmate in my arms, but I need to make sure this is over.

"We never have to worry about him again." She winks at me so adorably, unable to hide her huge grin.

"Did you—"

"Yes," she interrupts. "My wolf and I finished him. I just wish I could have done that long before everything fell into chaos."

"Sometimes things happen for a reason, and really, it should have been me who stopped him a long time ago. But it's done. Thank you for saving me out there."

She shrugs, almost bashful, which has me pulling her closer to me. "You would have done the same for me."

"In a heartbeat."

"How much longer?" I ask, pacing in Dušan's office, looking away from Lucien and Bardhyl. I can't stop worrying about what my blood results will show. That I'm still sick and it'll slowly wear me down? I haven't coughed up blood since transforming, so I'm praying with everything that my immunity to the zombies is some freak anomaly.

I keep glancing outside the window, where the sun shines brilliantly. Down on the settlement grounds, Ash Wolves are preparing for tonight's celebrations. It'll be a blue moon, and with it being a week since Dušan reclaimed his pack, there is a lot to party about. Mad and his dead followers were burned to ensure they didn't return as the undead and buried deep in the woods. Plus, tonight, Dušan will assure his pack that we are safe, that there is no cure as Mad claimed, but there will be changes to protect them all better. Those survivors who betrayed Dušan fled into the woods already, knowing death was coming for them. And add to all that, Dušan finally returned the serum Mad stole to the X-Clan to keep the peace.

Slowly, all the parts are falling back into place.

Except still, my stomach twists in on itself as I wait for news on my bloodwork. Footfalls approach me, and I turn to find Lucien standing behind me. Today he reminds me so much of when we first met by the side of the road. He's wearing his long-sleeved button-down shirt and those sexy dark jeans that hang low on narrow hips, and let's not forget his cowboy boots. His deep brown hair is swept off his face, and his gray-steeled eyes gleam. Every inch of him is spectacular. And there's a reason I fell for him the moment we met. He is a walking god.

"Come and sit with us." He takes my hand. "The blood results should be ready soon."

"Your pacing is making me tense," Bardhyl states from the three-seater couch where he lounges at one end, legs parted, one arm on his lap, the other along the back of the sofa. Something about him looks bigger today, broader, stronger. The white shirt he wears lays open at his throat, enough that the muscles below his collarbone flex each time he shifts around on the couch. Long white-blond hair drapes over his shoulders. A shadow of growth covers his chiseled jawline, and when he looks at me, he pats his lap, calling me to sit on him.

The corners of my lips involuntary curl upward in response. My body responds automatically to my soulmates it seems.

Lucien's fingers thread with mine, and he walks me around the table and over to the sofa.

I throw myself down on the middle cushion as Bardhyl hastily slips his arm around my back, and in a split second, I'm sitting on his lap sideways.

"My little Zombie Queen, don't even think you can get away from me," he says, keeping his gaze on me, while his fingers find my skin under my top.

"I'm totally okay to stay next to you," I answer, even if sitting in his lap has me burning up in moments, and already, I feel the bulge in his pants poking against my thigh.

Lucien makes little work of lifting my feet so he can slip in next to Bardhyl and hold on to my legs. Sneakily, he also raises my skirt for a peak.

"Hey." I slap his hand away. "I *am* wearing underwear."

He smirks devilishly. "Had to check just in case you were holding out on us."

I wrinkle my nose at him in confusion. "You think that I randomly decide to not wear underwear so I can surprise you?"

Both men look at me with an overzealous expression, the answer painted all over their horny faces. I shake my head at how transparent they are.

The door suddenly opens, and my gaze jerks upward.

Dušan strolls inside, and I glance behind him, half-expecting Mariana, the pack doctor, to be with him. Except he's alone, and my breath jams in my throat.

Does he have bad news and wants to deliver it to me on his own?

Bardhyl's grip around me tightens, like he senses my unease. But I push myself out of his arms and stand to meet my Alpha, my soulmate, my everything.

He greets me with smiling blue eyes, his black hair laying messily around his face like he's just run through the wind.

"Come here, gorgeous." He collects me into his arms.

I stare up at him, trembling. "Please don't make me wait. Just tell me. What did my blood results say?"

He cups the sides of my face and kisses me with a hunger like he's letting himself be rough with me once again. For the past week as we waited for the tests, we cleaned up the mess caused by Mad.

I push myself closer and kiss him back harder, hoping this means he has good news.

When I break away, breathless, I stare at him desperately.

"The result showed that you still have leukemia." His arms tighten around me.

A chill races down my spine and instantly, tears spring to my eyes. It's stupid how just a few words send a shudder right through me.

Lucien and Bardhyl are off the couch and move to stand on either side of me, their hands on me.

"Don't cry, beautiful," Dušan assures me. "You've always been special, and it seems that because you transformed so late, your first shift couldn't completely eradicate the disease. But it has made it dormant and inactive in your body."

I'm still processing his words, trying to come to terms with the results.

"It's why she's still immune to the zombies," Lucien adds, to which Dušan nods. "Is that how you're controlling them?"

I shake my head. "I don't really know. Guessing it's got to do with me biting them."

"Mariana seemed to think it's connected to your immunity and the bite where you exchange some of your saliva into their blood system. It changes their hunger to obedience to you," Dušan explains.

Bardhyl hugs me from behind, his whisper in my ears, "This is incredible."

"Are you sure?" I ask Dušan, so used to always hearing bad news that I now struggle to believe that in a roundabout way, everything turned out so well.

"Beautiful Meira. You have nothing to worry about." He grabs me and lifts me off my feet, and I'm laughing, my chest close to bursting with happiness. I don't remember ever feeling this way. Where I don't have to be constantly concerned about surviving. About someone wanting to kill me. About running away.

That's no longer who I am.

"I still can't believe how it's all turned out," I say as he lowers me to my feet. I'm surrounded by my three Alphas. "But I have one question."

"Go on," Dušan says.

"What happens if I have kids? Will they get sick too?" It's crazy to think this, but the notion popped into my head. But I don't need them to suffer like I did, and to have them safe from the zombies is what I really want.

No one responds at first, which has me blushing at the thought that I've somehow put them on the spot, talking about babies when we've only just found our freedom.

Dušan finally says, "Mariana told me it's not a hereditary disease, but it can happen. Except seeing as yours is dormant, it's very unlikely. And when the child transforms, which we will ensure they do, their wolf side will protect them as it has you."

I blink at him, and it makes sense, though I still worry. I exhale loudly. "It's so much to take in all at once. All these changes and what's going on with me. But you're saying I have no real cure for everyone against the zombies."

He shakes his head, and I didn't think it would be, but it's worth asking.

"You don't need to think about anything right now but settling into your new home, then helping us three run the pack. Plus, we have the Northern Wolves promising to return for a visit, and I want everything set up to give them no excuse to think we're weak in any way."

My eyes widen, and already a plan is forming in my mind. "I have an idea." I turn so I'm facing all three Alphas. "Let's position zombies around the settlement. I can command them to stay there. Anyone who dares come near our compound will be terrified to come any closer." I shrug. "I just think it's a great cautionary measure. Once they decay away, we replace them. Hell, there are enough of these things in the woods."

"I love that idea," Bardhyl states. "Back in Denmark, we'd do that with wild wolves. Keep them around our campsite. When they made a sound, we knew we had intruders, and most were scared away by them."

"Agreed," Dušan says.

I glance over to Lucien, who's been silent and staring at me strangely. "Are you okay?" I ask.

Sunlight from outside spills through the window, casting over him, giving him a glow. "I'm still back on our previous conversation." He clears his throat. "You're ready to have a baby with us?"

The softness in his voice, the tenderness in his eyes, undoes me because they aren't from someone scared, but someone dreaming of this day. I step toward him and hug him. "Maybe not right away, but yes, if that's okay with all of you."

His breath hitches. "It's everything I've always wanted."

He holds me against him, with Bardhyl and Dušan joining the hug. Me in the middle of these powerful men who love me, who want me in their future. But it turns out they're not the only strong ones. All along, I thought I lived with a monster inside me. But the real fiend was my own fear.

My new life is everything and I love them so much. For the first time, I have a purpose in life. And now, I have a family.

I will never be alone again, and my cheeks hurt from smiling so much that things are finally looking up for me.

"Who's up for practicing baby-making early?" Bardhyl asks out of the blue, which has me rolling my eyes.

Strong hands that I think belong to Dušan slide under my skirt, and I twist to face him. But the deviant is too fast. His fingers curl under the elastic of my underwear and in a violent tug, he rips them off me. I jerk from the movement, and suddenly, I have three sexually starved men staring at me.

"Are you ready?" he asks.

I back away from them, the heat between my legs already slick with arousal.

My breaths rush, and in an instant, I am craving them insatiably.

"Wait. I know we haven't had sex for a week, but—"

"Do you think she's trying to distract us?" Lucien asks.

"Definitely," Bardhyl answers, never lifting his gaze from me.

We've crossed the line from serious talk and into the heady need to release, and even I can't deny the desire igniting me from the inside out.

"Look, how about we all just talk about this first?" I say, trying to distract them.

As they sigh, I whip around and dart to the door, throwing over my shoulder, "Suckers."

The explosion of rapid movement has them charging after me, and I burst out of the room, unable to stop laughing as I sprint down the long corridor.

Everything I've ever dreamed of has come to life, and it still feels surreal, but I'm willing to make this work.

And who would have thought that even the most broken girl in the world could eventually find her happily ever after?

LOST WOLF

SAVAGE SECTOR

My fated mate sent me to my death

But I can't be killed easily.

Especially when four Viking Wolves awaken a passion within me that ignites fire through my veins and heat into my bones. They see my potential. See me despite my unique blend of darkness.

With me at their side, they want to conquer our broken wolf world.

But it's a deadly game, one I won't play without a few demands of my own--

Help me get revenge against my fated mate, no matter the cost.

ABOUT MILA YOUNG

**Find all Mila young books at
www.milayoungbooks.com**

Best-selling author, Mila Young tackles everything with the zeal and bravado of the fairytale heroes she grew up reading about. She slays monsters, real and imaginary, like there's no tomorrow. By day she rocks a keyboard as a marketing extraordinaire. At night she battles with her mighty pen-sword, creating fairytale retellings, and sexy ever after tales. In her spare time, she loves pretending she's a mighty warrior, walks on the beach with her dogs, cuddling up with her cats, and devouring every fantasy tale she can get her pinkies on.

Ready to read more and more from Mila Young?
www.subscribepage.com/milayoung

Join Mila's **Wicked Readers group** for exclusive content, latest news, and giveaway.
www.facebook.com/groups/milayoungwickedreaders

For more information...
milayoungauthor@gmail.com